PRAISE FOR
SCHOOLED

"Gossip Woman: Former private-school teacher Anisha Lakhani dishes the Upper East Side dirt in the bratty new novel *Schooled*."

—*Marie Claire*

"This sharply observed debut novel dissects life among the offspring of New York's absurdly rich." —*People*

"Lakhani gives readers a front-row seat as she exposes the secret world of private-school tutoring like only an insider can. You won't be able to put it down." —Cosmogirl.com

"Variations on Anna [Taggart] and her covetous ilk are likely to remain a mainstay of young adult entertainment." —*New York Times*

"*Schooled* isn't only a novel: It is a piece of sociology."

—*Wall Street Journal*

"The story slides between chick-lit banter and a more thoughtful tone that questions the NYC private school system and the children who are corrupted by it. Like *Gossip Girl*, *Schooled* is full of sparkling details—a 'faux mitzvah' with Kanye West performing, lots of text-message lingo, and an endless parade of brands, including Chanel, Marc Jacbos, Lanvin, and Prada." —*Page Six Magazine*

"*Schooled* is a biting teach-and-tell debut novel from Anisha Lakhani."

—*Redbook*

"An idealistic new teacher at an elite private school gets sucked into a material world. Four stars." —*OK!* magazine

"If you count yourself among those who eagerly await the second season of *Gossip Girl*, Anisha Lakhani's debut novel *Schooled* might be just the thing to tide you over." —SARA VILKOMERSON,
New York Observer

"Every bit the dishy, insidery look at private school privilege that one could hope for. Think *Gossip Girl*, but from the teacher's perspective."

—*Hamptons* magazine

"*Schooled* is witty, entertaining, and altogether tantalizing."

—*Town & Country*

"Fans of the CW soap [*Gossip Girl*] have to look elsewhere for their spoiled Manhattan teenager fix. Enter *Schooled* . . . a cheeky read about after-school tutoring in the rarefied 10021 zip code, where professionals are paid big bucks to help students plow through homework assignments—more often by just doing it for them." —*Women's Wear Daily*

"Biting, smart, and hysterically funny, Anisha Lakhani's debut book will have you laughing all through detention." —*Quest*

"*Schooled* easily finds its way to the head of the class."

—HANNAH SAMPSON,
Miami Herald

SCHOOLED

SCHOOLED

ANISHA LAKHANI

HYPERION

New York

A NOTE TO THE READER

The author was a teacher for almost a decade, and this story was inspired by not only her experiences, but also the experiences of fellow colleagues. Please remember that *Schooled* is a work of fiction and therefore none of the students she taught or tutored are featured in this book. Any resemblance to actual events or persons is entirely coincidental. Even the real New York City institutions are used fictitiously.

Copyright © 2008 Anisha Lakhani

Library of Congress Cataloging-in-Publication Data

Lakhani, Anisha.
    Schooled / Anisha Lakhani.
        p. cm.
    ISBN: 978-1-4013-2287-8
    1. Private schools—Fiction. 2. Middle school teachers—Fiction. 3. Tutors and tutoring—Fiction. 4. Rich people—Fiction. 5. Manhattan (New York, N.Y.)—Fiction. I. Title.
    PS3612.A433S36 2008
    813'.6—dc22

                                                    2008019190

Paperback ISBN: 978-1-4013-0996-1

Hyperion books are available for special promotions and premiums. For details contact the HarperCollins Special Markets Department in the New York office at 212-207-7528, fax 212-207-7222, or e-mail spsales@harpercollins.com

FIRST PAPERBACK EDITION

BOOK DESIGN BY CHRIS WELCH

10   9   8   7   6   5   4   3   2   1

For

HAROLD MOSCOWITZ

It was beautiful and simple as all truly great swindles are.

—*O. Henry*

PREFACE

W e just don't see how this could have happened.
We're paying you $250 an hour."

I focused intently on my heels and tried to come up with a response to Hunter Walker Braxton III's accusation. The truth was that I had written the entire paper on F. Scott Fitzgerald's *The Great Gatsby* while his daughter Whitney had gone through the March issues of *Elle*, *Harper's Bazaar*, and *Vogue*. We sat in the same room and, to be fair, Whitney had occasionally contributed a phrase I could swear she trademarked: "Make it sound more like me, okay?" So I changed words like *transient* to *brief* and cut out anything with more than three syllables. I had made it a point to cite three quotes incorrectly and to use four verbs in the wrong tense even though inwardly it killed me just a little. I think I spent more time dumbing down that paper than actually writing it. No easy feat considering that it needed to get a minimum of an A- without looking "too good" or "too smart" or, worst of all, "too tutorish." But the fucking thing had received an F with a big fat SEE ME on the top. Now it was 5:40 P.M. and I had four more tutoring sessions that evening. I didn't need this unexpected disaster.

"Now I have read the paper, Anna, and I have to say that I do disagree with this Mr. Rowen. We have a conference with him on Monday morning for which I will have to cancel my board meeting. My entire office will be compromised while I take care of this . . . *problem*. I don't have time for this. This is why we pay you. To bring out Whitney's potential." Hunter's voice was icy. I could see why *The Wall Street Journal* named him The Shark. (I Google all my parents just to check them out.) *Shit.* I was definitely getting fired.

"It just seems like such a harsh grade, Anna," Mrs. Braxton whined. "Whitney is devastated. Crushed. She told us how hard she worked on this paper, and all the helpful editing advice you gave her. We want you to accompany us Monday morning when we confront Mr. Rowen and his impossibly high standards."

I looked at Susan Braxton as calmly as I possibly could without betraying how utterly dumbfounded I was. Helpful editing? How hard Whitney had worked on this paper? Whitney hadn't even read the book, and the most bizarre fact of this whole meeting was that the Braxtons knew it: They had given me a cool $1,000 check to read the novel! Now it seemed as if this Mr. Rowen and I were going to take the fall. And Monday morning? *No way.* Not with a first-period seventh-grade English class to teach.

"Susan, don't be retarded. Obviously Whitney didn't receive an F on the paper," Hunter growled. "It's clear this Rowen is accusing our daughter of something much more serious." Susan wilted the minute her husband used the word *retarded* and I was torn between feeling sorry for her and agreeing wholeheartedly with him. Susan was the quintessential Park Avenue trophy wife (although to be specific the Braxtons lived in a townhouse on 78th Street between Madison and Fifth), and both husband and daughter seemed keen to acknowledge that the trophy had somehow tarnished. Hunter accomplished this with the subtle lift of an eyebrow, while Whitney took a more obvious approach, freely referring to her mother during our sessions as "dumb ho." It wasn't that Susan was sleeping around, it was just that words like *ho* and *slut* are as commonplace among Manhattan private school girls as *diplomacy* and *peace* are in the United Nations. Dumb ho was just Whitney's charming euphemism for the more probable reality: neglectful-anorexic-selfish-benefit-planning mother. I cleared my throat and reached for the mini Fiji water bottle the Braxtons' maid had put on the coffee table, thinking as quickly as I could. I had to come up with some seriously believable shit and get out of going to this meeting. It was 5:55 and my next tutoring appointment was at 6:00. If I could get out of here in five minutes, I could arrive ten minutes late, which wasn't too bad. This had to end *now*.

"Mr. and Mrs. Braxton, I think Mr. Rowen thinks that Whitney did not write this paper, and that is why he has simply put the F and the SEE ME on top. If it was an F quality paper, he would have marked it up with corrections," I declared firmly.

The Braxtons stared at me silently. Susan closed her eyes and sighed deeply. Hunter looked like he was going to sue me. His tell-me-something-I-don't-know face clearly spelled out that I had to get better, and fast.

"Which is ridiculous," I recovered, "because he simply has no proof. Whitney is an A student"—a lie everyone happily accepted—"and of course, when given the time to sit in her room and deeply reflect on the novel she read, is capable of writing an informed paper. My attending this meeting would be an admission on your part that she indeed *had* help. I would simply contest the teacher. I mean, what proof does he honestly have?" This was good. The Braxtons seemed calmer, but where the hell *was* Whitney? Why wasn't she here? And I just realized that my 6:00 was all the way over on the West Side. My only West Side tutoring client and he had to be next. I started to sweat.

"That's a very good point, Anna." Hunter seemed to be recovering his composure. "So you think I should just tell this guy to provide concrete evidence?" Thank God the tide was turning in my favor.

"Honey, isn't Mr. Rowen a new teacher? He doesn't understand we're a board family!" Susan wailed. Hunter looked at her with a flicker of admiration, and I jumped on the cue.

"She's absolutely right. In fact, I wouldn't even entertain a meeting with Mr. Rowen," I declared. "I'm sure you can put a call in to the head of the school and this can all be handled discreetly." I had learned that *discreetly* and *discretion* are favorite words among Manhattan's elite parents, particularly when plotting the best way to manage their children's latest *indiscretion*. The word had its intended magical effect: Hunter was immediately soothed.

Some distant part of me recognized how amazingly far I was willing to go to keep my $250-an-hour client. Here I was, calmly instructing impossibly wealthy and powerful parents to use their position to completely undermine a teacher. Not too long ago, Mr. Rowen had been me. Ready to put my job on the line in pursuit of fairness and honesty, I had accused a board member's child of cheating. Take that back. I had *known* for a fact he had cheated because I had run into him and his tutor at Starbucks and caught her typing furiously on his laptop while he sat idly. Even worse, she had been my colleague! Of course, I had taken the paper to the head of the department. In a matter of hours, the assignment in question had "disappeared." I had been thanked for my obvious concern and then told that the matter would be "taken care of." The whole episode was chalked up to my being green. In those barbaric pretutoring days, the prospect of losing my eighteen-hundred-dollar-a-month job kept me miserably silent. It also marked the end of my so-called teaching virginity. Now, being on the other side of that incident was a little like an out-of-body experience. I wasn't sure which side was more uncomfortable.

Hunter "The Shark" Walker Braxton III contemplated what I had just said. My phone was vibrating in my back pocket. I needed every ounce of willpower not to flip it open.

"That's an excellent idea, Anna. I'll do just that. I'm not canceling my board meeting for a stupid parent-teacher conference. Who does this guy think he is? I'll just put in a call." Hunter Braxton got up from the sofa with a disgusted snort and walked out of the room. If Mr. Rowen knew what was good for him, come Monday morning he would return Whitney's paper with an A and move on.

Just like that, the dark tutoring storm clouds that had threatened to destroy my afternoon suddenly cleared and I could breathe easily again. Susan gave me a glassy stare and smiled. Peace was restored, and I was free to hail a cab to Central Park West where I would write Joshua Levin's ninth-grade history term paper on Montesquieu's influence on the three branches of American government. I had already "drafted" the introductory thesis paragraph during my classes at school while I showed my unsuspecting students a film. As I waited for the elevator (the Braxton townhouse was, after all, five stories high) I remembered my cell phone and quickly flipped it open. It was a text from Whitney:

```
OMG I HATE Rowen!!!
Remind h-bag that she and daddy on school
board.
Did u c The Hills last night???
```

SCHOOLED

1

H ad it only been a year?

I vaguely remembered a desire to become a teacher and a belief that it was the most noble profession on earth. I was going to be Mother Teresa and Angelina Jolie rolled into one, motivated only by the desire to help others. Okay, and maybe wear cute little Rebecca Taylor skirt suits and look good while doing it. How could I have believed that the entire private school system was anything other than absolutely corrupt?

Just before graduation my singular goal had been to convince my parents that becoming a teacher was more important to me than any role I could ever hope to fulfill in my life. Their skepticism and disappointment had only served to further ignite my resolve. Our face-off had, like so many family arguments, been at the kitchen table. The lava had been simmering throughout dinner. The eruption was inevitable.

"I have never been so disappointed in all my life." One simple statement from my father, and I was liquefied. I looked across the table at my mother.

"Mom?" I started tentatively.

"I'm with your father, Anna. Honestly, what do you want me to say?"

"So this is it? This is your chosen profession?" I could swear the table was starting to shake.

"Yes. I'm going to be a teacher." *Stay calm, Anna*. I willed myself to look my father straight in the eye.

"Like in a school?"

"Yes, Dad, like in an actual school." I didn't get it. Where was all the disappointment and anger coming from? Wasn't this a *good* thing? Had I said I wanted to be a porn star? Or a poet?

My father's face was ashen.

"With metal detectors? And unions? P.S. pay nothing? P.S. screw you, Dad, for my Ivy League education?"

What?! Here I was, professing my decision to pursue a career that was considered quite possibly the most noble profession on Earth, and my father was . . . angry?

"Dad! I have such a passion for it. You should see me in my student-teaching class. I really get these kids and they love me!" It was true. I knew the word *passion* sounded cheesy, but it was appropriate. For the last two semesters I had been doing my student teaching at P.S. 6 on Manhattan's Upper East Side. Despite the constant supervision of the head teacher, I had basically been teaching a seventh-grade history class. I remembered the look of pain on my students' faces when I had told them we would be learning about the Bill of Rights in the Constitution, and how it had turned to excitement when I had announced that we would be creating rap songs to explain each amendment. A few eyebrows had been raised by teachers who passed my room in the hallway—there was music playing at any given time in my classroom with at least two kids standing on chairs performing their rap—but I got twenty-two initially apathetic students to understand the American Constitution by the unit's end. It was the proudest day of my life.

I took a deep breath and resolved to try a fresh approach.

"Dad, when I teach, I am the best of who I am." It was true. "I am never more proud of myself, more certain of my purpose, than when I'm with my students." He seemed to be softening.

"Anna, do you realize how lucky you are? You are going to graduate from Columbia. You can be ANYTHING. Do you remember how hard it was for all of us to get where we are? Your mother and I worked so that you and your brother could have the education that would allow you to lead comfortable lives . . . *better* lives than ours. One of my greatest achievements, Anna, is that I am in a position to pay for you to go to any law or business school in the country that you get into. Hell, you can *skip* grad school and I'll start you with an analyst position at Merrill Lynch. We can drive in to work together. Is this making any sense to you? Do you know how much teachers actually make? Less . . . than . . . a . . . gar . . . bage . . . man." My father said the last five words slowly, as if to chastise me with each syllable.

Before I had a chance to open my mouth, my mother chimed in: "Honey, we love you so much, and truth be told you've had a pretty cushy life so far. You really haven't had to pay for anything substantial. I know you think this is noble—your father and I do, too, but really, Anna, you can teach anytime. Go have a real career, and then teach after you've had your kids. Not now!"

I was furious. How condescending could they be? Apparently, I was a three-year-old more in need of a sippy cup than parental support. Teaching was not a fallback career. Okay, it wasn't *cash*-centered, but it was important. Very important. I suddenly looked at my parents through new eyes. Hypocrites. All my life I had heard my father complain about the long hours he spent at work. Phrases like *money means nothing when you are old and can't enjoy it* and *nothing beats spending time with your children* were thrown around our house on a daily basis by my mother. The beeping of the microwave, which signaled Mom reheating dinner in the middle of the night for my dad, was practically my childhood soundtrack. If I had a dollar for every teacher who thought my parents were divorced (my dad had the distinction of having never once attended a parent-teacher conference), I would have been able to retire by junior year. And now this? My parents wanted me to be an analyst? I was feeling deeply self-righteous and suddenly quite sarcastic.

"I'm sorry, Dad. You're right. Merrill Lynch. I can't wait to lead a lonely existence full of zero fulfillment. I'll be like all the other daughters of your friends who you are *so* proud of. I forgot that my sole existence in life is to please you and Mom. Gosh, how could I have been so carelessly independent?"

The look on my father's face was clear: I had gone too far. But I wasn't sorry. The direction this conversation had taken was entirely their fault. I had envisioned teary pride and heartfelt congratulations that they had raised such a well-intentioned, nonmaterialistic daughter. I hadn't announced that I was running away with my rock star boyfriend (not that I had one, but I *could* have). I hadn't made a dramatic declaration that I was going to join the Peace Corps. I opened my mouth to continue, but judging from my mother's face and her position right next to my father, I knew that anything I had to say was futile at this point.

"Okay. Go. Teach. But we're not helping you out one bit. Pay your rent. Buy your food. Ha—even more hilarious—pay your bills. Go have fun. We just wish you had told us you were going to take a Columbia University education and go teach. We wouldn't have bothered paying for it."

That did it. My parents were officially the most unreasonable people alive. Any desire to rationalize with these people was gone. They were mercenaries. Republicans. Supporters of the system that kept the working man (me) from ever getting a break.

"Fine!"

"Fine."

"FINE!"

I stormed out of the kitchen, brushed past my brother who had been eavesdropping in the hall, and went straight to my room. In a blur of tears and frustration I zipped open a duffel bag and crammed in as many clothes as I could, throwing my cell phone charger on top. I knew my parents were downstairs talking about me, but I was beyond caring. I was against everything they stood for. I didn't need them or their money. I would be fine on my own. I would make my own way. Okay, I guess that I would have to drive their BMW to the train station, but that would be the absolute last time I would drive a luxury car that promoted the evil empire. After that I would make my own way.

I couldn't stop thinking about how mean my parents were. Or how noble I was. If it weren't for people like me, the children of the world would never be educated. There would never be a cure for cancer, a car that would get sixty miles to the gallon, or a poet laureate to usher in the country's first female, African American president. I felt lonely, abandoned, and completely misunderstood. I had never had such a fierce argument with my parents, had never before left my house vowing never to look back. Well, actually, there was that one other time in the first grade when I had huffed my favorite Barbie chair all the way to the end of the driveway, sitting and stewing there till lunchtime because my parents had, in my wise opinion, favored my brother a little too much over breakfast. It was the smell of grilled cheese that had lured me back in that day. But there was nothing—nothing!—that could change my mind this time. I just knew I was right.

By the time I reached Grand Central, I was drained and homeless with only fifteen hundred dollars in the bank (an accumulation of graduation gifts) to last me for the summer. Or maybe a lifetime. Who else to turn to but Bridgette?

Bridgette Meyers was my best friend and sorority sister from Columbia. We had been suitemates in Carmen Hall—"suite" being Columbia's charming euphemism for a multi-occupancy cinder block cell—before upgrading into the Delta Gamma brownstone. Now Bridge had upgraded once more, and was living in a gorgeous doorman building in the East Seventies. She was an analyst at Morgan Stanley and was already making enough money to have decorated her entire space in subtle shades of sleek gray. I had visited her once over the summer, and even though I secretly felt like she had re-created a Maurice Villency showroom, complete with low couches, shag rug, and lighting fixtures that looked just like little spaceships, her apartment was definitely grown-up. Bridgette had been working part-time at the firm for the last semester; the week after graduation she moved to full-time. I really hadn't given much thought to what that had

meant until she opened the door to her apartment. Almost over-
night, Bridgette appeared to have aged a decade, but in that very
sexy twentysomething way. She had just gotten home from work
and was wearing a black pencil skirt, a fitted silk shirt, and what
looked suspiciously like Jimmy Choo heels. Suddenly I was very
conscious of my jeans and T-shirt.

"Hey, sis," she said warmly, opening her arms and engulfing
me in a big hug. "Are you okay?" One look at her I'm-so-sorry-
you-have-a-blue-collar-job expression and I was dangerously
close to bursting into tears. Seemed like the whole world was
either mad at me or felt sorry for me.

"Bridgette, I am seriously going to be out of here before you
know it," I promised, and I meant it.

"Sweetie, are you kidding? What are sisters for? But seriously, are you sure this is what you want to do?" Bridgette looked
sadly at my one lonely duffel, then directed me to the fold-out
couch. "I mean, all the Delta Gamma sisters thought you were
just messing around. Nobody thought you actually wanted to
teach."

"Why is everyone acting like I have a disease or something?"
I cried. "This is a normal career. Teaching. Normal. Some parents are actually happy when their children take this path! And
Langdon is the most prestigious school in Manhattan. Do you
know how lucky I am that I got this job?"

"I guess," Bridgette responded vaguely. "But Langdon is a
place people *go*. It's not like a place where you *work*. . . . Listen,
there's this thing tonight. Do you wanna go? You aren't going to
start at Langdon till the end of August anyway. Come, it'll get
your mind off . . . stuff."

Stuff. That's what my dreams had been reduced to.

"Where?" I was suspicious, and just a little resentful that a few weeks after graduation my best friend from college wore designer clothes, lived in a designer apartment, and had a "thing" she was invited to in Manhattan.

"Just this Morgan Stanley summer analyst thing at Bungalow 8. They like, I don't know . . . *rent* clubs and stuff. It's so lame, but lame fun, you know?" Rent out clubs? For summer analysts straight out of college? I may have gone to college in New York City, but my Manhattan had ended at Tom's Diner on 112th Street—fraternity and sorority parties on campus and nearby bars had erased my need to venture downtown. I was definitely not a New Yorker and the fact that Bridgette had beat me to it irrated me more than I was willing to admit.

"Downtown is too . . . far," I finished lamely. "They're just trying to impress you."

"Anna, listen, this is just how it is. In the i-banking world, first-year analysts work their butts off, but yeah, the hard work we do is appreciated. That's where the free dinners at Nobu and parties at Bungalow come in. Also, we're working so hard that it's only at these events that we can just hang and get to know each other!"

I shook my head in disbelief. How naïve could she be?

"Bridge, they're doing that stuff for you like a crack dealer gives out free shit to first-time clients! They want you to become addicted to this life so that they can use you. Once you taste how good a $400 meal at Nobu is, you'll be willing to put in whatever hours are necessary to be able to afford more dinners like that!"

It was all becoming so clear to me. I felt like I had been under a rock for twenty-two years. We were living in a society so blinded with fancy labels and exclusive restaurants that we were losing all sense of morality. What about happiness? Having time with your friends and family? Bridgette would be grinding away trying to raise millions for a company that might never know her name just so she could have a piece of ninety-dollar sushi and sashay her hips in a dark nightclub? Still, jobs like Bridgette's were rewarded with juicy salaries and addictive bonuses, whereas my role as teacher of America's youth would barely cover one month's rent.

We were replacing students with sushi.

"Okay, Anna, SERIOUSLY, you're taking this workers-of-the-world-unite thing too far. You want to teach. I get it. But are you coming with me or what? You'll love Bungalow." Bridgette gave me the same look I had seen on my mother's face: you're-going-through-a-phase-and-I'm-not-buying-into-it.

"No. You go." I pouted.

"Annie, at least teaching gives you the summer off. Come have fun with me . . . it'll be like old times," Bridgette pressed, clearly unconvinced that I had abandoned the old me who would have been out the door five minutes ago. I glared back at her, not even bothering to hide my resentment.

Bridgette sighed and came over to the couch to sit beside me. I crossed my legs defensively and stared at her blank plasma screen. If she gave me a sympathetic hug I was certain I would explode.

It came.

Ugh.

"Just go! I don't want your pity!" I shouted, jumping and grabbing my duffel. I could take anything but the pity hug. "This was a mistake. I'll find somewhere else to live."

"ANNA!" Bridgette ran to her door and blocked the entrance. "Okay. I get it. You're going to teach . . . I can't say that I don't respect someone who actually wants to go to work every morning."

Aha! The crack I had been waiting for!

"So you don't want to go to work every morning?" I challenged.

"I didn't say that."

"But you implied it."

"No, I—"

"Bridgette! This is *me*," I pleaded. "Since when did you have to impress me? I don't even recognize you with all this . . . this Jetsons furniture and analyst bullshit. Come down to earth, please?" Bridgette began twirling a piece of hair nervously, her eyes focused on a bizarre standing lamp that arched over her entire couch.

"The sound of my alarm clock every morning has already become . . . a . . . noose that seems to be tightening every day."

Her voice cracked when she said "noose," and there in front of me, finally, was a glimpse of my best friend from college. I almost wept with relief. After months of robotic "I love i-banking!" declarations, here was the lovable, lazy Bridgette I knew and adored. The girl who got herself through Lit Hum class at Columbia solely through SparkNotes and had her chicken cutlet sandwiches and Broadway milk shakes delivered from Tom's Diner even though our sorority house was around the corner.

"I can't go out because I'm flat-out broke," I admitted, but was starting to grin.

"The majority of my life is spent in a fucking cubicle," she shot back, grinning even wider.

"I've only been poor for a day and I hate it," I challenged.

"I don't even know what crunching numbers means," Bridgette retorted. "And I'm just waiting for someone to realize that I actually suck at math."

"You do suck at math."

"Well, you suck for implying I'm Judy Jetson!" Bridgette shoved me playfully.

She was back in full force. Beaming, I dropped my bags and lay down on her creamy shag carpet.

"Snow angels?" Bridgette dropped on the carpet a few feet away, and we both began to flap our arms and legs wildly as if we were lying in snow making actual snow angels. The tradition had started during our freshman winter at Columbia following a night of binge drinking at the West End. As we stumbled to our dorms, Bridgette had come up with the brilliant idea of making snow angels next to Alma Mater.

"Like a gift," she had slurred. "Angels for Alma Mater." Giggling madly, we ran up the steps toward Low Library and lay down on either side of Alma Mater, flapping our arms and legs and laughing so loudly that we didn't even notice campus security until they towered above us. After that, it was Bridgette who thought it would be funny to make snow angels while lying in the hallway of our dorm. Somewhere between sophomore and junior years she had managed to convince me that it was a hilarious activity.

Watching Bridgette from the corner of my eye as we both flapped, I was flooded with a sense of warmth. Her intimidating black pencil skirt had ridden up to her thighs, revealing an ugly pair of beige Spanx.

"You wear SPANX!" I screamed, sitting up and pointing an

accusing finger at the secret of her apparent slimness. Undeterred, Bridgette kept on hooting and flapping.

"I'm a Spanx-wearin' snow angel and I'm proud of it," she declared.

I looked over at Bridgette with affection. With all the stress I had endured from my parents, I hadn't given much thought to how Bridgette really felt about her new job. I might be broke, but at least I wasn't stuck in a cubicle twelve terrifying hours a day doing a job I wasn't even sure I knew how to do. Maybe this was the first time she had laughed in months? I had been a terrible friend and vowed that minute to make up for it. I sat up and poked her.

"Even though I'm broke, I'm going to splurge on pizza for us. It'll be like my last supper before a lifetime of ramen noodles," I offered grandly. All we needed to make the rest of the evening perfect was Bridgette's *Clueless* DVD. Bridgette stopped flapping.

"Um, actually I think I *am* going to go out. . . ."

Huh?

She hoisted herself up abruptly and smoothed her skirt back down, avoiding my eyes. Like the Spanx, my best friend was suddenly out of sight. Awkwardly she reached over to lay a hand on my shoulder.

The hand was even worse than the hug.

"There are just, like, people I promised that I would meet from my analyst class. Is that . . . cool? Anna, don't be mad."

Bridgette had disappeared.

"It's cool," I lied, smiling thinly and forcing myself to shrug. "I'm pretty tired anyway."

"I'm just so glad we had this time to bond," Bridgette said in her I-love-i-banking voice, and was suddenly engaged in such a flurry of activity that I couldn't help but wonder if she was annoyed with me for making her late. I watched her make a barrage of cell phone calls to new friends I had never heard of, and thirty minutes later all I saw of her as she walked out the door were the tassels of her obviously new Balenciaga bag.

It was going to be a long summer.

2

My interview at Langdon had been terrifying. All I had known about the school was that it was the breeding ground for everyone who had ever intimidated me at Columbia. Could I really belong here? The students had just been let out for spring break and the school was almost empty—just a few stragglers trailing around to say their good-byes to friends, only these stragglers wore low-riding designer jeans with $400 cashmere sweaters wrapped artfully around their shoulders. They sported casual hats worn backward over sun-ripened hair, and tans left over from a Presidents' Day weekend spent in Anguilla. Clearly these were not children whose lives were ruled by the weather.

"Bruce, I forgot my ID but can I please run up and get my BlackBerry?" I turned and watched as two high school girls holding Starbucks cups walked in through the front doors. Blowing the security guard a flirtatious kiss, the owner of the husky voice added, "We always go together," and nodded in the direction of her girlfriend. I couldn't take my eyes off them. It was as if Mischa Barton and Rachel Bilson had wandered off the set of *The O.C.* in search of a couple of caramel macchiatos. Mischa was wearing a slim, casually shredded jeans skirt that I knew was Chloé (I had seen it on the cover of *Elle*) and Rachel was wearing a Marni dress with an oversized pair of Chanel sunglasses perched atop her head. As they waited for the elevator I was uncomfortably aware that the girls were eyeing me too. Rachel looked at my pumps and mouthed *Ann Taylor* to Mischa. They both shook their heads sadly.

The elevator arrived and we rode up in awkward silence until the doors opened on my designated floor. I stepped out and the girls immediately started whispering; it was all I could do not to mutter a heartfelt, "Bitches." Thankfully, I managed to stop myself. These weren't the girls who had intimidated me at Columbia. These were children I was here to mold and teach the ways of the world. These weren't bitches. They were sad, misunderstood girls who didn't know better. I was clearly in private-school territory.

If the students at Langdon had come from the set of *The O.C.*, its headmistress came from Turner Classic Movies. With her gray, upswept hair, her heavy eyebrows, and deep red lips, Dr. Blumenfeld bore a striking resemblance to Joan Crawford. (Or was it Bette Davis?) She was intimidating and she knew it.

"Ms. Taggert," she stated coolly, extending a limp hand in my direction.

"A pleasure to meet you, Dr. Blumenfeld. You have no idea how grateful I am to have this opportunity to speak with you," I gushed. She appraised me evenly.

"You're very young," she said.

I took a deep breath and launched into the speech I had perfected in front of my bathroom mirror:

"I realize this, I assure you. But as I look forward to finishing my senior year at Columbia, teaching is the *only* career I see for myself. I am looking for a school that will give me a chance, and I will be loyal and true and absolutely dedicated."

Shit.

I sounded like a demented Girl Scout. The words had tumbled out too quickly, and I knew immediately from Dr. Blumenfeld's arched brow that she found it rehearsed, too. Nervously I looked down at my shoes, feeling like I had been sent to the principal's office and was now awaiting punishment. After a few painfully silent minutes (which she appeared to relish), Dr. Blumenfeld decided to speak again.

"We have a brilliant student body at the Langdon Hall School, and they all come from demanding households. I balk, Ms. Taggert, at the idea of giving you a full-time position at Langdon Hall without your having so much as one year of teaching experience."

Balk? That wasn't good.

I sat silently, staring back at her pastel twin-set and massive pearls. There was nothing for me to say, and Dr. Blumenfeld was obviously not finished.

"However, it is close to the end of the school year and a faculty member quit unexpectedly. I would like a replacement. I have never done this before, but your cover letter convinced me of your passion. Your education is immaculate. And I can see that you have a fire in your belly."

"Dr. Blumenfeld you have no idea—"

"I do, actually." She smiled a bit more kindly and took her glasses off. "Ms. Taggert, it was something you wrote in your cover letter. You said that teaching is your chosen path for life. That when you teach, and I quote," she paused and reached for my cover letter, "'I feel closest to my dreams.'"

A surge of courage rushed through my veins. It was true. I never felt more creative, energetic, or eager than when I stood in front of a class. Yes, I was intimidated by Langdon Hall and Dr. Blumenfeld, but I didn't walk into the building or this interview empty-handed. I knew I had much to learn about the profession, but if I could convince her to give me one shot, I would prove myself. Sitting up in my chair, I looked into her watery blue eyes and said simply, "It's true."

I sat in silence once again, watching as she scanned my cover letter. I noticed a small smile play at the corners of her mouth, and when she looked up her expression was almost warm.

"Anna, that's a bold statement for someone so young, but a worthy sentiment. Here at Langdon we pride ourselves on being progressive. That means we take chances when others may not." She paused. "I can extend you a one-year trial. I can make no promises that there will be a position for you next year, but for now the role of seventh-grade English teacher at Langdon Hall is yours."

Oh, my God!

This was happening! It was actually happening!

"Dr. Blumenfeld, I cannot thank—"

"My biggest concern," she interrupted, "is that you have absolutely no experience in the private school world. You will need a great deal of coaching—from how to handle your students to how to manage parent calls. Believe me, Ms. Taggert, there will be a great many parent phone calls, a great many expectations. I have a lot of résumés on my desk, but you are young and impassioned. We like that at Langdon Hall. I'm willing to take this risk."

"I am beyond grate—"

"Ms. Rollins, my secretary, will help you fill out the paperwork. Congratulations, Ms. Taggert. And don't thank me. The best thanks you can give me is to show me that I shouldn't re-gret this decision." I nodded furiously. As I reached out my hand to shake hers, she gave me an understanding smile.

"Oh, and Ms. Taggert, once a week our international chef creates a wonderful burrito in the cafeteria." I stared at her, baffled. "With *guacamole*," she added proudly, emphasizing the accent on the last *e*.

3

spent most of July tiptoeing around Bridgette. I had fallen into a miserable pattern of watching an unreasonable amount of Lifetime television during the day, and then watching Bridgette get ready to meet her new analyst friends each night. I pretended not to care that her earrings cost more than what was left of my dwindling summer money, or that she was spending lavish nights at the Waverly Inn and Bungalow 8 while I languished on her couch, but I don't think I fooled either of us. Our friendship was strained. That snow angel moment seemed so distant I found myself wondering if I had dreamed it. Had we really laughed ourselves silly over Spanx?

All the hours of Lifetime were taking their toll on me. I often woke up from my afternoon naps in a cold sweat: My parents were not my real parents, but a kindly couple from New Jersey whose own baby girl was now living with a family in Florida. Being switched at birth, I discovered after a particularly emotional four-hour movie, was actually quite common. I also found myself deeply distressed about the growing number of pedophiles preying on young girls in Internet chat rooms. I cried helplessly after watching the true story of the formation of M.A.D.D., and even harder during its rerun. There was also no doubt in my mind that all husbands had mistresses, and all mistresses had guns. Wives throughout America were in grave danger and nobody seemed to care. By the time *The Golden Girls* came on I was an emotional wreck. My life was in limbo, and Lifetime television was the only assurance I had that there were people in this world who were just as miserable as I was. Bridgette, however, seemed to have little sympathy for my situation. She grew increasingly hostile each night.

"*Quel surprise*," she drawled sarcastically. "Another busy day for Anna."

"It's not my fault that my job starts later," I said defensively. Why did Bridgette always have to walk in right in the middle of *The Golden Girls*?

"Ah, yes, the difficult life of teachers. These summers off can be such a drag."

"Don't you have to get to Bungalow 10 or whatever?"

Ha. That was a good one. Bridgette scowled and stormed off to her bedroom. I didn't always win our little confrontations, but the occasional victories saved me from going completely mad. I longed for my new life, my new students, and my new apartment.

On August 1 I was up before Bridgette and almost mad with excitement to get off her couch and begin to live my life again. I was teeming with anticipation at the thought of seeing my new apartment. Langdon Hall owned brownstones in the neighborhood, one-bedrooms that they rented to faculty members at affordable prices. Everything about Langdon was so incredibly over the top, and I was certain that my apartment had to be equally impressive. Okay, maybe not Bridgette-impressive, and maybe not equipped with a twenty-four-hour doorman, but still somewhere I would be proud to call home.

"Call me when you get to your new place, okay? I want to come see it," Bridgette said sleepily, still groggy without her morning Starbucks.

"Okay," I promised, reaching out to hug my very absent and increasingly distant summer roommate.

"I'll miss you," she murmured unconvincingly, giving me an icy hug.

"I'll call you," I replied equally unconvincingly.

And that was it.

I felt sorry for Bridgette. Who in their right minds would choose a life spent in a cubicle as opposed to a cheery class-room with colorful bulletin boards and a fresh, inviting chalk-board? Instead of Bloomberg terminals and maddening ticker tape, I would be surrounded by fresh-faced children, eager young minds ready to be expanded by my creative assignments. Maybe it was for the best that Bridgette and I were growing apart. I needed new friends who shared my passion. Already daydreaming of getting after-work margaritas with my new teacher friends and laughing about how adorable our children were, I splurged on a taxi to my new apartment.

There had to be some mistake.

The address—324 East 84th Street between Third and Lexington—was correct. But this was not an apartment build-ing. It was a single glass door with a crack. Rusty buttons on the side panel indicated that there might be apartments beyond the door, but the paint was peeled off and the numbers were un-readable. Beyond the dusty glass, all I could see was one very long staircase. No elevator in sight. And certainly no doorman. Steeling myself, I put the key Ms. Rollins had sent me in the keyhole and found that the glass door, besides having a charming crack, also apparently did not lock. It swung open, inviting residents and muggers alike.

I freaked out.

Nearly breathless and panting after climbing the first story, I was greeted with three sad letters painted on the wall: ONE. My destination, I realized with total clarity, was FIVE. Or HELL. By the time I reached the fifth floor, I hated Bridgette and her elevator and her doorman more than ever. Apartment 5A was a tiny studio masquerading as a one-bedroom. A cement wall that didn't quite make it to the ceiling separated the living room-cum-kitchen from what appeared to be the closet-cum-bedroom. Behind the wall-that-was-not-quite-a-wall was a bedroom that, with luck, could contain maybe a twin-size bed, a night table, and a small desk. That's if I wasn't planning on moving around a lot. I wanted to cry. How could I bring my parents here? How could I invite Bridgette to see this? Most sickening of all was how could I actually be paying twelve hundred of my eighteen-hundred-dollar salary for this tiny little hole? This was Langdon's idea of a faculty "break"?

Stop it!

I had been wasting away on Bridgette's couch for weeks waiting for this moment. No way I was going to allow myself to fall into another depression. I resolved to become the heroine of my own Lifetime movie: *Anna Taggert, The True Story of a Manhattan Teacher Who Battled the Odds.* A Lifetime heroine would use the three weeks before Langdon Hall's orientation to make the best of her apartment! She would spend time in

Central Park's Sheep Meadow with educational books, re-reading and highlighting passages on teaching technique! In the afternoons she would take blissful naps in the sunshine, lulled to sleep by the thought of all those gloriously empty penthouse suites towering over the trees. After all, most people who lived in homes like that had to work during the day so they could afford them. This Anna Taggert might be living in the tiniest hole on the island, but she was preparing for a career that was going to shape the minds of future leaders in this country.

God, I loved Lifetime.

The Spence-Chapin Thrift Shop was down the street, and I figured I could find some affordable pieces that would make my apartment more homey. The irony of a teacher being able to afford only the hand-me-downs of private-school families was not lost on me, but true-story-Anna-Taggert didn't let these things upset her. Even if I could find a simple desk and a night table I would be able to—

"Are you here to pick up Mrs. Carrington's Fendi?"

"Excuse me?" I blinked in confusion as an elderly man in glasses approached me frantically.

"Mrs. Carrington. Fendi mink. It got sent over by mistake with the other clothes. You're the nanny, right?"

So for one itsy-bitsy second the thought of saying "yes" and booking it out of the Spence-Chapin Thrift Shop with a Fendi mink did cross my mind. . . .

"Um, no . . . I was looking for a desk. And maybe a night table?"

"Oh. Yes, well, look around." The man gestured vaguely, losing interest. If I wasn't Mrs. Carrington or the Carrington nanny I was clearly not worthy.

In a corner labeled CAMP GOODS, I found a used blow-up mattress and a pack of unopened sheets from Gracious Home that once cost $650. The thrift store markdown now had them priced at $25. What kind of people tossed out unopened sheet sets with a thousand thread count? A stack of throw cushions for $10 each would make the mattress double as a couch (maybe my apartment could have an Arabian Nights theme?) and a slightly chipped but sturdy-looking desk might just be—

"DO YOU HAVE MY MINK?"

The elderly man shot me a nervous glance and then ran to the door. At the entrance stood a petite woman with curling blonde hair and enormous sunglasses. She was wearing a tiny white skirt with a tight black T-shirt that had big, interlocking C's on the chest. Little shining studs twinkled from the edges of her T-shirt and skirt. She looked like a BeDazzler-happy fourth-grader. With a very big head.

"Mrs. Carrington, we are *so* sorry!" the man gushed, holding up a long, caramel-colored mink.

"My nanny is *retarded*!" she sniffed in disgust, grabbing the coat. "What kind of human being can't tell the difference between shearling and *mink*? My husband got me this coat for Valentine's Day. He would have *died*!"

"We had a feeling there was a mistake. That's why we called," the man continued obsequiously. "We know how much your family donates to us, but of course we must all have perspective!"

Mrs. Carrington and her Fendi were already out the door.

"Excuse me," I asked, "can you do better than $150 for this desk?"

"*That*," the man sniffed haughtily, "is a Scully & Scully desk originally priced at . . . well a price you couldn't afford, my dear. I'd take it at $150 and not ask too many questions. Remember, we are a *charity store*, so your money does go toward a good cause."

I had a feeling he didn't mean teachers.

4

My first day of school, at last. Langdon's entry hall was full of teachers greeting and hugging one another warmly. I heard snippets of conversations—comments on new haircuts and summer vacations—while all around me people were breaking into loud shouts of laughter. Everybody seemed genuinely thrilled to see one another. A few of them were already poring over class lists and pointing at specific names with knowing looks and rolled eyes. I couldn't wait to be a part of it all. But first I was going to make friends with the Krispy Kremes. I moved toward the food: A hearty setup of donuts, muffins, and bagels covered one table; another contained pitchers of juice and urns of coffee.

"Please help yourself," a friendly voice greeted me.

I looked up to see a kind, gray-haired man with twinkling eyes and a Santa Claus beard.

"I'm Gerard Zimmerman, the school psychiatrist. We'll be touching base later," he said warmly, letting his eye scan down to my name tag. "Ms. Taggert."

"Oh, Anna! Call me Anna!" I said quickly.

"Okay, Anna it is," he beamed. "Ah, the kids are going to *love* you! We need a fresh young face around here."

I stood there grinning madly, happier than I had ever been.

I was a young fresh face! The kids were going to love me! Yes! Yes! Yes!

Teachers of all ages were now coming through the lobby in hordes, milling around the breakfast table and then heading into the auditorium in clusters. A few of them eyed me curiously, giving me tentative smiles.

I followed them into the auditorium, which looked more like the Majestic Theatre than a school. Red velvet seats in seemingly endless rows filled the room while the crimson and gold threaded carpet had all the opulence of Hester Prynne's scarlet letter. Thick, maroon drapes curtained the stage, and the balconies curved gracefully above, showcasing even more seating. I melted awkwardly into a seat near the back of the auditorium just as Dr. Blumenfeld took the stage. Conversation immediately died as all eyes turned to her. There must have been over four hundred people in the theater, and not a child to be seen. Were they all teachers?

"Good morning, everyone. It is my pleasure to welcome this amazing and talented faculty back to what promises to be another wonderful year at Langdon Hall," she said cheerily. The entire room broke into applause.

"Many exciting things have happened over the course of this summer. The math department enjoyed three weeks in Nepal and has wonderful slides from their trip to share in a later faculty meeting."

More applause.

"Our beloved Mr. Harry Agincourt published his first book on Caribbean literature, and Mrs. Rita Woodward received . . ."

Dr. Blumenfeld went on and on to mention accolades and

various trips that the Langdon faculty had made over the summer. The music teacher had adopted an Ethiopian baby. Two ninth-grade history teachers had teamed up to teach a Cantonese cooking class. I could feel my excitement rising. This was a school that truly supported its faculty. I could just imagine sitting here next year and hearing Dr. Blumenfeld tell the faculty about *my* important summer accomplishments: "Our cherished Anna Taggert had a book of poetry published this spring regarding her experiences in the classroom. What an amazing feat for our beloved first-year teacher!" I vowed right then to spend a good portion of my evenings and vacation days dedicated to this task.

"And now," Dr. Blumenfeld said suddenly, "it is my great pleasure and honor to introduce some new faculty members who will be joining all of you here at Langdon. As you all leave this meeting and head to your respective classrooms, I hope you will be sure to look out for these extraordinary individuals and make them feel welcome and at home."

More applause.

"First, I welcome Doori Iwahara, who will be our new high school biology teacher. Doori hails from Japan, and came to America when she was eighteen to study at the University of Pennsylvania. She will be teaching three sections of ninth grade and two sections of tenth grade. We welcome you, Doori. Please stand up!"

I craned my neck toward the far left corner of the room where the minuscule Doori stood, shyly waving. She was wearing a tiny black jumper with a white tank top, and had a shock of pink hair on the right side of her head. I loved that Langdon embraced the personal styles of its faculty! I wondered if I should get a few highlights as well. . . .

"Next, we have Ashok Mehta, who will be teaching sixth-grade math. Ashok comes to us straight from New Delhi as part of our Langdon Teachers-Without-Borders program. He studied at the Delhi Institute of Technology, and we are just thrilled to be welcoming you, Ashok! Please stand up!"

A large, dark-skinned man with thick glasses and wavy hair stood up and beamed. Unlike shy Doori, Ashok appeared absolutely thrilled with the attention.

"And finally, perhaps our youngest faculty member to be added to Langdon in a long time, I welcome the recently graduated and fresh-faced Anna Taggert, who hails from Columbia University! Anna will be teaching seventh-grade English with us this year, and we are sure she will bring her Mexican heritage to the classroom to make her lessons all the more enriching! Stand up, Anna!"

What . . . the . . . fuck?

I stood up and managed a faint wave.

"And finally . . ." Dr. Blumenfeld paused a bit awkwardly, "I would like to reintroduce the faculty to someone we already know and love. Our beloved Matthew from the language department has made an important life decision and would prefer to be known as Mary. Mary, we support and welcome you as always to our community, and we will *all* encourage our students to do the same!"

Huh?

There were a few shocked gasps and whispered exclamations, and then everyone broke into applause as a tall and very sturdy-looking woman stood up in the corner of the room.

"Langdon is a *progressive* school. Our children, faculty, and outlook on life are *always changing.* That is precisely what makes us so very unique in Manhattan's private-school world," she finished, beaming at the entire room. The Langdon faculty broke into enthusiastic applause, and then teachers started to exit the theater in small clusters. I could tell the science teachers from their short-sleeved collared shirts and thin ties. The art teachers had random bits of "flair," like purple tights or funky, pink-rimmed glasses. The room eventually emptied, leaving Doori, Ashok, and me to linger awkwardly. Where were we supposed to go?

"The new teachers can accompany me," said a tall, lanky man. "I'm Jerome. You will start in the technology lab. I'll give you your new laptops and set you up with faculty e-mail accounts."

"New laptops?" Ashok burst, hardly able to contain his excitement.

"Oh, yes, all our faculty are given laptops!" Jerome confirmed warmly.

"To . . . keep?" Doori asked, her voice a barely audible whisper. Oh, boy, the kids were going to eat her alive, I couldn't help thinking a bit smugly.

"To keep," Jerome affirmed, and then gestured for us to follow him.

The Langdon Hall technology room looked like it was about to launch a NASA aircraft. The room was stark white and devoid of any windows. There were two long metal tables with more Apple computers than I had seen even in the store. At the computers were geeky-looking guys typing furiously, their eyes glued to the screens. They were way too old to be students, and since they were not at the assembly I wondered who they were.

"Our computer support team," Jerome offered, his eyes shining with pride. "Here to assist the Langdon teachers in any and all technical support."

What did Langdon teachers do? Launch weekly spaceships?

"Wow . . . ," Ashok breathed, then looked me in the eye for the first time. His face was slightly shiny and plump, and his eyes sparkled with good humor. "Even at Delhi I.I.T. we did not have such highbrow stuff!" I couldn't tell if he was joking or not, but I was equally impressed.

"Our staff works hard to maintain teacher Web sites and other vital programs," Jerome said by way of explanation. "And your laptops are . . . here!"

Three large boxes from the Apple store sat in a corner of the room. As if he read our minds, Jerome confirmed that inside, wrapped in plastic and accompanied by complicated-looking instruction manuals, were shiny white laptops worth close to $2,000 each.

"Brand new? To keep?" Doori breathed reverently.

"To keep, really? When do we give these back?" I questioned again.

"Never. They're yours. Trust me, you'll use them!" Jerome laughed casually. Four hours later, I had a Langdon e-mail account, Anna@LangdonHall.edu, a teacher Web site, and enough knowledge to launch a rocket myself. On a laptop that cost more than a month's salary.

Orientation had begun in earnest and I had no idea I had already accepted a bribe.

Day One was over. I had an expensive laptop in my tote and my new apartment was only walking distance from the school. I was on cloud nine. Well, more like cloud eight. Truth was, I was dying to call my parents. I missed them more than I cared to admit, and the eager child in me couldn't fully enjoy the excitement of my new job without sharing it with them. I had informed them of the vitals through a perfunctory e-mail—address, phone number, location of school—and that was all.

Turning the corner of 84th Street and Third Avenue, I was so lost in thought that I failed to focus on the two people standing outside my apartment building.

"Anna!"

My parents!

And in that simple, magical way that you can go from despising your parents to absolutely adoring them, I melted. I ran toward them like a kid, arms wide open.

"Hey, there," my father said gruffly, engulfing me in a bear hug. My mother was teary and equally emotional.

"We wanted to surprise you . . . see your place. Sweetie, if this is *really* what you want to do, then what can we say? We're not going to lose our daughter just because she made one bad decision," my mother said sweetly. I was more than a little annoyed at the "one bad decision" comment, but what the hell. I was too happy to see them to give it another thought.

"Look at the laptop they gave me!" I exclaimed, pulling out the iBook from my tote.

"Anna! Oh, my God, this is New York City! Put that back before we get mugged!" my mother exclaimed.

"Mom, this is the *Upper East Side,* for God's sake." I rolled my eyes.

"I don't care. There are still rapists," she sniffed. "Now let's see your place. Your father and I have been waiting at the Starbucks across the street for the last hour. I'm dying to see your first apartment!"

I pulled out my keys and prayed the glass door was locked. Shit. It swung open before I even turned the key.

"It's UNLOCKED?" my father exclaimed.

"I'm sure it's a mistake . . . someone probably just walked out," I replied weakly. My parents were deafeningly silent as they followed me up the five stories. Gone was my *I'm just like Holly Golightly living chicly in her walk-up building* fantasy. Enter reality: I was heading up an endless staircase followed by not one, but two executioners.

"ANNA!" Mom screamed, somewhere in the vicinity of the second story.

"MOM!" I shouted. "DON'T SHOUT! GOD!"

"Anna," my dad huffed, his head suddenly emerging from the stairwell as he panted up the fourth-floor stairs, "this is barbaric. You cannot . . . ," he paused and breathed heavily, "*cannot* live like this." He was right. The stairs were killing me. The laptop in my tote felt like a ton of bricks. Too tired to speak or shout further, I continued the climb.

"Jesus," my dad stated, finally standing in the entrance to my apartment. There was nothing to do but let him in. He looked visibly pained as he started walking around the space, which he covered in a few strides.

"Oh, Annie," my mother sighed moments later, sweating and breathless from the climb. Her eyes welled up with tears. *That was the worst*. My mother was *crying* because this is what her daughter had been reduced to. I wanted to cry as well.

"Anna, we're going to Crate & Barrel. We're buying you furniture," my father declared firmly. I opened my mouth in shock. What happened to the *you're on your own* lecture? The *we're not going to help you* declarations?

"Dad, no, I'm fine, really. After a few paychecks I'll have enough saved up," I protested weakly. The truth was that I would have sold my soul for a couch.

"I know what I said, Anna. And I stand by it—I *told* you this would happen. I'm just buying you furniture so *I* can sleep at night. It's not right, how they pay teachers, it really isn't," he seethed, inspecting my cracking ceiling. Silent again, the three of us left the apartment, and I swallowed my pride as I accepted a sofa, armchair, coffee table, lamp, bed, night table, rug, desk, and chair from them. What a hypocrite I was, living on my own and accepting huge amounts of money from my parents. A part of me wanted to dance in glee that I finally had furniture, but most of me wanted to curl up and die at the thought that all these gifts had been purchased as charity. For me. Anna the charity case. If only I had had a doorman apartment with chic furniture like Bridgette to show them. What was she possibly doing at Morgan Stanley that caused her to earn so much more money than me? Wasn't she handling other people's money while I was actually molding their *children*? Feeling a twinge of resentment, I trailed after my parents to an even more humiliating dinner during which all I could do was thank them humbly and profusely. The evening ended with my mother asking a question that had all the makings of a dirty bomb:

"How are the deliverymen going to get that couch into your apartment?"

5

To a new teacher, entering into what is to be her classroom is like experiencing Narnia for the first time.

"Oh, wow . . ." I breathed, standing at the entrance of room 805.

It was . . . huge. French windows allowed the September sunlight to pour in, and with a shriek of delight I noticed I had my own personal air conditioner. In a corner was . . . my desk! It was invitingly bare. I could hardly restrain myself from running outside and buying an apple to put smack dab in the middle. I ran my fingers across the wood lovingly, thinking about all the grading and student conferences my precious desk would witness in the coming months.

Mine was the only desk in the room. The students were to sit at a long, sleek conference table that looked like it belonged in the head office of a Fortune 500 company. It was easier to imagine suited-up corporate types sitting around this table than a group of seventh graders. Still, I could picture myself seated at the head with my students all around, eager little faces, hanging onto my every word. What an amazing place for our literary discussions!

Across from the conference table was a long, green chalkboard that looked like it had never been used. It held all the same excitement for me as my first box of Crayola crayons had when I was little. Impulsively, I took a piece of chalk and wrote MS. TAGGERT in cursive with big, sweeping strokes. Even the smell of chalk was thrilling. This was . . . *my* classroom. I never wanted to leave.

"It's a nice room, isn't it?"

I whirled around and found Gerard Zimmerman's friendly Santa Claus face peering at me.

"The nicest," I confirmed, still starry-eyed.

"Yeah, I guess we get used to these rooms. Takes a newbie to remind me how gorgeous this place is," Gerard chuckled.

"I just love newbies," a smooth voice said, and with that a slender, black-haired man with wire-rimmed glasses and a pale face entered the room.

"Damian Oren." He smiled, extending his hand.

"Anna," I responded, returning his handshake. I smiled back even though I was a little grossed out by his clammy hand.

"So let's begin," Gerard announced, suddenly efficient. "I'm here to give you the background files on your students."

"Files?" I asked, interested. The more information I could get at this point, the better. Despite my excitement, I was a little nervous that in just a week orientation would be over and I would be standing in this classroom as the head teacher with a room full of children.

"Yes, Anna, files. Every student has one. They are sources of vital knowledge. In addition to past school reports and medical updates, they also contain every e-mail, detention letter, and private note written about the child or parent by teachers over the course of the student's years."

As if on cue, a frail, gray-haired woman entered the room

wheeling a trolley piled with files. Each file was the same hunter green, and each appeared stuffed to capacity with papers.

"Ah, Nancy, right on time. Thanks so much." Gerard walked over to the trolley and patted one of the files affectionately. "Okay, Anna, it's time to get acquainted with your fifteen homeroom children. I'll go through the files for some of your more high-maintenance students, and then Damian can stay with you while you read the rest. I have to get to Doori and Ashok today as well."

High-maintenance?

I glanced in Damian's direction, spooked to find his dark eyes focused intently on me. I couldn't read the expression on his face, but his lips were inexplicably twitching. Who was he, my babysitter?

"We never leave files unattended in a classroom," Gerard explained, reading my mind. "Damian is here in case you need to take a coffee break or visit the ladies' room."

So he *was* my watchdog! Was he going to stare at me while I read each file? How creepy!

"Oh, and Anna?" Gerard added. "While our parent body is aware that these files exist, they are told *only* that they contain school reports and medical updates. They are *never* to actually be given access to the files themselves as . . . er . . . they contain other critical information that is meant for only our eyes."

Understatement of the year.

The files certainly did contain "critical information" such as medical forms and school reports. But they also contained notes—some handwritten, some typed—from various teachers the child had had over the years. Some were signed, while others remained anonymous. These notes were often one or two lines, but their contents left me aghast.

Max Briggman:	*Mother is a freakin' lunatic who stalks the school.*
Charlotte Robertson:	*Gave bar mitzvah boy blow job in party bus.*
Chase van der Reedson:	*Made a pass at his nanny. Sexual deviant.*
Jacob Stein:	*Tutored in six subjects. Grand-father billionaire.*
Michael Worthington:	*Professional brownnoser.*
Blair Partridge:	*Made cover of Teen Vogue in sixth grade. Queen Bee Mean Girl.*

Three hours later, and I had been escorted through only three files: Max Briggman, Charlotte Robertson, and Jacob Stein. Already, I had about zero desire to meet any of these children. In fact, the very mention of their names exhausted me. How would I ever be able to give any of these children the chance to make a first impression? Already I was filled with judgment and harsh opinions toward three of my homeroom students. Gone was any need for an icebreaker activity or a getting-to-know-you game. In these files my poor students' lives were exposed and dissected like a frog in a ninth-grade biology class. Their contents smelled just as sickly, too.

"You know, I'm sure you and Damian have a lot of preparing to do for Monday. I could go through these on my own time.

Maybe take them home and read them at night," I offered generously. "I wouldn't let anyone else see them."

Gerard looked like he had been slapped across the face.

"Anna, these files are NEVER to leave the building, NEVER to be left unattended, and NEVER to be discussed with parents or students. This is HIGHLY sensitive material, and it is CRITICAL that you read them. Here. One by one."

"Sorry," I mumbled. Behind me I heard Damian make a sound that was a cross between a cough and a guffaw. Was he laughing at me? And Gerard was turning out to be Santa's bipolar twin, given to strange bouts of anger that disappeared as suddenly as they came. Now he was calmly stroking his beard and reading the file on Benjamin Kensington.

"Benjamin Kensington has acute, life-threatening peanut allergies. You are responsible if so much as a peanut, or anything in the vicinity of a peanut, enters the classroom. He could *die*." I opened my mouth to react but Gerard held up his hand. Unsurprisingly, there was more to young Benjamin. "He saw a therapist for most of fifth and sixth grade because his father had an affair with his yoga teacher." I sat up straight. Poor Benjamin! Kids never recover from something like that! I made a note to look out for him. Gerard continued, "There was a slight altercation with his older brother, Eric, involving drug use—his lacrosse coach found some, uh, materials in the locker. All of this was handled very discreetly by the school. Benjamin was very upset by this incident, and his parents want to be alerted if he ever mentions it to you. They are very good friends of the school and his mother is on the board." Friends? How can you be friends with a school?

I glanced at Damian. This time he was openly grinning at my discomfort.

"Let's move on to Jessica Landau. Her mother is a lesbian."

I sat there listening to Gerard go on and on, still weirded out by Damian's presence. His eyes seldom left my face, but he had yet to make a single comment. As Gerard droned on about the Landau lesbian scandal (Jessica was in the fourth grade when her mother left her father for a core-fusion teacher from Exhale) I struggled not to roll my eyes and squirm in my seat. I could just imagine how messed up Jessica would be after such a scandal. Benjamin sounded like an overindulged child who would probably think nothing of the sacrifice I would have to make in giving up my peanut M&Ms addiction lest I so much as *breathe* on him. And how I was even going to have a proper conversation with Charlotte Roberston, the blow job queen, was way past me. How the *hell* did any teacher find out about that tidbit anyway? And what kind of person actually took the time to document it and add it to a child's file? It was all so . . . invasive.

"Gerard, stop it. You're *killing* her!" Both Gerard and I looked up, startled by Damian's unexpected outburst. Thank God! He was going to put an end to this madness! Maybe he wasn't such a creep after all.

"Oren, take it easy. She's never been in this world before," Gerard growled. Damian was undeterred. With a wicked glint in his eye, he reached into his satchel and slapped a magazine-sized booklet onto the middle of the table.

"What is that?" I asked curiously.

"*That*," he smiled wickedly, "is the shortcut."

"Oren, GET OUT OF HERE!" Gerard barked, now furious.

There, in the middle of the conference table, was a booklet

entitled "Langdon Hall Friends." Desperate for a distraction, I lunged for it and was flipping through the pages before Gerard could stop me. Turned out to be one big disappointment. Just rows after rows of names, like a directory of sorts. What was the big deal?

"Is this a directory?" I asked, completely confused. Gerard looked supremely uncomfortable.

"You could call it that." Damian winked mischievously. "Or you could call it what I suggested . . . a *shortcut*."

"To what?" I was still baffled.

"Ahhh, a virgin. I love private-school virgins." Damian sighed dramatically. "If you look more closely, Anna—I can call you Anna, right?—you will see that above each page is a number. *A very special number.*"

"Oren . . . ," Gerard warned in a low voice.

Damian ignored him and sat down beside me, his eyes dancing with excitement.

"That number indicates how *friendly* that particular family is with Langdon Hall. So, say it happens to read twenty-thousand dollars, right? Well, then all the names underneath that amount are names of people who have been *friendly enough* to *gift* the school that very amount!"

Twenty-thousand dollars? I picked up the book again and looked through the pages more carefully before inhaling in shock. The donor names did not start with $20,000. The book opened with friends who contributed $100,000 *or more.*

"But how is this a shortcut?" I asked stupidly. Six months later I could recite the entire booklet in my sleep, but my initial encounter had left me awestruck.

"The last names on the first two pages are all that matter,"

Damian responded, deadpan. "If you have a student with one of those last names, give him an A. Hell, give him a fucking puppy. If her family name is not on the list, she's fair game for any special kind of torture you want to concoct for that day."

Was he kidding?

"Is this book sent to everyone in the school?" I was in shock.

"Try every family and every alum in the city."

I shook my head in disbelief. Was it really possible that Langdon published the names and donations of all the families attending the school? Why would they do something like that?

"Okay, Damian, that's enough. Get out of here!" Gerard boomed, finally springing to action. "Anna, please don't listen to him. That's not how Langdon Hall likes to think of itself. That is the *last* image we are trying to project here."

I didn't get it. Hadn't Gerard explicitly told me that Benjamin was to be treated with special care because his mother was a board member and because his family were very good *friends* of the school? Damian held his hands up in mock surrender and backed out of the room. *See me later in the faculty lounge*, he mouthed. *He's full of shit*, he added dramatically, pointing irreverently at Zimmerman. I couldn't help but grin.

"Inappropriate," Gerard grunted, still furious. "I'm going to talk to Blumenfeld about him—he should *not* be trusted with any new faculty. Now I have to stay here with you the whole time and go through the rest of them."

Oh, no.

Two torturous hours later, Gerard finally announced that we could continue my "orientation" tomorrow. I bolted out of the room and headed toward the high school faculty lounge. I had to find this Damian Oren. Strange as he was, I had a sense that he would be a voice of honesty in this world I apparently knew very little about. Gingerly opening the door to the faculty lounge, I was surprised to see that it was packed. Some faces were familiar, though I couldn't remember any names. A few curious glances were thrown in my direction, but I was largely ignored.

"ANNA!" Damian was at the other end of the room in a large reclining leather chair. "Hey." I smiled. "I thought I would take you up on your generous offer."

"Oh, yeah?" He smiled back, drumming his hands over his lean abdomen. "Have a seat." He gestured to the soft sofa next to him. The whole room was decorated in shades of neutral beige. An espresso machine and a tray of chocolate chip cookies rested on a corner table. I could get used to this!

"Damian, don't corrupt her," a friendly voice admonished, and I turned around to face an absolutely gorgeous woman. She seemed to be in her mid-forties, but Christie Brinkley forty, not your average forty.

"Hi, I'm Sarah Waters, ninth-grade biology." She smiled and extended her hand.

"Anna Taggert, seventh-grade English," I offered, quickly learning that Langdon Hall was big enough that teachers could easily get lost.

"Yeah, as if *I'm* the source of corruption here," Damian sniggered and rolled his eyes. "Hey, Sarah, I met Anna this morning getting the old file talk from Zimmerman."

"Oh, you *poor thing*! Don't pay any attention—we never actually read those stupid things unless we have a serious problem with a kid. Don't feel like you have to memorize them," Sarah offered helpfully.

"What about the Langdon Friends publication?" I asked, still reeling from Damian's dark shortcut tip.

"Okay, *that* we do look at," Sarah admitted. "It's hard not to be curious."

"Doesn't it make the kids whose families can't, you know, make massive donations feel like—"

"Shit?" Damian finished my sentence. "Probably."

"Then why do it?" I pressed.

"It creates a sick competition," Damian explained, suddenly serious. "Families try to one-up each other with donations. And what better way to make the exact amount they give public knowledge to the entire Langdon community than to publish it?"

Before I could ask another question, a palpable silence pervaded the room. I followed the sidelong glance of teachers and located the source: an impossibly thin, attractive brunette had flown in and headed straight for the espresso machine. She hadn't said a word to anyone, and was instead listening intently to whomever she was speaking to on her BlackBerry. This girl—model?—was all angles. Rail-thin legs were poured into skin-tight, stovepipe jeans that spelled out DOLCE & GABBANA in rhinestones on the butt pocket. The tight white tank, several skull necklaces, and massive Chanel glasses perched on the top of her head all screamed *Vogue*. Her oversized Marc Jacobs tote had already slammed into three teachers, who had simply shifted away in disdain without saying anything.

"Yes. Yes. Of course. I understand. Visual learning is key. *Oui, je parle français.*"

"The French teacher?" I whispered to Damian.

"*Mais non*," he responded, smiling widely. "I'm actually shocked to see Randi in here—a rare treat and a perfect way for me to begin the Langdon Hall behind-the-scenes lecture!"

"*Damian*," Sarah warned, but he looked too thrilled to care or be restrained.

"*That* is Randi Abrahams, and she teaches seventh-grade history. You'll be teaching the same students."

From the look on Damian's face he was clearly just getting warmed up. Why was she speaking French? What was up with that outfit? I opened my mouth to prod him further.

"Wh—"

"She bats both ways," Damian announced, clearly enjoying himself. I was shocked. I knew that phrase! She was bisexual! After an afternoon going through the files, I couldn't help but wonder . . . were there files on the teachers? I would have done anything to get my hands on hers!

"Not what you are thinking," Sarah interrupted quickly. "Damian has a special way with words that is amusing only to his juvenile students. What he means is that Randi, in addition to teaching at Langdon Hall, is probably the most in-demand tutor on the Upper East Side. When she's not here, she's in some Park Avenue penthouse tutoring a private school student."

"Langdon Hall kids?" I asked incredulously, my eyes glued to Randi, who was now downing an espresso as if it were a tequila shot.

"No, we're not allowed to tutor students who go to this school. She tutors kids from all the other schools." Sarah glanced at Randi again and continued, "It's not like she offers us this information, though. Frankly, she'll deny it if you ask her. Don't ask her, by the way. She's not very nice. But everyone knows because our kids have friends in all the other schools, and they tell them and then obviously it all leaks out."

"Yeah, next truth about private school world: everyone knows everything—teachers included—about two seconds after it happens. Nothing's a secret, so be careful," Damian warned.

"Damian, don't scare her! It's not like the Mafia! Honestly. Anna, just watch what you say and how much you choose to gossip, that's all. It's really not that bad, and the kids . . ."

I prepared myself for the worst when a soft, hypnotic smile spread across Sarah's face. "The kids are just *amazing*," she said earnestly. "They're brilliant and sweet and interesting. Truly."

This was the conversation I had dreamed of having all summer with another teacher. It almost made me forget for one brief minute about the files and even the Langdon Friends booklet. Until I noticed Damian furiously mouthing another message to me.

Sarah takes Prozac. A lot of it.

6

They put that kind of stuff in files?" Bridgette put down her peach Bellini and stared at me in horror. I was trying to stay focused on the conversation, but the place Bridgette had picked for my "celebration dinner" made anything aside from people-watching pretty impossible. Looking around the room, I felt like I was backstage at the MTV music awards with a sprinkling of E! I tried desperately not to fall into Bridgette as waiters shoved past me carrying trays of tiny little pasta dishes. The Gastineau girls were holding court at a corner table and I did a double take when I realized it was Harvey Weinstein sitting at the table across from them. According to Bridgette this restaurant was "the chicest" spot in Manhattan.

"Yeah, isn't that *crazy*? Do you think they had files like that on us in our high schools?" I wondered out loud. I could only hope that FBI-like student files were purely a Manhattan phenomenon.

"How interesting," Bridgette murmured. "Little Miss Teacher is uncovering some dirt in her perfect Teacher World." With a self-satisfied smirk, she downed her Bellini. Mine lay untouched. It was fourteen dollars. If Bridgette wasn't paying for this dinner, I would have to officially file for bankruptcy.

"Listen, Anna, I hope you don't mind. I invited a few of the analysts from my program over tonight—I think you know one of them 'cause she went to school with us," Bridgette trailed off, suddenly looking oddly uncomfortable.

"I thought it was just the two of us!" This evening was already going downhill and we hadn't even been seated. "We haven't hung out in so long, and I have so much to tell you!"

"You can still tell us everything," Bridgette replied, but she was looking around the room. "You'll love them. And you already know one of the girls so. . . ."

"Who is she?" I asked suspiciously.

"Belinda Bailey."

No way.

Not her.

St. Arthur's fraternity Belinda Bailey—the girl who had wooed me because she thought I had the "right look" for St. Arthur's, and then had dropped me the minute I admitted that there was no way my father was shelling out the monthly dues. I had spared her his exact words: "I'd rather buy a BMW a semester than pay to have you live in that Riverside prepster cult." My brother had chimed in, "Yeah, I heard one of their members committed suicide by hanging themselves with a ribbon belt."

Worst of all, Belinda had gone to Langdon Hall. Now I taught there. I was the help. The staff. We had both gone to the same college but apparently Belinda had moved into the glitzy world of investment banking and I had taken a step back—literally—into the world of high school. Her high school. For the first time, I wondered about my father's "you're going to regret this" comment.

"Anna, you're not mad, are you?" Bridgette asked.

"No, of course not," I lied. I was lying a lot lately. We stood there in an awkward silence in the middle of the boisterous restaurant and when a waiter gestured near an empty table, I thankfully turned in his direction. Sinking into my seat, I ran my eyes down the menu and grew increasingly faint as I saw the prices. Not only was I dreading seeing Belinda, if she looked anywhere as chic as Bridgette did in her black halter dress (or slip?) with her blonde hair slicked back into a tight ponytail, I would die. When Bridgette had told me to "dress cool," I had pulled out my staple jeans and black bar top. My bag was a fake Prada, and I had already caught some disdainful glances in its direction from the other flawless female patrons. They could smell a fake.

"Bridge?" A sexy, throaty voice interrupted my miserable thoughts.

"Ohmigod, Belinda, *hi!*" Bridgette got up and squealed (squealed?) and hugged Belinda tightly. Belinda wore a simple white strapless dress with zero jewelry and sported a tan that screamed St. Tropez. She looked more like Keira Knightley than she had in college. And thinner. She turned to me.

"You remember Anna Taggert, right?" Bridgette asked quickly.

"Um, sure. Hey." Belinda was making no attempt to hide her confusion. I was getting increasingly angry at Bridgette. This was supposed to be *my* celebration dinner! Why did Belinda look confused that I was there? And why were Bridgette and Belinda suddenly best friends?

As soon as Belinda sat down she and Bridgette huddled

together and began whispering furiously about the boys who would be joining us. I looked longingly at the sidewalk and had a wild impulse to run, but it had been so long since I had gone out with Bridgette that I was not about to give up so easily.

"So, Belinda, what have you been up to since college?" I asked brightly.

She ignored me. Maybe she hadn't heard me?

"Belinda! It's so great to see you!" I said louder, forcing a big smile. Belinda looked up and gave me a tight . . . smile? Bridgette, to my utter shock, didn't even look at me.

"I've been great," she responded coolly, then turned back to Bridgette. They clearly didn't want me here. I had nothing to do but pretend that the menu was the most fascinating reading I had ever encountered in my life. Somewhere between the forty-dollar Caesar salad and the sixty-dollar penne, four tall guys wearing suits walked in and smiled broadly when they spotted Bridgette and Belinda. I might have been invisible, but both girls appeared to have a radar for anyone they considered worthy. It rivaled anything Homeland Security could hope to own.

"Here come the guys," Belinda squealed, lighting a cigarette (apparently the no-smoking rule in Manhattan did not extend to this restaurant). Bridgette waved coyly and "the guys" ambled over to the table in a blur of gel, cologne, and blinding silk ties (think Donald Trump). I quickly excused myself to go to the bathroom. Neither Bridgette or Belinda seemed to hear because they were busy reaching out to hug "the guys."

Only I didn't go to the bathroom. I made a purposeful turn at the bar and headed to the entrance of the small restaurant.

In a moment of utter madness, or self-preservation, or both, I bolted from the restaurant and walked down West Broadway as quickly as I could. Actually, I ran. My cell phone started to ring and I knew it must be Bridgette but I ignored her. Crap, she must have seen me bust out of that place. Fourteen-dollar Bellinis. Forty-dollar salads. Belinda Bailey with a cherry on top. Three scoops of a sundae straight from hell. I found the nearest subway station and took the 6 train all the way to 86th Street, and then walked the two blocks to my apartment.

I was tired and embarrassed *and* I had school tomorrow. Trudging five flights of stairs in utter defeat, I stumbled into my apartment. Not even bothering to wash off my makeup, I kicked off my heels and curled into the mattress. I was a foreigner at Langdon, and tonight I may as well have been from another country with my supposed best friend. The last thought I had before I went to sleep (and I hated myself for it) was that I would have done anything to have had money and belonged tonight. Anything.

The remainder of orientation was spent preparing my room, typing up lesson plans, and attending inane department meetings and faculty workshops with titles like Deep Down We Are All Visual Learners and Your Student, Nanny, and You: Finding That Right Balance. I had assumed that a school like Langdon— springboard for the Ivy path, education bastion of the elite— would have a rich language arts curriculum.

I was wrong.

"You don't have an English curriculum?" I gasped when

Harold Warner, head of the middle-school English department, dropped a grammar and spelling textbook on my lap with a vague "I'm sure you'll feel your way around it."

"I wouldn't say that, Anna. No, I wouldn't say that at all." Harold looked more than a little irritated. "As I'm sure you were briefed during the orientation process, Langdon is a *progressive school. We cultivate a new kind of learning strategy.* If there is a war in the Middle East, then we talk about that. If our students are curious about a book they are reading, we discuss that. Sometimes we do some creative writing based on our discussions. It is all about discussion, Anna. That's what makes our curriculum so rich and deeply profound."

It sounded like bullshit to me. I wasn't alone. According to Damian, Harold was famous for doing absolutely nothing at Langdon Hall. He would ask his students to do three-month-long projects—"Go make a list of all the famous books written in the 1950s"—and send them packing to the library while he happily drank coffee and did his crossword puzzles. Like Sarah Waters, he was hugely popular among the parents because these long projects all received As and their students needed minimal outside tutoring. In fact, his Decades of Literature project was hailed as one of the shining examples of fine progressive education at Langdon. When I had pushed Damian and asked him how a teacher could avoid even grading, Damian had shaken his head and said two words: "Oral reports." Did the parents who paid Langdon's astronomical tuition ever bother to wonder what happened in the actual classrooms? I refused to be dictated to by such an obviously jaded man, even if he was my supervisor!

Easier said than done.

I quickly learned that Harold was going to do everything in his portly path to stop me from actually teaching any classes. When I showed him a lesson plan of which I was particularly proud—it consisted of leading my future class through all the modern-day references to *Romeo and Juliet*—he shook his head sadly.

"Harold, I really think this would show my students that Shakespeare is still relevant and alive," I argued.

"Anna, this is too *teacher-directed* a lesson," Harold disagreed, crinkling his nose as if my lesson plan gave off an unpleasant smell. "We can't have you having so many *teacher-directed* lessons. It makes the whole department look bad."

I was devastated. The lesson had taken me the better part of the morning to prepare, and what had kept me going was the anticipated excitement on my students' faces when they learned that my classes were going to be "cool" and "fun" as well as educational.

"Well, what should I have them do as a wrap-up for the Shakespeare unit, then?" I asked hopelessly.

"An independent project," Harold stated firmly. "Have them go up to the library. Give them a week to do it."

"What do I do while they're in the library?" I pressed.

"Plan for the next unit," Harold responded, looking a little bored. "Honestly, Anna, we have to teach our students to be independent learners. If we're always teaching them in the classroom, how are they going to become free thinkers? You have to let them go. Freedom. The freedom of a progressive education!"

More bullshit.

There was no way I wanted my students to traipse all over the building working on a pointless project. I had lessons I wanted to teach! I *wanted* to be in the classroom with them! Wasn't planning for the next unit something we were supposed to do when we weren't teaching? Disgusted, I got up to leave the English office.

"Oh, and Anna, one more thing. Remember we don't give grades at Langdon."

I stopped dead in my tracks. Nobody had told me this. I hadn't learned about this in my interview. Or on any orientation lecture. Even Damian had not informed me of this radical new way of assessment . . . or lack thereof.

"Damian said you give letter grades on your Decades of Literature oral reports," I challenged. What the hell did this guy mean, no grades? I was at a school, wasn't I?

"Oh, yes, we certainly provide our children with letter feedback on individual assignments. But the reports we submit to their parents never have grades. Ever. It goes against everything we stand for as a school."

"Then . . . how do I assess?" I felt like I was in the Twilight Teaching Zone.

"With comments," Harold responded, shaking his head in frustration. "Didn't you read any of the information about our school on the Web site? Grades are . . . titles. We avoid titles here at Langdon. We prefer to give valuable comments to our parent body."

"So the report cards just have comments about the students?" I asked curiously.

"Report cards?" Harold sniffed in disgust. "Report cards are for . . . public schools. We write informative essays on each of our students. With constructive comments."

Essays? On all fifty of my students? How long would that take?

"Don't worry, though. You can take your laptop home. That's what we use them for."

And just like that, I was a prisoner of my two-thousand-dollar laptop.

7

angdon Hall on the first day of school was as crowded as Morningside Heights on graduation day. Black Lincoln Town Cars were double-, triple-, *quadruple*-parked with not a traffic cop in sight. A line of bored-looking Latinas (nannies? housekeepers?) held the leashes of what seemed like an endless shih tzu and Yorkie parade. The women chatted to each other in Spanish as they waved good-bye to their young human charges, who greeted each other with the excitement that only the first day of school can provide. Amid all this bustle . . . *the Langdon Hall mothers.* These women—average height five-foot-seven, average weight 108—had assembled in loose packs of three and four. Some groups sported soft yoga whites that clung to their itsy-bitsy butt cheeks, others wore low-slung jeans with casual but expensive-looking T-shirts, while still others had slipped on trendy summer dresses with flip-flops. They looked like a casting call for a L'Oreal shampoo commercial. The highlights on these women—each and every one—were breathtaking. Everywhere I looked, hair seemed to be cascading, curling, and shimmering in the early September sunlight. And that's not all that shimmered. Each woman wore an enormous engagement ring. Four-, five-, and six-carat emerald-cut diamonds gleamed and twinkled as they waved *bye-bye* to their darlings. I was mesmerized.

"Wait till you see the dads."

I whirled around and there was Sarah smiling kindly at me. She nodded toward the scene and laughed. "I never get used to it either. It's quite a world, isn't it? Shall we dive in?"

"You first," I offered weakly, and watched Sarah approach a semicircle of women. The mothers closed in on her like paparazzi, surrounding her and giving her air kisses as if a celebrity were in their midst. Sarah looked positively thrilled, and I felt a surge of happiness. These mothers were wonderful! Any worries I had of teachers being treated like second-class citizens at Langdon were immediately eased. The families obviously respected us and knew that we were responsible for their children's education.

"Ahh, yes, our mothers do love Ms. Waters," Damian Oren sniggered behind me.

"What do you mean?" I asked, more than a little annoyed with his constant pessimism. These mothers seemed to genuinely love Sarah.

"She tells them all that their children are geniuses," he responded simply. "Even the dumb asses." With a shrug, he turned to watch Dr. Blumenfeld shake the hand of an adorable middle-school girl, and his face wrinkled in disgust. "She's such a phony I can't take it."

I didn't see anything insincere about the way Dr. Blumenfeld shook the child's hand. It was sweet, actually, that she took the time to personally greet all the students. I decided to take Damian's comments with a grain of salt and vowed never to become so jaded.

"Okay, Anna," he continued ominously, "let's do this—welcome to Dante's first level—the Langdon Hall Inferno!"

Clucking at his own cleverness, Damian walked toward the building. I followed him warily and felt a hundred eyes boring into the back of my head as I shook Dr. Blumenfeld's hand.

"Welcome to your first official day," she said kindly. And right then and there I decided to stay clear of Damian. He was a creep. This woman had given me a chance and had really done nothing unkind or phony. I was capable of making my own decisions. I entered the building, my head held high. Wait . . . did one of the mothers say something about me and Puerto Vallarta?

I stood near the entrance of my classroom, feeling like a Broadway actress on opening night. The scene I had just witnessed was a mere peep from behind the curtains. The moment had arrived and my performance was finally about to begin.

Congratulating myself for having come in during the long weekend to make photocopies of all my handouts, I felt ready to teach my first lesson. I refused to follow in Harold's footsteps. I had a full lesson prepared that required me to teach the class from beginning to end. My inexperience at teaching aside, I was adamant that seventh graders did *not* need to work on projects in the library so that they could become independent. They needed to be *taught*. In the classroom. By their teacher.

Before I could even extend my hand to shake each student's hand as I had planned, the seventh graders were upon me.

"THERE SHE IS!!!"

"Omigod, she's the new teacher!"

"She's, like, so young!"

"She's, like, our age!"

A deluge of students burst through the door, forming a circle around me. They backed me up against the chalkboard. I felt old and frumpy as twelve-year-old girls wearing neon Juicy skirts and Chanel ballet slippers raised their perfectly arched eyebrows at me. Did they *wax?* The boys—equally stunning—were in head-to-toe Abercrombie with white iPod strings dangling from their necks. It was as if an enormous circle of Ralph Lauren mini models were just breaking for lunch—and I was lunch.

"Hi!" I announced loudly, stepping out of the circle with a feigned confidence. With trembling knees, I walked to the board to write my name.

"WE ALREADY KNOW WHO YOU ARE!" Three girls shouted in unison, and if they had said they were all called Heather I swear to God I wouldn't have blinked.

"What are your names?" I asked sweetly, irritated with myself as I tried to step back from the ever-growing circle around me. This wasn't part of my lesson! Oh, God. I didn't even remember my lesson.

"Charlotte."

"Blair."

"Madeline."

I have to admit I gave Charlotte a closer look. She stared at me with wide, innocent blue eyes and the very idea that she even knew what the words *blow job* meant seemed ludicrous.

"Okay, girls," I ventured cautiously, "so you know all about me, huh?"

"YEAH! You're the new young teacher. You're pretty like Ms. Abrahams. You're going to teach English!" In spite of myself, I felt a foolish grin spread across my face. They thought I was pretty!

"Um, Ms. Taggert?"

A scrawny, red-haired girl with big braces and even bigger glasses peered intently at me. Poor thing. I would do my best to make this awkward little girl feel at home in my class.

"My name is Jessica Landau," she said confidently. "I just wanted you to know that Langdon Hall does not allow teachers to assign homework on Yom Kippur." Jessica made this announcement in a tone that would have humbled even the most stuck-up woman in my mother's bridge circle. So much for awkwardness. Jessica Landau . . . I did a furious search in my mental catalog of student files: Mother. Lesbian. And Yom Kippur?! That was, like, weeks away! Who was this kid?

"Excuse me?" I asked, trying to keep the sarcasm from my voice.

"Well," Jessica continued, pulling out a pink homework notebook with little glitter star stickers all over the front, "I just wanted to give you advance warning." She smiled frostily and held up her notebook to indicate the auspicious day on which I was not, under any circumstances, to give homework.

"Thank you, Jessica. I'll do my best to remember." I forced myself to smile.

A boy with sandy-brown hair and enormous brown eyes stepped in front of Jessica. "Um, my mother wanted you to know that my bar mitzvah is coming up and you should give me my work in advance so I can do it," he blurted. Before I could respond to his request, the group of seventh-graders all turned their attention to him.

"Omigod, Harry, when is your service?!"

"Next Saturday!"

"Shut up!"

"Seriously!"

"Where?"

"Temple Emanu-El."

"Sweet! Mine, too!" The voices came from every direction. I turned my head back and forth, trying to keep up. It was like watching the U.S. Open. My neck hurt.

"Are there so many bar mitzvahs coming up?" I blurted, a bit shocked. Nobody had warned me about this seventh-grade phenomenon.

"*Bat*," Blair spat out.

"What?" I asked.

"*Bat*. Boys have *Bar*. Girls have *Bat*."

Cover-of-*Teen Vogue* Blair. No wonder. She looked like she was already eighteen. Only the first day and already I felt as if I might hate one of my students just a little bit. That couldn't be good.

"I'm not having a bat mitzvah, but I have a chess tournament in a week so I may not be able to do my work then," said a small girl wearing tight black pants with the words so low stretched out across her butt. I had never seen these before. So many of the girls were wearing the same pants in different colors that I wondered if this was a brand beyond Juicy. Did the name not strike any of their parents as inappropriate?

"And next weekend I have a riding tournament so I'll be out of town and—"

"EXCUUUSSE ME!" I suddenly shouted. I had to remind them who was boss. Oh no! Had I yelled? Yes, I really had. I had yelled. I really had not wanted to yell. I had not wanted to be a yeller! I took a step boldly into the circle and started speaking as quickly as I could.

"Okay, here are a few things you need to know about me. One, you'll be learning a lot. Two, we're going to have fun. Three, I give a lot of homework. And finally, if you ever have an *individual* problem about why you can or cannot do your work, then please speak to me *individually* after class. Right now, I would like you to all take your seats. I would like to begin class."

After a moment of silence, my students began moving reluctantly toward the conference table. I noticed a few of them give each other little glances with raised eyebrows.

"Please just find a seat, okay?" I begged, absolutely detesting myself for being so nervous.

"Where?" Jessica asked.

"At the table," I responded stupidly.

"Um, yeah, we figured that one out. I meant, like, do we have assigned seats?" Jessica asked, giving Charlotte a little wink. I did not like that wink one little bit. If I didn't come up with a clever response, I was going to lose control.

Inspiration.

"This is a *progressive* school, Jessica," I replied slowly, giving her a knowing look. "I believe in giving my students the freedom to sit where they want with the assumption that they will sit in a place which will not cause them to be distracted. So I hope you, and everyone else, will think carefully about where you choose to sit each day."

They bought it. They had been hearing that word *progressive* since kindergarten, and I had a feeling that they understood it about as much as I did. But it was impressive enough to shut them all up. I made a mental note to store the word and use it for future ammunition. I watched with increasing wonder as they claimed their seats, marking their territories with Black-Berrys, cell phones, and iPods. The table looked like the scene of an illicit smuggling den, but these little muggers obviously saw nothing out of the ordinary.

"I'd like to start my class with a reading of Robert Frost's 'The Road Not Taken,'" I announced brightly after they were all sitting down.

"That's a poem about this dude in front of two roads. My brother told me every teacher is, like, obsessed with it." I looked in the direction of the latest disruption. It was peanut-allergies Benjamin.

"Benjamin, I need you to raise your hand when you want to make a comment," I responded sternly.

Benjamin raised his hand in a halfhearted effort to appease me, but he continued talking, "And poetry is something we did *all the time* last year and I *hated* it."

"Well, you will not *hate* this poem. It was *life-altering* when I read it for the first time, and it sets the tone for my class," I declared. "And now, I would like no more comments until I have read Frost's work completely." There, finally, was the moment I had been dreaming about. I was going to recite my favorite poem to my first class. Some demented part of me expected them to clap when it was finished.

I never realized how long that darn poem was.

Reading it alone in my apartment, I had been filled with the grandiose desire to take the more difficult path in life. I imagined myself as Frost's wanderer, caught in the crossroads. Yes, I could have taken the investment banking road, but I, why, I took the road less traveled and decided to become a teacher. And that, I had imagined at 3:00 A.M., while pacing back and forth in my apartment, would make all the difference. I had envisioned reading it to my class and having all my students become immediately inspired to always take "the road less traveled." I would be Robin Williams from *Dead Poets Society*! Instead of yelling "Carpe diem," my students would follow me down the halls of Langdon shouting, "Take the road less traveled!" Everyone would nod understandingly because they were "Ms. Taggert's kids," those unruly, unconventional geniuses who weren't afraid to pave the way. But as I read the poem to the class I was painfully aware of the shuffling and dramatic sighs being emitted from around the table. After what felt like an eternity, I reached the final line and read it with a burst of passion.

" 'And *that*,' " I looked around the room with conviction, " 'has made *all the difference*.' "

Silence.

Maybe they were letting the impact of Frost's words sink in?

Maybe they were too moved to speak?

Overwhelmed by its brilliance?

Forcing myself not to panic, I took a deep breath and waited for their reaction. I didn't have to wait too long.

"I don't get it."

"Are we going to be tested on this?"

"Is this guy, like, a *loner*? Why does he do all this walking by himself?"

"Yeah. He's like a total sketch ball."

"Like a stalker or something."

Terrific. Robert Frost was reduced to a sketchy stalker.

"This is a poem about taking the more difficult road!" I cried defensively. "It's about standing apart from the crowd, taking your *own* path. That is what I hope you will all do in my class!"

I had envisioned discussing the poem for at least fifteen minutes and hopefully drawing this conclusion out of them. What was wrong with me?

Blair raised her hand. I called on her warily.

"Maybe," she paused for effect, "maybe if you *drew* the poem out on the board we would all have a better sense of its . . . *intrinsic meaning.*"

"Blair, you want me to draw out the poem?" I was nonplussed.

"Yes. I'm a *visual learner.* If I can *see* the overarching themes *drawn out*, I can get a better handle on them. My learning specialist told me all about it," she finished smugly.

All eyes were upon me. The words *learning specialist* had been hurled at me like a seventh-grade grenade. I had to react. This time, however, my mind drew a blank.

I was defeated.

I approached the board and began drawing a stick figure facing two roads. I felt like an ass. Were they all watching me? I was dying to turn around to see, but instead I began to draw twigs and broken branches on one road.

"That's, like, the harder road, right?" Blair asked. A few girls in the corner began to giggle. I stopped drawing and nodded dumbly.

"Make a sun with a smiley face on the other road," Blair instructed. "So people can see that it doesn't have any obstacles. The sun is *symbolic.*"

Hating myself, I obediently began to draw a sun with large, exaggerated rays. Blair seemed to have quite a firm grasp on the poem's meaning for someone who had just loudly claimed that she didn't "get it."

"With a smiley face," Charlotte reminded, and shot a quick look at Blair. Both girls stared back at me with wide, innocent eyes. I had no choice but to fill in the sun's face, uncomfortably aware of the increasing giggles throughout the room.

"Is that better?" I asked, putting the chalk down. I had never felt like a bigger fool.

"That sun looks cracked out," Benjamin observed, and the entire room exploded in laugher.

At me.

I wanted to run. I wanted to cry. How was I ever going to win their respect after this? Even the stupid smiley-faced sun I had just drawn seemed to be laughing at me in all his demonic chalkboard glory. But if I ran out now I would become *that* teacher. The one who fled her classroom on the first day. I could just see Dr. Blumenfeld shaking her head sadly and telling me that she had made a mistake. I couldn't let that happen! Smiling weakly, I turned to the stack of *Romeo and Juliet* books I had stacked neatly on the ledge.

"This is the first book we will be reading this year," I announced as I began to pass them out. "Please write your name in pen on the title page in case you lose it."

"Can we use a pencil?"

"I only use gel pens. Are gel pens okay?"

"Do you have a black Sharpie? Sharpies are more *permanent*."

These kids were not seventh-graders. They were monsters with a predilection for bizarre writing implements.

"Use your judgment," I responded vaguely, not really caring at that moment if they threw the books out of the window.

"Isn't *Romeo and Juliet* a play?" Charlotte asked sweetly.

"Why, yes, Charlotte," I responded gratefully.

"That's what I thought," she said smugly. "You said *book*."

The rest of class was like an out-of-body experience. I heard myself give a monotonal description of Elizabethan England and then watched as I wrote a few key dates in Shakespeare's life on the board, pretending not to notice that nobody bothered to take a single note. We were all painfully aware of the clock—sixty seconds seemed like such an unreasonable amount of time to constitute a mere minute! Queen-Bee Blair yawned loudly and I didn't blame her. Even I was bored. I wanted them to leave so I could be alone and miserable. Maybe buy a pint of Betty Crocker vanilla frosting and lick the whole thing clean.

"Read the Prologue and write a summary of Act I, Scene 1, for tomorrow," I asked when the class finally came to an end. I knew I sounded like I was begging, but I was beyond caring. I just wanted them to leave!

Instead of rushing out, though, the entire class formed a line at my desk to discuss their *individual* issues. Why the fuck had I made that offer? One by one, they approached me with detailed explanations as to why I was to avoid giving them too much homework. Apparently these kids were busier than Zabar's on Saturday morning: Hebrew class, swimming lessons, yoga, ballet, painting, ice hockey, and the most anticipated and dreaded bar or bat mitzvah. A tiny boy wearing glasses was last on line, and I couldn't wait to get rid of him.

"I'm Michael. My mom told me to give you this," he said, handing me a small card.

"What is it?" I asked, curious in spite of myself.

"It's from my mother. She wants to have you come over for tea or something. She likes to meet all my teachers." I looked down at the heavy cream card:

> Sarah   Worthington
>
> 740 Park Avenue
>
> 212-546-7388

"Nice card stock, Michael," Blair called out casually as she left the room. Card stock? How did a seventh-grader know about card stock?

"It's really embarrassing," Michael offered, blushing at Blair's compliment.

"No . . . it's sweet. I'll call her. Thank you, Michael."

"You're welcome."

Michael kept looking at me. Why wouldn't this kid leave? Couldn't he see that I just wanted to bury my head in the desk and cry?

"Yes, Michael?" I asked, drawing on my last ounce of patience.

"I thought it was a really good poem. The Frost thing. I liked it."

Yeah, right. I was not going to fall for this again.

"I heard you laughing," I replied shortly, gesturing toward the door. "I'll see you tomorrow."

"Only Blair's posse and Benjamin," he conceded, then looked at me seriously. "But not everyone."

"*Everyone* was laughing," I mumbled bitterly, sinking in my seat. From my lowered vantage point, Michael no longer seemed so little. His brown eyes seemed almost wise as they peered at me behind the thick lenses of his glasses.

"Everyone does what those three do," he admitted, "but a lot of us find them annoying. And they always do stuff like that to new teachers and subs. They've been doing it since kindergarten."

I looked up at Michael gratefully, not quite sure who was the teacher at that moment. "So my lesson didn't totally—?"

"Oh, it totally sucked," he interrupted immediately. "I was just saying it wasn't all your fault. And the poem was kinda cool."

The bell sounded for the next class and I found myself grinning as I watched him dash out of the room.

"You shouldn't say *suck*," I called after him, knowing I sounded exactly like my mother. I didn't think he heard me, but all of a sudden I heard a locker door slam and a high-pitched "Sorry, Ms. Taggert!"

Ms. Taggert. That was me. I was a teacher at Langdon Hall. This was my dream job and I was not going to suck.

8

Resolve was one thing; momentum was another. After my first class—how did Michael put it . . . *totally sucked*—I was determined to do better. I squared my shoulders, took a deep breath, and prepared to approach my next lesson. Unfortunately, my next lesson wasn't for another three hours. A full day of classes was apparently too "public school" for Langdon, so its faculty taught just three hours a day. My students had all gone down to the science wing, and the halls were eerily silent. Not sure where I was supposed to go next, I wandered out of my classroom only to bump into Sarah Waters.

"Anna!" she gasped dramatically, putting both arms up. Maybe she needed to pop another pill and calm down?

"I was just trying to figure out what I should do with this time," I explained defensively. Hmmm . . . What was that smell?

"*Do* with this time? What do you mean?"

"Well, I'm wondering if there's a mistake in my schedule." *I know that smell. I know that smell.* "I mean, it looks to me like I don't have any classes till 1:25. Surely that can't be right?" God, that smell is *so* familiar. What *is* it?! "Would you mind taking a look at my printout?"

"Eeks!" Sarah threw her hands up again as I handed her my schedule. "Watch the nails!"

Aha! Nail polish! I knew it! Sarah's nails did indeed look unnaturally shiny and wet.

"We have a lot of time free." She grinned sheepishly. "Langdon teachers single-handedly support Blooming Nails."

"Blumenfeld allows that?"

"Anna, there's a lot of 'better-left-unsaid' over here. If you announce that you are getting your nails done during the three hours you are free, everyone will rush to point fingers. Sorry . . . no pun intended. You just have to, you know, learn to *disappear*." Sarah looked around nervously and gestured for me to duck back into my classroom. "We use words like *errand* and *bank* to sneak out of the building, and then it's up to you. Just avoid massages."

"Why?" I couldn't believe I was actually asking why getting a massage in the middle of the teaching day was out of the question.

"Because you have to keep the cell phone off. Essentially you can do anything just so long as it allows you to keep your cell phone on. I was getting my hair blown out once when the main office called to tell me that one of my students needed to speak to me."

"What did you do?"

"I said I was at the bank, put my hair up, and was back in the building in under five minutes."

"So I can just . . . leave?"

"Disappear," Sarah corrected, blowing on her nails. "Just master the art of disappearance. And *always* leave your cell phone on."

Alone in my classroom once again, I shook my head sadly at the thought of teachers needing to disappear. I had had all summer to myself. Why would I want to leave my dream job in the middle of the day? Feeling a bit sorry for Sarah, I decided to look for fellow teachers who also didn't feel compelled to leave. These would be the teachers I would befriend, the colleagues I would spend free periods with. Together we'd create innovative lesson plans. We might even team-teach. What kind of person found happiness at a nail salon in the middle of the day? No wonder Sarah needed Prozac.

I popped my head into the classroom beside mine. Surprise! It belonged to bat-both-ways Randi Abrahams, the warrior princess of the faculty lounge. How bad could she be if she spent her free hours in her classroom? Wasn't that the ultimate sign of dedication?

"Hi!" I smiled, suddenly feeling shy.

Randi closed the book she was reading and turned it over as if I had just caught her with porn.

"Hello," she said coldly.

"Was that *Romeo and Juliet*?" I ventured bravely, thinking how wonderful it was that Randi liked to be "in the know," that she liked to be aware of what her students were learning in other classes. Maybe I should ask her for a copy of her history textbook?

"No, it's not," Randi answered icily.

"Oh." I couldn't believe it. If any lie went down in the history of stupid lies, this had to be it. What was the point?

"I was just wondering what we were supposed to do now? I mean, I don't teach another class for *three* hours," I asked.

"When the school year progresses, there will be meetings. And this is also a time to call parents. Now, if you'll excuse me, Ms. Taggert, I really need to get back to what I was doing."

"Oh," I faltered, now scrutinizing her like a maniac, "of course. I'm sorry to bother you." But I just stood there, unable to move.

"Can I do something for you?" she asked coldly after a minute.

"Um . . . er . . . would you like to go to the cafeteria with me?" Ugh. I sounded like a middle-schooler incapable of going to the cafeteria by herself. Randi caught the insecurity with an almost imperceptible raise of her right eyebrow.

"I haven't decided when I'm going to lunch, Ms. Taggert. Now, if you'll excuse me, I really need to get back to my work." Randi turned back to her desk and pretended to become intently focused on the piece of paper in front of her. What was her problem? Maybe Damian Oren, with all his dark views on the private-school world, *was* the only voice of reason. I left the room, but not without one last glance at Randi's flawless highlights and Cartier watch.

The cafeteria was in the middle of a full-blown food festival. An Indian food festival. Bhangra music was playing loudly, and in the far corner professional dancers were doing a traditional dance in traditional costume. In the other corner of the cafeteria chefs tossed breads in the air in front of a sign that read: SAMPLE NAAN, THE TRADITIONAL BREAD OF INDIA! The lunch ladies were serving dishes that all had neat little signs beside them: TANDOORI CHICKEN. BASMATI RICE. CHANA MASALA. ALOO TIKKA. LAMB KEBAB. Lines of little ten- and eleven-year-olds mingled with adult teachers and high school students, all piling their plates with the exotic cuisine.

"I prefer Little Italy," a familiar voice sounded behind me.

"Damian!" I cried gratefully. "Sit with me?" I hated that once again I was sounding like a pathetic and insecure middle-schooler, but I just couldn't stand eating alone.

"Oh, no," he laughed. "I come down every now and then to see the show, but I live off coffee during the day. Come see me later if you're bored." He gave me a sardonic wink and wandered leisurely down the hallway, slapping high five to a group of high school boys.

Alone once again in the crowd, I stood in line and allowed the lunch ladies to fill my plate with basmati rice and chicken tikka masala. Before I could stop her, she added a samosa for good measure. Facing the sea of people in the cafeteria, I had a flashback of my first day in the cafeteria as a sixth-grader. Where would I sit? Where did I belong?

Snap out of it, Anna! You're being ridiculous! I forced myself to look around and notice the table arrangements. While students were sprawled in every direction, I noticed a small corner where two tables appeared to be reserved for faculty. I rushed over gratefully and slid into the first available seat.

"Hello!" I said brightly, and was greeted with cold nods. I hadn't seen any of these teachers at orientation or in the halls. They quickly returned to their conversations, while I sat among them, picking at my basmati rice. It was like being at that restaurant with Bridgette all over again, only worse because this time there was nowhere to run. I *worked* here.

"What do *you* teach?" I asked with exaggerated interest, hoping that one of them would respond.

"Math," a voice responded flatly.

I turned gratefully to my left and extended my hand.

"Anna Taggert, seventh-grade English," I said in my friend-liest voice. The woman I was facing appeared to be in her mid-forties with thinning brown hair that reached just below her chin level. Her watery blue eyes peered suspiciously at me and her thin lips were creased in a grimace. Since she was sitting I couldn't make out if she was simply large boned or overweight, and the shapeless brown tunic dress she was wearing made it even harder to discern. She looked supremely irritated that I had interrupted her lunch, and my smile began to fade.

"I *know* who you are," she said accusingly.

"I'm sure it's easier for *veteran* teachers to know who the new teachers are," I replied defensively, purposefully stressing the word *veteran*.

"I'm Dorothy Steeple," she continued, irritated. "I teach . . ."

She stopped midsentence and I watched with growing fasci-nation as she closed her eyes and sighed deeply.

"Seventh-grade math."

Oh. We taught the same kids. Was I supposed to know that?

"I see! We have the same students," I said with forced enthu-siasm. "I'm so sorry, I still haven't met all the seventh-grade teachers. And I've only had one section of my English class so far . . . the kids were pretty difficult."

"Um . . . ," Dorothy said slowly, closing her eyes again.

I was really starting to wish that I hadn't opened my mouth. What was I supposed to do when she closed her eyes? Wait with bated breath till she deigned to speak?

"The kids," she said suddenly, her eyes now wide open, "are not the problem."

There went the eyes again. If she was my teacher I would have killed myself.

"I never have difficulties in my classroom," she declared. "Ever."

"How nice for you," I muttered, feeling more depressed than ever. My drinking-margaritas-with-the-teachers fantasy was growing dimmer by the minute. Not only were two of the teachers in my grade level not interested in becoming friends with me, but they were openly hostile. Mumbling something about having to prepare for my next class, I picked up my tray and headed toward the garbage.

"Anna! You cannot throw away food from the mother country!"

Ashok Mehta stood in front of me with his hands on his hips, staring indignantly at my full plate. His face was even shinier than it had been during orientation, but it had lost its plumpness. Maybe his first class had also taken a toll on him?

"I'm sorry, Ashok, I'm just not hungry. I actually love Indian food," I promised, not wanting another confrontation.

"This is the time to stock up, though," he said seriously, stepping aside as I emptied my plate.

"Huh?"

"I don't know about you, but with rent and basic bills I barely have enough for dinner," he complained, falling in step with me as we walked out of the cafeteria. Lifting the flap of his satchel, he revealed several tin-foiled packages.

"No, you didn't . . ." I was torn between laughing outright that Ashok was smuggling his dinner from the cafeteria and the idea of doing it myself.

"You just—" Ashok paused and looked around furtively as if he were about to divulge a top secret, "—keep the Reynolds Wrap in your desk. One of the guys in the computer lab taught me this trick during orientation. We did the math. Not paying for dinner can save you a few thousand each year!" The thought of Ashok crunching these numbers with one of the computer lab technicians made me laugh outright. But he was right. Dinners *would* add up, and the free Langdon lunch was a perk we could make good use of.

"How was your first class?" I asked, changing the subject. The lunch smuggling had amused me at first, but I was starting to find the idea depressing.

Ashok's face immediately fell. "They hate me, Anna. I gave them one hour of homework and they looked at me like I was the devil. They all started complaining and yelling so loudly that I thought Blumenfeld would hear and fire me. I gave up and cut it down to twenty minutes. I don't understand it, Anna. Where I come from teachers are like gods. And only one hour's worth of math homework is a gift, not a punishment!"

The bell rang before I could answer.

9

t was Sunday afternoon and I had spent the last six hours scouring every retail store on the Upper East Side for a job. There was no doubt in my mind that I needed something to supplement my salary, and somehow I couldn't bring myself to follow Ashok's example and bring home the Langdon lunch. While Mom's check would carry me through (actually two—she had slipped another check into my purse as she and Dad had left), I just couldn't keep accepting their money. So I paraded up and down Third Avenue with my I'd-like-to-speak-to-the-manager-about-a-part-time-job spiel. I went everywhere. Ann Taylor. Banana Republic. Gap. Even Talbots. Nothing. I was ready to declare Manhattan the land of zero opportunity. Feeling self-destructive, I decided to drown my sorrows in a four-dollar pumpkin spice latte.

Starbucks was a rare treat for me these days, which was probably why the mere thought of waiting on line and jostling for a table had cheered me up. I was tired by the time I reached the Starbucks at 75th Street and Third Avenue, but in better spirits. Actually, I was feeling almost giddy at the thought of my latte, which might have been why I was considering the extravagance of a pack of madeleines to go with it. I was scouring the pockets of my purse to see if I could come up with more than five dollars, when I noticed peanut-allergies Benjamin sitting at a corner table. He was furiously texting with both fingers and didn't look up as I approached the table.

"Hi, Benjmain!" I said brightly.

Benjamin froze in midtext.

"It's me! Ms. Taggert!" I could say the stupidest things sometimes.

"Um . . . hey, Ms. Taggert," he mumbled, looking nervously toward the long line at the counter.

"I guess great minds think alike!" I continued, corny as hell.

"Um . . . great minds?"

"You know . . . you, me, this Starbucks? Great minds . . . we had the same idea so we both think—"

"Um, yeah, I got it," he said, still looking a little panicked. Had I scared him on the first day? Was there something off-putting about me? I had to learn to be cooler!

"Yeah, I can be such a dork," I grinned, rolling my eyes. "So it must be like the most embarrassing thing ever to run into your teacher outside of school, right?"

There! That was cool! I sounded more normal.

"I guess," Benjamin trailed off, now slumping in his seat.

"Benjamin, I got your text right in time! I changed it to a peppermint mocha!" Both Benjamin and I turned toward the familiar voice. It was Randi Abrahams! When she saw me, her entire body stiffened. Benjamin looked equally stricken.

What was going on?

Randi was holding Benjamin's peppermint mocha, so clearly they were together. If he was texting her . . . that must mean he had her number. Oh *GOD!* I knew what this was. I had seen it on Lifetime! This was the Mary Kay Letourneau story—a sick, twisted Manhattan private school version with peanut-allergies Benjamin and Cartier-wearing Ms. Abrahams as the principal players. I was going to report it immediately!

That's when I caught a glimpse of the computer screen on the little table.

"Isn't that a summary of the first act in *Romeo and Juliet*?" I pointed accusingly. A few customers had turned to look up with startled faces. I was making a small scene, but I didn't care. I might have been new, but I wasn't stupid. Is this how this sick woman seduced students? Was helping them with homework her version of perverted foreplay?

"Oh! Anna! Listen, let's catch up later? I'm just awfully busy right now." Randi laughed nervously and took a sip of coffee. Her hands were shaking just a little. I decided to ignore her and address Benjamin directly.

"I just kinda ran into Ms. Abrahams here," Benjamin replied, still refusing to meet my eyes.

"Anna, please, can we speak later?" Randi managed to ask while simultaneously smiling and clenching her teeth, her eyes shooting darts through my skull. We both stared at each other, frozen in an awkward silence. I looked at the screen:

One can ascertain that the animosity between the Capulets and Montagues stems from an ancient and inexplicable grudge.

There was no way a seventh-grader could have written that. The truth was starting to dawn on me. This wasn't some illicit love affair. Randi Abrahams was "tutoring" Benjamin for my English class! Was this what happened? Did teachers at Langdon Hall illegally tutor their students? Were my students CHEATERS?

"Well," Randi said finally, obviously defeated and more than a little pissed.

"Well. I'll see you tomorrow, I guess," I offered. I glared at Benjamin, whose left foot was now shaking with a nervous twitch. If he *dared* to hand in that paper, I was going to take it all the way up to Dr. Blumenfeld. Did Randi honestly think that I would believe that seventh-grade Benjamin Kensington would use *ascertain* correctly in a sentence?

Monday morning and I couldn't wait to collect my weekend's assignment. To Benjamin's credit, he could barely meet my eyes as he walked into class. The rest of the class was present and unusually quiet. The weekend's bar and bat mitzvah festivities had taken a toll, and most of them were slumped in their little chairs, looking quite adorable.

"Why don't you all take a minute and relax while I collect the papers? No homework tonight, okay?" I announced gently, enjoying the grateful smiles. Class went smoothly, and whether it was their sleepiness or my determination to explain iambic pentameter—perhaps it was a combination of both—at the end of the hour I felt, for the first time, a bona fide teacher.

And then I scanned Benjamin Kensington's paper.

I couldn't believe it.

I was FURIOUS, OUTRAGED, and GETTING RANDI FIRED.

Unsure of how to proceed, I found myself heading to Damian's classroom and hoping desperately that he wasn't teaching a class.

"Is that Anna? From the far outreaches of the distant middle school? What beckons you here?" I had never been more thrilled to hear Damian's sarcastic voice. I slammed a copy of Benjamin's paper in front of him.

"Read," I commanded.

Damian raised one eyebrow, skimmed over the first few lines, and grinned. Then his eyes raised to the heading of the paper to take in Benjamin's name and he shook his head in understanding. I couldn't believe it. Where was the look of disbelief? The outrage? The outright indignation?

"Anna, go teach your class. Leave this alone," he said almost gently, all sarcasm erased. "Honestly, it's not worth it. He's a Kensington."

"Okay, Damian, I know what you're going to say." I pushed forward. "I *know* Benjamin's parents are on the front page of that Langdon Hall Friends book. But I *saw* him doing this with Randi Abrahams at Starbucks. It's not like I *think* he didn't do this. I have actual *proof*." At Randi's name he looked up and stared at me for a moment and then he shook his head in disgust.

"So she's tutoring our kids, now. Amazing. Should have figured." Still calm, Damian went over to his desk and picked up a stack of papers. "Listen, Anna, I have a class in a few minutes, but I'm telling you that it's just not worth it. Where do you want to go with this? Get Benjamin in trouble? Randi fired? Look like a hero? Believe me, that's not going to happen."

Feeling betrayed, I stormed out of Damian's classroom and headed to Harold Warner's office in the English department lounge.

"Harold, I have something very serious to discuss with you,"

I stated firmly upon entering, and was greeted by his hulking back. He was focused intently on the espresso machine and let me go on with seemingly little interest.

"I have a paper by a student that was not written by that student. It was written by his tutor, who also happens to be a teacher at this school. I saw Benjamin Kensington and R—"

"SHHH!" Harold whirled around, espresso forgotten. He was suddenly in a hyperalert, hyperfocused state. "Anna, you are new here, so let me remind you that this is a *private school*. We do not mention names and drop accusations so carelessly or so publicly. Let me see the paper in question." I handed the assignment to Harold, and watched him skim the first few lines and take in Benjamin's name on top.

"Anna, I'll handle this from here. Thanks so much," he said curtly, putting the paper facedown on his desk.

"Are we going to contact his parents? I'd like to speak with Randi about this." I pressed on. "And what do I say to Benjamin? Do I return the paper ungraded?" Harold seemed to be lost in thought for a moment, and then responded, "I'll get back to you. And please, Anna, *no names out loud*!" He turned around and sat down at his desk. That was it. I had been dismissed. Utterly frustrated, I thought about Damian's question: Where do you want to go with this?

Where did I want to go with this? The unavoidable truth was simple: I wanted to hurt Randi Abrahams. And not because she had written one of my students' papers. It was because I knew with absolute certainty that Randi was obviously on the Kensington payroll, and for all the thankless, payless hours I would spend that year grading Benjamin-Randi's homework and essays, she would receive extra payment. So there it was—the answer to Damian's question that I could really only share with myself. Before I could even begin to grapple with this truth, I looked up to see Ms. Rollins, Dr. Blumenfeld's secretary, approaching me with a panicked urgency.

"Anna. Dr. Blumenfeld would like to see you in her office right now." I glanced at the clock at the end of the hall and calculated that no more than two minutes had gone by since my conversation with Harold. Whatever she wanted, it couldn't be about the paper. There was nothing to do but follow her down the hall.

Alone again with Dr. Blumenfeld, I felt just as intimidated as I had been the first time. She was seated behind her desk and was staring intently at her computer screen. She did not look up when I walked in.

"You can close the door," she ordered.

I was officially scared out of my mind.

I took a seat at one of the upholstered chairs opposite her desk and made a mental note that the number one way to intimidate someone is to ignore their presence as Dr. Blumenfeld was doing right now.

"Is everything okay?" I asked nervously. She ignored me. We just sat there, opposite each other, in her still, icy office.

"Anna," Dr. Bumenfeld said finally, prying her eyes away from the computer screen.

"Yes?"

"How was your first day? I heard the kids were enthusiastic in the halls after they left your class." I sighed in relief.

"It was actually really great. The parents, the kids, the faculty. I *love* it here!" I gushed effusively. Clearly I was back in interviewing mode.

"The kids are great, aren't they?" She smiled warmly.

"It's everything I imagined." I smiled back, beginning to relax. There was no need for me to be so paranoid. This wasn't the secret service.

"I understand you may have one concern, though?"

Fuck. There it was.

How had Harold gotten to her so fast? E-mail. I was so stupid.

"Um, actually I did have a small concern that I shared with Harold not too long ago," I conceded. "I hate to do this, especially to a colleague, but I witnessed Randi Abrahams essentially writing my student's paper at Starbucks." I had blown the whistle. She had to react. Something had to be done.

"Yes, Harold mentioned that," she responded coolly.

"Obviously my primary concern is Benjamin's education," I lied. "I need him to write his own papers. And I was also led to believe that Langdon Hall teachers cannot tutor their own students."

Dr. Blumenfeld opened her mouth to speak and was interrupted by a small sound on her computer that indicated a fresh e-mail. She returned to her screen. Minutes passed uncomfortably.

"Anna," she finally said, looking at me dead in the eye, "I thank you for your concern. You have approached the right people about this serious issue, and it will be handled according to our procedures. You have done all you can do, so please just return the papers—*even Benjamin's*—and grade it as if it were his work." Was that it? I opened my mouth to protest.

"But I'd like to speak with him directly, and possibly Randi as well about—"

"Anna, we are very thankful that you did nothing rash with this. We will speak to the Kensington family, and of course I will be having a conversation with Randi later. At this juncture there is very little you can do. Thank you so much." Dr. Blumenfeld gave me a tight smile and returned to her computer. I got up from the chair and walked out of her office. I had a creepy feeling that her eyes were boring into my back as I left, and I had a feeling that neither the Kensington family nor Randi Abrahams would ever be spoken to about this paper. Twenty minutes remained before I taught my next class, and I still had no idea what I was going to teach.

That's when I did a horrible thing.

There was an open computer terminal in the middle school office and I sat down and opened Word. On the blank document I typed: *Benjamin Kensington gets tutored illegally by Randi Abrahams.* There was a sixth-grade math teacher near me, but she seemed to be engrossed in an e-mail. I surreptitiously pressed Print, pulled the page out of the printer, deleted the page from the computer screen, and walked calmly over to the Langdon Hall files. I opened the K drawer, folded the offending page, and slipped it into the Kensington file. Any thoughts I had once had as to what kind of teacher added the fact that Charlotte Robertson gave blow jobs to bar mitzvah boys was answered. Some pissed-off, frustrated teacher who needed to tell the truth to someone, *anyone*, before the cover-up began. Guilty and terrified, I returned to the computer terminal to check if I had any e-mails. I had a new message:

Date: Monday, October 4, 2005 11:14 AM
From: "Lara Kensington" <lkensington@metropolitansoci
ety.net>
Dear Ms. Taggert,
Benjamin just raves about you. I would love to have you
over for tea. I have found that cultivating relationships
with my son's teachers through the years has been so
important in Benjamin's education. I hope you feel the
same.
Kind regards,
Lara Kensington

I glanced at the timing on Benjamin's mother's e-mail. 11:14.
Was it just a coincidence that she had e-mailed me at the exact
time that I was alerting the middle school headmistress about
her son's paper? Was this vaguely disconnected, disorganized
place just a front for a system that was more tightly woven and
interconnected than the CIA?

10

My furniture arrived the same day my cell phone was cut off. Apparently my ever-increasing pile of unopened bills contained a ransom note from Verizon. But what could I do? Between rent and food, I could barely afford a cab, much less pay off my three-hundred-dollar cell phone bill. And now the Crate & Barrel deliveryman looked like he might need a big fat tip to take my furniture upstairs.

"No elevator?" he asked, eyes widening.

"Listen, please. I'll help. I'm pretty strong—I HAVE to get this upstairs," I pleaded desperately. Fifty paragraph summaries of Act 1, Scene 1 awaited me, and I had no lesson plan for the next day. It was 6:00 P.M.—I was obviously his last delivery—and neither of us had any patience left.

"Listen, miss, nobody told me about this. We don't do staircases like those. I don't even think it's going to *fit*."

I wanted to sit down on the curb and just bawl. For six weeks I had been sleeping on a blow-up mattress in the middle of my floor. Every night around 2:11 A.M. it started to release air. Depending on my mood I would either ignore it or rouse myself to pump it back up. Apart from the desk and throw pillows it was my only piece of "furniture." Besides sleeping on it, I graded papers on it, ate my meals on it, and typed lesson plans on my ridiculously expensive laptop on it. I needed this couch. Today. This evening. Now.

"Please," I begged weakly. "Please try."

The deliveryman looked at his partner, who was supremely irritated.

"All right, miss, we'll give it a shot . . ."

Two hours later, I was almost manic with joy at the sight of the couch in my apartment. The poor deliverymen had averaged almost a half hour on every flight, urged on only by my very genuine tears (yes, I had cried). I had two twenty-dollar bills in my wallet that were to last me till payday, but I gave them each one. It seemed the right thing to do. Still, neither of them looked too impressed, and I began to regret the tip the minute they turned their sweaty backs to me.

Too tired to take the plastic off my brand new couch, I collapsed on the sticky covering and stared at my ceiling. I would grade my papers a little later, I promised myself as I closed my eyes to take what I sincerely believed would be the tiniest of cat naps. . . .

I shot up at the horrid sound of my alarm, my skin stuck to plastic. What the hell? The fearful reality dawned on me. I had fallen asleep. For the whole night. No papers graded . . . NO LESSON PLAN! And I had to be in school in forty-five minutes. What would I say? What would I teach? I was getting fired. I rescued a skirt from the floor and a crumpled-but-passable sweater I had thrown on a corner of my blow-up mattress. There was no time for a shower. I grabbed an elastic band and yanked my hair in a ponytail as I flew down the five stories of my building, carrying my heels in my hands. Fuck! Fuck! Fuck!

Hailing a cab was out of the question. I raced up to Park Avenue, and, turning right, pushed myself to average a block a minute. I was sweating and dirty and exhausted and utterly, utterly unprepared as I pushed through Langdon's glass doors. Usually I liked to be early so that I could have my classroom set up and be waiting for my students when they walked in. Today I entered with the full school rush.

"MS. TAGGERT!!!!"

Oh no. Please leave me alone. Please, please, please.

I looked up to see Benjamin Kensington standing beside a beaming blonde in chic white yoga pants.

"I'm Lara! Did you get my e-mail yesterday?"

"Ms. Kensington, of course. I'm *so sorry* I didn't respond earlier," I apologized, willing myself to stand still and not make a mad rush for the staircase. Did she know what it felt like to face fifteen judgmental thirteen-year-olds at 8:00 A.M.?

"Well, this is *so much better*! You can give me a date right now!"

"Excuse me?"

"For tea! Or better yet, let me take you to Sarabeth's. For a getting-to-know-you lunch. It will be so lovely—we'll discuss Benjamin!" She made it sound like discussing Benjamin over lunch was akin to being awarded a Grammy.

"Mom, you are so embarrassing," Benjamin muttered before running off to join his friends near the elevator.

Lara Kensington laughed like a madwoman. I joined her to be polite.

"Isn't he just such a *kick?*"

"Such a kick," I agreed obediently. "Ms. Kensington, you'll have to excuse me. I have a class in—"

"Ms. Abrahams is a *dear* friend of the family, and I can tell you will be just as *dear* to us, Ms. Taggert. I'm so happy that the two of you are Benjamin's teachers, and I'm sure you'll both get along famously." Lara Kensington's voice dropped ever so slightly as she became ever so slightly threatening. She was still smiling widely, but her blue eyes had turned to ice.

"I can't wait," I responded faintly, then tore up the now emptied stairwell two stairs at a time all the way to the eighth floor for a class I was not prepared to see or teach.

I thought it couldn't get any worse, but I was wrong. Rounding the corner to my class, I was met with shouts and shrieks— screams, really. I opened the door to . . . pandemonium. Benjamin Kensington (aka most high-maintenance kid ever) was sprawled on the floor heaving, and a circle of scared-looking seventh graders were looking on, appalled.

"Oh, my God, what is happening?!" I screamed. "Everyone STAY CALM! NOBODY FREAK OUT!" I screamed even louder, freaking out.

"Benjamin's having a reaction!"

"His peanut allergies!"

"He is going to DIE!"

Oh God Oh God Oh God. I turned around and fled to the main office. To my horror and relief Dr. Blumenfeld was just coming in.

"Oh, please!" I gasped. "Benjamin . . . peanut . . . help . . ." the words were hardly out of my mouth and she was already halfway down the hall with me miserably behind her. When I entered the classroom, Randi Abrahams was kneeling beside Benjamin, stroking his head calmly. In her right hand a strange-looking device—a glue stick? Tide to Go?—was rooted between the fingers of her right hand. What the hell was that?

"Ah, Randi, you have an EpiPen," Dr. Blumenfeld sighed in relief. "Thank *you*."

"Ms. Abrahams is the COOLEST!" Jacob yelled, while all the girls danced around Randi, gushing on and on about how she had saved Benjamin's life. Dr. Blumenfeld turned around and eyed me frostily.

"Ms. Taggert, I assume Dr. Zimmerman told you about Benjamin's allergies," she asked.

"Uh, of course!"

"Then is there any reason you did not get trained to use an EpiPen?" There were about a million responses to that question, all beginning with "What the fuck is an EpiPen?" but I chose to nod dumbly. He had mentioned something about training to use the thing, but it had completely slipped my mind. Of course Randi had one handy. She probably had a freaking hospital ward underneath her desk.

"I will take Benjamin to my office and call his mother." Dr. Blumenfeld gave me one last appraising look, put her arm around Benjamin (who looked healthier post trauma than he had all last week), and marched out of my classroom. Randi gave me a raised eyebrow as she followed the headmistress out, and I was left with fifteen hostile children.

"Benjamin's had that issue since kindergarten," Jessica said meanly.

"Yeah, he could have *died*," Madeline spat out maliciously.

"If the board finds out you could get *fired*," Blair declared.

How quickly they turned when one of their own was hurt! I looked around the room and searched desperately for a way to win them back.

"I like your hair," Charlotte finally perked up, and the kids looked at me as if they had never seen me before.

"Ohmigod I've never seen your hair up in a ponytail before!" Jessica squealed. And like Jack's mask in *Lord of the Flies*, my hair became a thing of its own behind which I hid. I might have been scared and incompetent, but apparently I looked good in a ponytail, so all was forgiven. With no lesson in mind, I found myself relenting when Blair asked helpfully, "Maybe we can watch *Mean Girls* in class today? I mean, just to calm everyone down and all? I don't think we're in the right *mind-set* to be learning much this morning." Blair produced the DVD from her Chanel tote, the little Upper East Side Aladdin. And with that, the spell of peace that only *Mean Girls* can achieve on a group of thirteen-year-olds was cast.

I allowed all my classes to watch *Mean Girls* that day. My mind was numb and I just couldn't concentrate. But I vowed that I would get back on track that night, and I couldn't have been happier than when I finally made it up my five flights of stairs that evening after what I considered to be an utterly wasted day of teaching.

Until I saw them. Eighteen voice messages. Something very, very bad must have happened. Mom! Dad! Had someone died? Hysterical, I pressed PLAY. *Oh, God, please forgive me. I will be a better person. I will be a better teacher. You are punishing me. I am taking for granted the job of my dreams.*

"Ms. Taggert? Hi, this is Lucille Windham, I'm Sam's mother? I just—"

I pressed the FORWARD button. I'd get back to her. *Oh God Oh God Oh God*. I had never prayed so fervently.

"Hello, Ms. Taggert, this is Maxine Landau, Jessica's mother. We would—"

I pressed the FORWARD button again. What the hell?

"Ms. Taggert, this is Lara Kensington. Oh dear, I really am stalking you now, but—"

I pressed the FORWARD button. Again. And again. And again. Eighteen messages from eighteen Langdon mothers. I was horrified. All these women needed to be called back, and I had no idea what they wanted. Even if I spent no more than ten minutes per parent, just returning these calls would take me around three hours. Luckily I had very little new grading to do because we had spent the day watching *Mean Girls*, but I did need to come up with some sort of a lesson plan for tomorrow *and* still had the summary paragraphs to grade. After all, I couldn't just keep showing videos. Or could I? My thoughts were cut off with the phone ringing. With a slight dread, I picked up.

"Anna speaking."

"Ms. Taggert, I'm so glad I caught you! This is Lynn Briggman, Max's mother?" I remembered Gerard Zimmerman's voice as he read the Briggman file: *stalker mother*. Great. I had to pick up for the worst one.

"Wonderful to hear from you!" I lied brightly, settling into the couch (still covered with plastic).

"Ms. Taggert, I won't keep you long. I was just calling because Max told me that you have spent today watching a popular movie in your English class?" I sat up quickly. Oh, shit!

"I have to say that while Max just simply *adores* your class, my

husband and I cannot understand the pedagogy behind showing the kids *Mean Girls*? I mean, for an English class in which
you are supposedly reading Shakespeare?" Lynn Briggman was
pissed and I couldn't blame her. If I was paying $30,000 a year
for my child's tuition I would expect the teacher to do nothing
short of resurrecting Jesus. But I had to save my ass.

"Mrs. Briggman, I so appreciate your calling me, and let me
say that I happen to *adore* Max as well," I said as sincerely as I
possibly could considering I was lying through my teeth. So far,
Max's most meaningful contribution to class had been a massive and crude fart after I had assigned the first homework assignment.

"The *pedagogy* behind showing the students this film"—*Think
fast! Think fast! Think fast!*—"was, er, was to provide students
with a *progressive lens* from which they could better understand
how rivalries are formed, which of course connects with the
Montagues and Capulets in *Romeo and Juliet*. And that topic," I
finished proudly, "is to be the focus of our next few lessons
and paper." I was spewing total crap. I was a fountain of
bullshit. Thank you, Harold Warner.

"Paper?" Lynn Briggman appeared to have heard only one
word. And her voice had lost its icy confidence. This was interesting. I sat up, aware that the ball had suddenly shifted into
my court.

"Yes. We will have a paper coming up," I said, warming up.
Anything that seemed to frighten Ms. Briggman was a very,
very good thing.

"Oh, well, Ms. Taggert, we should talk about when that will
be due. As I'm sure Max has already told you, he has a bar mitzvah coming up and anything you can do to help him plan his

time will be most appreciated. But you're so organized and helpful I'm sure you'll give him all the help he needs!" She was positively obsequious now. Aha! Intimidating me might have been a sport for this woman, but the thought of making sure her son wrote an English paper while doubling up on his Hebrew lessons hit a sore spot.

"*Of course* he told me," I replied smoothly, now lying like a champ. "In fact, since I have already told the students about this paper, I thought I would give them a break in class to watch a film so that they could use their homework-free evenings to get started on the paper. Max must be working on it right now." I had a crazy image of Lynn Briggman and me in an old Western flick. We were having a standoff in front of a dusty old saloon. I had just fired. She went straight down.

"That is incredibly thoughtful of you, Ms. Taggert. Most teachers are so insensitive to this special time in a Jewish home. And Max is hard at work on his homework right now!"

"I try to stay on top of things," I assured generously. "And please . . . call me Anna."

One down, seventeen to go.

11

My desk was covered with envelopes. Gilded envelopes. Colorplay envelopes. Lettra envelopes. Kate Spade envelopes. Crane envelopes. Mrs. John Strong envelopes. Envelopes in wasabi green, steel blue, ecru, lobster, and three different shades of celadon.

I picked up the largest envelope. It was an elegant cream, and very heavy. The postage had cost over six dollars! I looked at the script. My name flew across the envelope as if written by doves. *Ms. Anna Taggert.* Never in my life had I seen anything so elegant. I tore open the envelope and pulled out . . . a sheet of Lucite? What on earth? The Lucite was approximately five inches square, painstakingly etched with the details of Sue Wong's . . . bat mitzvah. Interesting. I didn't know Sue was Jewish. I was holding the invitation in my hand, but I still didn't believe it. It looked more like a paperweight . . . or a coaster. What on earth did one do upon receiving such an invitation? Well, RSVP of course. But after that? Did I throw it out? Frame it? Sell it on eBay? Those other envelopes . . . they were likely bar mitzvah invitations, too. No wonder Blair had been able to assess the quality of Mrs. Worthington's card stock from across the room. Likely these kids had spent as much time in Kate's Paperie as they had in Gymboree. Now I'd seen everything.

"Ms. Taggert." My reverie was interrupted by a little voice.

"Yes, Sue?"

"Did you open mine?"

"Well, yes, I just did! Are . . . er . . . are you having a bat mitzvah?" I was new to all this, but it did seem strange to me that Sue Wong, daughter of Korean immigrants, would be having a Jewish coming-of-age celebration.

"No, Ms. Taggert," she said, suddenly impatient. "I'm having a faux mitzvah."

"I'm sorry, did you say a faux mitzvah?"

Little Sue Wong looked at me with annoyance. I shrugged my shoulders By now I was used to visual learners and peanut allergies, but I have to confess, this caught me off guard.

"Like, my therapist says I have a complex? About not having a bat mitzvah and all? My parents want me to have a healthy sense of adjustment and a high self-esteem?"

Apparently Sue only spoke in questions. I decided to switch to answers.

"So this is a fake party. A *pretend* bat mitzvah."

"Didn't I, like, say faux? It's a *faux* mitzvah. Like there's no synagogue service? But we have the whole party and everything?"

"And you want me to come to the party and . . . everything," I trailed cautiously.

"Do you, like, want to? Because, like, you should only come if you want to? And if you, like, think you'll have fun?" Sue shrugged her tiny shoulders as if she didn't care either way, then left the room with Blair and Jessica. Michael Worthington looked at me with wide eyes.

"You should totally go."

"Excuse me?"

"To Sue Wong's faux mitzvah."

"Do other teachers *really* attend these events?" The last thing I wanted to do was to upset any of the faculty.

"Yeah, lots of 'em do. But Ms. Taggert, Kanye West is coming!"

Kanye West . . . hmmmm. Wait. A. Minute. THE RAPPER??!!

"Michael, how do you know?" I pressed, forgetting I was a teacher and completely ready to indulge in gossip with a twelve-year-old boy.

"Sue Wong's parents are like mad rich and all and her dad's in the entertainment industry so, like, you have to go. Plus you're, like, young so you'll like it," Michael responded excitedly.

It didn't take long for me to realize that I was going to have to call in reinforcements. This was more Bridgette's territory than mine so, somewhat reluctantly, I called her. She picked up on the first ring.

"Anna, do you *hate* me?" Shit.

"No, I don't hate you, Bridge," I said slowly. I think I did hate her a little, though. Things had definitely changed between us.

"What happened that night at the restaurant? You haven't returned any of my calls. What did I do? Are you mad that Belinda came? I thought you two could have talked about Langdon Hall together! I thought—"

"Bridge, honestly, please let's not talk about it, okay? Can you do that for me? I just started feeling really sick and I didn't want to make any awkward excuses," I pleaded, and something in my voice must have gotten through because Bridgette was immediately silenced. After an awkward pause, she spoke.

"I love you, Annie. Friends?"

"Friends," I returned, a bit relieved that the conversation I had been dreading for weeks was over. "Listen, Bridge, I have to go to this thing . . ." I won't lie, I did enjoy telling Bridgette that I had a *thing*.

"What thing?" Bridgette asked curiously.

"This fake bat mitzvah thing for a little girl I teach."

"Family name?"

"Wong."

"WHO?"

"The Wong family," I repeated again, although I could hear Bridgette hyperventilating on the other line.

"YOU'RE GOING TO THE WONG FAUX MITZVAH???"

"Bridgette, OW! Don't shout!" My ears were ringing. And when did *faux mitzvah* enter everyone's vocabulary accept mine?

"Annie, Stanley Wong is the new head of Mo Jam Records! This event was mentioned in *Entertainment Weekly*!!!"

"Guess what?" I couldn't resist, now getting really excited. "KANYE WEST IS PERFORMING LIVE!" I was screaming. And then we were screaming together.

"I'm coming. I'm totally crashing," Bridgette declared.

Yeah, right.

"I'm so sorry, Bridgette. It's a very strict door policy. I actually just wanted your advice on what I should wear," I explained, enjoying the silence on the other line. This was *my* thing. Cipriani on *my terms*. An evil little part of me *relished* the idea that Bridgette was not coming, and that she would probably tell Belinda and "the guys" that I was going to the coolest event in town.

"Definitely a dress," Bridgette answered finally, and refused to provide me with any more details when pressed. She suddenly said something about work and tried to get off the phone, but I had known her long enough to have known for a fact that she was jealous.

"Bridge, you're not mad at me because I can't get you in, are you?" I asked sweetly.

"No, I'm not," Bridgette responded in a cool voice, then added quickly "Gotta go, call me and tell me how it was."

I didn't get the advice I had wanted, still—and I hated to admit it—it was the most satisfying conversation I had had with anyone in months.

WELCOME TO WILLY WONG'S CHOCOLATE FACTORY!!!

I hadn't even entered the ballroom and already I found myself mesmerized by the huge banner. The words were covered with a shimmering brown glitter and I had a feeling that it was only the beginning of my chocolate-infused evening.

"Chocolate martini?"

There was nobody in front of me.

"Chocolate martini?"

The voice came from below. Standing in front of me were two beaming midgets dressed as . . . Oompa Loompas? They had the same elaborate wig, bushy eyebrows, and white overalls as in the movie. Their middle-aged faces blinking back at me were as terrifying to me now as they had been when I was little. Apparently the Wongs were sparing no expense.

I accepted my chocolate martini and allowed one of the midgets to escort me into the factory. WILLY WONKA'S AC-TUAL CHOCOLATE FACTORY!

Gigantic fountains in all four corners of the room spurted rivers of chocolate.

"Drink! Drink! Drink!"

Madeline and Charlotte were squealing near one of the fountains as Chase tilted his head and guzzled the liquid fudge like a frat boy at a keg party.

The dance floor was lined with huge lollipops and candy flowers. Strobe lights flashed and all over kids were dancing. On the side of this exclusive mosh pit lay a mound of stilettos, Mary Janes, and strappy sandals. Hard to believe, but there they lay—Jimmy Choos, Manolo Blahniks, Giuseppe Zanottis, and Christian Louboutins—the abandoned shoes of twelve-year-old girls.

"There's sushi for adults," one of the Oompa Loompas of-fered, shaking his head in disgust. "If you don't want to drink germ-infested chocolate."

"In the Nobu stall next to Build-a-Bear," the other Oompa Loompa explained. I gulped down my martini and allowed them to lead me to the row of stalls. Jacob was at the first one getting a wax replica of his forearm.

"What is he going to do with that?" I wondered out loud.

"Have another martini," the Oompa Loompa offered. "It'll make more sense." I took another glass and continued down the row. Make your own sterling silver ID bracelets. Create a perfume. Have your picture taken with Ashlee Simpson . . . and there she was! Michael Kors was at the Build-a-Bear stall with Fergie, the Duchess of York. They were arguing over a pink tutu.

"Bollocks, Michael! I want my bear to be the ballerina!"

"You English are so bossy," he huffed, making no signs of releasing the tutu in question. Everywhere I turned I saw another celebrity or model, and none of my students seemed impressed.

Dateless and more than a little overwhelmed, I noticed a woman about my age standing by the bar. She was dressed in a black strapless gown, and her hair was blown out in loose curls and held together with a diamond clip. A glittering Fendi evening bag dangled delicately from her wrists (I couldn't miss those interlocking F buckles), and red satin heels peeped from below her dress. I was mesmerized by her style, sophistication, and—

"Hey, Ms. Abrahams!"

The stunning woman turned around confidently and lightly kissed the cheek of my seventh-grader, Benjamin, who was now eye level with her breasts and showed no signs of departure.

Randi. Fucking. Abrahams.

Kids rushed from the dance floor to surround Randi as if she were her very own entertainment stall. I watched Randi throw back her head and laugh, exposing two four-carat diamond studs. She let Jessica Landau and two other little girls dressed in sparkling cocktail dresses lead her onto the dance floor, where she began to shake her hips and dance. All my supposedly successful lesson plans were long forgotten in this world. My students made it very clear that at this party they only had eyes for their history teacher. Little Amy Greenberg had given me a guilty wave from the dance floor, but otherwise I might as well not have been there. I felt the room swim . . . and spin. I was jealous . . . and maybe a little tipsy. Full-blown envy raced through my veins.

A minute later, seven adults dressed in sexy black tops and tight pants scattered themselves throughout the dance floor and started teaching my students some seriously X-rated moves.

"Oh, wow . . . I just love those motivational dancers . . . they were at the Schuler bar mitzvah," a woman next to me gushed as one of my seventh-grade boys allowed himself to be sandwiched between two of these professional dancers, sticking his tongue out and gyrating his hips against each woman. Gross. The more he wiggled, the more the parents, students, and other dancers cheered. Nobody seemed to find anything wrong with the fact that a twelve-year-old was *grinding* with two adult women.

"I'm sorry," I asked the woman next to me, unable to help myself. "Motivational dancers?"

"Hired dancers? To get people dancing?"

I looked at the woman next to me as if she was from Mars, but she was now peering at me curiously.

"Hey . . . are you Sue's new English teacher?"

"Yes," I responded carefully, keeping an eye out for my seventh-grader in the middle of the motivational sex sandwich.

"I'm Sue Wong's tutor."

"Excuse me?" I was now barely giving this woman any attention because I was convinced that young Benjamin had just grabbed a motivational breast.

"I tutor Sue in English and history!" the woman continued brightly.

"How nice," I murmured, edging away as politely as I could so that I could get a better view of the motivational sexual abuse, which I was now incapable of tearing myself away from . . . and why the HELL didn't Randi Abrahams stop grinding with some child's father and save young Benjamin's innocence? I was a split second away from stepping in when the room went pitch black. My students screamed in delight.

"YO YO YO LANGDON HALL IN THE HOUSE!"

My students screamed even louder. Michael Kors looked flushed with excitement. Parents and children were moving frantically toward the center of the dance floor.

"JESUS WALKS . . ."

The music started pounding.

"JESUS WALKS!!!" My students screamed back, and then one spotlight exploded on the stage and revealed Kanye West in a white suit and a top hat. *Oh, my God, it was actually him in the flesh.* I had read somewhere that he didn't make an appearance for less than a quarter of a million dollars.

"JESUS . . . WALKS . . . WITH . . . ME . . . , YEAH, YEAH, YEAH . . . BOW, BOW, BOW, BOW, BOW, BOW, BOW, BOW . . ."

Sue Wong was smiling calmly as her classmates were now roaring, "Go, Kanye" in such a frenzied delirium that I thought I might go deaf. Parents were shaking their hips as the seventh-grade class waved their hands back and forth and danced at their private Kanye West concert. The Oompa Loompas were equally excited, and a few had formed a circle and were taking turns going into the center and break dancing. Kanye West winked at Randi Abrahams while rapping "Diamonds from Sierra Leone," and motioned for her to approach the stage. Parents clapped in encouragement and the kids were screaming, "Go, Ms. Abrahams! Go, Ms. Abrahams! Kanye wants you!"

I turned around in a mixture of shock, disbelief, and confusion, and raced out of Cipriani 42nd Street, which I was convinced was Dante's final level of hell. Damian Oren was right about this world.

12

I was dreading my lunch with Benjamin's mother. She hadn't mentioned much about the peanut allergy debacle when I had called to confirm, and frankly I was surprised that she hadn't cancelled, or at the very least had me fired. Guiltily, I made my way up Madison and turned into the restaurant on 92nd Street. The restaurant had a chic but rustic quality: burgundy awnings, yellow French doors, pine tables and floors, and a bake-shop counter where cute little rows of jams and home-baked pies were lined up on proud display. I felt like I had just entered a quaint bed-and-breakfast in Maine. One quick glance at its patrons, however, made one thing very clear: This was *not* Maine. Sarabeth's was the playground of the Langdon Hall mothers. Lara Kensington had invited me here for one specific purpose: to be seen with me. When I finally saw where she was seated—all the way at the back of the restaurant—it became abundantly clear that she wanted all the other mothers to see me heading over to *her* table. I greeted the room as if I were Bill Clinton—shaking hands and exchanging smiles—and could feel the curious stares from the few women who were not Langdon mothers. They may have thought I actually was a celebrity!

When I finally reached Lara's table she extended her hand as if she were Queen Elizabeth. For one wild moment I contemplated kissing it. Instead, I just took it in my own hand and waited for her to rise three quarters out of her seat so we could air kiss. Everyone was staring.

"Wow, so many of the other class mothers are here," I offered helplessly.

"Oh, are they?" Lara asked innocently. "They must like the food as much as I do! Please have a seat!" Gratefully, I sank into the seat opposite her. A waiter appeared and asked if we wanted tap or sparkling, and Lara interrupted my "Ta—" with a cool "Sparkling." I made a mental note *never* to order tap in Manhattan.

"I am *so* sorry about the other day—" I began immediately. I planned to begin with my apology so it wouldn't linger over the entire meal.

"Oh, Randi was there," Lara waved her hand carelessly. "And honestly, you're new. You can't be expected to be a super teacher *and* a lifesaver, now can you?" she asked charmingly, her white teeth glistening like a shark going for the kill. I inhaled.

"And speaking of great teachers," she leaned in closer to me, "that is *exactly* what you are. A gifted teacher. I've never seen my Benjamin get so excited over a class. Never!" At that moment we were approached by Gillian Stein, Jacob's mother.

"Ms. Taggert, is that you? What a lovely surprise!" A cloud of annoyance passed over Lara's eyes. She might have wanted to be seen with me, but she did *not* want to be interrupted.

"So nice to see you, too," I said, feeling Lara's now very dark, annoyed blue eyes penetrating my skull.

"My son just adores you!" Gillian exclaimed. I felt like a man caught between his wife and mistress.

"He's such a terrific kid," I replied lamely.

"Oh, how lovely of you to say!" Gillian gushed, clearly enjoying herself. "And he was so proud of the A he received on his first paragraph!" She air kissed us both, and returned to her table where another blonde who was not a Langdon Hall mother was eyeing us curiously.

"Gillian can be so flashy and in your face. I apologize for her," Lara said sweetly as she watched Gillian walk away. Something had happened between these two women in this brief interchange, and somehow, I was very much a part of it.

"She's nice," I defended, but not too strongly. "Shall we order?"

Lara was perfectly charming for the rest of the meal, asking me questions about growing up, college, and how I came to be at Langdon Hall. No check came at the end (a house account?) and as if she had never had to pay for a thing in her life, Lara got up gracefully and beamed at me.

"Anna, this was *so* much fun! We have to do this again!" I nodded yes, but was still mystified. We had not spoken about Benjamin. We had not spoken much about Langdon Hall. It had been all about me. I felt like I had been on a very lavish date with a man who was clearly trying to seduce me. Only Lara gave me one last innocent air kiss before getting into the Town Car that was waiting outside for her.

"Are you sure I can't offer you a ride home?" she asked, but I shook my head. I wanted the walk and I needed to figure out what had just transgressed in the dark, murky waters of the Sarabeth's cesspool.

I walked into school on Monday morning with three resolutions:

1. I would rededicate myself to being the best and most creative teacher I could be.

2. I would not allow Langdon mothers to dictate my life.

3. After returning Benjamin's paragraph with an A, I would never remain quiet about a cheating incident again.

Filled with good intentions, I forced myself not to cringe when Benjamin screamed, "Yeah, baby!" and held up his paper for the class to see when I returned it. I couldn't believe it—not a shred of remorse! That shaking, twitching boy in Starbucks was completely erased from his memory, and I watched him from the corner of my eye as I returned the other essays (which were all surprisingly sophisticated) as he made little raise-the-roof gestures with his hand to express his joy.

"Today I am going to give you all a card," I stated firmly, then began to circle the table so the class had to keep turning their heads to keep their eyes on me. I had discovered that the busier and more confused the students were, the less able they were to call out or distract.

"On each card," I continued, "will be a name. A *very special* name."

"Whose name?" Madeline blurted, unable to restrain herself.

"Madeline needs Ritalin," Jacob sneered.

I ignored them both.

"The name is someone from *Romeo and Juliet* and *that* person is who you will *be* for the rest of class. But you cannot show anyone this name. It is a *secret*." I had planned this lesson down to its tiniest detail. It was flawless. I opened my mouth to continue.

"I don't want to do this," Jessica complained.

"Yeah, this sounds very complicated," Sue agreed.

"Just *listen*," I urged. "You will *love* this activity! And—"

"I want to watch *Mean Girls* again," Max announced.

"Yeah, this card thing . . . *sucks*," Benjamin announced devilishly.

I had spent *hours* planning this activity! I had gotten to school early just to cut out the damn cards! I had bought fucking Hershey kisses as miniature prizes! With my *own* money. Then it happened. From the corner of my eye . . .

One.

Hot.

Tear.

"THEN DON'T DO IT!" I snapped, and stormed out of the room, leaving fifteen stunned students sitting in the classroom. I ran down the long corridor toward the girls' bathroom, tears stinging my face. Pushing open the door to an empty stall, I pulled myself up on the toilet seat so nobody could see my legs beneath.

That's when someone else started to cry.

Sniffle. Sniffle. Gasp.

It was from the stall next to me. Slowly I lowered my legs and unlocked my stall. I gently knocked on the door next to mine.

"Hello?" I asked gently, forgetting my own ridiculous behavior. Had I really just run out of my classroom?

The sniffling stopped. Like me, the occupant of this stall had raised her legs so it would appear empty.

"It's Ms. Taggert," I prodded. "Are you okay?"

Silence.

"You can talk to me if you want."

More silence. I had to give her something more.

"I just stormed out of my class," I offered stupidly.

"You did?" a little voice squeaked.

I nearly jumped in surprise.

"I did," I admitted. "I got scared and I just left in a panic."

"That . . . was a pretty . . . stupid thing to do," the voice stated between hiccups. Wait. I *knew* this voice. It belonged to Amy Greenberg from my third-period class.

"Amy?" I asked tentatively.

"Yeah," she confirmed miserably.

"Amy, can I please come in? Or will you please come out? I won't tell anybody that you cried," I promised. The door unlocked, but Amy made no sign of coming out. Gently, I pushed the door open and found her huddled on the toilet seat, her pale skin streaked with tears. She turned her big green eyes upward.

"Hi, Ms. Taggert."

"Amy, sweetheart, what happened?" The drama of my mad exit from class was completely erased from my mind. It was all I could do to stop myself from engulfing this little girl in my arms.

"It's so stupid," she sniffed, looking away.

"No, *stupid* is a teacher running out of her classroom," I corrected, and we both giggled.

"Okay, well, if you want to know the truth I'm scared . . . for . . . lunch." At the word *lunch* Amy started quietly sobbing again.

Why would the idea of lunch provide reason to panic? Was she anorexic?

"Amy, you have to help me out here . . ." I was completely in the dark.

"Ohmigod, Ms. Taggert, have you ever seen our lunchroom?" Amy cried, still shaking. "I . . . I *don't know where to sit!*"

"But there are so many seats, Amy," I replied ridiculously, not grasping that the number of available seats was not the issue.

"Okay, like, I always sat at this one table with Blair and Madeline?" Amy began, now ready to share her soul. "But then they were, like, Jessica is going to sit here, too, and that means basically they don't want me? So, like, now I have no *group* and lunch is next period!"

I felt a smile creep into my face, and I squashed it like a bug. I had *forgotten*. Oh God. In my desperate need to be a teacher I had forgotten what it was like to be a student. There, in that stall, Langdon Hall and my role in it made perfect sense to me.

"Amy, how would you like to skip lunch next period and go get a slice of pizza with me on Lexington Avenue?" I asked.

She looked up, shocked.

"We can't do that," she stated firmly.

"Yes, we can. I'm your teacher. I will tell the main office and Dr. Zimmerman that we needed to have a girl talk, and you are having lunch with me," I stated, equally firm. "Now, how about you go back to your class and I return to mine?"

Amy smiled. It was the first genuine smile I had received at Langdon. We left the bathroom together with a plan to meet in the lobby at noon. When I returned to my classroom, I was surprised to note that everyone was still seated at the table. Many of the kids were looking a bit sheepish.

"We're sorry," Jessica said softly.

"We want to play your game," Madeline added.

I paused for effect, and then launched into the most heartfelt speech I had given since I got to the school.

"Actually, we're *not* going to play a game," I declared. "I am tired of being tested. I'm your teacher, and you can either be grateful that I put time and energy into my lessons, or you can just do assignments all year that I will, so help me God, photocopy out of some very boring manual and let you do while I sit at this desk and read magazines. Your choice. Now, I am going to assign your home-work, and you are going to spend the rest of class working on it. If anyone," I took a deep breath and glared around the room, "*If any-one* talks or so much as calls out, you are going straight to Dr. Blu-menfeld's office. Are we clear? And then, I am not calling your mothers. I am calling your *fathers* at work and I will let them know how you are behaving."

No one said a word. The class worked in silence until the end of the period, and only when my last student had left my class did I allow myself to smile.

I learned more during my short pizza excursion with Amy Green-berg than I did during all of my education classes at Columbia put together. We had signed out in the main office and gone across to John's for slices.

"This is super cool of you, Ms. Taggert!" Amy had gushed happily. "Lunch is, like, the *worst* part of the day for me."

"So, it's still that important, huh? Sitting at the so-called right table?" It made me sick to realize this was still going on. I remembered spending some of my middle-school lunches hiding out in the library because there were no seats left at the "cool" table.

"It's, like, the *most* important thing," Amy admitted. "I would, like, *never* tell this to my mom, but sometimes I pretend to be sick in the morning if I know I can't sit with Blair and Madeline."

"Amy, how in the world do you know before school starts whether you are going to be sitting with these girls or not? And last time I checked, the lunchroom was made up of long rows!

Surely there's room for you?" I looked over to the petite, brown-haired girl with affection.

"Okay . . ." Amy started, pausing to dab her pizza with a napkin to wipe the grease off. "So, at night? We all go online? Wait—you know what IM'ing is, right?"

"I'm not that old," I laughed, rolling my eyes.

"Well, that's, like, when stuff gets decided. Like who is sitting with who. And who is dating who and who likes who."

"Sounds like a lot of who-who," I joked, but Amy was staring back, deadly serious.

"And there's only one end of the table where the popular girls sit, and that's where Blair and Madeline sit. *They* decide every night who to invite to sit there," Amy finished, now looking a bit miserable.

"So what happened last night?" I asked gently.

"Like, *everything*!" Amy exclaimed, her eyes welling up with tears. "So my mom is really strict and all? And she, like, doesn't like me being on IM past 10:00 P.M., so she made me get off, and everyone decides all this stuff at, like, 11:00 or midnight!"

The image of my entire class sitting in their separate bedrooms IM'ing each other at night flashed through my mind. I could almost see them—little faces bathed in the luminous glow of their computer screens as they ferociously secured lunch seats and dates for the next day. And parents wondered what their kids were doing up so late at night!

"So it's all about the IM, huh?" I asked.

"Well, yeah, being allowed up late helps. Which is a lot easier for the kids who have tutors and can get their homework done in time."

"Tutors?" I urged. The word was beginning to taunt me.

"Yeah . . . but, Ms. Taggert, omigod, you, like, *can't* tell anyone I'm telling you this," Amy said seriously, leaning forward. "Everyone has tutors!"

"So, what exactly do the tutors do?"

"Well, they're supposed to help with the homework . . . and *stuff*." Amy was looking increasingly uncomfortable.

"Amy, this is just you and me," I promised. "I'm not going to say anything." I meant it, too. I had to learn the truth about this tutoring thing, and I had a feeling that only a student was going to be able to give it to me.

"So, there're three kinds of tutors," Amy began slowly. "The first kind helps you organize your binders and tells you how to manage your time and stuff."

"Like a secretary," I encouraged.

"Yeah, like a secretary. Then there are the tutors who help with the actual homework."

"Help?"

"Well, some tutors help a little, like telling kids how to do certain math problems or editing their papers and stuff. But they don't last very long. Not like the popular tutors."

Amy's face was completely flushed. There were *popular* tutors.

"So, what does it take to be popular?" I pressed, but I already had a sick feeling in my stomach.

"They're the *third* kind of tutors. They . . . sorta . . . well . . . they *do* the work," Amy admitted. "Ms. Taggert, you cannot tell *anyone* I told you this!"

"What do you mean 'they do the work'?"

"The ones you can convince to . . . you know, sorta *do* your homework," Amy responded uncomfortably. "But we should get back now 'cause lunch is almost over?"

I trailed after Amy with a million questions running through my mind. How many of my students had *popular* tutors? Who were these immoral people? Was Randi one of them? Did they know they were undermining everything we teachers were trying to accomplish in the classroom?

More importantly, could I pay this little girl to be my spy?

13

That night I found myself staring resentfully at my source-book, *Shakespeare, the Classroom, and You!* Before I had met my students I had honestly believed that this single book was going to be my lifeboat. Now, it seemed hokey and boring and very 1950s. My students had been grudgingly turning in their assignments and occasionally participated when called on, but most of their glazed attention was on the clock above the door. One thing was certain: None of them cared about Romeo. Or Juliet. Jacob Stein had put it most eloquently:

"Maybe if they didn't speak like they'd been slipped a roofie we'd understand what they were saying."

Madeline had followed more gently:

"Jacob, you're so retarded. That's how Italians speak English."

I had to find a way to get to them. To make the play come alive. Obviously my students thought their scene summary assignments were the dullest things imaginable. At least they didn't have to read them. (If Amy was right about this tutoring racket, most of them didn't.) Each summary took me fifteen minutes to go through, at least. I had bought stickers—smiley faces, stars, emoticons—for the papers that were particularly well done. But it was hard to come up with helpful comments when I realized that I could be grading the seventh-grade work of an Ivy Leaguer. If only there were a way to know for sure!

Spending fifteen minutes on a homework assignment might not sound like a big chore, but multiply fifteen minutes by fifty students and that's well, twelve and a half hours! I had to divide the workload over the course of two nights. That meant that even with the many free periods at Langdon I had to work the minute I got home, usually until bedtime. Bridgette had long since given up on me and I had quickly found that my dreams of getting after-work margaritas with my friendly faculty friends were just that: dreams. Nobody had approached me at the end of the day or stopped by my classroom for a friendly chat. By 3:00 the school cleared and I usually found myself walking home alone. Now, as I flipped through the pages of the sourcebook, I tried to view the lessons from Amy Greenberg's point of view.

"Okay, Anna, you're a seventh-grader. What do you care about?"

I closed my eyes and willed myself back to my thirteen-year-old self. Like Amy, I had been obsessed with where I sat at lunch. It ranked right up there with my desire to get a boyfriend, have a cool birthday party, and convince my parents to let me get my own phone line. But school itself? To my horror, I realized that I couldn't even remember a single name of any of my seventh-grade teachers! Sure, there were a couple standouts in high school and elementary school, but the middle school teachers were one big blob. And that was what I was destined to become one day as my students tried to reflect back on their seventh-grade teachers.

Unless I did something drastic.

Come Monday morning I was ready and waiting when the seventh-graders filed in. The mood was almost solemn. The weekend's six bar and bat mitzvahs had taken their toll, especially for girls like Blair and Madeline, who had made appearances at each one. Hiding behind enormous Nicole Richie sunglasses, the girls slinked in with their shoulders slumped. They looked suspiciously hungover.

"Everyone come in, have a seat, and clear your desk except for a pen or pencil," I stated brightly.

"Are ge—"

"Gel pens are fine. *Any* writing implement will be fine," I cut off Jessica, the gel pen queen.

"Are we having a test? You never said!" howled Jacob.

"Poor Jacob, is your tutor not here to take it for you?" Benjamin snickered.

"Immediately!" I ordered, straightening myself up and standing at the head of the long conference table. "I want nothing on this table in front of you except a writing implement. There is nothing to discuss." A large grin threatened to escape from my lips, but I pursed my lips stubbornly. This had to be executed perfectly.

They actually looked a little afraid.

"I want your cell phones off, too. Not on SILENT or VIBRATE, but OFF. There will be *no* under the table texting during this class, and if you have to go to the bathroom, you are going to hold it till the end." Their eyes widened and I waited as many of them took their cell phones and pressed the OFF buttons, creating the little dwindling cries cell phones make when they've been shut off.

My first experience with UTT, or Under Table Texting, had occurred while I was attempting to explain the significance of Romeo and Juliet being star-crossed lovers. Nanny molester Chase van der Reedson had appeared to be looking intently at his crotch and both his hands had been moving furiously in the same direction . . . under the table.

"Chase! What are you doing?" I had shouted, horrified to feel my cheeks flaming. Of course, I could depend on Benjamin to catch on to my mortification. He was absolutely delighted to scream, "Ms. Taggert thinks Chase is jacking off!"

The class erupted. Jacob fell off his seat. Blair and Jessica ran out of the room claiming they were going to "pee in their pants."

"I was just . . . sending a text," Chase had mumbled, as embarrassed as I was. That day I, too, avoided the cafeteria for fear that the jack-off incident would have spread throughout the seventh grade by lunch. Naturally, my worst fears had been confirmed by one of Damian's charming e-mails:

Date: Monday, October 24, 2005 12:10 AM
From: "Damian Oren" <Damian@LangdonHall.edu>
High school is in uproar about some middle school teacher
finding a student masturbating in class. Did you let the
poor guy finish at least? These things can be quite painful
if interrupted . . .

"In fact, I *never* want to catch anyone texting in my classroom again," I confirmed, staring pointedly at Chase. This time, *he* blushed alone.

"I am going to pass out a quiz," I announced, starting to walk around the room. "It will remain *facedown* until I say you can turn it around. Then, and *only then*, may you all begin." I relished the horrified silence as I put the quizzes I had prepared at 2:00 in the morning in front of the seventh graders. I was mad with excitement.

"Begin!" I cried with a flourish, and then waited with delight to see the expressions on their faces. Benjamin burst out laughing first. A few girls giggled.

"What the . . . ?" Jacob blurted, then looked at me, grinning.

"No talking. It's a quiz. If you cannot finish, you can come take it after school," I declared, willing myself to look stern. Delightedly, my seventh graders filled out the "quiz" questions:

What is the most annoying reality show on TV?
What candy would you die without?
What song do you sing the most often in the shower?
Which synagogue in Manhattan has the shortest service?

Nobody looked at the clock or gave me a glazed expression of boredom. My students weren't quite sure why they were taking such a quiz, but the questions intrigued them and they were enjoying themselves thoroughly.

"We're going to share our answers when you're done, so absolutely no talking to each other till then!" I reminded them, circling the room and enjoying the looks of happiness. They were having fun.

I may have been sacrificing one day's worth of teaching, but I would learn a lifetime's worth of information about them in this one lesson. And these would be the very bits of pop culture and personal interests that I would weave into my lessons for the rest of the year. For all three of my classes, my students seriously shared their views on topics ranging from reality TV and current music to candy and favorite movies. That night, my grading consisted of taking notes on their "quizzes." I was never more interested or focused. Because out of these quizzes came the lessons I had always dreamed of teaching. Sourcebook be damned! From now on my grammar quizzes would feature sentences about Miley Cyrus and I would always know what kind of candy to reward as prizes for *Jeopardy!* games. They would finally see how much I cared and then, maybe *then*, they would love me.

"Ms. Taggert! Quick! Where's the dictionary! Omigod!"

"Jessica! Don't scream!" I cried, but smiled warmly as I rushed over to her group to hand over a dictionary. The class had been divided into three groups of five, and each group was responsible for rewriting Romeo's first lines describing Juliet in the style of a rap song. I had learned from their quizzes that Kanye West and 50 Cent were among their favorite artists, and when given the challenge of translating Shakespeare to rap, never were they more engaged or focused.

"Yo yo yo she do be teachin' the lights to burn bright, yeah yeah yeah . . . ," Max Briggman was bouncing up and down in the corner with one hand raised in the air, while his group jutted their necks out and made little rhythmic noises with their mouths. I had to admit, they sounded pretty good.

"It seems she hangs like a mad rich piece 'o BLING in an Ethiop's ear, bow wow wow . . . ," Max continued.

"What does *doth* mean?!" I heard Sue ask urgently.

"Look it up in the Shakespeare dictionary Ms. Taggert gave us!" Jessica cried, rushing to find her binder.

The classroom was a flurry of excitement and energy. They had been told that they were presenting in twenty minutes, and the group to catch the meaning of the monologue with the greatest accuracy and creativity would receive bonus points on the next quiz. I was walking around the room making sure everyone was on task, but found that to my utter delight the lesson was running on its own. When the students finally presented, I found I had tears running down my cheeks. I had never laughed harder, and wasn't quite sure if Shakespeare would be rolling in his grave or delighted that his work was the cause of such delight to a group of jaded Manhattan seventh-graders. As the class filed out, Max Briggman gave me the one compliment that made it all worthwhile.

"Pretty dope class, Ms. Taggert."

14

Thus began my teaching honeymoon. In the evenings I crafted lessons that would fuse elements of my students' interests with the text of *Romeo and Juliet*. Kids actually started coming to class early to find out what I had planned. My favorite lesson involved the creation of a "missing scene" between Romeo and his first love, Rosaline, and then having the students write Dear Abby letters giving Romeo love advice. My favorite letter came from Charlotte and Michael:

> Dear Romeo,
>
> Maybe if you weren't so conceited and so obsessed with being such a pimp, girls would like you better. Like, when you say Rosaline should open her lap to your "saint seducing gold," that is actually very obnoxious of you. Like, who are you to say that your penis is like gold that can seduce a saint? Girls don't like that kind of talk. Also, it's really inconsiderate how you're being all depressed and bipolar just because Rosaline won't sleep with you. Your Mom and Dad AND your cousin Benvolio are so worried about you! There are other fish in the sea. You really need to bounce and stop being such a freak. Get out of those sycamore trees and join the human race!
>
> Sincerely, Charlotte and Michael

Wow. They got it. They really got it.

Even more impressive, they had touched on how melodramatic and inconsiderate Romeo was being toward his parents simply because Rosaline would not sleep with him. Sure it was a little unorthodox to allow them to use words like *pimp*, but in context it actually was used appropriately. And isn't that exactly what Shakespeare did—use the common jargon of his day to attract all kinds of audiences? My students were so eager to share their letters and hear what others wrote that once again, the play was alive and all around us. As they filed out, I was in a state of pure bliss.

That's why I was surprised to see Harold Warner standing outside my classroom with an ugly grimace on his face.

"Hi, Harold!" I said brightly, refusing to let my newfound confidence be challenged.

"Anna, we have to have a talk . . . about . . . er, your latest lessons," Harold began, looking around my classroom suspiciously. Over the course of the past weeks I had put up various student assignments and interesting posters and bulletins I had found. The room was cheery, bright, and everything I had dreamed my classroom would look like.

"It seems as if all your lessons have been quite self-involved."

What?

"Excuse me?" I asked, honestly confused. "Self-involved?"

"Yes. Self-involved. Anna, it is my duty as the head of the department to tell you what other teachers have been saying about you."

That last comment was like a wound in my heart. As much as I had started to really love my job at Langdon, I had noticed that not a single teacher had reached out to befriend me. I was greeted with polite smiles in the faculty lounge, but nothing more than that. Usually the other teachers would find a way to sit just a little away from me so that while I was never alone, I was never a part of any of their conversations.

"What have they been saying?" I asked, my voice quivering. Harold was unmoved. In fact, he almost seemed pleased that I was upset.

"They say you are a show-off. That you are scoffing at our progressive ideals and teaching lessons that are centered around you. Students come running into other classes speaking of *games* they are playing in your class. And . . . *talk shows* in which you are *Oprah Winfrey.*"

"Harold! If these kids think these are games, then I have delivered them successfully!" I exclaimed hotly. "The *Jeopardy!* boards and talk show games take hours to prepare, and yes, they are extremely fun, but in the joy of it the students have to read and memorize lines straight out of the unabridged version of *Romeo and Juliet.* We *are* having a blast in here, and if they don't look at my class as work, it's because what *I'm* doing is *working!*"

"This is not a *game*-oriented school, Anna," Harold went on, completely ignoring my arguments. "There are to be no more *games* in your classroom. Not every teacher can play *games* in their class, and we can't help but feel as if you are doing this to become a popular teacher. None of us likes this rivalry. Now I suggest you find a way to make your classes more academic. More *progressive.*"

The conversation was over. Harold marched out of my room. I slumped at my desk, sick with disappointment and anger. A recent *Jeopardy!* game *had* been quite loud. I had divided the class into boys vs. girls and there had been shouting and competitive finger pointing, but I was confident that every student walked away with full lines from Act Two completely memorized. I nearly fainted with joy when Amy had boldly stated that she wanted the Balcony Scene for $500.

" 'A rose by any other name'," I had begun, and the room had fallen silent, all eyes on Amy.

" 'Would smell . . .'," she began cautiously.

"You can do it, Amy," her teammates urged.

" '. . . as sweet so Romeo would, were he not Romeo called. Retain that dear perfection which he owes without that title. Romeo, doff thy name, and for that name, which is not part of thee, take all myself.' "

The room had been pin drop silent, then we were all screaming and hugging Amy while the boys good-naturedly booed and stamped their feet. Yes, it had been a game, but for a seventh-grader to recite lines like that? I could have burst with pride! So what if they had had fun in the process? And that damn board had taken me the entire evening to create, not to mention the forty dollars of my own money I had spent on poster board, glitter, and markers at Duane Reade. Wasn't progressive education about trying to find new ways to educate students?

But Harold had a point. My classes were loud, and perhaps I had been spoiling the students with candy prizes and promises of new games every day. I would tone it down a bit and give them a project they could work on independently—Harold would like that. Hopefully I might even start making some friends in the faculty.

"What game are we playing today, Ms. T?" Max yelled, flying into the room like an airplane and zooming around the table with his arms spread open.

Maybe I *had* let them run a little wild.

"You'll find out, but take a seat first." I smiled, grinning as he "flew" into his seat and landed with a thud. My other students came rushing in equally boisterously, but quickly grew quiet and found their seats when they eyed the boom box I had resting at the head of the table.

"I think Ms. T is going to let us listen to Z100," I heard Benjamin whisper to Blair.

"That would be *so* cool," she squealed.

I waited. And waited. When the seventh-graders realized they weren't getting a peep out of me until they were silent, they gave up. Walking to the front of the room, I turned off the lights. I had already lowered the shades so the room was pitch black. I turned on the flashlight I had been holding in my left hand and shone it on the board.

"Oooohhhh," Madeline sighed. The rest of the class was too shocked to react.

"The spotlight is on," I announced dramatically. "Enter Romeo and Juliet." I pressed PLAY on the boom box and the Bee Gees "How Deep Is Your Love?" began. The room was immediately filled with the 1970s ballad that most of my students, I was certain, had never heard before.

"There's a disco ball twirling," I announced, circling the table. I could make out the shape of fifteen little heads looking upward at the imaginary disco ball. "Romeo enters in a white leisure suit. Juliet is across the stage, wearing . . ."

I turned on the lights and shut off the music.

"Hey!"

"Wearing what?"

"Where are they?"

I ignored all the cries of frustration, which I had happily anticipated.

"Max, what year was that scene?" I asked instead.

He looked confused. "Um, I mean if it was Romeo and Juliet, then it was like the 1500s or whatever like you said . . . but that music sounded kinda seventies. And that disco ball and leisure suit description also sounded kinda seventies," he responded.

"Exactly!" I beamed at him, and he looked thrilled. "Music, lighting, and costuming are just some of the ways you can make a scene from a play appear to take place in *any* era."

"That's so cool," Jessica breathed.

"And for the next two weeks, *you* are all going to be directors!" I was positively floating with excitement as I saw the thrilled expressions on my students' faces. "You are going to take your *favorite* scene in *Romeo and Juliet*, and without changing any of the text, you are going to create a director's book. It's going to include stage directions, costuming, lighting, music, and all the other details listed on this assignment sheet."

Without missing a beat, I started passing around an assignment sheet. The project would require them to basically memorize and take control of an entire scene in the play, and then redirect it through the lens of another time period.

"You have to get your time period approved by me," I continued, "but I want you to be creative! Do they meet at a dude ranch? At the Parthenon in ancient Greece? At a clambake in the Hamptons?" The last suggestion received a sprinkling of giggles.

"You will have class time and of course, you will work on this at home. In two weeks, the most realistic and detailed director's book will be given the honor of getting staged by the entire class!"

For the next forty-five minutes, my room was a hive of productivity. Papers, markers, and texts of *Romeo and Juliet* were furiously produced as my students searched for the scene they most wanted to direct. They ran to corners of the room to create private work spaces and I was an air traffic controller trying to control fifteen little planes all trying to land at one time.

Surely this was what Harold Warner had meant when he requested more serious lessons?

A week later when I saw fifteen messages blinking on my answering machine, I felt more confident than I had in a long time. My classes, I knew for a fact, were going spectacularly well. The students rushed in every day with huge smiles on their faces, and I could barely contain myself until I told them what I had planned for that day. The room had gotten a bit messy with all the colored paper, glue, and scissors we had been using for our director's book project, but I had never seen the students more inspired and excited to work. It was about time I could sit back and enjoy some good news from the Langdon mothers!

I picked up the receiver and started with Gillian Stein. She answered on the first ring.

"Ms. Taggert, I'm so glad you called. We're having a huge meltdown here."

"Oh, no! Ms. Stein, what's going on?" My mind started racing. What had Jacob's file said? He wasn't also a peanut allergies kid, was he? No—that was only Benjamin. He was. . . . Aha! Jacob Stein was the "tutored in six subjects grandfather billionaire boy"! What could possibly be their problem?

"Jacob has been working on your director's book since he returned from school," Gillian replied accusingly. "And he worked on it for most of Sunday as well."

"That's wonderful!" I exclaimed. If I hadn't seen Jacob work so hard on it in class as well, I would have sworn that Gillian had been lying. I hadn't seen Jacob work hard on *anything* till this project.

"No, Ms. Taggert, it's *not* wonderful. I'm sure from your point of view your class is the only class these children take, but I assure you that is not the case." Gillian's voice was frosty.

"Um, no, I'm aware they take oth—"

"All the mothers who have children in your class have signed a letter I drafted yesterday. We are taking it to Dr. Blumenfeld. We were wary of her decision to hire such an *inexperienced* teacher to begin with, but now we are certain that our fears were warranted."

Oh, God! I felt those hot tears rise up again in the corners of my eyes. I wasn't sure what exactly I had done wrong, but a letter to Dr. Blumenfeld? Signed by every parent? I was getting fired!

"Ms. Stein, please," I begged, "I don't understand. I've never seen Jacob, or any of my other students, so excited to be in my class and work on this project!"

"How *dare* you question our judgment!" Gillian shot back furiously. "I hate to speak for other mothers, but do you know Lynn Briggman walked into her son's room at 10:00 P.M. last night and Max was still working on his project for *your* class?"

For one second I allowed myself to be delighted. Good for Max! I could think of worse things than a child staying up till 10:00 P.M. working on an English assignment. Shouldn't his mother also be delighted that he was doing schoolwork rather than IM'ing and text messaging?

"Ten at night!" Gillian exclaimed.

"Ms. Stein, I assure you that many of my students are up *much* later than that watching TV and IM'ing each other," I cried defensively. What was going on here?

"Obviously you're not willing to be reasonable. We'll just let Dr. Blumenfeld explain it to you. Good night, Ms. Taggert."

Click.

I sat there looking at the receiver, which was still in my hand. Did I just get shouted at for giving too much homework? That couldn't be right. I finally believed that I was becoming the teacher I always dreamed of being, only to discover that this Langdon mother seemed intent on ruining me. I was just very unclear as to what exactly I was being accused of. Too depressed to call anyone else back, I dove into planning the next day's lesson.

There was a note on my desk when I walked into my classroom the next morning. There, on a little yellow Post-It, in red ink, were the dreaded two words: SEE ME. In the lower right corner Dr. Blumenfeld had signed her scrawly signature. My first class was scheduled to start in fifteen minutes. With my heart sinking to my stomach, I headed toward her office. Had that evil Gillian Stein gotten to her already with that signed letter?

Her office door was open when I arrived, and she was sitting at her desk waiting for me.

"Close the door behind you, Ms. Taggert, and have a seat," she ordered sternly. "I have here," she began immediately, pulling out a sheet of paper with a single typed paragraph and several signatures below, "a very serious complaint. From *every* parent who has a student in your class."

I gulped.

"I'd like to share the contents of this paragraph with you first, before we decide what to do," she went on. "And don't worry about your first-period class. I've asked Mr. Warner to tell your students to report to the library for a work period."

Oh no! If I missed my first-period class then I wouldn't get to provide my students with the final instructions for their project!

"I really need to teach my class! Their projects are due next week and tod—"

"Please read, Ms. Taggert."

Clearly, I had no choice.

Dear Dr. Blumenfeld,

Over the course of the last two weeks, Ms. Taggert has taken it upon herself to assign a minimum of two to four hours of homework nightly. Our brave and hardworking students haven't voiced a single complaint, but as concerned parents we realized that some adult intervention had to be taken. Our children are staying up as late as ten in the evening, and many of them have voiced reluctance to attend social engagements on the weekends. We can only imagine that they are nervous about completing Ms. Taggert's assignments. Furthermore, we also question the content of these assignments, many of which require a shocking amount of art supplies. Is this English class or camp?

We ask you to please look into the situation and rectify it immediately. We also ask that should Ms. Taggert teach eighth-grade English next year, none of our children be placed in her class. Another year of such an inexperienced teacher would be just too detrimental to our children's learning experience at Langdon. Below are the signatures of every parent at Langdon whose child has Ms. Taggert as their English teacher.

Sincerely,
Parents in Ms. Taggert's class

Motherfuckers! I was absolutely enraged. For the first time, their children were actually excited about an assignment. And yes, I could tell that some of the work I had been receiving lately had been the product of several hours, but only because the seventh-graders were inspired to work harder. And art school??? Just because the director's book required some colored paper and scissors?

"It's been a long time since I had a teacher who received a letter like this," Dr. Blumenfeld continued, a bit more gently. "Obviously, whatever it is that you are assigning must come to a halt immediately. You will draft a letter that I will then make sure gets mailed to all these parents. Another letter like this, Ms. Taggert, and I simply cannot extend you a contract for next year."

"Please let me explain myself!" I cried, standing up. "These women are cr—"

"I have back-to-back meetings this morning, Ms. Taggert. This conversation is over. There is nothing you can say that can cancel or refute the voice of so many parents at this school. Frankly, you should consider yourself lucky that I am extending you a second chance. Good day."

Dr. Blumenfeld dismissed me with her back and I had no choice but to exit her office. I found my classroom empty—Harold Warner had apparently gotten to them already—and I was in no mood to go up to the library to find them. I just didn't get it. For weeks I had thrown lessons at the students that came straight out of teaching manuals written in the 1970s. They were uninspiring, dry, and arguably bored me even more than they had bored my students. I had finally found a project that was meaningful. Now, when I was sure that my students were not only enjoying my class, but actually *learning* the material, I was getting chastised? It almost seemed like Langdon supported the notion that children simply be sent to the library to "work" and be given simple little assignments that might be boring but nobody questioned. From the meeting I had just had, the message seemed clear: Give up the director's book project immediately. But my students loved it! Amy Greenberg had told me just the other day that they had gotten in trouble in the cafeteria because she and a group of girls had tried to work on it during lunch. I had witnessed Max Briggman reciting the Friar's lines from Act III, Scene I, just so he could pencil in appropriate stage directions. My students were living and breathing Shakespeare, and their mothers were annoyed?

"We have spent quite some time working on the director's book," I started as calmly as I could when my next class began, "but I'm going to collect them today and assess them based on where you are."

"But we're not done! You said they wouldn't be due till the end of the week!" Blair yelled wildly, jumping out of her chair.

"Blair, sweetie, please sit down," I replied as gently as I could. I was broken-hearted. I knew Blair had been extremely proud of her project, and had even told me that she thought she might win the privilege of having hers be the one we all performed.

"I thought this was like some big thing! I was going to win!" Jacob screamed, and the look on his face convinced me that Gillian Stein had never consulted her son before making that phone call or drafting the letter to Dr. Blumenfeld.

"It *is* a big thing," I affirmed, trying to stay calm. "Hey, listen, how about we just take a break from them? Give me a week to see where you are, and then maybe revisit them?" I asked weakly.

"What are we supposed to do in the meantime?" Madeline asked suspiciously.

"We're going to work on essay writing structure." I prayed they wouldn't smell the scent of fear on me.

"Essays are boring."

"Yeah, we want to play a game."

"Didn't you bring any candy for us?"

Shit.

I had been spoiling my kids. I looked at the fifteen hostile seventh-graders glaring at me, and I glared back.

"Well, we *have* to learn to write essays. We cannot play games and have candy every day. So, everyone, please clear your desks and get ready to focus on the assignment sheet I am about to pass out."

Groaning, the class began shuffling binders and pencil cases under their seats as I passed out the three-page essay assignment.

"Charlotte, please read the first paragraph," I instructed firmly.

"Over the course of the next week, we will be writing a five-paragraph essay in class—"

"WHAT?!" Jacob Stein shouted.

"Excuse me, Jacob, don't interrupt me while I'm reading. It's very disrespectful," Charlotte sniffed haughtily.

"Jacob, you may *not* call out," I trailed after Charlotte, who was clearly a better teacher than I would ever be.

"We are writing this in *class*?" Jacob's face was red.

"I can't do that!" Benjamin followed, his right leg starting to twitch nervously. I looked around the room. They were panicked. What was it about writing an essay in class that had them in such an uproar?

"Guys," I said calmly, "it's only on the Balcony Scene. You know it cold! What's the problem?"

"I think," Jessica began helpfully, "that many of us like to write essays at *home*. In the comfort of our own rooms and our own laptops."

"Yes, Ms. Taggert," Blair added in her sweetest voice, "we love to learn about essays in school, but it's much easier to write them at home!"

I tried to catch little Amy Greenberg's eye, but she was looking nervously at her binder. Even she had apparently deserted me.

"I could have my mom call and explain it to you," Benjamin offered evilly.

That did it. I couldn't handle another encounter. Or fifteen phone calls. Weakly, I told the class that indeed the essays could be written at home, and we would just spend the time in class going over various skills. The seventh-graders were relieved and eager to discuss essay strategy, but their enthusiasm was eerie. As if they were putting it on just for me while laughing behind my back. The bubble of built-up confidence I had experienced in the last month unceremoniously and officially popped. I might have gotten back on the track of winning over their parents, but I had lost the students once again.

15

I was doing my best to get used to Langdon—the visual learners, the Prozac-popping teachers, the cafeteria food festivals, and the "progressive" learning—when another door opened and, like Alice, I fell down the rabbit hole. It all began with a simple question.

I was waiting for the elevator to go up to my homeroom when Francine Gilmore, Langdon Hall's learning specialist, came and stood next to me. Close to me, in fact. Very, very close to me. I gave her a polite smile and discreetly stepped away. She stepped closer. She looked around furtively. She whispered, "Do you tutor?"

"Pardon?"

"Do you tutor?

"Umm . . . yes?" When in doubt, always answer *yes*. That much I knew.

"I have a family. Child goes to Chapin. I'll e-mail you the number and the mother's name. I prefer you not mention this to anyone."

"Ummm . . ."

"And charge a minimum of two hundred dollars an hour. They'll think you're not worth it otherwise."

The elevator door opened and closed, and Francine Gilmore vanished like a true fairy godmother. I was incapable of moving.

Two hundred dollars! I didn't make that much in a *day*. In TWO days! And then it hit me. In a flash of blinding clarity I knew the secret of Randi Abraham's success. If she tutored just five students a week, she made one thousand dollars. Four thousand extra dollars a month. And that's if she only tutored five students. What if she tutored ten students? Or twenty? I was going to lose my mind. I thought I might throw up. Throughout the day I lunged for every available computer terminal and checked my e-mail like a crazed woman. When Francine Gilmore's e-mail came with the contact information, I slipped into an empty classroom and called Chapin Mom immediately.

Pick up pick up pick up.

The ringing was endless and my heart stopped beating for a split second every time a ring was ignored.

"Hello?"

"Hello, this is Anna Taggert. May I please speak with Mrs. Carleton?"

"Mrs. Carleton is indisposed at the moment," a snooty voice sniffed.

Indisposed? Who talks like that?

"Oh . . . could you please tell her that I called?" Shit! A long silence ensued and just when I was beginning to think the woman had hung up on me, she returned, this time with a much friendlier tone. "I'm sorry, Ms. Taggert. Actually, Mrs. Carleton was expecting your call. Just a moment, please."

Two minutes and an eternity later, Mrs. Carleton breathed *Hello*. "Thank *you* for calling!" she gushed. "You come *so* highly recommended. Francine is a good friend, and she says the children just adore you at Langdon! I'm *delighted* you called. Just delighted!"

"Wonderful! I'm thrilled to be in touch with you, too!" God, I sounded so fake. Could Mrs. Carleton tell from my voice that I would trade my kidneys for this job?

"My daughter is in the seventh grade at Chapin. She's very bright, but just needs some help with organization and getting her homework done."

"Wonderful!" I had forgotten every adjective but one.

"Why don't you come over and meet Katie. We'd love to get acquainted with you and figure out a schedule. My address is 801 Park Avenue, Penthouse A. Can you come over after school today? Say around 3:15ish?"

"Wonderful!" That word again.

"Marvelous. See you then!"

Click.

That was it. She didn't even allude to an hourly rate. I guessed that in the Carletons' world payment was considered a vulgar topic. The day passed in a blur. When it finally ended, I was right on Randi's heels as we raced down the staircase and flew out of school. Neither one of us spoke as we both turned left onto Park Avenue, walking separately and incredibly fast, until Randi disappeared into a large building with a green awning and white-gloved doormen.

I passed three kinds of people on my way to the Carletons: children clad in private-school uniforms; slightly overweight, brown-skinned women in white uniforms; and a slew of anonymous-looking men and women carrying huge totes stuffed with papers. They *had* to be teachers! Could it be possible that after the hour of three every day, teachers became tutors who marched up and down the Upper East Side like a quiet, purposeful, underground army? I caught the eye of one young woman who looked about my age and we exchanged a cold glance. I had this unreasonable surge of anger. Who was she tutoring? How had she found this person? I wanted her job. She wanted mine. This was war. As I passed her, I couldn't help but also notice that she was in the same Juicy Couture tracksuit that Randi had been wearing at Starbucks. Was this the uniform? Pop in a telephone booth after school, rip off her skirt suit, and emerge as Super Tutor, a la Juicy Couture?

I turned into the building on 77th Street and felt, for the first time in my life, a rush of pure, greedy adrenaline burst through my veins. I was on a tutor high, and the addiction was so instantaneous that I was hooked even before the doorman announced me.

The door opened before I had a chance to knock. A woman about my age was giving me the once over. She must have been the snooty-voiced woman on the phone.

"Ms. Taggert?"

"Yes, I'm here to see Mrs. Carleton," I announced, refusing to be intimidated by this strange girl.

"Of course. Let me escort you to the living room. Mrs. Carleton and Katie will join you in a moment."

I followed the girl down a long corridor lined with very expensive-looking artwork—was that a Chagall?

"Anna?"

I whirled around to see . . . Oh My God! This was Cindy Crawford's apartment! There she was, impossibly tall, in tight designer jeans, a simple white tank, and her glorious hair falling down the length of her back.

"I'm Amanda Carleton!"

LIAR!

"Oh! Has . . . anyone ever told you that you look a lot like—"

"Omigod, PLEASE don't say Cindy Crawford," a voice drawled behind the supermodel. A slightly smaller, but equally stunning girl emerged and stood next to "Amanda." Apparently, it was Katie. Both mother and daughter were checking me out. Katie seemed particularly bothered by my scuffed Nine West pumps.

"You're gorgeous, too! You look a bit like Jessica Alba," Amanda Carleton declared. "Where are you from originally?"

"New Jersey," I offered awkwardly, knowing that it would probably offend young Katie as much as Nine West.

"My old nanny was from there," Katie announced. "And yeah, you totally do look like her." She was starting to smile. I knew I wasn't Randi Abrahams gorgeous, but I had lost a little over ten pounds over the summer on my teacher salary diet, and I was back into my high school jeans. I looked okay. But Amanda and Katie Carleton were clearly pleased that I passed at least one important criteria.

"Please sit down! So, how long have you been teaching at Langdon?" Amanda smiled and ran a hand through her glossy mane. *She even had that famous mole on the upper corner of her lip!*

I lowered myself gingerly on what looked like a throne for a French king. "I just started this year after graduating from Columbia."

"Cool! I knew you looked young!" Katie smiled, but was now looking at me more critically than ever, as if she were giving me a makeover.

"Well, I can see you and Katie will get along very well." Amanda beamed. When did that happen?

"Katie would like to see you on Mondays, Wednesdays, and

Sundays for an hour, with the option to see you for two hours if the workload increases. Between her voice training and media expressions class she's not home until 5:30. Are you free?" Amanda asked, immediately getting down to business. She crossed her long legs, uncrossed her toned, tanned arms, and leaned forward. Once again, I felt as if I were being propositioned.

"I'm recording a CD," Katie explained.

"W-wow," I stammered. Was my student going to be the next Britney Spears?

"Awesome! Mom, can I go now?" Katie asked quickly, already getting up. It was a done deal.

"Katie, in a MOMENT!" Amanda silenced her daughter with a fierce look and then turned back to me. "Well?"

"I'd LOVE TO!" I nearly screamed, doing mental math so quickly that I wasn't sure I would be able to walk and talk at the same time. Wait a minute . . . payment. What about payment?

"Shall we discuss payment?" I asked nervously.

"Oh, just write me a quick handwritten bill every week or so, and I'll write a check," Amanda waved her arm breezily. Apparently the hourly rate was of no concern. She joined her daughter by standing up, which was my cue to stand as well, and before I could say another word, the strange girl who had shown me in ushered me back out into the one-door hallway.

I floated down the elevator and onto Park Avenue like Peter Pan on crack. I gave the doorman a mad grin as I was leaving. He looked a little scared. Jesus. H. Christ. If I did as Francine suggested and charged $200 an hour, I would be making a minimum of $600 a week. That would be $2,400 a month. That was more than my monthly teacher salary. I could eat! I could shop!

I could pay my rent on time! What had just happened? What had just fallen into my lap? Was this legal? Did other people know? Should I ask for more? I was like a mother seeing her baby for the first time: filled with awe and wonder and bliss. It was sick of me, I knew, but I felt total and complete joy. It was like the skies had opened and rained money all over me. Randi Abrahams wasn't the enemy . . . she was a survivor. A *genius*.

16

M onday morning I sauntered into Langdon wearing an aqua terry-cloth tracksuit. I would be starting with Katie Carleton that afternoon and I had spent a glorious Sunday afternoon shopping. Jessica Landau had informed me that the place to get the newest Juicy was Henri Bendel, a veritable bastion of socially acceptable clothing for private school teens and the select group of über-cool teachers, tutors, and hot moms. I had winced at the two-hundred-dollar price tag for two pieces of towel, but judging from the approving glances I was getting from kids in the lobby, it was worth it. Besides, I could chalk up the whole purchase as one Carleton session. Not bad. I knew I needed Chanel flats to complete the casual chic look, but the $450 price had me waiting. But not for long!

"Ms. Taggert?!"

It was nanny-groping Chase van der Reedson.

"Yes, Chase?"

"Tell her! Tell her!" A group of boys at the end of the hall were grinning madly. Chase flushed with embarrassment.

"Chase?" I persisted.

"Um . . . my friends think, that, um . . . you look really . . ." Chase faltered and was staring wildly at the lockers to the right of him.

"That you look MAD HOT, MS. TAGGERT!!!!!!" The boys at

the end of the hallway called out in unison and then dispersed in five different directions. Chase followed as fast as his legs could carry him.

I started to dart after them, then stopped suddenly. They thought I was hot. A hot teacher. Like Randi Abrahams! And I felt hot. And cute. And very, very private school. I wasn't sure what was happening to me, and how this change was being implemented before I had even had my first tutoring session, but I was grinning when I walked into my classroom.

"Ms. Taggert, ohmigod, I love your Juicy *so* much!" Jessica announced as she settled into her seat and opened her glitter binder.

"Why, thank you, Jessica! I took you up on your suggestion and bought it at Bendel's!"

"Ohmigod, did you see the new Tibi resort line there?" Charlotte jumped in.

I had my hand raised at the chalkboard and had been about to write out the homework assignment, but I found myself drawn to the table where the girls were sitting. Charlotte's eyes widened with delight as I pulled a chair next to her.

"Actually, I *did* see the bikinis, but they seem really revealing . . . you know . . ."

"We know, but honestly if you try them on they're like super flattering on the butt," Madeline offered sagely.

"Yeah, *all* the boys like it when we wear them!" Blair laughed.

By now the class had entered the room and I had to get up and start the lesson. I was amazed by how reluctantly I got up from the table. There were so many more questions I had for these girls! When could I talk to them again? At lunch?

"Oh, Ms. Taggert?"

Jessica Landau was sitting up straight and raising her hand.

"Yes, Jessica?"

"I thought your assignment last night was, like, sooo fun."

"Yeah, I did, too!" Benjamin grinned.

I looked at my students in amazement. I had not asked them to do anything spectacular—just some reading and answer some basic questions. Something was definitely happening here. They didn't just seem to like me. They wanted to be my friend. They thought I was hot. And well dressed. And cool. And therefore a really, really good teacher. My four years at Columbia had gotten me through the doors at Langdon Hall, but one visit to Bendel's had launched me into superstardom.

I reached Katie's apartment five minutes early, shockingly more nervous than I had been for my Langdon Hall interview. What if she didn't like me? What if I got fired after one session?

"I'm in my room!" Katie shouted from the end of a long corridor, which was lined with artfully framed family portraits. Amanda Carleton was nowhere to be found, and Katie obviously saw no need to come greet me. I followed the clicking of her keyboard down the corridor and into her room. I gasped. In all my life, I had never seen a room like this. A large white canopy bed with sheer white curtains took pride of place in the middle of the room, right under an antique crystal chandelier. The shaggy white carpet was spotless, and the walls were covered in thick pink and white pinstripes. In the corner was a seating arrangement consisting of two white silk club chairs, a mirrored table, and a rock crystal lamp with an outrageous fringed lampshade. Adjacent to it was a large desk that was distressed with white and gold foliage. A vanity table with a little stool and a Venetian mirror graced another side wall. As if that weren't enough, the entire room seemed to be under the spell of an enormous bay window draped in endless yards of silk and held back with threaded tasseled cords. The effect was nothing short of spectacular.

Katie was seated at the desk, typing furiously, eyes locked on the screen of her white iMac. Next to that her Sidekick, adorned with bejeweled stickers, glittered and buzzed with a life of its own. A lime green iPod lay forgotten under her chair. A white painted chair with a pink cushion sat empty beside her. (For me?)

"I'll get off in like two secs, I promise," Katie assured, not missing a beat as I sat down next to her. There wasn't much to do but look at her computer screen. Four little boxes popped up:

Couturegrl246
Westsideplaya69
Dadyzprincess4evah
Cuteepie55

Suddenly two more boxes popped up and Katie responded to both with speed and ease. I was baffled.

"Hi, Katie!" I said brightly, hoping my first tutoring session would not begin with a battle to get my student off the computer.

"Heeeyyyyyyy. . . . ," Katie drawled, eyes a bit glazed, but still intently focusing on the screen.

"Wow . . . you're a fast typer!" Ugh. I was so pathetically

chipper. But somehow I could not bring myself to stop this impish IM monster. There was something about the way Katie's fingers flew across the keyboard that had me mesmerized. She could have been an air traffic controller. I just could not stop looking at her. Her light brown ponytail was secured with an elastic band with a little ball that read: I LOVE DIOR. Her tight T-shirt said: ANYTHING BOYS CAN DO GIRLS CAN DO BETTER. She had on the So Low stretchy pants and pink Livs (the new Uggs, according to my girls). Twenty rubber bracelets hung on each of her wrists. Encompassed in this little body, I couldn't help but realize, was the very heart of the Upper East Side. There was something fantastic about her. I had to say something. I had to get her attention.

"I love your Dior ponytail holder."

Katie turned and faced me, her blue eyes widening.

"I have another one I can give you!" Before I could say a word, she furiously typed GTG in all seven IM boxes, clicked off her AOL, and opened a desk drawer. In a flash, her little palm displayed a Dior elastic band identical to the one she was wearing.

"I couldn't take that! But you're SO sweet."

"Take it, please!" she insisted.

"I couldn't wear that. It seems a little young for me, don't you think?" I was weakening, and she sensed it.

"Pleaaassssseeee? It'll look sooooo good on you, I swear."

"Okay, Katie, I'll borrow it till our next session, okay?"

"Okay. Will you wear it when you come?"

"Totally. I'll wear it to school tomorrow!"

"Ohmigod, your students will LOVE it!" Katie gushed.

I could just imagine the levels of ecstasy Blair, Charlotte, and Madeline's clique would undergo if I walked into class wearing Dior hair accessories. I was strangely elated by the thought.

"You're right, they will. I can't wait to wear it. Do you want to start now?"

Katie grinned at me, I grinned back, and suddenly I was having as much fun as I had had that morning discussing fashion with the girls in my class. Somehow I had tapped into that same almost-impossible-to-hit moment when you and your student are suddenly . . . friends. I was sitting in a fantasy room with Katie Carleton, and all she wanted to do was become my personal stylist. . . .

I snapped back to attention.

We HAD to work! At the end of the day, if Katie failed out of school, I would be out of this gig.

"Okay, Katie, I *really* want to start now," I begged. "Can you show me your binders and school planner so I can see what you have to complete this evening?"

"No, so, wait . . . like, omigod, you teach seventh grade? You're like an actual teacher, too?" Katie asked, her blue eyes wandering up to her ceiling as she tried to run through a list of names in her head. We both knew she had heard me, and we both knew that she would not be doing any work that afternoon.

"Do you know Charlotte Robertson and Max Briggman?"

"Yup. I teach both of them."

"Ohmigod, wait, I bet I know so many more people you know . . ." Katie turned back to her computer and began to log on to her AOL account.

"Wait! What are you doing?" Oh, crap! I had just lost her again!

"To go through my buddy list," Katie answered matter-of-factly. "I, like, have to tell everyone you know that I know you too. Duh!"

"Katie, listen, let's do it later, okay? Let's make sure we do your work together really well so your mom will be impressed, okay? Please?"

Katie paused. She clicked off AOL but didn't look up. *Did I say something wrong? Did I piss her off? Oh, my God, did she hate me?*

"Katie, c'mon." I hated that I sounded whiny. And needy. I felt like a complete loser.

What was happening? My heart was beating so fast I thought it would explode out of my chest. I wanted to throttle her! Did this little brat know that on a whim she could decide whether or not I would be paying my cell phone bill this month?

"Katie?"

Nothing. I had lost her. Just like that. I had to try something else.

"Okay, Katie, listen. Do you want to start your homework in, like, fifteen minutes and just talk first?"

Apparently, those were the magic words.

Katie jumped off her seat, flew across her room to a door, and swung it open to reveal the largest walk-in closet I had ever seen, complete with a pink shag rug and *another*, smaller chandelier inside.

"Do you want to see my clothes?" she asked happily, causing me to wonder if she was bipolar. Still, I was willing to go with it. I was willing to go along with *anything* that kept me in the Carleton apartment for an hour. I felt enormously guilty because it was almost a hundred dollars, er, thirty minutes into the session, and we had accomplished absolutely nothing.

Shrugging helplessly, I followed Katie into her closet and watched as she pulled each article of clothing off its hanger, draped it against herself, told me a small history of where and when the article was purchased, and then grandly dropped it onto the rug.

"I got this shirt in Palm Beach last spring break. We go to the Breakers every Christmas.

"I got these cute stretchy sweatpants from this amazing Web site called shopbop. It's, like, the best thing ever!

"These shoes are Prada and I stole them from my mom 'cuz we have the same shoe size already!

"These are the dresses I wear to bar and bat mitzvahs. I have three a weekend at least."

As Katie went on and on endlessly the closet went from a state of spectacular organization to total chaos.

"Katie, this is so messy now! Your mom will be mad!" I felt completely and utterly out of control. If Amanda Carleton saw this closet she would have *empirical* evidence that we had done absolutely nothing during our session.

"Oh . . . yeah . . . don't worry, Papita will clean it. Do you want to work now?"

Papita? So now she was ready to work? Mysteries I might never solve. Before I could even begin to venture a response, Katie wandered over to her desk and casually turned her Chanel tote upside down. Gum rappers, gel pens, mechanical pencils, books, binders, and an endless array of little scraps of paper poured out. Katie smiled, shrugging her shoulders and rolling her eyes in a move so smooth that it held me oddly captivated. I forced myself to return to the task at hand.

"Should we start with this?" I took the emptied bag as a white flag. Katie was ready to allow me into her secret world, and I was *dying* to look at the scraps of paper. I saw my students pass them around, and even though I had done the same thing in middle school, seeing an updated note was the most compelling thing I could think of doing in that moment.

"You can read my notes if you want," Katie graciously offered, then sat down and logged on again. Apparently I was meant to clean out her bag while she socialized online. Was the right to read her notes meant as some sort of privilege? That was *not* going to happen. I refused to be the Papita of the tutoring world.

"Okay, Katie, let's start with cleaning out your bag. Let's chuck all the crap and then go through your binders and make them look all cool, 'k?" I was trying my best to sound like the girls in my class, and apparently it worked. Katie studied my face for a second and nodded. She sat happily engaged for the next few minutes while I threw her notes away, went through her binders, hole-punched loose papers, and filed and organized until her binders were neat little masterpieces. They looked terrific—organized and neat.

"There! Doesn't that look better?" I felt triumphant. Katie was clearly pleased, and as a reward she opened her desk drawer, took out a pink sticker with a skull on it, and stuck it in the middle of the binder.

"Katie, this is a skull." Of all the stickers I had ever seen in my life, this was definitely the most weird. A skull???

"Ohmigod, skulls are like the new hearts," she dismissed and then looked as if she was about to go back to her computer when both of us heard the front door open. Katie's head cocked to one side like a little dog and she listened intently to the heavy footsteps before bolting out of the room yelling, "Daddeeeeeeee!"

I was alone in the room. Helpless. Abandoned. I needed Katie. Because without Katie, what was I doing there?

Daddy Carleton appeared in the room a minute later with his arms around his daughter. The man was, in a word, stunning. He was basketball player tall and dressed in a suit with a crisp white shirt. He shared Katie's sandy brown hair and sparkling blue eyes. He looked like a member of the Kennedy family.

"Hello, err . . . ?" He looked at me blankly. It suddenly dawned on me that fathers who pay private-school bills, tutoring bills, voice training bills, cell phone bills, therapist bills, and all the other extracurricular activities that their children partake in probably had very little understanding of these activities apart from how much they cost. I stood up and extended my hand.

"I'm Anna Taggert, Katie's new tutor."

He shook my hand warmly and then turned back to his daughter.

"So Katie Pie, what have you accomplished so far?" His voice seemed friendly, but I was nervous, certain that if Katie responded truthfully he would fire me on the spot. But Katie was a master of deception.

"Daddy, look at how organized my binders are!" Daddy's little girl exclaimed proudly. Mr. Carleton walked over to Katie's desk and thumbed through the binder I had just organized. My heart was pounding so hard I felt as if I was going to pass out right there. My palms were sweating. I dreaded the obvious follow-up question: "What else did you do, considering I'm paying your tutor two hundred dollars an hour for her services?" Any half-intelligent man would have asked it. All sorts of excuses were rushing through my head.

"Wow, Katie, I'm SO PROUD OF YOU!" he exclaimed, giving me a grateful look. He was?

As I tried to comprehend what had just transpired, he kept talking:

"Listen, err . . . , I rarely come home early, so if you're finished here I'd love to spend some time with my daughter. Please charge us for the time you had planned on staying, of course, and we'll just see you next time."

Daddy Carleton put his arm around Katie Pie again, and both of them turned on their heels and walked happily out of the bedroom as if I had simply disappeared the minute I was told I could leave. I was flabbergasted. I had just made two hundred dollars doing pretty much nothing. And I had a Dior elastic band. What's more, Katie appeared to really like me. At least enough to lie for me. If the money had fallen out of the sky onto my lap I couldn't have been more astonished. Was this tutoring business really this ridiculously, wondrously simple? Had I really just made more money than I did in my entire day at Langdon Hall? As I walked down Park Avenue, I imagined Katie sitting in the kitchen with her father, laughing and joking and watching Papita make their dinner. An hour later Mrs. Carleton would come home from her yogilates class and the three of them would eat a healthy, carb-conscious meal. I didn't care. I might be going home to Lean Cuisine and the latest episode of *The Hills*, but I could sleep easy knowing that my bills were no longer a problem.

It turned out that the Dior band was as big a success as Katie had promised. The minute I walked into my classroom Blair and Charlotte came running up to me and grabbed my ponytail.

"Ooh, Ms. Taggert, this is SO cool!" Blair gushed.

"Yeah, when did you get it? There's, like, a waiting list for those!" Charlotte announced indignantly.

"I have my ways," I smirked, enjoying the jealous expression on the girls' faces. *Oh God*. What was happening to me? It was inexplicable, but post Juicy Couture, Dior, and tutoring, my students at Langdon were starting to really respond to . . . *me*. They were more focused than ever during my classes, and actually rushed to talk to me afterward. I was . . . popular. But I wasn't sure if I was a popular teacher or a popular student masquerading as a teacher. I went to the board to write down the day's schedule, but not before eyeing Blair's Cartier watch . . . just like Randi's. It didn't bother me for some reason that a thirteen-year-old girl was wearing a Cartier watch. What bothered me was that I really, really wanted it.

17

Once I started tutoring it was like they could *smell* it on me. I knew that "they" were the Upper East Side, but I wasn't sure what "it" was. Still, I had this sensation of being subtly tracked and hunted. Since tutoring Katie Carleton, I was no longer in debt and had even bought a flat screen TV. Henri Bendel had replaced Ann Taylor, and my Nine West pumps went out with last week's trash. While sitting on my couch trying to get through the ever-growing stack of papers to grade, I absent-mindedly reached for the ringing phone without even checking the caller ID.

"Hello. This is Laura Brandeis from Ivy League Tutoring. I may have a client for you." I was mystified.

"May I ask how you got my number?" It was the only logical question I could muster.

"You were referred, and come highly recommended," Laura assured briskly, "and I have a job for you." I shut up. It didn't matter that I had no idea who Laura was, nor that it was absolutely creepy that she knew how to reach me. Or that I tutored. Bottom line: Laura has a job for me.

"Okay, I'm interested."

"The family lives on the Upper East Side, which I know you prefer because it's in your neighborhood." I was convinced Laura was across the street with binoculars.

"The boy is in ninth grade, and the mother says she wants only the best for him. Both the parents went to Princeton and they insist that his tutor has an Ivy League education," Laura continued.

"How do you work . . . ?" I was in completely new territory. What was in it for Laura?

"I started Ivy League Tutoring four years ago. Manhattan private school parents prefer Ivy League—educated tutors, so I organize and manage a group of tutors who fit this criteria. I refer the tutors and take twenty percent off the top," Laura explained.

"So you don't actually do anything besides make the connection?" I asked incredulously. Laura paused. *Awkward.* A part of me wished I had never asked the question. It was rude, but it had just slipped out.

"Well, actually I do a lot," Laura sniffed, clearly offended. "I take care of the business side, which is actually quite time consuming for you. Once a month, I will mail you a check for the hours you tutor. You won't ever have to hound the parents for money. You just show up and tutor. Period." Wait a minute. This woman was a con artist! What a setup! She sat on her ass at home while her Ivy League "tutors" ran all over Manhattan tutoring children and gave her 20 percent?!

"I'd want to make a minimum of two hundred dollars an hour, so you would have to make sure this family is willing to cover that extra twenty percent to pay you," I stated firmly, sure that Laura would slam the phone down.

"Of course. That will not be an issue. The family is willing to pay anything for your combination of skills."

"Excuse me?"

"You are Ivy League, *and* you teach at one of the most exclusive private schools in Manhattan. I have more than enough eager Ivy graduates trying to pay off their college debts by working for me. Teachers are a bit harder to come by. So you will get the sum you wish for, Ms. Taggert," Laura responded professionally.

"Laura, I really must ask how you got this phone number," I declared firmly.

"I really am not at liberty to say. I just want to know if you are interested in this potential opportunity." All that was missing was a dark alley and a trench coat.

"I am."

"Terrific. You'll be hearing from me." The line went dead.

Turned out I didn't need a lesson plan for that day. Or the next. When I walked into my classroom at 9:00 A.M., most of my students were slumped listlessly around the conference table. Glassy-eyed and silent, they didn't even acknowledge me when I walked in. For one crazy minute I wished I could just take a seat around the table as well and just disappear. It was so unfair that we teachers were expected to perform every single day. Be bright. Be cheerful. Provide entertaining lesson plans.

"Hey, guys," I offered, pulling up a chair at the head of the table. "I'm exhausted." It was the most successful opening to any class I had ever taught. Instantly, heads perked up and students started to smile.

"Ohmigod, *me too*!" Jessica sighed dramatically.

"Yeah, Jacob's bar mitzvah party didn't end till, like, one last night," Max Briggman explained, and all of us looked over at Jacob's vacant chair. I had learned that it was utter foolishness on any teacher's part to expect even a glimpse of the bar mitzvah child in their classroom a week before or the Monday after the big event.

"Yeah, it was at Capitale. The motivational dancers were so hot," Jeff Zuckerman said loudly.

"And so was that one camp friend he had over—that Allison girl," another voice chimed in.

"What was the theme?" I asked, immediately interested. I had a wild impulse to just chat with my students for the rest of class.

"He's obsessed with *Entourage*," Charlotte explained. "So the whole thing was like very Hollywood, and they even had Adrian Grenier and Kevin Connolly make an appearance. Adrian is soooooo hot."

"I think so, too," I admitted, hating Jacob Stein for not inviting me. And then, because I couldn't help it, I asked, "Was Ms. Abrahams there?" The class looked at the table uncomfortably, and a few heads nodded. I hated that I was a little jealous.

"Don't feel bad, Ms. T," Amy soothed. "It's just cause Ms. Abrahams is family friends with the Steins." *Family friends*. How the hell did she get to be family friends with the Steins? She probably tutored the little shit. Come to think of it, his last paper had been exceptionally well written.

"I'm not in the mood to teach today," I confided.

"I have *Zoolander* in my locker," Jessica offered cautiously. All eyes were on me.

"We can't just see another movie . . . can we?" I asked hopefully. They could smell me weakening.

"It's about social pressure. We could discuss that afterward," Jessica chimed intelligently, already equipped with a Ph.D. in Langdon Hall's *progressive education* standards.

"Ms. Abrahams lets us see movies all the time," Benjamin offered.

"I love that movie." I was weakening. "And yes, we can have an important conversation afterward." *Bullshit*.

In under three minutes, my kids and I were blissfully watching a movie we had all seen four hundred times. For a moment I was nervous that someone would walk in and catch me, but then nobody had come to observe my classroom yet. I turned the air conditioner on high, followed my students' example and put my feet up on the conference table, and watched the movie. When class came to an end, they groaned sadly.

"We love you, Ms. Taggert. You are the coolest!" Benjamin cried, and I could have hugged him. It wasn't his fault that Randi manipulated him, and I wished that I could be the one to tutor him. Forty-five minutes of *Zoolander* and I was in a better place.

"Thanks, Benjamin, this was fun for me, too," I admitted.

"We're finishing the movie tomorrow, right?" Jessica asked suddenly, and the students all froze and looked up at my face. That's when I realized that I was not only going to get out of teaching today, but tomorrow, too! I couldn't just show *half* the movie. And this was only one of my classes! Two more classes would expect to see the movie, and then it would happen all over again tomorrow.

"Only if I can keep your DVD for the next two classes!" I exclaimed sweetly, and everyone cheered. I was a hero. The best teacher ever. I would grade the rest of my papers while the next two classes watched *Zoolander*. Maybe I would take a quick field trip to Blooming Nails during my next break and treat myself to a mani pedi. Suddenly I didn't care about Benjamin's paper or Randi Abrahams or finding a moral high ground at Langdon Hall.

I was going to Blooming Nails. All I was focused on was whether I should go with Ballet Slipper or Angel Food Cake Polish.

Laura Brandeis's call came between my second and third viewing of the first half of *Zoolander*, a movie I could now recite perfectly, much to my students' delight: *I'm really really good looking.*

I even launched into a full-blown "modeling" competition with Chase, Max, and Benjamin while the girls giggled uncontrollably.

"Ms. Taggert does the best Blue Steel!" Madeline cried.

"I love your nails. Is that Angel Food?"

"Ballet Slipper," I corrected sweetly, then snapped my neck dramatically and puckered my lips. "I'm a male model!"

The class howled.

Since I had my phone on VIBRATE, I missed Laura Brandeis's message. Apparently I was scheduled to be interviewed that afternoon by Elizabeth Herring, Princeton graduate and hyperinvolved mother of Jake Herring. Jake attended Collegiate on the Upper West Side, and was in the ninth grade. They lived on 87th Street and Park Avenue, and I was expected at 4:00. I was to call Laura Brandeis after this initial meeting and discuss specifics. That's all she gave me in the rather curt and businesslike message.

The prospect of securing another tutoring job filled me with joy, but I must have had some misgivings because I hadn't told my parents about this tutoring-on-the-side part of my job yet. In fact, I hadn't told *anybody* about my job with the Carletons because, well, it just seemed so obnoxious to tell a fellow teacher,

"Hey, I got a job that pays twice in one hour what we make in a day." What were they supposed to say? Congratulations? If someone told me that, I would tell them to go fuck themselves. Or give them a fake smile and then talk about them behind their backs like Damian and Sarah talked about Randi Abrahams. But then who was to say that Damian and Sarah didn't tutor themselves? Maybe their scorn for Randi was a mere cover for their own lucrative side business? Or maybe they were just burning with jealousy that they had to live off their miserable teacher salaries while Randi enjoyed all the luxuries tutoring afforded? Langdon Hall's private world was unfolding like a poisonous flower and the heady scent was intoxicating.

Getting to the Herring residence on time proved more challenging than I had ever imagined. Gone were the days that I could enter and exit the school with relative anonymity. As I walked past the heavy French doors and into the afternoon sunlight, the Langdon Hall mothers descended on me.

"Ms. Taggert!"

"We're so excited to meet you!"

"I've been hearing your name in my house all semester!" I looked around at the golden-haired beauties and didn't know who to speak to first. The tallest one stepped forward.

"I'm Dana Robertson. I called you a few weeks ago?"

"I'm so sorry, I have meant to call you for ages," I stammered. I noticed two of the other mothers glancing at each other with a look of irritation that Dana and I already had been in contact, but the glance was fleeting and replaced almost immediately with broad Cheshire cat grins.

"Don't be silly, sweetie. Would you care to do it now? We can hop over to Sarabeth's for a late lunch—it would be fabou!"

Fabou or not, I had to get to the Herring residence in under fifteen minutes.

"Can we take a rain check? I'm actually running to a . . . a doctor's appointment," I said quickly, once again aware of the fact that I was absolutely incapable of admitting to anyone that I tutored.

"Are you okay?"

"Pregnant?"

"My husband has a practice! He'll take wonderful care of you!"

I took a step toward Park Avenue and smiled politely. The mothers stepped with me. *Oh God.* "No, really, just a checkup, but it's been booked for ages. Why don't I give you my cell phone number? We can speak later?" In my desperation to make the interview, I had unknowingly walked into the lion's den of the private school circus. BlackBerrys and cell phones came out in blinding speed and heavily bejeweled fingers stood poised and ready for action. I quickly rattled off my number, flashed Dana Robertson an apologetic smile, and tore up to Park Avenue. I was completely annoyed that I had to take a cab once again, but one look back assured me that unless I made a quick getaway, the mothers would be upon me again. But not before they had each saved my cell phone number for all of posterity.

Jake's building was one of those grand Park Avenue landmarks with a lobby that seemed to stretch endlessly. A white-gloved doorman hustled to open my cab door as it pulled up to the building, but then looked incredibly disappointed to see me step out.

Could he smell tutors? Did he know that no tip would be involved and that it was entirely possible for him to abuse me? He turned around and went back into the building, forcing me to open the door myself.

"Excuse me?" I asked meekly, irritated by the Manhattan hierarchy. Doormen over tutors in the lobby. I was catching on to this insane world. He raised one gloved finger and gestured that I should wait. When he finally deigned to look over, I said even more meekly, "Herring residence, please."

"Who may I say is calling?" he asked, looking terribly, terribly bored.

"Um, Ms. Taggert," I mumbled, not looking him in the eye. Why was this stupid doorman doing this to me??!

"Who?" Bastard. He *totally* heard me!

"Anna Taggert," I answered more firmly this time. With a look both disapproving and suspicious, he announced me. After a moment he gave me a withering glance and told me to go right up.

As I started down the lobby, he called out:

"Do you know the way?" His tone was clear. I had no right, absolutely no right at all, to be in this building.

"Yes," I responded curtly and swept up the imperious lobby as if had lived there my entire life. I could feel him watching me disdainfully from behind.

"Actually," he called, "it's the other way."

I mustered up the dignity to sweep past him one more time. I hated him. I really hated him.

There was another elderly man in white gloves and a green suit in the elevator. Edward, according to the brass name tag on his breast pocket. Edward didn't ask me where I was going.

Turned out he knew. The doorman situation was as cryptic a system as Laura's tutoring agency, and I was just going to have to get used to it. He pressed a button and then turned and faced the elevator door as if it was the most fascinating thing he had ever seen. He didn't even make small talk about the weather. I hated Edward, too.

The elevator opened into a beautiful little hallway. A Baccarat chandelier hung from the molded ceiling and a Venetian glass mirror rested above a dark cherry console table. These items were simply hallway decoration. I hadn't even entered the Herring apartment. Before I could knock, the door was opened by a young woman who was wearing the same French maid's costume I had worn for my fifth-grade Halloween party.

"Missus Herring eez in the libraree," she politely informed me, ushering me down a long foyer lined with two more chandeliers and into an impressive library with wood moldings from floor to ceiling. I thought I was alone in the room until I saw one of the sofa cushions appear to move. It was Mrs. Herring. She blended into the room so perfectly that it was impossible to discern where the couch ended and she began. She was wearing a cream, sleeveless shift dress and sitting with her legs elegantly crossed on a cream couch flanked with gold and cream cushions, her perfectly bronzed legs poured into creamy heels. I imagined that even their money must be cream, minted, perhaps, at a dairy farm.

"Hello, dear, why don't you have a seat?" Mrs. Herring whispered.

"Okay," I whispered back, and lowered myself into a chair that looked like a throne for someone named Louis or Napoleon or Henry.

"Of course I know all about you, so I want to begin by telling you all about my son, Jake," Mrs. Herring whispered again. Was she really, really affected or was something seriously wrong with her?

"All good things, I hope!" I smiled warmly.

"That you come very highly recommended by Laura Brandeis, and she selects only the best tutors to work for her. All my friends call her when they want only the best for their children," Mrs. Herring confided.

"Mrs. Herring—"

"Mimsy, please."

Mimsy?

"Oh . . . okay, thank you. Mimsy, I would love to hear more about Jake." I gave up. Laura's cover was airtight. Mimsy Herring's eyes became watery. I wondered if she was going to cry.

"Well, I want to begin by telling you that he is a beautiful boy."

Jesus Christ. She paused and tucked a stray piece of pin-straight cream hair behind her ear. A diamond stud the size of a golf ball was exposed. "Sensitive, thoughtful, and very, very sweet," Mimsy continued.

"Wonderful!" Apparently I was back to *wonderful*.

"And smart. Jake is very, very smart. He just struggles a bit to harness that intelligence and focus it, if you know what I mean." Mimsy began to tear. I felt like rolling my eyes, but instead I forced myself to nod sagely. If I was going to get this second job, which would bring me into a completely new tax bracket, I would have to start thinking differently. I was an Ivy League Tutor. I worked for Laura Brandeis, a woman I knew for some reason I would never meet but was sure I would work very hard for.

"Wonderful! I'd love to meet him!"

Mimsy looked aghast. Although honestly I wasn't sure what expression she was after. Her face was so botoxed that it was difficult to distinguish aghast from merely surprised.

"Oh, no! He's not home, of course. Jake is with his learning specialist right now. Besides, I had hoped to give you some more information before he interviewed you," Mimsy whispered.

Before *he* interviewed *me?* I briefly wondered whether I should charge for interview time. And what did a learning specialist do? More importantly, did they make more money than a tutor? At that exact moment, a beep sounded in the room and Mimsy calmly pressed a button on a cream phone next to her. She listened for a moment and then whispered, "Just a club soda with a slice of lime, dear. Can I have Conchita bring you anything?" She turned expectantly to me. Oh. People in this apartment called each other from different rooms. On phones.

"I'd love a glass of water," I offered. I felt as if Mimsy wanted Conchita to bring me something. I was in a total trance. Mimsy gave the instructions to Conchita, who I guessed was the uniformed maid who let me into the apartment. She then turned to me, winked, and leaned over.

"Let's have a look at Jake's room, shall we?"

"Excuse me?"

"Just a quick snoop. Come, come!" Suddenly Mimsy got up and floated off her chair, gave me another wink, and exited the library like a cream-colored Casper the not-so-friendly ghost. I followed her down a long hallway and into Jake's room. Already prepared to be amazed after my experience with Katie's room, I suddenly felt old and experienced. But when the door to Jake's room was opened, I realized that no amount of experience could prepare anyone for a room like that. Sunlight poured in from the gigantic window overlooking Park Avenue. A queen-size bed that was *clearly* not made by Jake (judging from the showroom-perfect bedding and arrangement of cushions) rested grandly in the center of the room. Just like Katie's room. Every sports star that had ever lived had apparently given Jake a picture of himself, and had taken the time to sign it. These personalized, autographed photographs covered the walls. They all read, "Dear Jake," followed by a personal message that suggested that Jake was not just a starry-eyed fan clamoring for an autograph, but someone the star clearly wanted to please.

> *"Jake, you're the man! Live the dream!"—Michael Jordan*
> *"Jake, you sexy beast!"—Lindsay Lohan*
> *"You're my genie in a bottle, Jake."—Christina Aguilera*

Besides a built-in desk with two chairs neatly pushed in (two chairs . . . just like in Katie's room!) there was a flat screen TV hooked up to surround sound and a TiVo. But Jake's room had an additional surprise. On a shelf above the huge flat screen TV were a series of photos of him with Britney Spears, Jessica Simpson, Kelly Ripa *and* all her kids, . . . and (gasp!) Paris Hilton. All these photographs were taken on beaches in exotic locations, and judging from the scantily clad celebrities laughing with their arms happily around Jake, after the picture was taken, they probably took a dive into the hotel pool *with* Jake, actually hung out *with* Jake, and then exchanged cell phone numbers *with* Jake. Who was this kid?!

"Oh, those," Mimsy laughed. "I'm afraid my son is a bit of a ladies' man."

A bit of a ladies' man? This was ridiculous. And Jake did not look like a ninth grader. Jake was gorgeous. He had obviously inherited his mother's thick, creamy blonde hair, and his eyes were a startling green. From the photographs, he looked like he was easily over six feet. His abs were—

I was sick! What was I doing? I could not comment on his abs! But there they were, in photograph upon photograph! Six-pack after six-pack.

"I told you he was a beautiful, beautiful child." Mimsy smiled proudly, actually seeming to bask in the fact that her son's future tutor was gawking at his shirtless photographs. Jake looked more like a twenty-year-old Calvin Klein model than the pimply ninth grader I had expected. Mimsy led the way to Jake's desk and opened a neat binder.

"See, he is really very organized. He just needs a bit of help staying on task."

The binder was a work of art. Jake had even taken the time to type out the labels for each of the sections, and he clearly took thorough notes in class. What an unexpected treat! It looked like Jake might be an easy child. Bless Laura Brandeis! I looked at the ghostly woman beside me with growing affection. I could see the beginning of a very perfect, symbiotic relationship.

"Can Jake interview you tomorrow afternoon at 4:45?" Mimsy asked suddenly. I realized the snooping session had come to a close. (Who scheduled children in forty-five-minute increments?)

"Wonderful!"

"I should warn you, though . . . Jake has been through six tutors. He's very, very sweet, but he accepts only the best," Mimsy informed, her whisper becoming even softer.

SIX tutors?

"But he'll love you. You're gorgeous in an exotic kind of way. Boys find that so sexy these days." Mimsy smiled kindly and I swallowed. EXOTIC? I let it go. She was beaming at me as if she had just given me an Oscar. I had a feeling that "gorgeous in an exotic kind of way" roughly translated to: *My son will find you sexy and therefore he will flirt with you instead of fighting with you. He will look forward to studying and then he will leave me alone. You will help him do his homework in the same way Conchita brings me my sparkling water.* Blinking back my outrage, I smiled politely at Mimsy, accepted the glass of water Conchita brought, and penciled Jake into my planner. Mimsy gave me a creamy smile and graciously allowed Conchita to show me out. The minute I got out of the building I went straight to Bendel's to buy the new skinny Sass & Bide jeans Jessica and Charlotte were talking about in class. It was time to celebrate my new job. My cell phone rang nonstop with calls from the mothers, but since I was still on my tutoring high, I chirped merrily about lunches and coffee dates as I shopped. The teachers didn't want to be my friends, so what was stopping me from befriending the mothers, who so obviously liked and appreciated all my hard work?

18

The crisp November air was a welcome change, and I was enjoying the looks of envy I was getting as I marched up Park Avenue to school. The Sass & Bide jeans *did* cling pretty low on my waist, and the saleswoman at Bendel's had assured me that they were sold out all over the city. Walking past the horde of Nightingale, Chapin, Brearley, and Spence girls (all distinguishable by the patterns on the über short skirts of their uniforms), I had a wild impulse to carry a sign that read: NEED A TUTOR? CALL ME AT (212) 555-8290. How else would I get these kids? I was tutoring Katie and Jake that afternoon, but that was only two hours. I could take *at least* two more clients easily. As I approached Langdon, I passed a group of Spence girls who went quiet as they eyed me up and down. If they were focused on the label on my ass, I was even more focused on their quilted Chanel schoolbags. Chanel as a schoolbag. How impossibly chic. I swung my Kate Spade tote (a gift from my mother for getting the Langdon job) to my right side so the girls wouldn't see it. I felt dimly guilty that I was competing with fifteen-year-olds; still, it took all of my willpower to teach my class when all I wanted to do was run to Chanel and charge the bag on my credit card.

Lynn Briggman and Maxine Landau beamed at me as I approached. Both were wearing tight yoga pants and carrying identical Louis Vuitton yoga mat holders as totes.

"Anna!" Lynn smiled, her Fendi sunglasses sparkling against her honey highlights. She was holding up an envelope that was half the size of the imposing French doors. "I wanted to give you the invite in person!" Maxine's eyes narrowed and she looked positively evil for a split second, then her face smoothed into a serene smile.

"You must come to Jessica's as well. It's in December," she urged, her white-blonde ponytail bouncing like a fifth-grader's. *Jessica Landau: Mother is a lesbian. Ran away with Core Fusion teacher when Jessica was in the fourth grade.* Was Maxine going to meet her lover at core fusion class after she dropped Jessica off at school? I shook my head and forced myself to focus.

"You're both too kind." I grinned broadly, thrilled to see that Dr. Blumenfeld was watching me intently from the lobby. Maxine had simply welcomed me and begged me to "keep social tabs" on Jessica because "Charlotte and Blair can be so cruel and exclusive."

Standing in front of Langdon Hall and chatting with Lynn and Maxine, I felt a sense of *belonging* to this school, to these people, to this world. That letter of complaint had been a mere bump in the road. Now these women really liked me (I had lost count of all the coffee and lunch invitations I had been offered) and my next three weekends were filled not only with bar mitzvahs at the city's most exclusive venues, but with lunch and coffee dates at Fred's, La Goulue, and Le Bilboquet. I had never been to any of these places, but the thought of going to them as the guest of some of the city's most beautiful and influential women was thrilling to me.

"I *really* have to go," I finally said, giving both women an apologetic smile. They immediately leaned in for air kisses (air kisses with *Langdon Hall Friends* in front of old Blumenfeld!) and I delightedly air kissed them back. Blumenfeld pretended not to notice me as I walked past her in the lobby, but I watched her dart out of the building and give both mothers a warm hug. It seemed like I wasn't the only one who had memorized the first few pages of the "Langdon Hall Friends" booklet.

As I rode up the elevator to my class, I couldn't help thinking about my favorite 80s movie, *Working Girl*. Trade in the shoulder pads for Juicy and skinny jeans, and I was Melanie Griffith. In September I had moved into a fifth-floor walkup and was staying up all hours of the night trying to come up with interesting lesson plans. Now I was wearing three-hundred-dollar designer jeans and making enough money to reschedule another dinner with Bridgette. This time I would drink as many fourteen-dollar Bellinis as I wanted! Admittedly the quality of my lessons had started to slip, but my students seemed to adore me even more. In fact, every immoral step I made at this school brought me respect and adulation from my students *and* their parents. That's why I hadn't even given it a second thought last night when I put a big fat A in red ink on the top of another Benjamin-Randi paper.

I hopped, skipped, and jumped to the Carletons that evening, unaware that my tutoring session might as well have been on the *Titanic*. Right when it hit the iceberg.

I was the *Titanic*.

I was greeted (confronted was more like it) by both Amanda and her husband. I could see Katie in the background, sitting in the living room with her eyes all red and puffy.

"Is everything okay?" I asked weakly, knowing full well that everything was obviously *not okay*. Maybe this was it. The pin that would prick the crazy bubble I had been floating in for the last few weeks.

"Anna, Katie received a Friday report," Mr. Carleton said gravely, looking at me dead on. What the *hell* was a Friday report?

"I'm sorry?" I asked, hoping for further clarification.

"*A Friday report!*" Amanda cried, and then whipped around and glared at Katie. The Carletons walked toward the living room where their daughter was sitting, and I followed mutely behind them. Dare I ask what a Friday report was?

"It turns out that Katie did *not* hand in her *Lord of the Flies* paper," Mr. Carleton finally said. Ahh. Friday reports were probably like the alert forms we sent home if a student didn't turn something in or was in danger of failing. At any rate, how much trouble could I be in? Katie had never even told me about this paper.

"YES, I DID!" Katie suddenly screamed, and we all jumped. "I WORKED ON IT WITH ANNA LAST TIME. REMEMBER, ANNA?" Katie was hysterical. The Carletons turned to face me, and I caught a glimpse of Katie's pleading face behind their backs. *Please* she mouthed to me. While I preferred to take the honest route and just tell everyone that I had no idea what was going on and that Katie was a freaking LIAR, I knew that alienating her could result in losing this tutoring job. After all, wasn't Katie sort of my boss? I was so screwed.

"What happened to it?" I asked Katie calmly, and then gestured a bit more wildly at her when I was sure both her parents were focused on her face. *What the fuck?* I mouthed back. I felt no remorse for swearing at a twelve-year-old equipped with fully matured manipulative abilities.

"I *e-mailed* it to myself and now I can't *find* it. Ms. Hyatt is such a freakin' *bitch!*" I winced as Katie cursed out loud, and braced myself for the yelling that never came. Neither Carleton seemed in the least bit fazed that Katie had just called her teacher a bitch.

"We need this resolved, Anna. I am going to believe my daughter because I know Katie does not lie. But she does need to write another paper," Mr. Carleton said firmly.

"Apparently if it is not turned in tomorrow it gets lowered a grade. We figured that since you helped her with it, you could, ah, just help her more than you normally might just so she gets it done," Amanda said in a strange voice.

"More than I normally would?" I echoed. This lie had gone so far that even I was beginning to recollect writing this phantom paper with Katie.

"Well, not *write it* per se," Amanda said quickly, "but just help *more than usual*. You probably remember most of it anyway, so writing whatever you remember will just make it a little easier for our daughter to get it completed."

"Or Katie could dictate and you could type," Mr. Carleton suggested. "We have an important family dinner with friends tonight, and I really would like the paper completed before you leave. Obviously charge us for however many hours you are here."

All three Carletons stared at me as I tried to take in what was going on. First, I needed to basically write a paper. Second, the paper had to be done by this evening, and done well or else I might be deemed an incompetent tutor. Third, apparently we had already *written* the paper in our last session so rewriting from memory should only be a breeze. I was seeing Jake Herring for the first time in two hours. I had figured that I wouldn't be with Katie for more than an hour and a half, and had generously budgeted thirty minutes to walk over to Jake's and maybe even get a Starbucks in between. I didn't even have the Herring number in my cell phone. Fuck and double fuck. And then I heard a voice that sounded exactly like mine:

"We'll get it done, won't we, Katie?" I was a maniac. A raving maniac. The Carletons looked positively thrilled, and Katie breathed a sigh of relief.

"We'll leave you two be," Amanda said happily. "Anna, we don't know what we would do without you."

I followed Katie into her room like a prisoner on death row. As soon as she closed the door, I opened my mouth to start shouting, freaking out, *anything* to convey how I felt.

"Before you speak!" Katie interjected. "Before you speak I want to say that I am, like, so sorry. I totally forgot about it! Ohmigod, my parents are so annoying!"

"Katie! You just put me in the WORST position!" I didn't know why, in that terrible moment, I started to smile. God knows I found nothing remotely funny about this situation. Maybe it was the sheer ridiculousness of how a seventh-grader had managed to completely dupe her parents. Or the lengths one had to go when their boss was a seventh-grader. Katie started to smile, too, and suddenly we were struggling to muffle our laughter. I collapsed on her bed and felt the tears roll down my eyes. I think we were both just a little hysterical.

"You're the best, Anna," Katie finally said, looking at me with genuine affection. It was the world's sickest way to bond with a child, but there it was. Our moment.

"Okay, listen, we can go to SparkNotes or GradeSaver," I finally said, eagerly endorsing the cheat sites teachers were warned about in education programs. They featured full summaries and intelligent analyses of almost any book taught in the American school system. "*Lord of the Flies* has to be on them. Have you read the book at least?"

Katie looked at me with a guilty smile and shrugged. I had my answer.

"Just sit here, okay?" I ordered briskly, and Katie obediently sat on the chair next to the computer. I took the main seat and went directly to the SparkNotes Web site and typed in *Lord of the Flies.* "Get me the assignment sheet your teacher gave you on this essay thing," I muttered, reading faster than I had ever read anything in my life. "Then come over here and read the summary so at least you have some idea of what we are doing."

Katie jumped to action and began pulling binders out of her bag. She finally pulled out a tattered sheet indicating that a two- to three-page double-spaced paper with an original thesis on *Lord of the Flies* was to be turned in last Friday. It had been assigned the first week of school. I wanted to give Katie a lecture, but the thought of getting to the Herring residence on time silenced me.

"It's about these stupid boys on this island," Katie offered.

"Shh. Just read the summary—I printed it out for you." I began typing furiously. Katie was quiet for a few minutes, but after I finished the introductory paragraph she perked up.

"Anna, you forgot to type my heading."

"I think you can manage that," I returned sarcastically, moving on to the second body paragraph. "Go to chapter three in your book and skim until you find what page Jack taunts

Piggy on," I ordered. "We have to cite the page number." I was now typing at such an alarming rate that Katie was staring, open-mouthed.

"Ohmigod, you'd be like the fastest IM'er," she breathed.

"Just find the quote, Katie," I ordered, still typing.

"Anna?"

"Hmm?"

"Don't make it too good, okay? I usually get Bs."

I made it out of the Carleton apartment at the exact time I was supposed to be at the Herring residence. I figured if I took a cab I would be five minutes late, and five minutes was hopefully acceptable. Amanda Carleton had given me a grateful smile and slipped me an envelope as I had said good-bye.

"We cannot thank you enough," she had said warmly. I'm not sure what I had mumbled in my rush to get to the elevator, but now, as I sat in the back of the cab and headed up Park Avenue, I couldn't shake the reality of what had just happened. I had done *exactly* what Randi Abrahams had done for Benjamin. Now I felt overwhelmingly sorry for her. Who knew what pressures had been on her to get Benjamin to complete my assignment that day at Starbucks? Tutors were the diplomats in the wars waged between parents and children, and for the sake of diplomacy I realized a certain amount of papers just had to . . . "get done." By any means possible. It went with the territory. I was dying to open the envelope that Amanda had put into my bag, but the cab pulled up at the Herring building and I didn't have a minute to spare.

I was nervous for my interview with Jake. Clearly this was no ordinary freshman. As I walked up to the building, I noticed that the doorman from the other day was on duty. Crap. But this time I was prepared.

"Herring," I declared.

He raised his eyebrows and announced me. I turned left confidently and walked down the long hall to the elevator. Edward was still in the elevator. Had Edward even left? When I reached the floor, ANOTHER maid opened the door and informed me that Mrs. Herring was "not home." Oh, God, it was just me and Jake. Alone. Yet another maid (I was losing count) led me down the hallway into Jake's room, and there, lying on his bed wearing nothing but a pair of Abercrombie sweatpants, was Jake. He had a remote control in his hand and was casually switching channels. He grinned at me.

Oh, shit. Suddenly I was nostalgic for sweet seventh-grade Katie.

"Hey," he drawled sexily.

"Hey," I croaked, my mouth feeling very dry.

"So you're like my tutor number one thousand." He rolled his eyes.

I had to come up with something shocking to catch him off guard.

"Why? Did the others just fucking suck?" I was gambling with this approach, but after Mimsy had told me that Jake had gone through six tutors, and after I had heard Katie use the word *bitch* with no repercussions in front of her parents, I was beginning to learn that cursing just might prove to be the golden ticket.

It worked. Jake shut off the TV and turned to face me. I felt the same joy I experienced when Katie had logged off her AOL, like a dog who had just been given a second and unexpected liver treat. Jake got up from the bed and reached for a T-shirt, trying to be casual, but I could tell the swearing had taken him off guard. He was probably debating whether he should rat me out to his parents and enjoy watching me get fired, or accept that I might be that cool tutor he always wished for.

"Yeah . . . you know . . . ," Jake muttered finally, shrugging his shoulders. I sauntered over to his desk as if it were my room, purposefully sat down on the second chair, and looked at him. Jake appeared to have one more trick up his sleeve.

"Did you see this picture of me and Paris in Hawaii?" he asked nonchalantly, nodding over to the shelf with his celebrity photographs. I blessed Mimsy and her snooping because I was no longer a gawking fool.

"She's cute. I saw her at Barneys the other day," I lied casually. I had never seen Paris Hilton in my life, and I had never been to Barneys.

"So, like, you're rich or something?" Jake eyed me curiously.

"What?"

"I mean, none of my teachers shops at Barneys."

"How do you know?" I challenged, trying to buy time.

"C'mon. You know what I mean."

"I have no clue what you mean. It's not really your business, but whatever. My dad gave me a trust fund. I just tutor because, you know, I like kids." I could just see my father rolling on the floor and laughing at me. I had a trust fund, all right—a trust in my ability to do without a single one of his funds!

Jake and I stared at each other. He blinked first.

"No way," Jake finally said, and then blessed me with a dazzling smile. "So, like, you teach and tutor for fun?"

"Yeah, you know. I did the whole spend-money-all-day thing, but it got old." I was starting to have fun. I was also starting to become a pathological liar.

"Yeah. I know what you mean," Jake commiserated.

"So, why don't you give me a rundown of all your classes and the work you have to do . . . and we'll, uh . . . check that out and see what we can bang out in one session." I forced myself to speak as if I had never been more bored in my life, which put Jake on the defensive. He started to stutter.

"Well, uh, um, okay, like my parents put a lot of pressure on me? And m-my sister went to Princeton like them? And I mean, we have connections and stuff but I still need to pull my own?" Jake didn't meet my eye as he answered my question. And whether it was because he sounded so desperate, or because I was pretty in an "exotic kind of way," or because I had just lied and cursed like a sailor, he was *letting me in*! It was like when Katie gave me her Dior elastic bands. As Jake began getting out his binders and assignment pad, I couldn't help but hope that if things went this well for a week or two Jake might introduce me to Paris Hilton. That would *kill* Bridgette. Before I left, Jake looked at me shyly and asked me if he could take my picture.

"I just, like, have pictures of all my friends," he explained. I melted. As he innocently clicked a picture with his digital camera, I smiled gamely.

19

I know I should have probably saved my first week of tutoring checks, but for some reason, going blonde and acquiring a Chanel handbag had jumped to the top of my to-do list. It was Saturday morning and I didn't think twice before allowing the magical revolving door to suck me into the world of Bergdorf Goodman. Bridgette and I had browsed through the handbag displays and had lingered over the Hermès scarves in college, but I hadn't ventured back. The memory of the $400 scarves scared me even more than the $14 Bellinis. But now, armed with Amanda Carleton's $1,000 "thank you" check, I marched in confidently. The John Barrett Salon was *the* place, according to Charlotte and Blair, to get your hair cut and highlighted. Only I wasn't going for mere highlights. I wanted the whole thing: double process, bleached, glistening, platinum blonde. I wanted to *shimmer* like the Langdon Hall mothers, and I wanted this accomplished before my series of lunch dates. Walking past the Valentino handbag display and the precious jewels section, I found my way to the elevators. On the way up to the ninth floor, the doors opened and closed on almost every floor, allowing me glimpses into mini-salons that read Gucci, Dolce & Gabbana, Prada. When the doors finally opened on 9 I was hardly surprised to be greeted by a lanky, doe-eyed girl holding a tray of Pellegrino in tiny green bottles with even tinier little straws.

"Hello, welcome to John Barrett. Who is your appointment with today?" she asked brightly, offering me a drink.

"John," I said as casually as I could, pretending to ignore the widening of her eyes. Getting an appointment with John was absolutely impossible unless you knew someone. And now I knew someone. After mentioning my desire to get highlights to Max Briggman's mother, she had followed up with an e-mail the next day finalizing my appointment with John. I chalked it up to one of the perks of teaching at a private school.

"Why don't you change into a robe and I will lead you to his seat," she offered, now practically bowing. Two blonde women walked by, both carrying the already iconic YSL Muse bag.

The white-haired and debonair John Barrett appeared minutes after I was seated, followed by his faithful dog, Chaser.

"So, you want to be a blonde?"

"How did you know?" I asked, looking at his image in the large mirror that reflected his face and all of Central Park in the background.

"Lynn Briggman is one of my favorite people." He waved his hand in a casual gesture. "She told me that you want to be a platinum blonde." As I nodded, he deftly ran his fingers through my hair, called over two assistants, and fired off instructions for Ross, his master colorist. (Apparently, John did not do color. He would be giving me a cut to suit my new head of highlights.)

"You'll have to have two different processes today because you have dark brown hair," he said almost to himself as he continued to lift and fuss with my hair, "but if you will be patient, you will leave here today a Bergdorf Blonde." He grinned as he referenced the novel, which was suspended in a glass case in the entrance of the salon. Ross nodded in agreement and fired instructions to his assistant. I had lost count, but it seemed as if no less than five people would be attending to my hair today.

I leaned back in my chair and took a sip of Pellegrino.

I could be very patient.

Thanks to Ross, my highlights were Jennifer Aniston–worthy, and John's expert scissors had created bouncy waves that showed off each golden strand. I was so busy trying to catch a glimpse of myself in every mirrored surface, I hardly heard the receptionist when she gave me my bill.

"Excuse me?"

"Nine hundred and fifty dollars."

Crap.

How could a few artfully placed waves and some blonde streaks cost close to a thousand dollars?

"I only got a haircut and some highlights . . . is there some mistake?"

"Four hundred for John, and you didn't just get highlights, Ms. Taggert. You got a *double process* with Ross and a deep conditioning treatment."

I had anticipated it costing more than the $200 my mother usually spent to cover up her gray, but this was beyond anything I was expecting. Even in my newly discovered tutoring riches, I never thought my hair could eat up all of the Carleton bonus.

I reached for my bag when another receptionist interrupted. She gave me an obsequious smile and said airily, "Oh, Ms. Taggert. It's been taken care of . . . compliments of Ms. Briggman."

"Oh . . ." I managed, looking helplessly from one receptionist to the other. There was no gray area for this one: I was accepting a bribe plain and simple. I could just imagine how disappointed my parents would be if they knew.

"I feel terrible . . ." I replied weakly as if it were the receptionist at John Barrett who would be deciding my fate come Judgment Day.

"We love Lynn," she replied as if that was the only answer I needed. I sheepishly accepted and walked toward the elevator in a trance. My hair was bouncy and frothy and shimmery. I looked a little like a Langdon Hall mother, and I *felt* heads turn as I walked. And just like that my guilt evaporated. I would never be brunette again. So what if I had to return every two weeks for a touch-up? By then I would be able to afford it easily! The John Barrett Salon now owned me in a grip that was both deadly and orgasmic.

"Oh. My. God."

The voice was unmistakable. Damian Oren. I had arrived at school early because I needed to check out some library books for the paper Jake needed to write that afternoon. In my rush I had forgotten that my hair was making its debut.

"Do you like it?" I grinned a little self-consciously. Hair that glittered on a Saturday afternoon at Bergdorf's now seemed a bit X-rated under the fluorescent lights of the school library. There's never a dimmer switch when you need one.

"So, you competing with them now?" He tried to act casually, but I could tell from his eyes that he was serious. And a little disappointed? I couldn't make out.

"Can't a girl change her hair color?" I retorted equally casually, catching a gigantic curl glimmer from the corner of my eye. My hair really had taken on a life of its own.

"Nice Juicys," he shot back, and then, just like the sun coming out, he was all laughter and smiles again. Had I imagined the disappointment?

"So, you know you're famous, right?"

"Huh?"

"You're totally a hot commodity. It's all over Facebook," he answered, staring hard at me. I returned his stare blankly.

"Wait. You're kidding me." Damian tilted his head back and howled. "An actual, living, breathing specimen who doesn't know what Facebook is. I love it. I *fucking* love it!"

"Okay, Oren. Don't be such a wiseass. I know what Facebook is. I just don't know what you're talking about." I was irritated. He was undeterred.

"Nice book. Nice book on Edith Wharton. I'm sure your seventh-graders just *love* Wharton's prose," he taunted, pointing to the book under my arm. Needless to say, Jake's paper on Edith Wharton's *Age of Innocence* was due next week.

"Is it for Jake?" Damian asked innocently. I felt like I had been shot through the heart. What?

"Excuse me?" I sputtered. How did he know about Jake?

"Jake Herring, kingpin of the Upper East Side juvenile drug world? Celebrity whore, teen fucking Jake Herring?" Damian was clearly having the time of his life torturing me.

"How the hell—"

Damian sighed dramatically, took my arm and ushered me to a nearby computer terminal. Looking around furtively to make sure nobody was near, he logged on to Facebook. What happened next was too fast for me to keep track. Whether Damian had an account or logged in as someone else, I don't know, but all of a sudden we were on Jake Herring's Facebook page looking at a picture of . . . me!

CHECK OUT MY HOT TUTOR his wall read. Apparently, they did.

Snoop2D4: yo Davo you have to tap that.

TuLegit88: nice lessons, man.

Skaterboyz: get me her digits NOW.

Before I could respond, Damian clicked the album SATURDAY NIGHT PICS and opened up a digital album of Jake and all his friends apparently out on a Saturday night: closeup with a girl in a cab; shot of same girl pretending to give Jake a blow job and grinning madly; shot of all the guys doing a shot in somebody's living room; closeup of Jake smoking a joint. I opened my mouth to react, but Damian was too quick. He simply brought the cursor to the point in the picture that focused on the nameless girl's face, and all of a sudden we were at her homepage! That's how easy it was. Just click on someone's face and you were at their homepage. Click. Click. Girl kissing another girl. Same girl in bra holding shot glass. Another shot of girl kissing another girl.

"Um . . . how many lesbians are there in the private school world?" I was wide-eyed.

"They're not lesbians. They're just lesbian *chic*." Damian winked.

"What the hell is lesbian chic?" I hated how Damian seemed to know everything. And how he purposefully responded in enigmatic phrases that forced me to beg for more information.

What kind of person honestly believed that lesbian chic was a perfectly understandable explanation?

"Lesbian chic, Anna," Damian paused dramatically, "is heterosexual girls who take girl-kissing-girl pictures to get all the boys excited."

"Oh . . ."

"Works for me." He flashed me a wicked grin.

"Damian! STOP!" This was getting out of hand.

"Yeah, crazy, isn't it?" Damian shrugged agreeably, logging off. "These punks post all this compromising stuff and they have no idea that any teacher with half a wit can log on and see what they do."

"But how do you have access to all these students' walls? Don't they have to friend you first?"

"Nope," Damian announced with undisguised glee. "Half these geniuses we teach never alter their privacy settings. With our Langdon teacher accounts we can go on and see their pages, what they write to each other on their walls, and, of course, the holy grail—the pictures!"

"So, you actually *check* this stuff?" I asked, torn between thinking Damian was the biggest loser in the world and desperately wanting to do some spying of my own.

"Hell yes! Like last night I was just checking up on one of my students' Facebook page because he honestly looks high every time he comes to class, and sure enough there were about a dozen pictures of him holding a joint and getting high with his friends this weekend. And then he said something about this kid Jake's tutor being hot, so I clicked on Jake thinking I'd see Randi's face, and then, well, then you know," Damian looked me in the eye. "So you really got into the swing of things, huh. You learned fast, I have to say."

I couldn't quite tell if he was judging me, congratulating me, or condemning me, but a bell rang and a few older students walked into the library so our chat was clearly over. I followed him wordlessly out of the library and then we parted ways, my blonde hair attracting every student's attention as it bounced and shone and reflected off all the lockers. But I was over the blonde hair already. I wanted quiet time to go on Facebook. Did Katie Carleton have a page? Did my students? Could these kids get arrested? Did the police know? Did the parents of these kids know about this . . . bastion of information? So many questions!

I couldn't wait to confront Jake in our next session. I had wrestled with the idea of not telling him and just spying on him, but I also had my self-respect. This time the doorman did not bat an eye as I walked past him; nobody asked where I was headed. The hazing period was over and I was clearly Herring staff. Once again I was led to his room by a fully uniformed maid. And once again Mrs. Herring wasn't home. Jake's room was empty but I could hear his shower running. How transparent was this kid? His need to be in a state of seminakedness at all times was unbelievable.

Refusing to get ruffled, I went to his desk, clicked on the Internet, and opened it to his Facebook account. Smirking back at me was Jake's own face. Where the hell did my picture go?

"Dude! What are you doing!"

I whirled around to face Jake, dripping and indignant in his white towel.

"How did you get on that?"

"I have my ways. I saw the picture you posted of me. Not cool." I tried as hard as I could to remain annoyed, but Jake's right-out-of-the-shower move had me a little distracted.

"You should thank me for that. Do you know how many people are going to call you now?" he asked seriously, shaking his head and reaching for a T-shirt.

"Aren't you in the least bit curious how I can get onto your page?" I asked.

He paused for a minute and then shook his head. "Nah, I mean, whatever. I had heard some teachers knew how to do it, but who cares. Let 'em know how we roll on the weekends. It's funny." He sat down on the chair beside me, pulled off his towel (thankfully there were boxers underneath), and looked right into my eyes.

"You look different."

"Yeah, I colored my hair." I touched it self-consciously and felt myself blush.

"I like it."

"Thanks."

"A lot."

"Shall we get started on the Edith Wharton paper?" I was relieved to find that at the mention of the paper, Jake was sixteen again, and completely helpless.

"Yeah, we better . . . Anna, I can't bring myself to read the thing. I *can't*. It *sucks*. My mom wants to talk to you about that when we're done anyway."

"About what?" I asked suspiciously.

"About prereading the books I have to read so then you can just tell me the story, you know, *verbally*. I'm just a lot more *verbal*," Jake responded seriously. "She'll probably offer to pay you. My last tutor got a grand a book." *A grand a book?! Hello highlights!*

"What happened to her?" I asked as casually as possible.

"She was boring," he responded evasively. "And oh, Anna?"

"Yeah?"

"Don't tell my mother about the Facebook thing. She still hasn't figured it out. She thinks it's, like, a place pedophiles go to find teenage girls. They don't know we all have our pages."

"It *is* a place pedophiles go," I retorted.

"Yeah, well, good for them. Just don't tell my mom, okay?"

"Yeah, okay." I figured for $1,000 a novel (could I ask for $1,500?) Elizabeth Herring could be kept in the dark about the Facebook thing.

Like clockwork, her phone call came that evening as I was sitting down to plan the next day's lesson.

"Anna, dear, it's Mimsy," she whispered. If this woman wasn't already so wealthy, she could make a killing as a phone sex operator.

"How are you?" I asked politely, relishing the fact that I wasn't nervous. She was obviously calling about my prereading Jake's books, and I was looking forward to how she would manage this as a perfectly respectable and normal request.

"Jake just adores you, dear. He finds you so intelligent and warm," Mimsy gushed. "He . . . *we* . . . are both so lucky to have you in our lives."

Classic.

"I feel very lucky, too," I affirmed, going through a pile of menus. I still hadn't ordered dinner, and this conversation could go on for a while.

"I heard Jake spoke to you about his . . . *dyslexia*," Mimsy breathed the last word as it if were a rare form of cancer.

"No, he didn't mention that." I refused to make this easy for her.

"Oh, dear, the poor boy must just be so . . . *embarrassed*. What destroys his father and me is that simply for this one fact, a brilliant boy like Jake is going to be hurt academically. It's been a Herring family struggle for so long," Mimsy sighed tragically.

"I had a friend in high school who was dyslexic," I said truthfully. "But there are some wonderful programs he can—"

"Oh, Jake is much too embarrassed to go through all of *that*," Mimsy dismissed. "His father and I were wondering if you could preread the books he has to prepare for English class so you could verbally cover them for him."

"Would Jake read the books as well?"

"Of course he would, but one can never tell how much he . . . *internalizes*."

Mimsy was a genius.

"Perhaps I can read them to him?" I shot back cleverly.

"Oh, dear, how embarrassing for him . . . It's hard enough to be in his . . . *predicament*, but having to be read to as if he were in kindergarten would be so terrible for his fragile self-esteem, Anna. You do understand? We would of course pay you for however many hours it takes you to read these books."

"Ms. Herring—"

"Mimsy."

"Mimsy," I echoed, "some of these books are quite hefty. They could take four, even five hours to read."

"Money is no object when one is talking about one's children's education." Mimsy sighed nobly. "No object at all."

Reading Jake Herring's books, I realized, would allow me to

move out of this apartment and into a doorman building. Have a nightlife. Pay back my parents for all the furniture. Perhaps even give Bridgette a run for her money. Reading Jake Herring's books also went against everything I had believed in when first applying for a job as a teacher. I would be condoning a system of cheating. Even worse, I would be enabling a child to override the system just because his parents could afford it. I opened my mouth to tell Mimsy Herring that this proposal went against every moral fiber in my body.

Then I saw a roach the size of a puppy scurry across the living room floor and under my bed. I meant to scream, but what I said instead was, "I'll do whatever it takes to help Jake."

I needed to get out of this apartment, and Herring checks were my fastest ticket.

20

Y ou're making how much an hour?"

"Two hundred dollars."

"Do you ride in on a pony?"

I glared at my father across from the turkey. Here we were, sitting at the same table we had initially had our first argument about teaching. Only this time, there was no argument. My parents were staring at me, mouths agape. My brother looked delighted.

"Can I get in on this action?"

"Shut up, Jonathan!" we shot back in unison at him, and he raised both arms in defense.

"Sorry, guys, but I'm becoming a teacher when I graduate."

I shot my brother a dirty look and turned back to Dad. First he hadn't believed that I could make a living off teaching in this country. Then he had felt sorry for me and bought me furniture. Now, *finally,* when I was telling him that I had found a way to pay the bills and maybe move to a decent apartment on my own, he still wasn't happy.

"I'm sorry, Anna. I just don't understand. It sounds illegal."

"I agree with your father," Mom chirped irritatingly, pouring gravy on my brother's turkey and passing me the mashed potatoes. "Eat, honey."

"I will NOT eat! God, Mom!" The world could be coming to an end and my mother would still find a way to offer a cookie with the gas mask.

"Let me get this straight, Anna. You get two hundred dollars an hour to sit down with other teachers' students and do their homework?" Dad was not letting this go. Ever the businessman, he had this habit of questioning any topic that became his target until it lay dying, gasping for air on the kitchen table.

"I don't *do* their homework," I protested hotly. "I *help*."

Jonathan guffawed and spat his Coke back into the glass. "Anna, honestly, that even sounds retarded. An Ivy League–educated teacher sitting in a room with some spoiled twelve-year-old and a single homework assignment doesn't sound like helping."

"Fuck you, Jonathan!"

"ANNA!" My parents both screamed.

"Okay, okay, sorry," I muttered. I had gotten so used to hearing Katie curse around her parents that I had forgotten that I could be fifty years old and still be slapped if I so much as said "shit" around either one of mine.

"Awesome vocab, teach." Jonathan smiled demurely and popped a sweet potato in his mouth. I hated Thanksgiving.

"Your brother is right, Anna. How come none of us knew about this before? This . . . this *tutoring* business? Finish your stuffing." Mom was relentless.

"Mom, honestly. How much did any of us know about this private school world? I went in knowing nothing." I briefly contemplated telling them the whole truth. That the more work I put into my lessons, the more the parents seemed to hate me.

That I had never been more beloved or accepted than when I eased up on the teaching and wore the expensive clothes that tutoring afforded me.

"Anna, let me turn this around. Put yourself in a different pair of shoes," Dad began, leaning forward.

"Dad, cut the Atticus Finch routine. I'm a great teacher, and tutoring is a fun thing on the side that allows me to shop a little. Period."

He was undeterred.

"Think about *your* students being tutored by someone much like yourself. Pick any student in your class. Let's call him Jack. Imagine that after school every day, Jack has Stanford-educated Jill come over and help him do the homework you assigned. Then *you* grade this perfect assignment and give Jack an A. Only it's Jill's assignment. So, how do you know if you're really a good teacher? What if all the teachers in Manhattan are doing each other's homework and none of the kids are learning anything at all?"

We were all silent.

"Jack and Jill went down the hill and Anna came tumbling after!" Jonathan interrupted, looking enormously pleased with himself.

I stared at my plate a little guiltily. I thought about how furious and betrayed I had felt the first time I had run into Randi and Benjamin at Starbucks. That had been only two months ago. How had I, in such a quick span of time, gotten over that incident? I had joined the enemy and was no better than Randi Abrahams now. Yet somehow, I had never felt more accepted by my students.

"Then, again . . . ," Jonathan began, raising his fork thoughtfully and finally serious, "what if all these Jills make seventy bucks a day? Honestly, if Anna and all these teachers can pull in a grand in an afternoon, I'm not sure what I would do."

I looked at my brother gratefully. We were four years apart, and he was a freshman at Yale. Those four years allowed us enough distance that we could rag on each other and give each other a hard time, but we always came through for one another.

"A thousand dollars in an afternoon?" Apparently that was all Mom heard.

"Well, I'm not *there* yet," I began, "but yeah, if I see Katie for an hour and a half and then Jake for a couple hours, I can make an easy seven hundred."

"Hell, you should support all of us," Dad joked, but his eyes weren't smiling. "I just don't like it, Anna. It doesn't mean that I think what teachers make in this country is right. But—"

"Two wrongs don't make a right!" Mom exclaimed fervently, pushing the cranberry sauce in my face.

Saturday night I was back in my apartment, still downcast from my long weekend at home. I had decided to come back to Manhattan early and do some retail therapy on Sunday to cheer myself up. The conversation at the Thanksgiving dinner table had been repeated throughout the weekend, and it always ended in a stalemate. Dad was right, I couldn't deny it . . . except to his face, of course. It did bug me that my students were probably turning in such perfect work because other teachers like me were doing it for them. But it also irritated me that, regardless of how much I put into my lessons or how carefully and promptly I graded the assignments, my students never responded to me in the same way they responded to Randi Abrahams. Until I started to morph into her.

Maybe that was it.

I needed to talk to Randi Abrahams. Really talk to her. Until now I hadn't made a single friend in the faculty. Damian was constantly lurking with his sardonic comments, Sarah Waters always passed me with her Prozac-induced grin, and Dorothy Steeple's weird habits continued to bug me. I had yet to find a real peer. Randi taught the same grade, the same kids, and appeared to be only a few years older than me. True, she had been nothing but cold to me at the beginning of the year, but I was willing to give it another shot. As a teacher I was lonely, but as a tutor I felt like I was lost at sea. Okay, maybe out at sea on a really expensive yacht.

My mother always told me that if you can articulate what you want, then the entire universe will conspire to get it for you. Too bad she didn't write *The Secret*. The universe decided to pull through for me the very next day at the Chanel boutique.

It was the first time I had ever walked into a Chanel store with the intent of purchasing a handbag. Chanel was for window-shopping. Or splurging on a gossamer lip gloss. But it was the Sunday after a very depressing Thanksgiving holiday, and I was quite certain that a quilted handbag upward of fifteen hundred dollars would do wonders to cheer me up.

"Welcome to Chanel," the doorman said with a glint in his eye, as if he too knew that today was the day.

"I'd like to see totes," I told the elegant saleswoman. A perfect leather Chanel tote to carry my schoolwork in.

"Of course." She smiled, and began pulling down two of the softest bags imaginable in a black and a brown. The gold, interlocked Cs gleamed under the store's lights and my heart skipped a beat.

"I like the brown," a voice offered casually behind me. Randi Abrahams.

I couldn't believe it. Had I literally conjured her up?

"It goes better with your boots. Black's kind of harsh, you know?" Randi was being . . . nice? Charming, even! And helpful! And . . . smiling!

"The brown is cute," I mumbled awkwardly, eyeing her chic figure clad in skinny jeans and high boots. Slung casually over her shoulder was the $3,000 shearling Chanel tote.

"I was just looking for sunglasses, but maybe I'll get the brown, too. Unless you're getting it for school?" Randi asked, looking genuinely interested in the bags before us.

"I was thinking . . . for school?" I managed weakly.

"Yes, it would be perfect!" Randi agreed, handling the bag and sticking her hand in its roomy insides. "Plenty of room to stuff grading and papers."

The saleslady looked inquiringly at me, and I nodded. "I'll take it."

"I'll take one, too," Randi called from the sunglasses counter. "Don't worry, Anna, I won't be using it for school! You don't mind, do you?"

I nodded dumbly. This was not at all how I had envisioned my Chanel encounter.

"Add these sunglasses," Randi added, then looked at me brightly. "Fun, isn't it? Are you free to grab a quick bite? It would be nice to finally get to know one another."

"Sure," I replied. We were buying the same bag! We were on equal footing! Why had I ever let this woman intimidate me?

"Perfect. I'm going to go outside and smoke a cigarette and wait for you. We can walk over to Fred's," Randi said brightly, smiling as she accepted a glossy black Chanel shopping bag from the saleslady. Randi smoked? I watched her from the corner of my eye as she stood outside the big glass doors, all legs and boots and leather.

"Enjoy your bag, Ms. Taggert," the saleslady said as brightly to me as she had to Randi, and I tried not to think about the price tag as I joined my colleague outside of the boutique.

"Whew . . . eight hours of tutoring," I ventured shyly as I approached her, placing the tutoring subject boldly between the perfect smoke rings Randi was exhaling.

"You can't think about it that way, Anna. Let's get lunch. You have *a lot* to learn." She smiled casually and nodded toward Madison Avenue. "Shall we?"

"Let's," I agreed equally casually, walking alongside her. As we turned the corner, I caught a glimpse of us across the street in the Coach store windows. Two girls enjoying a cold November Sunday, shopping on Madison Avenue. Our twin Chanel shopping bags hung merrily from our shoulders. We could have easily passed as young versions of the Langdon mothers. Randi caught me looking.

"Ugh. Coach is so public school."

It was?

I decided to keep my mouth shut and my favorite Coach wallet out of sight. The only Barneys I had ever been to was at the Riverside Mall in Hackensack, and that was only a CO-OP. Nothing like this Madison Avenue shopping heaven. Randi led me expertly passed the Lanvin jewelry counter and headed straight for the elevators. Fred's, on the top floor of Barneys, was Manhattan's luncheon Mount Olympus.

"I could live in this store," she sighed happily as she pushed 9 and grinned wildly. Clearly she was in her natural habitat, and like an expert hunter, she had sniffed me out as prey.

"I've never been here," I admitted, and she only appeared more delighted.

"We're hitting *every floor* after lunch," she declared, marching confidently out of the elevator and into the glass doors of the restaurant. A gray-haired man who appeared to be the restaurant's host greeted her with a hug, and I noticed the aggravated looks on the people who were lined up at the door.

"Randi!" he cried obsequiously. "Your usual table?"

"Max, you're a darling," she breathed, suddenly sounding very British. "And this is my *dear* friend Anna. You have to be *very* nice to her." She laughed hysterically as if she had said something very funny, and Max turned to kiss me on the right cheek. When I pulled back, he looked like he had been slapped.

"We do both cheeks!" Randi trilled, walking ahead of us as I dutifully offered Max my left side. Randi's usual table was near a window in the middle of the room. Though large enough for four people, it was only set for two.

"Two glasses of Sancerre," Randi told the waiter, who nodded as if she had just granted him the biggest favor in the world. I was finally face to face with Randi Abrahams.

"So . . ." She smiled, leaning forward.

"So . . . ," I echoed, crossing my arms and looking around the room.

"Don't you just *love* it here?" Randi was orgasmic.

"It's a far cry from the Langdon cafeteria, that's for sure," I smirked, attempting to adopt her obvious disdain for all things un-Barneys.

"Ew, gross. I ate in that fucking cafeteria *once*, during my orientation, and I *never* returned. You actually go there?" she asked in disbelief. I had to laugh at Randi's use of our seventh-graders' vocabulary and her dismissal of a school cafeteria that I believed must rival some of the city's top restaurants.

"Sometimes," I lied. The truth was that I actually couldn't wait to go there every day. Even if I sat with a group of glassy-eyed teachers who refused to speak to me, I always enjoyed the spectacle. "Little Italy and Little Thailand are my favorites," I admitted.

"Gag me!" Randi laughed dramatically, and then sighed happily as our wines were brought to the table. "Oh, thank God, alcohol!" She took a long sip, closed her eyes, and sighed again. "Heaven."

"This is weird, being here with you," I started, feeling my face flush. "You have to admit, we didn't get off to the best start."

"Oh, let's not talk about that," Randi dismissed with a laugh. "You can't be negative at Fred's. It's, like, a *rule*. Let's just be happy that we met at Chanel and ended up here drinking wine!"

I was so happy I took an unnecessarily huge gulp of the Sancerre. It went straight to my head. Randi was lonely, too! Of course! I had just misunderstood her! Maybe we could help each other in this crazy world. Maybe we could get those margaritas after work! Part of me wanted to delve deeper into the Benjamin Kensington episode at Starbucks, but things were going so well and I didn't want to risk losing this new and friendly version of Randi, who, I had to admit, I was already loving.

"Call me superficial," she went on, "I like nice things. I'm not about to spend the rest of my life in that building walking up and down the halls in some Ann Taylor suit and dorky Nine West pumps. What is there, like some unwritten code that teachers have to know their place and adhere to some dowdy uniform?"

"I know what you mean," I replied quickly, trying not to wince at her spot-on description of my teaching uniform for most of September and October. Pretutoring days, of course. I took another large gulp of wine for confidence and asked her the question I had been dying to ask from day one.

"Why did you become a teacher?"

All of a sudden a shadow crossed her face and her eyes narrowed. I immediately regretted the question. What was it about me that couldn't let go and have fun? Why did I have to be so intense?

"You don't have to answ—"

"No, no!" Randi waved her hand again, her face brightening. "Totally fair question. I was just thinking. I haven't been asked that in a long, long time. Let me see . . ." She paused dramatically, turning her eyes up toward the ceiling. "Why did I want to become a teacher?"

Did she want me to answer?

"I was a really awkward kid in middle school, you know?" I nodded sympathetically as she leaned over on the table and propped her chin on her elbows.

"Me, too," I admitted, thinking back to the slightly plump, pimply teenager I had been. "Who wasn't?"

"Yeah, but I was a serious *nerd*," Randi confided, her eyes widening. We both laughed at her use of the word, which seemed somehow taboo to come out of the mouth of a teacher. "Totally not *popular*."

"So you didn't sit at the cool table at lunch?" I shot back, warming up.

"Are you fucking kidding me? I was in social Siberia!"

A waiter came by and Randi gestured for him to refill our wineglasses, nodding impatiently when he asked if we were ready to order. I was so riveted that I hadn't even glanced at the menu.

"So you're trying to be cool now?" I asked in disbelief. It was like a pin had just pricked my Randi bubble and I was watching it deflate before my disappointed eyes. She couldn't be that pathetic . . . could she?

"God, NO!" she cried, picking up her wineglass and reading my mind. "How pathetic would that be!"

The bubble started to mend.

"My parents always told me that schoolwork was the most important thing," she went on, breaking a small piece of bread and swirling it in olive oil. "So that's all I did. Worry about homework and grades. They told me that all the other things—you know, like friends, clothes, and having fun—was for later. So I just buried my head for the first thirteen years of my life and worked my ass off. I was absolutely miserable."

I noticed that Randi was still swirling the piece of bread but had yet to put it in her mouth.

"My parents were like that, too," I confided. "I was told in no uncertain terms that getting into a good college was my number one priority."

"Yeah, me too, until I realized that was a miserable way to go through school." Randi laughed, putting down the bread and looking at me. "I snapped out of that mind-set pretty fast and it was because of a teacher."

I gave up trying to find a connection. Randi was too full of surprises, and I just wasn't fast enough.

"You lost me," I grinned, putting up both my hands in mock surrender. The waiter approached again and I hurriedly looked at the menu.

"We'll both have the Gotham salad," Randi said curtly, then turned back to me. "Trust me, it's amazing."

"Sounds go—"

"Anyway, so this *teacher*," Randi went on, warming up to her story, "taught eighth-grade math at my school. Ms. Lavery. I still remember her name. I'll never forget how she walked into class that first day, dressed in tight jeans and the most amazing cropped jacket you have ever seen."

Randi was looking at me, but her eyes seemed far away and I could tell she was back in that eighth-grade math class, transfixed by the sight of this amazing Ms. Lavery. I tried to imagine her as well, and an image of Randi on that first day I had seen her in the faculty lounge came to mind.

"I mean, a *cropped* jacket!" Randi emphasized, breaking another small piece of bread. "And she had this amazing hair that looked like it was professionally blown out, and the highest heels I had ever seen a teacher wear."

"Sounds like you," I laughed.

Randi wasn't laughing.

"So here was this gorgeous woman who defied every stereotype of how a teacher was supposed to look. Kids in my class were starting to exchange glances and we were all waiting for her to be a total ditz. But she wasn't! Ms. Lavery turned out to be the hardest and," Randi paused for effect, "smartest teacher we had ever had."

"Wow," I responded unnecessarily. Randi wasn't finished.

"I mean, she just had this *way* about her. Like she was someone you wanted to impress in class but also talk to about personal things. The popular kids loved her because she knew all about the songs and TV shows they obsessed over, and kids like me respected her because she thought being in the math league was the coolest thing in the world. Ms. Lavery just . . . leveled us. We *all* loved her. Here was a teacher, for the first time, we could actually imagine having a life outside of her job." Randi's voice had become positively reverent, but I was now a little unconvinced that this Ms. Lavery was worthy of such worship.

"All because she dressed well?"

"Yes and no." Randi raised one manicured finger. "If she had just dressed well but done a lousy job in the classroom we wouldn't have all been so into her. It was just that she was . . . the whole package. For me, it was the first time I had a teacher who defied the expectations of what a teacher should be. She was good at math. But she also liked fashion and music and all things pop culture. It didn't have to be one or the other, you know?"

I was beginning to catch on.

"I could care about school and things like math class, but it was okay to concentrate on my appearance. I could be in the math league, but I could also listen to Poison and sneak out to a party. It seems simplistic now, but to an eighth-grader whose parents had always led her to believe that it was one way or the other, I swear to God Ms. Lavery was a fucking liberator!"

Randi's face was flushed, and I wasn't sure if it was from the wine or the speech. Before I could respond, two enormous bowls of salad arrived and neither of us objected when the waiter refilled the wineglasses. Again.

I was getting a little tipsy. But my understanding of Randi was clearer by the minute.

"You want to be Ms. Lavery," I said simply.

"You got it," Randi responded equally simply, stabbing a piece of lettuce with her fork and then waving it triumphantly. "I love history. I loved it in college, and I love it now. But I love all of *this*—" She gestured around the room. "And what I fucking hate about our profession is that we're somehow not allowed to."

I took a bite of the salad and chewed thoughtfully. It was delicious.

"Why do you think that is?"

"Anna," Randi began to play with her lettuce, "don't you get it? That's why Ms. Lavery was such a Lone Ranger and took us by such surprise. When you pay teachers just enough to, well . . . *breathe*, any of them who look like they have means to an alternate life become the enemy."

"Is that where the tutoring comes in?" I asked, understanding. *Means to an alternate life.*

Randi didn't answer directly.

"Look, the only friend I had at Langdon was the teacher you replaced," she replied.

"Who was she?" I was curious. I hadn't heard much about her. Nothing, in fact.

"Her name was Jenny Rivers. She was my absolute best friend in that place, but then she quit in the middle of the summer. She was married and had one little girl, and then she got pregnant."

"So she wanted to spend more time with her kids?"

"She couldn't afford day care so she quit to tutor full-time," Randi replied flatly. "Anna, c'mon. Don't be naïve. You know what the salary is like. Jenny's husband was also a teacher at a private school in Manhattan, and even between the two of them they couldn't pay for day care. It's too bad, because I have to admit she was an incredibly talented teacher."

"But how can she tutor full-time? Kids don't get out of school until three in the afternoon at the earliest!"

"Please." Randi grinned again, signaling the waiter for another glass of wine. "Don't forget the high school kids throughout the city. They have so many free periods that half of them are running around the city taking long lunches at Bilboquet and shopping on Madison Avenue. Or getting high in one of their apartments. If they have a paper due, though, they're willing to meet at anytime throughout the day."

"So that's where you disappear during our free periods?" I was beginning to understand.

"No, I go to the cafeteria for Little Thailand's pad Thai noodles," Randi responded sarcastically. "If I have an hour, better I earn two hundred and fifty dollars than sit on my ass listening to Harold Warner or Blumenfeld or some other douche bag hold court at a lunch table and go on and on about progressive education."

I was open-mouthed. Two hundred and fifty! Maybe it was time for a raise. . . .

"Listen," she said, her voice softening, "I've seen the change in you. I *know* you know what I'm talking about. Getting to that place all starry-eyed and 'I'm going to mold the minds of the future' happy. I *get* that. But I also get standing in front of a roomful of students knowing that their individual tuition is more than you get paid in a year. It's fucking *degrading* and nobody has the balls to say it. And the more you put into your lessons, the more pissed off the faculty gets, the more unhappy and nervous the mothers get. Nobody wins. And this goes on for years until you wake up and you're sixty and the same kids you thought you molded don't even remember your name. All the while you have no other memory or experience of anything outside of the four walls of your classroom."

I gulped. Here I was, listening to another teacher voicing my greatest insecurities. I was Odysseus lost at sea, and Randi's voice was like the Sirens. Her reasoning was irresistible.

"Oh, I think the kids are a riot, don't get me wrong," she said cheerfully, picking at the side of lettuce next to the chicken. "Sometimes I teach great lessons. But everything in moderation. I'm not going to put my twenties on a shelf just to stay up till two in the morning grading papers and planning lessons.

I make sure I have a fabulous life outside of school. It's good for me, and it's also healthy for the kids."

"Why the kids?" I challenged.

"Oh, Anna, c'mon. These kids are literally taught to view their teachers as part of their staffs. You know. Nanny, therapist, driver . . . teacher? We're all on the payroll and we do as we're told. It does them a little good to see a teacher dressed better than their mothers. Shakes them up. Makes them nervous."

"I did notice that Charlotte started paying me a lot more respect once my wardrobe got a tutoring-salary boost," I admitted.

"Yeah, the blow job queen!" Randi hooted, throwing her head back and laughing. I noticed two men at a table next to us look at her admiringly. She looked like a supermodel with her long hair and even longer eyelashes. I allowed myself to laugh with her, relieved to be able to *finally* talk about the students we had in common.

"But," Randi said, leaning closer and lowering her voice, "the tutoring allows *you* to have a life. Get real. All these kids are getting tutored. And if you're not going to do it, someone else will. So you have a choice. You can teach and live in some miserable walk-up, or you can find a healthy balance and have a little fun on your own. Besides, I think what I earn in tutoring is what I deserve as a teacher, so it's a nice little payback for me."

Randi was unapologetic. I wondered if I could hire her for the weekend to take on my parents. Why hadn't I thought of all these points? A part of me knew that Randi's reasoning was utterly self-serving, but the other part of me that was relishing my Gotham salad and Chanel bag agreed wholeheartedly. Why not have some fun and take care of number one? *Moi!*

"You have to meet my friend Bridgette." I smiled sweetly, finishing my wine. Randi smiled back and nodded happily.

We spent the rest of the afternoon and evening hitting every floor of Barneys. On the Co-op floors we ran into Jessica Landau shopping with her cousin who went to Spence.

"Ohmigod! Ms. Abrahams! Ms. Taggert!" she had squealed delightedly, and then proudly introduced us to her cousin as "the coolest teachers *ever*." Randi then proceeded to instruct me on her picks for the fall season—Marni, Zac Posen YES, Pucci and Versace NO. The latter, she explained, were too "Long Island mother trying too hard." I had followed in wonder as we tried on seven-hundred-dollar shoes and slipped on twenty-thousand-dollar chinchilla vests. The second floor was having a resort trunk show, and the saleslady, obviously egged on by our Chanel shopping bags, handed us glass after glass of wine. I had never drunk alcohol and shopped before, but Randi informed me that in-store parties were quite common at Barneys and easily downed three more glasses of wine before we left.

By the time we left the store, it was already dark. I could barely walk.

"Shall we share a cab? Which way are you heading?" Randi asked, then dropped her handbag on the sidewalk. "Oops," she giggled, "I'm drunk like a skunk!"

"I'm on 84th between Third and Lex," I offered, trying to focus on her fallen handbag. The sidewalk was tilted at an obscure angle.

"Perfect, I'm on 76th between Madison and Park—just drop me off!" she exclaimed, bending down to pick up her bag.

We collapsed into the cab and I allowed Randi to tell the driver the two stops he was to make. As I watched the Madison Avenue stores whiz by, I looked over to the beautiful, leggy girl beside me who was now someone I could call my friend.

"I had the *besssst ti . . . meee*," she slurred, her eyes half shut.

"Me, too," I responded truthfully, watching her exit the cab at 76th Street. As I leaned back in the taxi and waited for my stop, I made a formal decision to find a new apartment. And not throw up in the back of the cab.

21

dragged myself to school Monday morning more hungover than I had ever been in my life. After getting home from Barneys the night before, I had collapsed on my bed and passed out cold. No papers. No lesson. But before I started to panic in earnest, I saw Randi turn the corner of Park Avenue looking equally lethargic. Enormous sunglasses covered half her face. Her body looked frail, barely able to hold the gigantic Marc Jacobs bag that caused her to tilt to one side.

"Anna . . . oh my God . . . ," she called out dramatically.

"Ms. Lavery!" I cried back, delirious with joy that we already had an inside joke. I noticed several of the mothers look our way curiously, and for once I was thrilled to have someone on *my* team. For some reason they were more reluctant to intrude when two teachers were talking. Maybe because they couldn't smell the fear.

"Randi, what did you do to me?" I moaned dramatically, enjoying the curious looks my Chanel bag was receiving. As soon as she approached me, Randi linked her arm through mine and whispered, "We're sending them to the library."

I sighed with relief. Not only did I have Randi backing me, untouchable Randi who even Dr. Blumenfeld was afraid to chastise, but I would have a friend to gossip with the whole day. We remained with our arms linked as we walked through the

lobby past Dr. Blumenfeld's raised eyebrows and Damian
Oren's disgusted smirk.

Randi's expert dismissal of our students made Machiavelli
seem innocent. She collected both of our classes in her room
and stood by the board with a glint in her eyes.

"Ms. Taggert and I have something *very* special planned for
you today," she gushed. "But we're not going to announce it
until each and every one one of you is very, very quiet."

The entire room was silenced in an instant. Even I couldn't
wait to hear what this surprise treat we were apparently giving
the children would be. Randi looked over at me and winked.

"Shall I tell them, or will you, Ms. Taggert?"

"By all means, you tell!" I was admittedly as caught up as the
kids.

"Well," Randi said slowly, starting to pace from one end of
the board to the next, "Ms. Taggert and I were discussing how
stressed so many of you are after your weekends. And we've
gotten so many calls from your parents requesting that we not
give any homework as so many of you can barely keep up after
your exhausting bar mitzvah partying."

The seventh-graders were wide-eyed and waiting with bated
breath.

"And we also know that some of your *other* teachers are not as
understanding . . . so we have decided to allow you to spend
the entire history and English class times today in the library
catching up with your homework for your other subjects!"
Randi finished triumphantly.

The room broke into applause and our kids started making a
mad dash for the door. I started to panic at the thought of fifty
students tearing into the library.

"Excuse me!" Randi exclaimed, expertly blocking the door. "But Ms. Taggert and I have *one* more thing to say. We are treating you like *adults*. Like *college* students. If you run down the halls and burst into the library like banshees, then you're never going to be invited up there again. If either of us get a single complaint about your behavior today, we will not only never allow you this opportunity again, we will make it a *point* to share with you the names of your peers who acted out and kept you from ever doing this again."

Randi was a genius. The kids immediately started hushing each other.

"Yeah, Benjamin, you better not be all hyper," Charlotte ordered.

"Shut up, ho," Benjamin shot back.

"Be good!" Randi ordered, beaming as the last student left the classroom. Immediately she shut the door, turned, and faced me.

"Starbucks?"

"It's like they don't want their kids to get an education," I said in wonderment, sipping my peppermint mocha.

It was a week before we got let out for winter break, and Randi and I were at the local Starbucks having our midday mochas, which had become a daily ritual. As usual, Randi looked impossibly chic in her gray J. Mendel chinchilla vest and black cashmere sweater dress. Soft knee-length boots in black suede completed her look.

"It's all about entrances. They just care about entrances," Randi replied, stirring her coffee. "Entering the right nursery school. The right private school. The right college. They don't give a hoot what actually goes on post entry. Honestly, what do you think Lara Kensington would rather do, hire a tutor to deal with Benjamin's failing English grade or simply hear that he's doing 'just great' and that his teacher even gives him time to work on other subjects in school?"

"But Randi, they're not *all* like that, are they? I mean, are you saying that every single Langdon parent just doesn't want to be bothered by their child's education?" I found Randi's sweeping statements very difficult to believe. Yes, I was enjoying this new lifestyle she had introduced me to. My afternoons were spent tutoring and shopping, and I had even started to look for a new apartment. But every now and then I felt a twinge of guilt about the fact that I had taught my students absolutely nothing in the last few weeks. Even the great Ms. Lavery had apparently taught some incredible lessons.

"Let's just say that my experience has been that all these parents just like hearing how *brilliant* their kids are. Look at it the other way. If you actually told any one of them the truth, what do you get out of it? They either hate you, or even worse, they *believe* you. If that's the case they want to have five hundred meetings that involve you, their child, their child's therapist, learning specialist, or worst of all, tutor. And honestly, Anna, after that three o'clock buzzer goes off, you can either go tutor and make some serious cash, or you can sit like a chump and have after-school meetings. Remember, you're not paid extra for caring."

It was hard not to wince at Randi's brashness.

"The parents *have* been a lot nicer to me after I backed off on the homework and heavy workload in class," I agreed slowly, still cringing a little at her last statement.

"Trust me, Anna. Just go on and on about how you've never quite come across a kid like their child, and everyone goes home happy. You worry too much. They're not paying you enough to worry."

"I guess," I responded, not entirely convinced that caring and worrying came with price tags. Randi didn't hear me because she was now immersed in her BlackBerry, furiously texting. There seemed to be a never-ending stream of people who needed to get in touch with her all day.

Living in Randi's Langdon was life altering. We sent our students to the library at least three times a week, which allowed me ample time to plan and grade papers for the actual two days I did teach. On those days, I continued to strive to make my lesson plans interesting and action-packed out of sheer guilt, but I no longer felt the stress of performing on a daily basis. Most surprising were the phone calls and e-mails from grateful Langdon mothers who thanked me for being "one of the few understanding teachers" and "so in tune with the needs of our overworked seventh-graders." I had to admit that without this extra time, I would never have made it out of report writing alive.

While I had been told about Langdon report writing during orientation, nothing prepared me for its brutal reality. We were meant to write in-depth little essays about each of our fifty students by the second week of January. These essays were to be submitted to the parents, who we then faced in one-to-one conferences in March. Harold reminded me in a curt e-mail that these essays were to be informative, descriptive, and under no circumstances to mention a grade. Randi and I were both sitting in my empty classroom working on them while our students were blissfully in the library.

"I refuse to write these fuckers on my own time," Randi had stated matter-of-factly. "Find a way to write all your reports in school."

"Maybe I'll just write mine during winter break when I have more time," I mused.

"Slog your ass off while your students fly down the slopes of Aspen or tan on their parents' boats in Anguilla? And get nothing out of it?" Randi countered in disgust. "No, thank you. My winter break is my busiest tutoring season! These reports need to be done well before. You'll see. Yours will be, too."

"I thought they all went away," I said, confused. "Besides, no Manhattan private school encourages homework over winter break. Who are you tutoring?"

"You'll see," Randi replied mysteriously. "You can make up to ten grand if you're good and work full days."

I had no idea what she was talking about, and absolutely no winter break tutoring lined up. Plus, my parents would *kill* me if I wasn't home for the holidays. I was also getting a little tired of Randi's "they're not paying you enough" line, which I was quickly learning was her reasoning for every private-school corner she cut. Lately I had been spending less time with the kids and more and more time with Randi at Starbucks, Sarabeth's, and Fred's. Finding ways to get around teaching and discovering tutoring clients who would pay the most were her favorite *and only* topics of discussion.

I couldn't argue that she had a point. There seemed to be no repercussions at Langdon for being a lax teacher. Contrary to Dr. Blumenfeld's intital interview during which I had truly felt as if she would keep a very close eye on me, no one had ever entered my classroom. In fact, the only time I had been chastised at Langdon was when I *had* been teaching. Just last week I had passed Harold Warner in the halls and he had given me a beaming grin.

"Saw your kids hard at work in the library, Anna!" he had congratulated me.

"That's right!" I had grinned back, inwardly cringing at his transparency. As long as my classes weren't being taught well, I was not a threat to him. I did not upset the Langdon balance. The few teachers who apparently were giving work were constantly ragged upon by the students.

"I *hate* Ms. Steephill," Max moaned on another day I allowed my students to have a "work period." He was referring to the math teacher, Dorothy.

"Yeah, my parents think she's *such* a bitch," Jacob growled, furiously punching numbers in his calendar.

"Jacob, don't call teachers a bitch!" I had ordered, but quickly followed up with, "Why?" I was curious.

"She gives like *hours* of math homework every night, and even my tutor doesn't understand how to do like half of it," Madeline whined. "Plus she's weird and keeps closing her eyes and saying 'um' which totally freaks us all out."

"I know, my mom said that she's spending a *fortune* on my math tutor," Max groaned, erasing the equation he had just written on his graph paper. "But they *love* you, Ms. Taggert. You *get* us."

Since I seemed to be doing everything lately with Randi, it was no surprise that she wanted to start writing reports together. The first report I tried to tackle was Benjamin Kensington.

> Benjamin is a wonderful young man. He is very enthusias-
> tic and loves coming to school. He really liked the Shake-
> speare unit, and found *Romeo and Juliet* to be very interesting.
> It was clear he understood the text and he made some won-
> derful contributions in class.
>
> Benjamin's writing is coming along very nicely. He clearly
> likes to write.

I stared at the blinking cursor on the screen. Randi was across the table writing feverishly.

"How can you write that fast?" I sighed. "I haven't even finished one report."

"I'm on my twentieth," she replied proudly. Her eyes looked oddly bright.

"Let's take a Starbucks break?" I asked, desperate for any procrastination.

"No coffee today, love. We are finishing these babies! I told you, winter break is going to be busy, and with the kids at the library and then at gym for the rest of the afternoon, we *have* to get the bulk of them done. Trust me. It's easy, Anna. First paragraph commendations, second paragraph recommendations." She returned to the screen and began typing again, her fingers flying across the keyboard at a manic speed.

On a wild impulse, I decided to write from the heart and see what I came out with.

> Benjamin Kensington is fabulous at being a pampered
> pain in the ass. He flawlessly disrupts class constantly and
> often makes perfectly obnoxious comments. He seems to
> have made it to the seventh grade, but I'm not even sure if

he can read at a fourth-grade level. This is truly an admirable feat.

I recommend that Benjamin be put back at least two grades. I recommend that he start doing his homework by himself. I also recommend that he be grounded for a good two weeks.

Grinning, I pressed PRINT and slapped my "report" in front of Randi with a flourish. She didn't look up.

"Randi!" I cried. "Check this out."

"Mmm?" Her typing was now blindingly furious.

"Look at my Benjamin report," I said, laughing.

She finally looked up at me with the same expression she had given me the first time I entered her room. I took a step back, alarmed. What had happened to my new friend? Grimacing, she reached into her purse and pulled out a bottle of Tylenol.

"Do you have a headache?" I asked, now utterly confused by her erratic actions. Wordlessly, she snapped open the bottle and shoved it in my face. Inside the bottle were tiny little cream-colored pills.

These were not Tylenol.

"Ritalin. Take one," she ordered.

"Randi!" I exclaimed. "I don't have ADD!"

"Obviously you don't," she said impatiently. "I stole these from a kid I tutor. They work even better if you don't have ADD. Pop one in and your reports will literally write themselves."

"What if . . . I have a reaction?" I asked weakly.

"Anna, don't be a baby. God! Just pop one and please shut up."

I had never done a drug in my life. I was now doing drugs. But her "pop one and your reports will literally write themselves" line was just too tempting. Guiltily I put the tiny pill in my mouth and swallowed. I waited.

"Nothing is happening," I said with certainty. I felt no compulsion to return to report writing.

"Tell me that in an hour," Randi retorted, rolling her eyes. "Now, no talking."

Before I could open my mouth to protest, I felt the oddest sensation. I was in a long, black tunnel and the only thing I could see was the computer in front of me. I wanted to write those reports more than I had wanted anything else in my life. After I finished them I would write a novel and maybe a few poems. Why wasn't everyone addicted to this beautiful life-solving pill?

By the end of the school day half of my reports were written. I had used words like *charming* and *promising* at least six hundred times, and even though most of the reports were utter bullshit, I was proud of myself. The Ritalin had to be wearing off, though, because once again I had reached the point that I could not possibly write another word.

"You got another one?" I asked, embarrassed.

"I have plenty, but I'm not giving you any for the evening. Reports are to be written in school. Now go and tutor—you're on your own time!"

I nodded obediently. I had Katie and Jake to tutor, one right after each other, and I wasn't in the mood to handle reports anyway. I believe that if Randi had asked me to go jump into the Hudson River, I would have seriously contemplated it. As long as she gave me another report-writing pill tomorrow.

22

Conchita looked nervous.

"Missus Herring no here," she explained, staring at her feet.

"That's okay. Is Jake in?" I asked brightly.

"Jake here . . . he in room. With . . . friend," Conchita replied, now blushing.

"Okay, Conchita, I'll go find him," I said, walking down the long corridor that led to Jake's room. She trailed behind me, making little clucking sounds.

"You knock, okay?" she called, finally halting near the kitchen. Clearly Conchita was not going any further.

"Of course!" Whatever. If "Mimsy" wasn't home, I wasn't going to knock! I wasn't Jake's Conchita. I was his tutor, and I had spent a good eight and a half hours reading *The Age of Innocence* so that I could "explain" it to him. I opened his door confidently.

Ooops.

There was Jake, half-naked (of course) with a half-naked girl (this was a bit of a surprise) straddled on top of him. They were making out furiously. I stood there dumbly, rooted to the spot.

"Oh, hey, Anna," he said in a raspy voice. "Just a sec, okay?"

"Um, okay," I responded awkwardly, then quickly shut the door. Poor Conchita . . . she had tried to warn me! I looked down the hall and saw her standing there, wide-eyed.

Instead of embarrassed shuffling in an attempt to get dressed and look decent, I was shocked to hear loud moaning coming from the room. Moaning? It seemed the make-out session had entered an even *heavier* dimension, spurred on by my entry. Angrily, I knocked loudly on the door.

"Jake! I have someone after you! I can't stay longer!" I shouted.

"Oh, Jake, yes!" I heard a squeaky voice call. "Yes, yes, yes!"

I knocked even louder.

Silence. Shuffling. A piece of paper was slipped under the door. Wordlessly I bent down and opened it. It was his assignment sheet for *The Age of Innocence* term paper!

"Jake!" I screamed, now banging on the door. "I am NOT writing this paper. Now, either you open this door this minute or I'm calling your mother. I mean it!"

"Chill . . . chill," Jake muttered, opening the door in his trademark boxer shorts. I looked around the room for signs of the thin little blonde who had been attached to him just moments ago.

"Alison's in the bathroom," he offered.

"*Alison* needs to go home," I retorted.

"Yeah, she will, give her a break. She's just washing up," Jake replied, wandering over to his bed casually. Lying down, he reached over to his drawer and pulled out a pack of cigarettes. I watched with mouth open as he expertly lit one up and blew a perfect circle of smoke out of his mouth.

"Jake!" I exclaimed.

"I'm sorry, Anna. Where are my manners? Would you care for a smoke?"

I couldn't believe what was happening. This was out of some bad movie. I had a half-naked man-child of a student lying on his bed smoking after he had just made out (had sex?!) with his girlfriend (friend with benefits?!) who was still in the bathroom "washing up."

"No, I DO NOT want a smoke," I snapped. "I want you to get dressed. I want Alison to go home. I want you to be seated at your desk or I will *not* explain this book to you," I said flatly. No amount of money in the world was worth this.

Jake put both his hands up in mock surrender and took one last drag of his cigarette before putting it out.

"Hey, Allie," he called out, "I need to use the bathroom, too. You almost done?"

"Coming, baby!" a voice squeaked, and I closed my eyes and tried to calm myself down.

"Hey, Anna, don't get mad. I'll be, like, three seconds, and then I swear I'm going to be such a good boy you'll fall in love with me," Jake promised smoothly.

I kept my eyes shut.

A minute later Jake was in the bathroom and I was alone with Allie.

"Um, are you Ms. Taggert?" she squeaked again. I opened my eyes and found myself face to face with the source of Jake's entertainment. Now dressed in a pair of jeans and a dark, cashmere hoodie, she looked like a pretty and angelic high school student. Her blonde hair was pulled back in a ponytail and she was staring at me with big blue eyes that did not appear to be in the least bit embarrassed.

"Yes. Who are you?" I had no intentions of being kind or friendly with this little slut.

"I'm Charlotte's older sister, Alison Robertson," she replied. "I'm on break from Penn for the winter holidays. Charlotte adores you!"

Ahh. Of course this made sense. Charlotte gave blow jobs in party buses, so clearly her sister Alison had sex in the afternoon with high school boys.

"Are you Jake's girlfriend?" I asked, raising an eyebrow.

"Jake? Oh no," Alison laughed casually. "We're just good friends. I mean, sometimes we kiss a little, but otherwise he's like a *brother* to me."

"How nice," I replied sarcastically.

"I know, he's so sweet," Alison gushed, the sarcasm clearly over her head. "I'll tell Charlotte I saw you! She'll be *so* excited!"

Grabbing her purse, Alison blew me a kiss and exited the room with her ponytail bouncing. Not missing a beat, Jake entered in sweatpants and a U of Penn sweatshirt. Still grinning, he sat Indian style on his bed and faced the desk.

"Can we compromise? If I sit up on my bed, can you just teach me from over there?" he asked sweetly.

Giving up, I pulled out the copy of *The Age of Innocence* that I had "preread." What I really wanted to do was preslap him.

"So, how do you want to do this?" I asked, a bit confused. "Do I just tell you what it's about?"

"Yup."

"Just curious, but there are Web sites, you know . . . like SparkNotes and GradeSaver that do the same thing. Why have your parents pay so much to have someone do what is already available for free on the Web?"

"Those fucking summaries are, like, as long as the book," Jake complained. "I like to *listen*."

"Let me guess. You're an *auditory learner*."

"Exactly! How'd you know?"

There was nothing I could say to someone who could actually complain with a straight face that reading SparkNotes was too much effort. I began to relay the story. Since I had read it so recently, I was able to go into the details and found myself almost enjoying talking about the book. Every now and then I would pose questions and share what I enjoyed most. Jake was shockingly engaged. I found him incredibly interested, and I was thrilled by the way he would jump in with questions and insights.

"It's incredible how a country founded on the principles of, like, meritocracy could, on so many levels, like, mimic the very class-conscious world it, like, totally strove so hard to totally break free from, you know?" Jake mused at one point. "I should, like, write my paper on that. Whaddaya think, Anna?"

"I think you should have read the book if you're that smart," I shot back, shaking my head in disbelief. This kid never ceased to shock me. Beyond the string of "likes" and "totallys," Jake had actually made an intelligent point. "But I have to go. I'll finish the summary on Thursday, and then we can get started on the paper over the weekend, okay?" It was 5:15, and I had to be at Katie's apartment at 5:30.

"Wait, no!" Jake howled. "I'm really, like, *into* it now . . . can't you stay for another hour and just finish it?"

"I *told* you that I had someone else after you, Jake," I reminded him. "And remember that we had a bumpy start to the session."

"Oh, yeah." He grinned, allowing himself to lie back on his bed. "Okay, we'll finish on Thursday. But you should, like, allow more time between your clients in case we need you for longer," Jake advised. "And there's an envelope for you in the foyer. Mom told me to remind you."

"Where is your mother, by the way?" I asked curiously.

"No clue. See ya, Anna." Jake lit up another cigarette as he simultaneously reached for his BlackBerry. I was clearly dismissed. Sure enough, on the way out was a thick envelope with my name scrawled on it. I was dying to open it in the elevator, but Edward was peering over my shoulder as if he, too, were burning with desire to see just how much Mimsy had left me.

Alone outside the apartment building, I quickly tore it open.

Dear Anna,

What a lifesaver you are to our son! Thank you for reading the book. Enclosed is the reading fee, and a little extra thank you. I realize that Laura Brandeis does all the billing at All Ivy Tutoring, but we can keep this between us.

Big kiss,
Mimsy

Enclosed in the note were so many hundred-dollar bills that I was afraid to count them on the street. My hands shaking, I hailed a cab to the Carleton apartment and began counting in the backseat. One, two, three . . . five . . . seven . . . twelve . . .

fifteen . . . twenty! Twenty hundred-dollar bills. I wanted to find Jake's English teacher and kiss her feet for assigning such a big fat book. At the same time, I just couldn't figure out this world I was now so immersed in. On the one hand, the schools and the parent bodies found every possible way to keep the teachers miserable and underpaid. After school, however, they fought tooth and nail to seduce these very same people with massive sums of money and bribes. Did they honestly think we wouldn't catch on?

The afternoon before Christmas break I was standing in the faculty lounge for our "holiday party." Cheap little decorations from Duane Reade were stapled to the bulletin boards, and cups of Minute Maid fruit punch and cookies rested on a stainless steel cart. Damian Oren was walking around with a Santa hat tilted on the side of his head, holding a mug of creamy liquid that smelled suspiciously like heavily jacked eggnog.

"Merry Christmas," he slurred to me. "Or in Langdon tradition, I should also say, Happy Hanukkah . . . and a big fat Happy Kwanzaa, too."

"Are you drunk?" I asked curiously, certain he was not drinking the fruit punch.

"Shhhh." He grinned, putting a finger to his lips. "Where's your best friend?"

"Randi didn't want to come," I responded defensively. Damian had the completely wrong idea about Randi. Without her I would never have survived Langdon for so long!

"Faculty! Gather round! I have a surprise for you!"

We all looked toward the entrance of the lounge. Dr.

Blumenfeld had just entered, wearing a plain red skirt suit with enormous pearls. She was smiling graciously and beckoned for all of us to find seats near her.

"I want to thank you *all* for the hard work you all put in this semester! Now, as you know, Langdon does not allow its parent body to give gifts. It's our *progressive* way of showing that what we do comes from our hearts!" She beamed.

What? No gifts?

"But that doesn't mean we don't have holiday spirit! I have gift certificates for all of you!"

I relaxed. That was a really nice touch. Not that, after the generous "gift" I had received from Mimsy Herring the other day, I was in need of anything, but still, we teachers did deserve some recognition.

"Now I want you all to line up," Dr. Blumenfeld ordered, as if she were talking to a second-grade class. "When you come up and receive your gift, we will cross your name off the list. We don't want anyone getting a gift twice," she joked, and a few teachers laughed uncomfortably at the insult. The line started to form, and Damian made a beeline for me.

"Ah, the bread lines of St. Petersburg . . . ," he breathed into my ear. I shrugged him off, irritated. Poor Blumenfeld was trying to be nice for a change. He whistled annoyingly as we stood in line, and when my turn came, he whispered, "Alms for the poor, alms for the poor."

"Thank you, Anna. I'm so happy you have made such a turnaround and become such a beloved member of our faculty." Dr. Blumenfeld smiled at me and handed me an envelope.

"Thank *you*," I replied, overwhelmed by her public compliment.

Holding the card in my hand, I walked out of the lounge with a light heart.

Until I opened the card.

A twenty-dollar Barnes & Noble gift certificate.

Not even enough for a hardcover. Or a single pearl from Blumenfeld's necklace.

Alms for the poor indeed.

The desk in my classroom, however, revealed a completely different story. It was piled high with shopping bags from Barneys, Bergdorf's, and Hermès. Boxes of all shapes and sizes were covered with elaborate wrapping paper with coordinating ribbons. This was all for . . . me?

"In case the Barnes & Noble certificate doesn't cut it," Randi said behind me. "I'd gather those up pretty quickly before Blumenfeld sees. Those are your real gifts."

"I can't even carry these home, Randi," I replied, still shocked. I reached for an orange Hermès bag.

"ANNA! Empty the gifts into this," Randi ordered, holding up a Hefty bag. "Open them when you get home. Hurry!"

"But why can't we—"

"We're not supposed to get gifts, Anna. And *trust* me, not all teachers get this treatment. If you want to keep them, just do as I say. Once freakin' Dorothy Steeple walks by and sees the display, she'll sic Blumenfeld on you like a rabid dog."

In a panic, I began emptying the endless array of bags into the Hefty bag until it looked like Santa's pouch on Christmas Eve.

"Merry Christmas," she winked. "Let's get out of here. Call me when you open everything and we'll talk about what we got." I noticed another big black Hefty bag at the entrance of my classroom. I smiled in understanding and then we both dragged our loot down the hallway toward the elevator.

"Cleaning out the rooms, hey?" Harold Warner smiled knowingly as we passed him in the hall.

"They get so messy!" Randi replied without skipping a beat.

Two hours later my bedroom was littered with Prada bags and Hermès scarves, Chanel wallets and Gucci clutches. Many of the gifts, I knew, cost more than one month's rent. The little cards that accompanied each other were tiny and simply had innocuous little messages like HAPPY HOLIDAYS, WITH LOVE THE BRIGGMANS or JUST A SMALL THANK YOU FROM THE ROBERTSONS! Of course I called Randi immediately.

"I just got the new Chanel clutch!" she screamed without even bothering to say hello.

"Me, too! From the Roberstons!" I shouted back, delirious.

"Oh." She was temporarily deflated. "Weird they gave us the same thing."

"Randi!" I exclaimed. "We just won't wear it at the same time when we go out!"

"You're right," she replied, brightening. "What else did you get?" We spent the next twenty minutes gushing about every gift we received until a thought occurred to me.

"Does every teacher at Langdon get these gifts?"

"Yeah, right," Randi scoffed. "I'm willing to bet we're the only two. I mean, maybe Sarah Waters gets some good stuff, but really we're a select breed, you and I."

I marveled at the notion that in four months, I had become part of a "select breed."

"Now come meet me at the shoe section at Barneys to celebrate. I'm sure the Worthingtons got you a nice little gift certificate from there?"

"I'm already out the door."

When I arrived at the second floor of Barneys, Randi was already surrounded by a pile of shoe boxes. She waved me over happily.

"After this let's eat," she suggested. "So where should we go for the best Mexican, Rosa Mexicano or Dos Caminos?"

"I'm hardly the expert, either one." I shrugged, watching as she slipped her foot into the new Prada stilletos.

Randi looked up at me curiously.

"Um, Anna? Aren't you like a quarter Mexican or something?"

There it was again! And this time I was NOT letting it go.

"Okay, we have enough secrets between us that I can ask you something, right? Something you won't breathe *a word* about?"

"Anna, of course," Randi laughed. "If you don't like margaritas just tell me!" We both paused for a minute, momentarily distracted as a salesman brought me a pair of Marni pumps to try on.

"No, Randi, it's not that," I replied, admiring the shoes. They fit perfectly. "Since the first minute I entered Langdon, people have been going on and on about my Mexican heritage. Blumenfeld even alluded to it during the interview. Only I'm not Mexican whatsoever, so what the fuck?"

I noddedly absently to the salesman and gave him my credit card. I wanted the shoes *and* an explanation. Randi was grinning from ear to ear.

"No shit!" she exclaimed.

"What does that mean?"

"You're really not Mexican?!"

"No!" I yelled a little too loudly, ignoring the curious looks I was getting from the other shoppers.

"My, my, my," Randi laughed, extending her leg to admire the knee-high suede Marc Jacobs boots she was trying on, "What a shocker."

"Randi," I asked seriously, sitting on the soft couch next to her, "I'm not fucking around. I really need to figure this out. Please tell me what's going on? Whenever I felt the impulse to tell the truth, everyone always seemed so thrilled that I was Mexican that I just shut up. The truth is, I have no idea how they got the idea or why they're so happy about it."

"You really don't know?" Randi asked, unzipping the boots and finally turning to face me. "After all this time? You still don't get it?"

"Randi!" I exclaimed. "Just tell me!"

"Langdon is like a corporation," she said finally. "They're selling a product. And that product is entry into an Ivy League college. Or an equally prestigious university. Parents will pay thirty grand a year for their child from kindergarten to twelfth grade if they have some level of assurance that their child is going to go to an Ivy League school."

"Okay," I nodded. "So they need Mexicans to help them do that?" I failed to see how Randi's explanation was going to lead to my supposed ethnicity.

"And Ivy League schools are all into this affirmative action thing," Randi went on. "So Harvard is not likely to take twenty white Jewish kids from Langdon Hall. But . . ."

"They'll take a bunch more from one school if they have various ethnicities?" I asked, catching on.

"Exactly. So by bragging about a diverse faculty, Blumenfeld hopes to attract a more diverse parent body. All in the pursuit of being able to say that Langdon sent more students to Ivies than the other private schools. Which, in turn, keeps applications to Langdon high enough so that the school can have the luxury of accepting only the families they want."

I signed for my new Marni pumps in wonderment.

"Just look at every private school in Manhattan," Randi went on callously. "Why is it that in the last two years almost all of them put a person of color in a leadership position? Or how come they're so hell-bent on hiring teachers from diversity conferences?"

"You really think that's why?" Was it really that . . . calculating?

"But what's even better," Randi rattled on, focusing in on a pair of purple Gucci loafers across the room, "is that they're all still run by very old and very racist white people. But that's just my opinion."

"But how did Blumenfeld make the leap and assume I'm Mexican?"

"I don't know . . . ," Randi shrugged. "Your complexion is a little on the dark side, and your hair *was* dark brown. Maybe she confused your résumé with the ones from the diversity conference. Mabye it was just wishful thinking on her part."

There was only one appropriate response.

"My people prefer Rosa Mexicano."

Laura Brandeis called at 9:30 P.M. that night. I had just gotten home from dinner at Rosa Mexicano with Randi, and was preparing to pack. My mother was picking me up the next morning and giving me a ride back home. For once, I was going to shower her with expensive gifts!

"Anna Taggert," I replied automatically, not even bothering to check the caller ID.

"Anna, this is Laura Brandeis calling."

I focused immediately. Yikes! Had Mimsy complained about me?

"Is everything okay?" I asked nervously.

"Everything is wonderful. I'm calling with good news," Laura answered. I was convinced she could win the lottery and still remain deadpan.

"What's up?" I relaxed, eyeing the Chanel clutch and wondering if I could bear parting with it. Mom would love it.

"What are your plans for winter break?"

"Um, I was actually going home . . . tomorrow morning?" What could Laura Brandeis possibly want from me during winter break?

"Please let me know if that is set in stone. I have twelve clients for you. Just for the break. They are college students with papers."

"How can college students have papers? The semester is over. Their classes are over," I argued. Twelve clients?

"That may very well be. But not all students were successful in completing their courses. For some of them, well, let's just say that their return to campus depends on completing their papers over the winter break. For college students you can charge $450 an hour, and you can keep $360. If you decide to accept, you will be tutoring up to seven hours a day."

"I'm not really trained to tutor college students . . ."

"Ms. Taggert, you did go to Columbia University?"

"Of course I did!" I responded hotly.

"And you did major in English?"

"Yes, of course. . . ."

"Then all that I need to know is if you are willing to accept these clients. I have three other teachers who I know will gladly accept. I'm calling you first as you have had such success with Jake Herring, who I know is a very difficult client."

"I accept," I said automatically, finally realizing what Randi was talking about. I spent the next forty-five minutes taking down names, addresses, assignments, and other vital information from Laura. A part of me couldn't help but think that in five years I would be taking down Benjamin Kensington's name. Having coasted on a tidal wave of his parents' influence, he would graduate Langdon with top honors and go to whichever Ivy his parents had the most connections at. Once admitted, however, he would realize that entrance to a prestigious university didn't automatically result in growing a brain over the summer.

23

What do you mean you aren't coming home for winter break? Your brother is home! Everyone is with their families!" Mom was unrelenting.

"Mom! I'll come for Christmas Day!" I shouted back into the phone.

"Oh, thank you ever so much," she said sarcastically. "Wow. Really? The whole day? Nobody wants to be tutored on Christmas? Are you sure? You better check carefully with your guru, Laura Brandeis."

"Well, they might . . . ," I answered fairly, wondering how much I could charge.

"I'm putting your father on the phone." I could hear her covering the mouthpiece and mumbling something to my dad. Ten seconds later, he was on the phone.

"How much?"

"What?"

"Anna, I'm so disgusted that I'm even saying this, but how much? I'll write you a check. It will break your mother's heart if she knew I was asking this, but I can't stand to see her disappointed this way. Christmas is her favorite time of year and you are killing her."

"Close to ten thousand dollars," I whispered hardly believing the sum of money myself.

"Excuse me?"

"Close to ten grand," I repeated more firmly.

I heard him whistle. "And you're sure this is legal?"

"Dad, I'm working through a company! They're writing me formal checks. Yes, it's totally legal. I'm not sure how *moral* it is," I admitted, "but honestly, working this break will let me finally get a new apartment. I really want that. And I want to pay you and Mom back for all this furniture."

He was silent.

"Okay, Anna. You're an adult now and these have to be your decisions. I'll explain it to your mother. I still don't like it, though. Something about this just doesn't smell right."

"I can't win with you, Dad! When I'm making no money you feel sorry for me, and when I actually find a way to make a decent living as a teacher you question me!"

"I'm just not sure what you're doing is called teaching, Anna."

The phone line went dead.

My winter break clients had three things in common:

1. They were going to fail a class if they didn't turn in a paper by January 1.
2. They were in a deep depression about having to skip their family vacation to write that paper.
3. They were physically incapable of writing said paper.

"I feel like it's not worth it," I grumbled to Randi on the phone. "I've never had such a splitting headache and I can't keep any of these papers straight. They're all starting to blur into one gigantic term paper for the University of Spoiled Brats."

"It *is* worth it," Randi urged confidently. "Believe me, when you move into my building, you won't be crying then. Just push through it. Think of it like . . . a really hard spin class."

Spin class my ass.

Twelve stacks of books were piled neatly in my living room. In essence, I was writing twelve term papers for "students" who were only a few years younger than me. Each student, and their parents for that matter, seemed to have been produced by the same dysfunctional assembly line: Create child, send to 92nd Street Y nursery school, bribe head of admissions at select private school, then coat all assignments and work with a glossy tutor. Drive smoothly off conveyor belt and straight to Harvard!

My first client, Emily Schwartz, had set the tone for the others that followed. In fact, it was difficult to differentiate between them.

The Schwartz family lived on Park Avenue in the high 80s. No surprise there.

"Are you Anna? From Ivy Tutoring?" A frazzled but attractive woman stood in front of me in minuscule tennis whites. It was 20 degrees outside.

"Um, yes, I'm here to see Emily?"

"Oh, Emily." The woman rolled her eyes. "What are we to do with Emily? Please come in and meet my husband. We only have a few moments before we have to leave—we're going to the Dominican Republic—but Larry and I do want to touch base with you. After that, the two of you are on your own!"

I nodded mutely and allowed the already tanned Mrs. Schwartz to lead me into an oak-paneled room that appeared to be her husband's study. Larry Schwartz was sitting at his desk reading the *Wall Street Journal.* Cigar smoke spiraled up from behind the paper.

"Oh, Larry, really! So early in the morning!" his wife sniffed with disgust. The newspaper crinkled and lowered to reveal an attractive man in his mid-fiffies. He, too, was wearing bright tennis whites. I imagined that the Schwartzes would go straight from their limo to their private jet to the tennis courts in the Dominican Republic.

"The tutor," he sighed. "The million-dollar tutor. Can I work for you?" he chuckled madly.

"I'm Anna," I replied, extending my hand.

"Larry Schwartz," he grinned gamely. "And you already met my wife, Bunny. Bun, where's Pookie?"

"Emily's in her room, dear. She's depressed."

"I would be, too, if I had to miss winter break!" Larry laughed uproariously, as if this whole scenario were exceedingly hilarious. "Those bastards don't cut these kids a break. Now listen here, Anna, my daughter's a smart cookie. A real winner of a girl."

"I can't wait to meet her!" I said brightly. Winner. Yeah, right.

"She just had the bad luck of getting one stinker of a professor at Yale this past semester. Won't let her out of this one damn paper," he continued, shaking his head in disgust.

Bunny Schwartz nodded in agreement, her blue eyes tearing. Were these people mad? This was *Yale* they were talking about. Forget Yale, I couldn't think of *any* college or university that would consider a professor a stinker for making a student write a paper.

"What's wrong with Emily? Why couldn't she do it?" I asked, then immediately regretted the question.

"Anna, I'm going to ask you to please refrain from speaking about that which you do not know," Larry said, suddenly icy. He sat up in his chair and peered at me. "There is nothing *wrong* with my daughter. On the contrary, you will find her to be quite bright—*brilliant*—actually. She's just *depressed*. She needs motivation and encouragement. She needs a . . . work buddy. That's where you come in."

"You'll be like a big sister," Bunny agreed. "My Emily knows what to do, she just doesn't want to stay home and write it all alone. Larry and I are much too responsible as parents to take her along for the vacation. If she doesn't finish the paper, she must face some level of repercussion."

"It's called tough love!" Larry boomed, getting out of his chair and swinging a tennis racket over his shoulder.

"Emily's in her room, Anna. I know you'll get along famously."

And with that the tennis players bounded out of the apartment.

"They're such fucking assholes."

I whirled around. In front of me was a girl who looked exactly my age. She was still in her pajama bottoms and was wearing a tight Yale T-shirt. Emily.

"Hey . . . Emily. I'm Anna."

Emily looked me up and down. No doubt about it, she was appraising me.

"Are you, like, my age?" Emily asked accusingly.

"Twenty-two," I answered. "How old are you?"

"Twenty-one." She suddenly grinned. "It's my last year. Just my luck I get this fucking English professor who couldn't cut me some slack. I have this goddamn Yeats paper to write. It's supposed to be twenty pages." She headed down the hall toward what I guessed was her room.

"I love Yeats," I responded honestly. "I wrote a term paper on him at Columbia!"

Emily whirled around and looked me square in the face. "Do you have it? I swear I won't tell my parents. They'll still pay you for the week."

"Emily, I can't!" I cried, appalled. We were only a year apart. If she got caught, then I got caught, and that was the last thing I wanted to deal with.

"Just kidding!" She grinned, although I caught a glimmer of annoyance in her eyes. I followed her into her bedroom, which looked like it hadn't changed since she had been in the seventh grade, with its massive pink canopy bed and array of stuffed animals.

"So . . ." Emily looked at me with interest. "You one of those high moral tutors who's gonna make me write this paper, or are we gonna get it over and done with and take advantage of this empty apartment for the week?"

"I mean, I don't think I could *write* this for you," I replied awkwardly. "How about you tell me how you got into this mess, anyway?"

Emily shook her head in frustration and flopped onto her bed. Leaning over to her bedside drawer, she took out a pack of cigarettes.

"Ciggie?"

The last thing I was in the mood for was a cigarette, but I figured that since Juicy Couture was compelling to a seventh-grader, sharing a cigarette might help me bond with this world-weary college student. I nodded and Emily quickly popped out a neon pink lighter, thrilled.

"Thank God, you're not totally Mother Teresa," she drawled, inhaling deeply. "Okay, so here's what happened. I try and stick to the lecture classes that require one test at the end of the semester. I'm an *amazing* listener, I really am. Like, I have a *photographic memory*. But these papers fucking kill me. Usually I have this kid who helps me with them on campus, but I totally forgot about this one until it was too late. And wouldn't you know it that damn kid got mono and went home in November and I got totally stuck."

"You have a kid who writes them for you?" I echoed.

"Just this guy who's, like, *obsessed* with me." Emily rolled her eyes. "But he *likes* to do it, so it's not like I'm forcing him or anything. Anyway, so I thought my professor would just let it go. I went to like fifty *zillion* office hours begging him to let me do something oral instead. I'm *amazing* at oral assessment." She looked me in the eye and grinned suggestively.

No. No. No . . . she didn't mean . . . she couldn't?

I forced myself to put the image out of my mind.

"But he wouldn't go for that?" I asked, dryly. I thought of the hours I had spent on my papers at Columbia. The idea of having someone else write them had never crossed my mind. But I was quickly learning that Emily was of the same breed as most of my students at Langdon: They found tutors to do their work in high school, even more tutors to get their work done in college, or in Emily's case people who were "obsessed with them," and parents who paid every bill, no questions asked.

"No! Would you believe it?" Emily wailed. "So listen, I'm not, like, a total *cheater* or anything. It's basically on the poems he wrote that involved Greek mythology—like "No Second Troy," "Leda and the Swan," and . . . some other ones I can't think of. And weave in some outside stuff about his life and how it relates and all. Maybe you can just . . . write the introductory paragraph, conclusion, and all the topic sentences for the rest of the paragraphs? If I have topic sentences, I'm *amazing* at writing the rest of it."

For someone who had clearly never written a paper in her life, Emily's self-esteem was rock solid. Write all the topic sentences? That would mean researching the whole paper and basically outlining and, well, writing most of it.

"My mom ordered a bunch of books from Amazon," Emily said quickly, nodding to an unopened box on her desk. "You can have them all if you want. And yeah, any quotes you can pull out from them that we can sprinkle through would be great. Finding quotes is the only other thing that I can't really do."

"So what are you going to do while I do all of this? Your parents booked me for three-hour sessions a day," I asked, completely bewildered. The pile of books glared at me menacingly.

"Well, today we can just have a quiet work session. You can start thumbing through the books and getting yourself familiar with the subject. Maybe get the introductory paragraph and a couple topic sentences done?"

"What are *you* going to do?" I asked, already knowing the answer.

"Well, today there really isn't anything I *can* do," Emily responded, looking at me as if I had asked the dumbest question in the world. "I'll just be in the other room. You can use my desk, and if there's *anything* you need, just ask Tildy—she's in the kitchen. You'll love her."

I sat there, frozen. Had I been ordered to sit here and re-search Yeats alone? I heard the TV go on in a distant part of the apartment and it was pretty safe to assume that it wasn't Tildy who was watching the *E! True Hollywood Story of Nick and Jessica*. In under three hours I had to report to my next client, Jonas Lippman. Furious at myself for being in this predicament, I texted Randi:

> Am sitting here alone researching a paper. Is this what u deal with?

She responded immediately.

> Writing paper on War of 1812. Think of new apartment.

Miserably, I opened the first book and started scrolling the index. Five minutes later, I snapped the book shut. This was ridiculous. I marched out of the room and followed the sounds of *E!* Sure enough, Emily was sprawled on a leather couch, her wide blue eyes riveted to the biggest plasma screen I had seen in my life.

"Emily."

"Hey, everything okay?" she asked calmly, her eyes not leaving the screen.

"Emily, why don't you sit with me? If you're not good at finding quotes, maybe I can help show you the process. You know, *teach* you how to do it?" I struggled to keep the sarcasm out of my mouth.

She turned and looked at me.

"Oh, Anna, I can't do that," she said simply.

"Excuse me?"

"If I was capable of doing that, my parents wouldn't be paying for your help. If this is not something you want to do, please tell me. I can call Mom and Dad right away. I'm sure their plane hasn't left yet." Emily reached for her cell phone on the table.

New apartment. New apartment. New apartment.

"No, that's okay, I just wanted to offer," I said quickly.

"Oh! Thanks, Anna. No, really, I'm fine. We'll work together tomorrow, I promise," she responded sweetly, turning back to the TV.

Christmas Day I was back at the dining table, facing a family that had grown increasingly hostile since Thanksgiving. I was slumped in my chair, nursing a headache that had started with Emily and had continued through all twelve clients. Tomorrow I would be back in the city. Too bad for me, not one of my students had any intentions of completing their own papers. Emily had compromised the most by dictating paragraphs to me while lying on her bed. A brilliant bullshit artist, she found a way to repeat the topic sentence I wrote for every paragraph in fifteen different ways, and then would ask me to "sprinkle in a couple good quotes," as if I were merely providing the seasoning.

"You look terrible," Mom said flatly.

"Exhausted," Dad agreed. "Are you sure you're not just in the city going out and drinking every night?"

"You don't look that bad," Jonathan said sweetly. I looked

over at him gratefully, but was immediately betrayed. "Kinda heroin chic."

"Jonathan!" Dad yelled, not amused.

"Anna," Mom began, placing a heaping spoon of vanilla custard in my dessert bowl, "your gifts this morning were amazing. I loved the Chanel clutch. Your father has never had a Cartier wallet. And Jonathan's Barneys gift certificate is beyond generous. We are *overwhelmed* by these gifts."

"But Anna," Dad jumped in, "these gifts mean nothing to us if you're going to come home looking like this. I take everything Mom and I said in the beginning back. If you want to teach, go for it. Please. If it brings you true joy, then we're not going to stop you. I was just concerned that you wouldn't be able to afford a lifestyle that Manhattan dangles in every twentysomething's face."

"And clearly it did get to you," Jonathan pointed out, now looking serious. "I mean, if you truly wanted to teach for the love of it, why would you care about all this other . . . stuff? I mean, you never really gave a shit before."

"Don't say *shit*, Jonathan," Mom ordered. "But your brother is right. If anything, maybe your dad and I were being a bit materialistic when we thought you shouldn't teach. We just wanted you to have everything you wanted in this life. But this . . . tutoring. Winter breaks spent alone. Running after school to different apartments to help kids do work they should be doing alone. I've never heard of anything like it."

"Okay," I relented, "I'm a little tired, too. But there's an apartment open in my friend Randi's building. A *doorman* building. What I've made so far, with this winter break's money included, will allow me to move in January. And most of these gifts, I have to admit, were gifts I got for free from families."

"These were gifts?" Dad's eyes widened. "Anna, these look like bribes to me. Is it okay for you to be accepting two-hundred-dollar handbags from families who have kids you're still going to be teaching for the next semester?"

"Honey, that Chanel clutch is over twelve hundred dollars," Mom corrected him. I winced as I saw my father gasp. "I agree one hundred percent with your father. These are bribes. We all like expensive things we see in magazines, Anna, but neither your father nor I brought you up to think this was okay. I never thought I'd say this, but it's almost like teaching has . . . *corrupted* you. You were always the hardworking good kid. The one your father and I were always so proud of."

"Hey!" Jonathan cried. "Thanks, you guys."

"This is not about you, son," Dad silenced Jonathan, who put both his hands up in his signature mock surrender. "Anna, you're an adult. We are way past the point of telling you what you can and cannot do. But once again, I find myself in the position of telling you that everything you are describing *does not sound okay*. It's like you didn't hear a single word at Thanksgiving, and you've gotten even worse. More obsessed."

"Dad, it's just this break. I completely agree, the college thing is totally out of control and nothing I want to do ever again. I just need to finish what I started and chalk it up to experience," I vowed.

"And then what?" he argued. "Just this spring break? Just this summer? This 'thing' you've gotten yourself involved in seems like an insatiable monster that keeps popping his head up for more, more, more."

He was right, of course. I was obsessed. After this bout of college tutoring, though, I would go back to just working with Jake and Katie to maintain my new apartment. Once I got a decent place to live, I would be content. There wasn't really anything else I wanted.

Or so I thought.

24

I returned to Langdon exhausted, my twelve days of Christmas spent on twelve college term papers. No pipers piping or swans a-swimming for me. I had been consumed by Bolsheviks a-revolting and Wordsworths a-rhyming. Still, I had parlayed those term papers into a new lease, and I was due to move into Randi's building in January. I tried to hold on to that thought on the first day back from the holiday break, but the sight of my tanned and glowing seventh-graders proved too depressing.

"Ms. Taggert, you're like a ghost!" Madeline cried.

"Yeah, were you sick?" Charlotte asked, sporting tightly woven cornrows with little beads hanging at the end.

"I like your braids, Charlotte," I commented, desperate to change the subject. I was well aware I looked like death.

"Thanks. I got them in Jamaica," she said proudly, tossing her head.

"I think you look ghetto," Benjamin smirked.

"Benjamin, you are a racist idiot," Charlotte retorted.

I was too tired to say anything to either of them.

"Why don't you all have a seat," I ordered weakly. "We're going to start a new book. I think you'll like it—it's called *Lord of the Flies*."

My students settled down as I passed out the books. Cries to borrow gel pens and markers filled the room. I took a seat at the table. l was on intimate terms with *Lord of the Flies* thanks to Katie's paper, and decided to teach it as it was still fresh in my mind. Still feeling a little guilty from my parents' justified disapproval, I was determined to put in a few good lessons. Besides, the irony of teaching Langdon kids a book about children who resorted to hunting for human flesh was not lost on me. I drew up my last bit of strength and began circling the room.

"Hello! And welcome to the island!" I said in my best Moviefone operator voice. "Imagine you have just *crashed* and all adults and supervisors have died! It's just you and—"

"I need to be excused!" Madeline screamed dramatically.

"Madeline, *why* do you need to be excused?" I was beyond irritated. Why couldn't I ever finish a single announcement without getting interrupted?

"I'm in *therapy* for my fear of flying," she announced dramatically.

"Then how'd you get to Hawaii, swim?" Benjamin shot out automatically, and for once he took the words right out of my mind.

"I was given *pills*, idiot," Madeline retorted. "Anyway, Ms. Taggert, I *cannot* read a book about planes crashing. I have to leave the room *immediately*."

"Okay, Madeline, why don't you step outside for fifteen minutes? It's only on the first page. The rest of the book is all about what happens *on land*." Madeline got out of her seat and dramatically dove for all her materials as if the room were on fire.

"It's too bad, though, because my introduction activity involved quite an interesting game," I called out, lying through my teeth. Sure enough, little Madeline halted at the door and turned around.

"What kind of game?" she asked suspiciously.

"I can't tell you because I'm afraid it will *upset* you," I taunted. After an entire winter break of being manipulated, I was not about to start the new year being outmaneuvered by a seventh-grader.

"Maybe I could do some of my breathing lessons and participate," Madeline relented, returning to her seat, engaging in a case of heavy inhales and exhales.

Ignoring her, I passed out a blank sheet of paper to buy some time, certain that a game would come to me by the time I finished. That's when I saw a robot (a robot?) whiz past the classroom.

Just a minute.

"Can you all please hold on a sec?" I requested weakly before rushing out of the classroom. There, in front of me, was the strangest sight I had ever laid eyes on. Dorothy Steeple was calmly walking down the hall next to a blue, new age ET. It had a large, bulky body with an oversized head. Two plastic hands in a neon orange color moved back and forth rhythmically, and it made a whizzing sound as it rolled obediently next to Dorothy. At any minute I felt like it would put one of its orange hands around her. I had pretty much avoided Dorothy Steeple since our cafeteria incident. But now I was glued to this strange pair—she shabby and threadbare, like something from the past, he shiny and new, like something from the future. Reluctantly, I returned to my classroom where my students greeted me with mysterious smiles.

"Ha, ha, so you saw it!"

"Tweebles! Tweebles! Tweebles!"

"You know about this . . . robot?" I asked stupidly.

"Yeah, that's Tweebles!" Jacob yelled, absolutely delighted.

"Amy, what's going on?" I turned to my little friend, hoping for a more rational explanation.

"Um, that really *is* Tweebles," she said awkwardly.

"Ha ha ha!" Benjamin laughed obnoxiously, then purposefully pretended to fall off his chair laughing.

"Go on," I urged.

"Well, Sue Wong went to Korea to visit her grandparents," Amy continued, "and her parents don't want her to miss any classes. She's not coming back for another month. So Tweebles is an interactive robot that will allow her to hear and participate in all her classes."

"Yeah, you should see when Tweebles raises its hands!" Max yelled.

"Ohmigod, it's *so* scary," Charlotte gushed. "My mother says that it's really inappropriate of the school to let this happen. She feels like it's interfering with my education."

"It gives me panic attacks," Jessica affirmed. "Really serious ones."

"Don't worry, Ms. Taggert. You'll know all about Tweebles really soon. It's coming to your next class!" Benjamin called from under the table. He was now lying flat on the floor, with tears streaming down his face. "You're so lucky. I wish Sue Wong was in all my classes. That Tweebles is mad whack."

Dorothy Steeple was the last person I wanted to befriend at Langdon. But prompted by the impending visit of Tweebles in my afternoon class—not to mention sparking the curiosity of the entire high school—I found myself standing at her door. Dorothy was sitting at her desk, bent over a pile of papers. Soft strains of opera music were coming from her laptop, and her red pen was making large and furious marks all over some unfortunate child's paper. I made a coughing sound. She didn't look up. Entering gingerly, I walked over to her desk.

"Um, Dorothy?"

She continued grading as if she hadn't heard me.

"Dorothy?"

Nothing.

"Dorothy!"

"Um," she sighed heavily, then closed her eyes dramatically. "I can *hear* you. I'm not deaf."

"Oh." God! She was still doing that thing with her eyes and the *um*s. "I just didn't realize you knew I was here."

"People need to *realize*," she pronounced slowly, "that the world does not revolve around them. You cannot get someone's undivided attention just because you ask for it."

She was talking to me like I was a seventh-grader, and it was working. Miffed, I sat down at one of the empty desks and squeezed my feet under it. I mumbled a "Sorry" and waited. Dorothy went back to her grading. I found my gaze lingering on her pastel T-shirt and floor-length denim skirt. Under the skirt she was sporting white tube socks that were squeezed into tight sandals. Ugh.

"Yes," she said suddenly, looking up. "What brings you to my room? For the first time?"

"I heard . . . that there is a robot you will be bringing to my next class?" I asked, the corners of my mouth twitching.

"Tweebles is *not* a laughing matter," she said sternly. "Sue Wong's parents expressly asked me to make sure that he works perfectly for the first week or two and that all her teachers get accustomed to it."

"It is a little bit funny," I pushed. "A robot in the classroom? That looks like a little blue person?"

"Um," Dorothy closed her eyes again.

I still wasn't quite sure what to do when she said "um" and closed her eyes. It was a Langdon mystery for the ages.

"Mr. and Mrs. Wong are deeply concerned about education. I applaud them for making sure that Sue remains up to date with all her schoolwork."

"Oh, c'mon, Dorothy," I attempted once again, "these are the people who hired little people for their daughter's faux mitzvah. I would hardly call them responsible." (I wondered if the Oompa Loompas had been the inspiration for Tweebles.)

"I don't go to their parties," Dorothy said superciliously. "I believe there is a *line* between students and teachers, and I, for one, don't go around crossing it like some *other* people at this institution. What happened at Sue's party is of no interest to me. Her ability to keep up with my math class, however, *is*."

It wasn't just Dorothy's curious manner of speaking that made her annoying. It was her attitude. She had a holier-than-thou aura about her. Dorothy seemed to take pride in her shabby appearance, as if she had better things to do than keep up with the latest fashions and, I don't know . . . moisturize? Five minutes with her and she had managed to make me feel more guilty than both my parents combined.

"Okay, okay. So basically this Tweebles comes to my class. Do I, like, call on it? How does it work? And why the name *Tweebles?*" I didn't want to spend another minute with this woman.

"Um . . ." She closed her eyes again. I could have slapped her.

"Tweebles is actually the name of the *technology* company that manufactures this unit. Tweebles will come to your class whenever Sue Wong is scheduled to be there. *I* will roll it in, turn it on, and make the appropriate connections. Then you will see Sue's face in the screen. She will be watching from her own computer screen in Korea. Both of you will be able to hear and see one another."

"What about the time difference?"

"Sue stays up at night for her scheduled classes," Dorothy stated. "Her grandparents are very serious about her education."

The thought of Sue Wong being woken at three in the morning to attend her Langdon classes struck me as utter madness. And the image of her little face peering at me from Tweebles's "screen-face" creeped the shit out of me.

"Awesome," I muttered, and walked out of the room, determined never to enter or be in Dorothy's presence again. Ever. I also wondered whether I should ask my father to invest in this Tweebles company.

25

Bridgette promised to meet me in the lobby of my new building on Saturday, I think more out of curiosity than anything else. Thankfully I had come up with enough excuses to avoid her ever having to see my first apartment. Bridge had been quiet on the phone when I had mentioned my new address. I would be living two floors below Randi's apartment and right around the corner from the Carlyle Hotel. I knew it killed her.

"You should move, too," I said sweetly, unapologetically relishing how the tables had turned. "We can have coffee at Saint Ambroeus every morning. We could go shopping at Intermix."

"Yeah, well, looks like I'm not as rich as you! I'm sorry, did I somehow miss the memo on how teachers are all of a sudden making more than investment bankers?" Bridgette's tone was sarcastic, but I could tell she was jealous.

"I'm tutoring quite a bit," I responded as casually as possible. Secretly I was thrilled that Bridgette was jealous. This wasn't a one-night affair like the faux mitzvah—this was a lifestyle I could afford while Bridgette now watched from the sidelines.

"Are they paying you in *diamonds?*" Honestly, she was relentless.

"It's pretty good," I answered, determined to be evasive. This was my "thing," and at last I was able to feel . . . *even*. "And you can meet one of my best friends at Langdon," I had finished, thrilled at the prospect of introducing Bridgette to Randi. I had hung up the phone daydreaming about going back to that nameless restaurant, just the three of us, and finally being able to foot the bill.

"Welcome, Ms. Taggert."

It took every last bit of resolve to keep from hugging the doorman. *My* doorman. I beamed at him and proudly led Bridgette to the elevator. My apartment was not large when compared to Bridgette's, but it seemed palatial to me. It had two large windows in the living room that reached all the way to the ceiling. The smell of fresh white paint greeted us, and the dark wooden floors gleamed. One of the windows overlooked the hotel across the street and since I was on the third floor, tree branches were charmingly visible. I felt like I was in Paris.

"Wow," Bridgette managed, "this is really nice, Anna. I'm impressed. Have you given any thought to how you are decorating it?"

Leave it to Bridgette to try and burst my bubble. Okay, maybe my Crate & Barrel couch and Spence-Chapin Thrift Shop furniture weren't quite *Elle Décor*, but I was proud of my new apartment! Bridgette was probably just jealous that it was in a better location than hers.

"Maybe down the road," I shrugged, then added meanly, "At the end of the day, I'd rather have Madison Avenue than Maurice Villency."

I had hoped to crush Bridgette with that last comment, but I had underestimated her.

"I don't know . . . ," she trailed doubtfully. "Looks like it needs a zebra rug at the very least. Otherwise it seems so . . . *plain*."

I hated Bridgette, I really did. Come Monday morning, I would see if Francine could hook me up with another tutoring client so I could buy new furniture. I knew I shouldn't let Bridgette get to me, but she did. Somehow that was her greatest skill. And my continual downfall.

Francine Gilmore looked like a telemarketer. Wedged behind her desk, talking into a headset while scribbling furiously into her datebook, she might have been taking orders for QVC—something from the Judith Ripka collection, sterling silver, perhaps, eligible for six easy payments. Only she wasn't. Francine was brokering a deal for a tutor, and I listened with complete fascination.

"Let's see . . . you want a physics tutor . . . male . . . I have someone for $250 an hour, but he isn't attractive . . . Yes, I understand Sarah prefers attractive tutors. That's Sam Walters, but he's more expensive."

Forget QVC. Francine sounded like she was taking orders for an escort service! What kind of parents put a premium on attractive tutors, anyway? After jotting down a few more notes, she finally got off the phone and smiled at me brightly.

"Anna! What a pleasure! How's Langdon treating you? I hear good things!"

"It's been amazing," I gushed, giving her my best fake smile. "I *love* it!"

"Good, good. I'm so glad when we find loyal faculty," she replied. "And the Carletons? I haven't heard from them so I assume no news is good news?"

"That's actually what I wanted to talk to you about," I began awkwardly. All of a sudden Francine was all business. Her face darkened and she leaned forward in her chair.

"Is everything all right? I usually don't make poor matches."

"No, no! Actually I *adore* little Katie, and the Carletons are lovely," I answered quickly. The truth was that since the *Lord of the Flies* incident manipulative little Katie was doing virtually zero work and finding ways to get me to finish all her assignments. I could see her growing up to be exactly like Emily.

"What a relief! I had a feeling they would really like you," Francine smiled, relaxing.

"The thing is," I felt myself flushing, "I was wondering if you could . . . could maybe recommend me to a few more clients? I really enjoy tutoring and have some free time in the afternoons."

"Ah." She smiled again, then looked at me curiously. "Are you sure you can take on a few more clients? In addition to your teaching position?"

"Oh, absolutely! I'm really getting the hang of teaching, and tutoring just allows me to continue my passion for teaching," I affirmed. We both knew I was bullshitting. And from the gleam of the diamond studs that sparkled from each of her ears, it appeared that Francine Gilmore had a few "clients" of her own.

"Well, let's see," she said slowly, thumbing through the enormous datebook she had in front of her. Now I really felt as if I were with a Hollywood madam.

"It's a bit difficult midyear as most families set up their tutors in the fall," she said slowly.

My heart stopped beating.

"But . . ."

"Yes?" I asked urgently. I was willing to take on a hundred Jakes and Katies.

"Things change drastically after March conferences."

"Why is that?" What did parent conferences have to do with tutoring?

"That's when parents start calling again," she stated matter-of-factly. "When they get updates on their children, many of them give me a call if they hear anything of concern. And," she gave me a little wink, "they *always* call."

"I'd really really appreciate that," I gushed.

"It's my pleasure, dear," she said kindly. "I'll be e-mailing you very soon. And just remember, be *sure* to e-mail *me* after your conferences so I know which of your students may require a tutor. After all, that's my job!"

"Hey, neighbor. Guess who I am," Randi asked devilishly as I opened my apartment door. She made little whizzing sounds and entered with rigid, awkward movements. When she got to the center of the apartment, she raised her right arm in an abrupt, swinging fashion.

"Tweebles!" I screamed, and we both doubled over with laughter.

"The fucking thing gives me nightmares!" she cried, tears streaming down her face. "Every time that awful Dorothy rolls it in I want to punch her *and* the robot."

"What about when you see Sue's face in the screen, how do you keep a straight face?"

"Forget her face, what about when that little freaking neon arm goes up and you have to call on it!"

We were both hysterical now. Through my tears, I looked over at the woman I had been so ominously warned against in September. Who would have thought she would become my best friend and saving grace at Langdon? Because of Randi I was living in a beautiful apartment, wore designer clothes, and had somehow attained the status of beloved English teacher.

"Should we eat out or order in?" I asked finally, getting up from the couch and walking toward my stack of menus I kept in the kitchen. "I could go for some pasta from Patsy's."

"Yeah, let's order. I'm *exhausted* from my tutoring today. I had four in a row." Randi sighed, leaning back on the couch and reaching for my remote. "Let's watch something mind numbing."

"*America's Next Top Model*," we screamed in unison.

As I thumbed through for the Patsy's menu, I couldn't help but feel a little envious again. Four tutoring jobs. Randi probably made a grand that afternoon. My two clients seemed like peanuts.

"I need some more tutoring clients," I admitted. "I only have two."

"Just ask Francine," Randi answered automatically, her face riveted to the TV screen.

"I *did*, and she said she has nobody right now. But she will after parent conferences. What's her deal, anyway? What do you want from Patsy's? I'm calling now."

"Thin crust margarita. Francine's *deal*? I thought you got it?"

I finished ordering and went and stood in front of the TV.

"Hey!" Randi yelled.

"No, I really want to know," I said seriously. "I have no idea. Remember, I'm still new at all of this."

"Okay, okay," Randi grumbled, turning off the TV. "This is how it works. She gives you a couple of clients, until, you know, you get *hungry*. Like you are now. Then, when you ask for more, you quickly realize that she's not giving you any more people until you refer some of your own students whose parents think they need tutoring."

"And this happens at parent conferences next week," I finished, catching on.

"Exactly. So, pretty much you will find that you will get tutoring clients from her in the exact ratio of how many Langdon families you refer to *her*. She calls the other learning specialists at the other private schools with the referrals and they hook them up with their teachers. They, in turn, give *her* names and numbers of families at their schools who need help."

"So, what's in it for her?"

"She keeps the best ones for herself," Randi answered. "Duh."

"And she doesn't have to teach. She just sits there . . . and networks," I thought out loud in amazement. "Classic."

"You got it. So make sure when you have your parent conferences that you push for the tutoring thing," Randi advised. "Only you don't suggest it. If the parents ask if you think their child could use more help, just nod. Then e-mail Francine. It's easy."

"So, it's all about working the parent conferences."

"Exactly!" Randi beamed triumphantly.

"So, how did you get Benjamin Kensington?" I asked bravely.

I saw a shadow cross her face for a split second, but admirably Randi answered honestly.

"Blumenfeld set it up. Benjamin was failing out of school and Langdon didn't want to lose the Kensington donations. He told his parents he flat-out refused to work with anyone except me. So the school made an exception."

"Just like that?" I asked in amazement.

"Just like that. But hey, you don't have to wait till after parent conferences for a new client. I can give you one of mine."

"Um, yeah, I would love it!" I enthused. "But . . . how come? You don't want this kid?" I couldn't believe how generous Randi was being.

"Her name's Jennifer Parker. She's actually great—she's an eighth-grader at Spence. The family's ridiculously wealthy and you can charge $300 an hour." Randi was now warming up to this idea, and sat up straighter. "I just have too many clients right now, so I'd be happy to refer the family to you. They'll do whatever I say."

"Randi, this is way too generous! Why are you giving me such a lucrative client, though?" I was still a little suspicious. Randi usually guarded her client list like a mother hen.

"She's just more your type," Randi answered evasively. "I'll have Dottie Parker call you tomorrow. Enough tutoring talk. I'm turning Tyra back on."

Parent conferences started at 7:00 in the morning, and parents buzzed in and out all day from the Langdon beehive. I was expected to sit in my class all day as parents flew in and out in twenty-minute increments. Nobody seemed to care that teachers were expected to talk nonstop for hours. Even worse were the divorced parents who *refused* to sit in a room together. These special cases received *forty* minutes as I was expected to relay the information twice.

"Here's your list of appointments," Alicia Rollins said brightly as I stood in the office with the rest of the faculty, awaiting our lists.

I was scheduled straight through the day till 8:00 in the evening, with one thirty-minute break at 1:00 for lunch.

"What if I have to go to the bathroom?" I asked, horrified.

"You can go at lunch," she replied, laughing. "My goodness, Anna, you sound like one of your students! Just hold it!"

I walked out of the office, clutching my list with a growing sense of dread. The thought of meeting all these parents alone and unprotected left me feeling exposed and vulnerable. How the hell was I supposed to talk nonstop for the entire day? And what was I supposed to talk about? I walked past Randi's room and saw her talking animatedly to a chicly dressed couple. The father looked like Pierce Brosnan in his sleek, pin-striped business suit, and the mother could have easily passed for Kelly Ripa. All three of them were leaning toward each other and laughing. Randi appeared to be having the time of her life.

"Keep them light and vague," Harold Warner had ordered. "Offer no specifics. Give them nothing."

I had rolled my eyes. What the fuck was the point of these conferences if everyone sat in a room and bullshitted about the students? Passing Dorothy Steeple's room, I was surprised to see the same scenario of a gorgeous couple facing the teacher, only the three of them looked miserable. Dorothy's expression was steely and the mother looked like she was going to cry. I quickly vowed to keep mine light and frothy like Randi's.

"They're all brilliant, they're all brilliant, they're all brilliant," I muttered silently to myself as I entered the execution room. It was to be my mantra for the entire day. Unless, of course, the parents thought their child needed a tutor. Then I would most passionately and vehemently agree.

Lynn Briggman and her husband Andrew were my first conference. I got up from the table nervously and extended my hand.

"Oh, Anna, kisses, kisses! We're all friends here!" Lynn objected, dismissing my hand and giving me a kiss on both cheeks. I looked over at her husband and was happy to find that he looked just as awkward as I felt.

"Kisses it is," he shrugged, leaning over and giving me a quick peck on one cheek.

"Look at her hair, Andrew! Isn't it gorgeous! I had her go to John!" Lynn continued, grabbing a handful of my hair and holding it up to show her husband.

"Lynn, let's not completely molest the teacher," he joked, relaxing a bit. "So, Ms. Taggert, give us the damage. What has our devil been up to?"

"Oh, Max is one of my most enthusiastic students," I began. "He is such a delight. An absolute pleasure."

"Can you move in with us? That's not the kid we know," Lynn exclaimed, and she and her husband both started laughing again. So this was the game. I had to sit and compliment the children while the parents made little jokes about their child to appear modest and grateful.

"How's he with the ladies?" Andrew Briggman asked suddenly.

Excuse me?

"I'm sorry?" I asked, completely caught off guard.

"I mean, does he have a girlfriend? Is he a ladies' man?" Gone was the awkward and shy father who had entered the room. "I was quite a ladies' man at his age."

"Oh, Andrew!" Lynn began giggling like a schoolgirl.

"Oh, the girls love Max," I assured. "He's so charming." Just yesterday Max had warned the class that he was about to lay a silent but deadly and had blessed the entire class with the most vile and lingering smell I had ever experienced in my life.

"The little stinker! He never tells us anything!" Andrew cried, looking enormously pleased. Little stinker indeed.

"Now, Anna, I have to ask you something," Lynn said, her face becoming deadly serious. "Max spends an inordinate amount of time at the computer doing his homework each night. I worry about that."

"Are you sure he's not just IM'ing?" I laughed, feeling comfortable for the first time.

Neither Briggman laughed back. Oops.

"Our son is one of the most honest human beings I have ever met," Andrew replied, his face darkening. "If he says he's doing his homework, I believe him. And I agree with my wife, two hours a night seems quite excessive for a seventh-grader."

I would have bet my apartment that Max was either IM'ing or playing video games, but clearly this was not something either Briggman parent was willing to consider. Just when I thought there was no way out of this one, Lynn Briggman showed me an escape route.

"Do you think he needs another tutor? Someone to help him, you know, *plan* his time better? Get a bit more organized? He has one, but she only comes twice a week. Maybe he needs someone on a *daily* basis."

"Well . . . um . . . ," I couldn't help but falter. Was she really handing this to me on a tutoring silver platter? I forced myself to recover and take advantage of the opportunity. "It couldn't hurt. I'll let Ms. Gilmore know, and she'll get in touch with you," I replied immediately. Yes! Yes! Yes!

"Oh, that would be wonderful, Anna," Lynn gushed. "Not all the teachers at Langdon are as understanding as you and Ms. Abrahams. Thank God you give him manageable work."

I smiled back sweetly, but victory was short-lived. Lara Kensington was at the door with a grimace on her face. She was looking furiously at her watch.

"Um, I think our time is up," I said, although neither Briggman was showing any sign of moving.

"What about friends? Who is Max hanging out with these days?" Andrew asked. Lara knocked loudly on the glass panes of the door and pointed to the watch.

"I'm sorry, Mr. and Mrs. Briggman, I *really* have to try and keep on schedule," I stated firmly. "Mrs. Kensington is at the door and her conference time already started."

"Lara is so selfish," Lynn muttered spitefully, then immediately appeared to lighten up and gave me an enormous and exaggerated hug. I was quite sure it was for Lara's benefit. Just as I was pulling away, she entered the room.

"We are starting two minutes late, Anna, so we're staying two minutes longer," Lara warned, then turned to the Briggmans with an enormous smile on her face. "Lynn and Andrew, how naughty of you to eat up my time! Robert and I must have you over for drinks!"

I watched the women air kiss while the men shook hands and clapped each other on the back like they were fraternity brothers. One minute later I was replaying the same scenario, only I was facing Benjamin's parents.

"We're starting three minutes later," Lara reminded me again. "Every minute I spend with Benjamin's teachers is precious. Don't you agree, Robert?"

"Absolutely," Robert Kensington agreed, then gave me a wicked grin that made him look exactly like his son. "And can I just say that you are even *prettier* than he mentioned. No wonder he loves your class so much!"

Right at that moment I felt a warm hand on my knee. Horrified, I quickly crossed my legs and pushed my chair back. Robert Kensington gave me a knowing wink.

The day stretched endlessly ahead.

26

My e-mail exchange with Francine Gilmore played out like a perfectly orchestrated drug deal, only instead of a dark alley, it transpired via e-mail. Names and phone numbers were shared, and in under a week I had eight new clients. Counting Jake and Katie, I now had ten private students all of whom wanted a minimum of two sessions a week with the option of Sunday, which I realized was clearly The Day of Homework. With so many clients and times to remember I had copied Francine and purchased a simple paper datebook from Staples. I looked at my Monday afternoon schedule with delight:

3:30–5:00	Katie Carleton
5:30–7:00	Jake Herring
7:30–9:00	Keith Morgan
9:30–11:00	Whitney Braxton

Keith Morgan and Whitney Braxton were both juniors at Horace Mann, and their parents were in search of tutors who would be willing to work late in the evenings and even into the night if required. Both sets of parents had impressed the importance of Keith's and Whitney's receiving no less than an A- on any assignment. All in a day's work for Super Tutor.

If having ten clients was good, then having eleven was even better. That's what I told myself when I received a call from Bettina LaVera. Mrs. LaVera had phoned me earlier in the week, claiming that her daughter had procured my cell number from one of her classmates. Pre–Laura Brandeis, I might have wondered how my number was floating around the classrooms of the Upper East Side. A growing addiction to the checks I was earning, however, caused me to hold my tongue and simply schedule the prerequisite interview for the next day.

The LaVeras lived in an old, prewar building around the corner from the Metropolitan Museum of Art. Standing across the street, I noticed that the doors were a thick gold and looked like they belonged in the entrance of a vault. Two gloved doormen stood side by side with expressions that could have rivaled the Windsor guards. Strangely nervous as I approached the building, I took a deep breath before announcing myself to both men.

"I'm here to see Bettina LaVera," I declared in my most confident voice. "I'm Anna Taggert."

One doorman continued to stare straight ahead as if he had never heard me, but the other one nodded slightly and pointed to a large door a few feet away from the building's entrance.

"The service entrance is through there."

Service entrance? I blinked in confusion and quickly glanced down to recheck my outfit. Jil Sander suit. Jimmy Choo heels. Certainly not nanny material. What the hell was this doorman trying to imply? And was that a sneer I just detected?

"Unless your doors aren't working, I'm sure I don't know what you mean," I said firmly, looking him straight in the eye. "I have an appointment with Bettina LaVera."

"Mrs. LaVera told us that she was expecting a . . . *tutor* for her daughter," he said silkily. "All staff goes through the service entrance." He was now making no attempt to hide his broadening smile.

I wanted to kill this asshole! Who the hell did he think he was? No way I was going to enter this building like some nanny or cleaning lady. I wasn't . . . staff! Not when my outfit probably cost more than his monthly salary. I crossed my arms and glared back defiantly.

"Please call Bettina," I challenged, purposefully using her first name. "I would like this to be her decision."

"You're not the tutor?" His arms were now crossed as well.

"Unless you are a building resident posing as a doorman, I suggest you do your job and let Bettina know I am here," I retorted icily, refusing to budge.

"Anna?"

The voice came from behind me and all of a sudden the doorman's sneer vanished. I turned to face a petite woman in frayed jeans and an oversized sweatshirt. She was smiling hopefully at me while balancing two grocery bags from Eli's. Her mousy brown hair was pulled up into a tight ponytail held by a scrunchy (yes, a scrunchy) and her lips were chapped. Now *this* was a candidate for the service elevator! How did she know my name?

"Let me get your bags, Mrs. LaVera," the doorman gushed. Both men jumped to attention and I stood speechlessly as they took her bags and opened the golden vault.

"You're . . . Bettina?" I asked weakly, now feeling awkward and overdressed. With a Fifth Avenue address and a name like Bettina LaVera I had been expecting a Botoxed yoga goddess clad in cashmere and stilettos. Not *Ugly Betty*!

"I'm so happy to meet you," she replied warmly, grabbing my limp hand and shaking it vigorously. "It took forever to catch a cab and I was so nervous I'd be late for our appointment! Let's go in."

Still furious at the doorman, I shook my head with feigned awkwardness and looked toward my latest archnemesis. "I think he . . . ," I paused and glanced at him pointedly, "wants me to use the service entrance."

"Oh, Anna, don't be silly! Last I checked I lived in this building and Hector was the doorman," Bettina dismissed, barely glancing at the now scowling Hector as she ushered me into the lobby. I gave him a triumphant smile and followed Bettina into the elevator.

Prepared for an apartment that was as shabby as its owner, I was stunned when the elevator doors opened directly into a grand marble foyer. Dark wood paneling covered the walls, and two tastefully upholstered benches graced the ends of the room. It reminded me of an entrance to one of the Newport mansions. Bettina casually kicked off her sneakers and padded down one corridor, gesturing for me to follow. I trailed after her, cringing at the sound my heels made against her floor. Should I have taken them off? Before I could ask, we were both standing in the living room.

I gasped.

Enormous French doors opened into an expansive patio overlooking the Met. On the opposite side of the room a grand piano stretched luxuriously behind an oversized plush couch flanked by two brocade love seats. Similar seating arrangements were repeated throughout the vast room while coffee tables and armoires boasted impressive china and crystal collections. Beneath us was the largest Persian rug I had ever seen. The room looked like it was straight out of *Architectural Digest.*

"Your apartment is amazing," I said honestly, looking around in wonder. "Believe me, I see so many apartments but this is truly breathtaking."

"You have *no* idea what that means to me, Anna!" Bettina replied proudly, looking around the room with me. "I decorated it myself—picked each and every fabric—and I have to say I love it, too. As long as we are giving compliments, let me tell you that I feel like a frumpy housewife compared to you! What a gorgeous suit!"

"Thanks so much," I replied awkwardly, still feeling over-dressed. I watched her walk over to the couch and gesture for me to join her. She surprised me once again by putting both feet up and crossing her legs Indian style. I lowered myself gingerly into an armchair, unable to figure out how this woman could decorate her apartment so stylishly and look the way she did. As soon as I sat down, Bettina jumped up and slapped her forehead.

"I'm so rude, Anna! Can I get you something to drink? Water? Coffee?"

I looked around the room for signs of a maid. It was so huge that it was entirely possible one had entered without my noticing.

"Water would be great," I replied, still craning my neck to see beyond the piano. Where was she?

"Just give me a sec, I'll be right back."

I watched in growing wonderment as the shoeless Bettina padded out of the room briskly and returned moments later with two bottles of Fiji water.

"Catch," she said cheerfully, tossing me a bottle. It flew dangerously near a crystal figurine and I lunged for it. How could this woman be so casual in a room like this? Unaffected, Bettina flopped back on the couch and took a long swig of water.

"Ahhh," she breathed happily. "Feels good to finally sit down. I've been running errands all afternoon! How was your day?"

"My day?" I had never been asked this before in an interview.

"At school," she clarified, tugging at her scrunchy and running one hand through her hair. The ends were unkempt and greasy. "I can imagine how much work goes into being a teacher!"

"My day was . . . wonderful," I replied, reverting to my favorite interview adjective. "I love teaching."

"That's so great to hear," she enthused. "From some of the stories my Vanessa tells me, my husband and I sometimes wonder why anyone would want to teach in a Manhattan private school!" Bettina's eyes were now wide and she was shaking her head in commiseration. "Just last week she was telling us how one of the girls in her class actually told their English teacher that her parents paid for his salary so he essentially worked for *them*. Can you imagine? And the girl didn't even get in trouble!"

"Many of the students don't seem to have respect for teachers," I agreed sympathetically, secretly thrilled that my students would never dare say something like that to me. As long as my tutoring checks afforded me a wardrobe envied by even the Langdon mothers, they could never speak to *me* like that. I felt a renewed love for my Jil Sander suit.

"It's such a shame," Bettina went on. "My husband and I

literally cringe when we hear how disrespectful the kids can be. The worst part is that so many of Vanessa's friends have parents who enable this behavior. Would you believe that this morning three mothers called me and wanted to start a petition to stop the science teacher from giving a quiz on Monday!"

"Why?" I asked, curious in spite of myself.

"Because it's someone's bar mitzvah party on Sunday night!" Bettina exclaimed, pulling her hair back again, this time into a tight, messy bun. "Here we were, telling Vanessa she had to leave Sunday's party early so she could come home and study! I'm telling you, Anna, sometimes I'm not sure I can tell the difference between the kids and their par—"

"Wow, that's too bad," I interrupted abruptly, eager to change the subject. It was making me a little uncomfortable to hear her voice so many of the frustrations I had felt in my first few weeks at Langdon. I thought this was a tutoring interview! What kind of dirty trick was she playing?

"I know! I just keeping wishing that someone would stand up and say—" She had to be stopped. This was going too far.

"What kind of *tutoring* help does Vanessa need?" I interrupted again, making sure to emphasize the word *tutoring*. Had she forgotten that was why I was here in the first place?

"Help?" Bettina looked confused.

"In our future tutoring sessions," I reminded her, beginning to think that she might be a little loony.

"Oh!" Bettina slapped her forehead again and gave me a how-could-I-be-so-out-of-it look. "I'm so sorry, Anna. When you're up at six trying to get the kids and the hubby out the door in time, we mothers start to lose it a little by midafternoon!"

I was convinced at that moment that the Langdon mothers could, if given the opportunity, devour Bettina LaVera for lunch. What kind of private school mother was she? Why was she dressed like a suburban soccer mom? And more importantly, where were her maids? There was no way she was from Manhattan.

"The truth is," she went on, sitting up a bit straighter, "Vanessa does not actually need any help. She's a terrific student. At least she *was* in her old school before we moved here . . ."

Aha! I knew this family was not from here!

"Where did you move from?" I asked, back on solid ground.

"We just moved a year ago from Pleasantville," Bettina explained, "from Westchester. 'Ness was doing so well academically that we figured she'd have no problem adjusting to a new school, and living in Manhattan just made more sense since my husband's law firm is located here."

"The standards in Manhattan private schools are quite high," I affirmed gently, getting up and walking over to the couch. Sitting down next to Bettina, I looked sympathetically into her eyes. "The adjustment can be so hard. I can help Vanessa catch up."

"Oh, no! You misunderstand me." Bettina chuckled grimly. "If only that were true! The public school 'Ness attended had incredibly high standards, and the work they are expected to do here is comparable. What she is struggling with is—"

"Being the new girl," I finished expertly. "Navigating the private-school world can be tricky. We've all seen *Mean Girls*!" I began to laugh knowingly, but stopped when I realized Bettina was not joining me.

"Anna, I'm going to be very frank with you," she said slowly, her voice becoming low and serious. "Vanessa's father and I do not believe in tutors. We have always taught her to work independently. If she ever needed help we were here for her, but we always encouraged her to seek out her teachers as well. We figured that's what they were there for. You know, to teach."

"I see," I replied curtly, looking at my watch. What a waste of time! "I guess there was a misunderstanding. When we spoke on the phone you mentioned that you wanted to interview me as a potential tutor for Vanessa." I was unexpectedly nostalgic for Mimsy Herring and her fervent belief in the necessity of tutors.

"I don't *want* a tutor for my child," Bettina corrected earnestly, "but we *need* one in order to level the playing field. Anna, almost every child in her class has a tutor. So, no matter how much effort our daughter puts into a homework assignment, or how impressive her writing may be, Vanessa can't . . ." Bettina's voice cracked, "compete."

"Against who?"

"Against all the students in her class with tutors! It doesn't matter how capable my child is, Anna. At the end of the day she is thirteen years old. Anyone in her class who works with a tutor on the same assignment has a clear advantage. We tried to convince 'Ness that as long as she worked hard the grades didn't matter. But now we're getting letters from the school telling us she's not turning in work. When we confronted her, she told us there's no . . ." Bettina's eyes started to tear, "no point. No matter how hard she works nothing she does compares with her friends' work. She's calling us *cheap*. Saying we're too cheap to hire a tutor." She looked around the room and laughed bitterly. "I'll tell you what's cheap. Hiring a tutor and teaching your child that even homework has a price."

I didn't know what to say. Selfishly I couldn't help but think that Vanessa sounded like an ideal client: bright, capable, and just in need of a little guidance. As a teacher, however, I knew that Bettina was right. The few homework assignments I had my students turn in were suspiciously devoid of any errors. But what was I supposed to do? Tell them they had to do their homework by themselves and risk the wrath of the Langdon mothers? I could just *hear* Lara Kensington saying, "Benjamin has trouble with *beginnings*. His tutor helps him find his true voice. How *dare* you suggest that we endorse cheating in our household?" I shivered at the thought of such a confrontation, suddenly irritated that my interview with Bettina LaVera was turning into a moral crusade that was threatening the very source of my newfound wealth.

"So Vanessa needs someone to help her just polish her assignments?" I asked brightly, determined to play dumb. I could not afford to waste another minute philosophizing about the evils of the tutoring industry. If it was so bad, why didn't all the private schools just ban it?

"Just polish," Bettina echoed, looking a bit defeated.

"I charge $250 an hour," I stated flatly. "I could see her twice a week on Mondays and Wednesdays from seven to eight."

"Money's not a problem," Bettina responded evenly, her voice matching my businesslike tone. "Vanessa will be thrilled."

Randi could barely conceal her jealousy when I told her about my new tutoring client. She wasn't even surprised when I told her how reluctant Bettina LaVera had been to hire me in the first place.

"Those are the *best* ones," she argued. "All you have to do is some basic editing and then sprinkle in some sophisticated ideas. They do most of the work. God, Annie, you're so lucky."

"But you should have heard this woman," I pressed. "Part of me didn't even want to take the job! She kept going on and on about how she had no choice but to hire me and that she and her husband didn't believe in tutors . . ."

"Like I said," Randi was now grinning broadly, "those parents are the best. You know what it means for us if even the parents with bright kids are desperate for tutors?"

"What?" I asked, playing along. I couldn't help but start smiling as Randi began to do a little dance in the middle of the classroom like a Fendi-clad Rumpelstiltskin.

"Every parent feels compelled to hire a tutor!" she exclaimed with glee, clapping her hands together. "And there's only so many of us! Which means we, my dear Anna, can charge whatever we want!" Randi's face was flushed with enthusiasm and I longed to be as swept away as she was. I just had one lingering question that I couldn't ignore.

"But then none of our students are doing their own homework, are they?" I noticed a shadow flicker briefly across Randi's face, but seconds later she was beaming triumphantly.

"If the parents don't care, then why should the teachers?"

A week later I found myself in Randi's classroom, so exhausted I was barely able to keep my eyes open.

"Just have them come to your house," she advised after I

shared the horrific details of my schedule with her. "That transition time you have blocked in is just stupid."

"I don't want them in my *apartment*," I argued. "Isn't it better just to keep them a little removed?"

"Sure," Randi responded, shrugging. "But the thirty-minute transition times you have scheduled in there amount to two hours. That's two hours of schlepping around in cabs or walking up and down Park Avenue. You could be making five hundred bucks instead."

"So, you have them all come to *you*? At *our* building? Back to back?"

"Exactly. If they're late, you're still on the clock. And if they're not done, the next student is at the door so there's no drama about them begging you to stay later. It's clean, it's easy, and you can just sit in one place. These are Manhattan kids. They take cabs. They have drivers. *Trust me*, they are extremely *mobile*."

"And what if the parents refuse? I'm afraid some of my new parents prefer that I come to them," I argued.

"Just get them hooked then. Go to their place for a month or so, and when their children find that they can't do without you, that's when *you* call the shots. Lay down the law. Raise your prices. The key is to get them hooked."

Randi was making sense, but once again I was a little appalled by how mercenary she could be. This did seem like the only logical solution, but boy, she really did have this system down pat. She was clearly Super Tutor, and had both Langdon and the tutoring world spun around her little pinky finger.

"I feel bad sometimes," I admitted, heaving myself on the ledge that ran around her classroom.

"About what?" Randi was expertly putting great big stars in a red magic marker on a stack of assignments. I noticed that she barely glanced at the contents of the papers.

"Like *that*, for instance," I replied, pointing to the papers she was supposedly grading. "I barely have time to read what the kids write anymore. I haven't planned a real lesson in weeks. Sometimes I miss it. Yeah, the money is *awesome*, but I don't even have time to spend it. I'm so fried by the time I get home each night. My friend Bridgette keeps asking me to dinner and I keep turning her down. I can't believe that I'm working till eleven each night, and *she's* the banker."

Once again, that same look of irritation darkened Randi's perfect face. She put her marker down and sighed. "Anna, remember, this is always your choice. You were the one who wanted more clients. It's not like you have to tutor. You can go back to just being a *teacher*," wrinkling her nose at the word. "You're making me feel like I'm a bad influence or something. Don't make me feel guilty."

"No no!" I cried quickly. "Are you kidding? I don't know what I would do without you! And honestly, it seems like the less I teach the happier everyone is. The kids and the parents, that is. It's just that . . . ," I trailed off, searching for the right words.

"Just that *what*?" Randi pressed, glaring at me.

"It's just that I never imagined it would be like this," I said softly, looking down at the Dior pumps I had purchased last week. They were worth three tutoring sessions. I was calculating everything in tutoring sessions lately. The rent was twelve sessions of tutoring. My Prada blazer was four sessions. A week's worth of cab rides and all the Starbucks I could drink was one session. For the last week I had found myself tutoring like a madwoman, often way past eleven at night.

Every morning I had slept through the alarm clock and had ended up running to school and arriving late. Although Randi and I *had* made up for all our hard work with a Saturday afternoon shopping spree on Madison Avenue.

"Just think of this Saturday and many more to come," Randi said as if reading my mind. "Let's face it, *nobody* likes to work. We'd all like to be millionaires who sleep in late every day and spend their days doing whatever. But can you honestly tell me that when we lunch at Barneys and walk up and down Madison buying whatever we please that you don't feel like it's all worth it?"

"I guess," I replied, still not fully convinced. I didn't know what was wrong with me. "Forget it, I'm just feeling down today." Maybe I needed some of Sarah Waters's Prozac.

"Anna, it's fucking *boring* and *annoying* to sit and do homework for hours on end with these kids. Believe me, it's not like I'm having a blast. But personally, I get to forget all about it for a day and a half every week, and I certainly make the most of it. And wait till the summer . . . then it'll *really* be worth it!"

"I know, I can't wait," I confessed. "Three blissful months of no tutoring." Randi spit back the coffee she had just sipped and started laughing.

"No tutoring? No, babe! Much more tutoring! But a different kind of tutoring . . . and a different location," she added mysteriously.

Oh God. Not the college kids again?

"*Hamptons* tutoring. Actually, I meant to bring this up with you because we need to jump on the timeshare thing pretty quickly. I was thinking a two-bedroom in Southampton?"

"Whhhaaatt?" I stared at her in disbelief. "The Hamptons?" Randi was suddenly glowing with excitement.

"Yup! I learned all about it from Lillian Summers. You've never heard of her?"

"Noo . . ." From the way Randi said her name, this Lillian Summers sounded like her role model. Was it possible that somebody else was the reigning queen of tutors in Manhattan?

"Lillian Summers *owns* the Hamptons tutoring scene. She's so good she quit her teaching position at Chapin. Now she barely even has to tutor during the year because she makes so much in the summer. She's actually my idol," Randi admitted, her pupils widening in excitement. "I met her last year at a cocktail party the Kensingtons throw at the end of the school year, and we had a very interesting conversation. She rents a beautiful house in Southampton every summer and tutors all the kids whose families summer there. Manhattan families. Celebrity families, you name it. She drives around in a little navy blue coupe, and basically spends the summer tutoring, but she also treats herself to daily private tennis lessons, massages, and sickening shopping sprees. And come fall," Randi was now flushed with excitement, "she only keeps a few select clients just to have a little extra cash."

Now I was also in awe of the mighty Lillian.

"So she really doesn't teach anymore?" I persisted, suddenly very envious. "I thought people only paid the big bucks for private-school teachers."

"Oh, you put in the time," Randi dismissed, running her hand through her freshly highlighted mane. "I still have a few years to go, and you should consider staying at Langdon for at least two more years. But once you have your clientele and a solid reputation, you can just leave. Tutor full-time."

"But what is she teaching in the summer? Summer school? I don't get it," I pressed, now dying to meet this Lillian Summers. With a last name like that, she was clearly destined for her infamous role as the Hamptons Tutoring Madame.

"Summer tutors are like fancy babysitters for the rich," Randi explained. "Parents want their free time, and along with horseback riding and tennis lessons, they also book tutoring sessions. Since these kids aren't at school, Lillian says you can basically *make up* your lessons. Read books with them. Practice writing. You know, whatever."

"Have you ever done this?" I was wide-eyed. I had never been to the Hamptons before. In fact, it was only this year that I had learned why the word was plural. It was Madeline who had provided the lesson. "But Ms. Taggert," she had scolded, "there are only *two* that are acceptable. South and East. *That's it*. Like, Amy's family just bought a place in *West*. Ugh."

"Nope, but we're doing it this year!" Randi exclaimed, paper-clipping the papers she had "graded." "That is, if you're game?"

"Where are we getting these fancy and famous clients?"

"You'd be surprised how many of your yearly clients will jump when you mention you're available for summer tutoring," Randi replied. "And I've been doing some networking at Core Fusion with *this*." With a flourish, Randi reached into her wallet and pulled out a tasteful-looking cream card that looked exactly like the one David had presented to me on the first day of school. Good card stock, I couldn't help but notice. Only this one read as follows.

Randi Abrahams

Reading and Writing Specialist

Hamptons
Randi@LangdonHall.edu

I stared at it in amazement. She was handing this out at Core Fusion? The same workout spot that Charlotte's mother met her lesbian partner?

"Core Fusion is private school mother *mecca*. It's *the* greatest place to get clients," Randi swooned. "I have to take you. You just lie down and basically do a million little crunches and leg lifts, and then in the locker rooms it's network city! I see Katie Couric there all the time!"

"So you already have clients, then?" I had never wanted to take an exercise class so badly.

"I have *too* many," Randi grinned. "That's why I'm asking you. I'll give you half of them. Who wants a summer timeshare without her best girlfriend?"

Her last two words erased all the caution and guilt I had been feeling earlier in our conversation. Randi had called me her best girlfriend! I was going to the Hamptons! (Thankfully "South!") *And* I was going to meet this Lillian Summers, who would clearly be someone else I could bond with about the tutoring world.

"I'm sold," I replied, laughing happily as Randi jumped up to hug me.

———

That afternoon I had my first interview at the home of Randi's referral, Jennifer Parker. It began like all the others: Townhouse, check. Elevator, check. Flawless furnishings, check. Uniformed maid, check. Impossibly thin, blonde, and tanned mother, check.

"Mrs. Parker, I'm Anna Taggert," I said smoothly. Gone were my days of spurting out monosyllables and repeated "wonderfuls." I was surfing the tutoring wave now, and this was just another crest I had to skim before I rushed to the other clients I had that evening.

"Anna, it's so lovely to meet you in person! Diana Parker, but you can call me Dottie. Won't you sit down?" She smiled, gesturing to the couch. In stark contrast to the room, "Dottie" was wearing a bubblegum pink Lilly Pulitzer dress with white polka dots. She looked like a fourth-grader with a fondness for Botox.

"As we discussed on the phone, I have an eighth-grader at the Spence School. I just wanted to make sure she has access to all the resources possible so that she can reach her potential. That's why, when Ms. Abrahams quit so unexpectedly, I was desperate to get in touch with you."

"Did Ra—I mean, Ms. Abrahams give any reason for leaving?"

"Not really . . . she just said she was busy with teaching and that she was slowing down on her tutoring after school."

I struggled to keep my expression neutral. Something was fishy here. Randi would not just drop a well-paying client for no apparent reason.

"What was Ms. Abrahams helping her with?" I pressed, hoping for some clue to the puzzle.

"Anna, can I be frank with you?" Dottie asked, leaning forward at her desk and looking at me square in the face. "My daughter has always been an *excellent student*. Straight As, in fact! Until this year, and then only in one class. Unfortunately she got the worst English teacher in the school, and there simply isn't anything we can do. Her grades have been dropping dramatically!"

"Didn't working with Ms. Abrahams help?" I asked, secretly hoping to hear that Randi was not the perfect tutor she touted herself to be.

"Actually, and this *is* a bit awkward as I know she is your colleague," Dottie paused, clearly searching for a tactful response. I was thrilled. Finally, a crack in Randi's seemingly flawless tutoring armor.

"Ms. Abrahams is clearly very talented and obviously brilliant. I mean, you have to be if you're hired by a school like Langdon Hall. And she's been with us for years! But for some reason, Jennifer's grade in English was simply not going up this year. One little bit. I mean, Jennifer *adored* Ms. Abrahams, but my husband and I have a sneaking suspicion that Ms. Abrahams gracefully stepped down when she saw that her help wasn't . . . paying off. When she mentioned that you are actually an English teacher, it just made us feel so much more comfortable."

I was certain something had to be wrong with little Jennifer Parker. Even the most incapable students I worked with saw a rise in their grades simply by the homework I was able to help them "polish." The word, admittedly, had become a personal favorite in my vocabulary. It was an all-purpose word, something of a Swiss Army knife capable of replacing all sorts of words, such as *do, write, create*, and especially *finish*.

"Does Jennifer have any learning issues?" I asked expertly, donning my best concerned expression. Eight months at Langdon and I could talk endlessly about ADD, Ritalin, Concerta, dyslexia, and spatial issues, the latter of which was code for nothing-is-wrong-we-just-need-something-that-sounds-good. "Some visual, *spatial* issues, perhaps?"

Dottie shook her head. "We went over this with Ms. Abrahams. Jennifer was recently tested and she appears to have no learning disorders. My husband and I are convinced it's the fault of the teacher, Mr. Richards."

"Have you complained to the board?" I asked sympathetically. "Remember, the teachers work for you. It's not right when they hinder your child's ability to learn and excel." Sitting there in my Lanvin belted dress and Gucci stilettos, I felt very much on the side of the mothers. Who did this Mr. Richards think he was?

"Many of us have!" Dottie cried, now getting excited. "We've written endless letters signed by all the class parents! But they do nothing. I'm sure Langdon would never ignore such a bold statement from its parent body."

"Never," I agreed vehemently, willing myself to forget my own little "incident" not too long ago in Dr. Blumenfeld's office.

"Unfortunately," Dottie continued, "this man has been there for ages, and truthfully he doesn't seem to assign too much homework or give us anything concrete to complain about. Anytime we do complain, he brings in essays written by our children that are, admittedly, quite poorly done. We just don't understand how his class is the only class children perform so poorly in. It's quite maddening," she complained, throwing her hands up in frustration. "Believe me, if he was a high school teacher and the grades he gave actually got reported to college, we would be up in arms. But it's eighth grade . . . you know the middle-school years don't really count. Still, we just don't want Jennifer's self-esteem to suffer, you know?"

I bristled slightly at the "middle school years don't really count" comment, but there was nothing to do but agree with Dottie.

"I will do my best," I promised. "Shall we say Tuesday, Thursday, and Sunday for an hour and a half?"

"That would be perfect," Dottie beamed. "We'll see you this Sunday. And you're adorable just like Ms. Abrahams. One hates to be . . . superficial, but you know it's important with these young girls to have a, what do they call it, cool tutor?"

"I'll take that as a compliment!" I laughed, enjoying Dottie's double take as I stood up and smoothed out my dress.

"Is that Lanvin?" she asked curiously.

"I think so," I replied as casually as I could, and then allowed the maid to escort me to the elevator. I could feel Dottie's eyes curiously boring into my back as I exited the room. Lanvin trumped Lilly any day of the week.

Sunday afternoon found Jennifer Parker sprawled on her carpet, arms propping her head up. Her terry-cloth pants had JUICY PRINCESS written in huge pink letters across her tiny butt, and of course she was wearing the matching hoodie in a deep, chocolate brown.

"What'ya reading?" I asked casually by way of introduction. I joined her on the floor and sat Indian style.

"*US Weekly*," she mumbled reverently, not looking up. "It's like, my *Bible*."

"Oooh, is it the new one?" I asked, peering over her head.

Clearly the magic question. Jennifer sat up and gave me a huge smile. "Yup! I get it on my way home from school every Wednesday. I'm *obsessed* with Lindsay Lohan."

"*Mean Girls* is one of my favorite movies!" I exclaimed.

"OHMIGOD shut up. No it isn't!" Jennifer cried, sitting up. "*Shut up!*"

"I swear!" I laughed, then held out my hand. "I'm Anna, by the way. Your new tutor."

"Thank *God* you're cool! Randi said you'd be cool. I was, like, *so* pissed when she quit because she was, like, my *best* friend!"

"Why did she quit?" I asked, hoping for a more honest explanation.

"I'm not sure," she answered, lowering her eyes. "I mean, she said it was because she needed more time for grading and stuff, but I hear she still tutors a bunch of my friends. I think my parents, especially my dad, were putting some pressure on her about my English grade."

"Your mom was telling me a little about Mr. Richards," I said carefully, not wanting to get too serious. "Since this is our first session we can just hang and talk, you know, bond? Whatever you want to do, Jennifer."

"Oh, God, call me Jennie. Only my parents insist on calling me Jennifer. And yeah, I wish we could just hang, but my dad will go through the roof if I don't raise my English grade. He cares about stupid stuff like that." While she was talking, I watched as Jennie reluctantly closed the magazine and slumped toward her desk.

"Should we start?"

Wow.

This was new. No talking? No long, drawn-out bonding session? No wasting time? Whoever this Mr. Richards was, he had clearly instilled the fear of God into little Jennie Parker. I pulled up the chair from her vanity table and joined her at the desk. She shuffled through her quilted Chanel schoolbag and finally emerged with a copy of *Romeo and Juliet*.

"I just taught that last semester!" I exclaimed. Score! I wouldn't even have to prep or put a minute's effort into my tutoring sessions with her. I knew that play backward! Before she could reply, there was a knock at the door.

"Excuse me, Miss Jennifer." The same maid who had escorted me up and down the elevator was standing at the door. "Your mom want me to bring snack."

"Thanks, Maryella! Love you!" I smiled as Jennie stood up and planted a kiss on the older woman's wrinkled cheek as she set down a silver tray on the desk. It had two glasses of milk and Oreo cookies. Maryella looked pleased and ruffled Jennie's hair with obvious affection. She smiled at me and then quietly retreated.

"Maryella's been with me since I was a baby," Jennie explained, returning to the desk. "She still brings me milk and cookies. I *hate* milk and I can't have the Oreos, but you should totally help yourself."

"Thanks." I hadn't had an Oreo in . . . years. Out of habit, I broke it in two and began licking the cream. It was heavenly. "Why can't you have them?"

"You're such a kid!" Jennie accused as I blissfully licked the cookie, but she looked pleased. "Are you kidding? I'm on a *diet*. I'm such a *chunky monkey*." She promptly lifted her hoodie and attempted to grab a handful of flesh from her tiny stomach. I was horrified. The girl could not have been more than ninety pounds.

"Sweetie, you can't pinch an inch. Your stomach is absolutely flat. Just have a cookie." I dangled a cookie in her face. "And besides, one of the kids I tutor, Jake Herring, said just the other day that boys *hate* girls who try to be stick thin." That was a necessary white lie. I hated to invoke someone who, I was sure, would one day wind up on "To Catch a Predator," but Jake's reputation cast a wide net, and this was important. What Jake had really said was that he hated skinny girls because they had no boobs.

"You tutor Jake Herring?" Jennie asked, her eyes widening.

"I'm only talking if you eat a cookie," I replied with mock seriousness. Jennie relented and stuffed one in her face.

"Mmm," she closed her eyes in delight. "I haven't had a cookie in *months*. So, tell me about Jake. I mean, all the girls at my school think he's the hottest boy in Manhattan. We all kind of have a crush on him."

"He's charming, I suppose," I replied neutrally. "Do you know any kids at Langdon?" I reached for another cookie and leaned back in my chair. This was more like it. But once again, Jennie Parker surprised me.

"Can we talk about that next time? I really *really* need to do my English with you."

Aha! That word *do*! Mr. Richards probably assigned huge sums of homework and Jennie just wanted to find a way to get me to do most of it!

"Let's see the assignment before we read," I suggested.

"The assignment is to read the prologue," Jennie replied simply. "We just started it today."

Wait a minute.

"Just the prologue?"

"Uh huh."

"That's only fourteen lines. That will take five minutes," I said flatly. "Why are you so nervous?"

"Because Mr. Richards doesn't give *homework*," Jennie grimaced. "He gives *schoolwork*."

"I don't understand," I pressed. "He gives *no* homework?"

"Well, yeah, he gives us reading to do, but never anything that we turn in the next day," Jennie explained. "I hate him! He doesn't understand that I work so much better at home!"

"So you actually have to know this prologue pretty well, then, huh? Because you'll do the assignment in class tomorrow?" I was in completely new territory.

"Yeah," Jennie said glumly. "So we can't just read it, okay? You have to help me understand what every line means. And even then I have no way of knowing what he's gonna ask tomorrow."

For the next hour, Jennie and I pored over the prologue. We read and reread it until both of us had memorized it perfectly. Then, line by line, I led Jennie through the translation.

" 'Two households, both alike in dignity,' " she read slowly.

"So what does that mean?" I urged.

"So there are, like, two houses, and they're both equal?" Jennie shrugged.

"Pretty good," I nodded encouragingly. "But he's not just talking about houses. He uses the word *households*. How does that change the meaning?"

"Oh, so there're, like, a lot of people in the two houses?"

"Close," I smiled. "He's actually referring to two large families. These *households* can include relations beyond the basic family unit, like aunts, uncles, cousins, and even servants. So there are two households that comprise many individuals, and what they have in common is that they are absolutely equal. Now, that word *alike* is loaded. What do you think it means?"

"That they're both rich?" Jennie wondered.

"Yes, absolutely. You can infer that. But the word *dignity* that follows it suggests social status as well."

"Well, you can't have, like, that great of a social status if you're not rich," Jennie argued.

"Maybe," I relented. "Shakespeare is most likely referencing two very wealthy families. But then he could have just said they were both alike in wealth. But the word *dignity* does one thing wealth doesn't. . . ." I lingered, watching Jennie as she returned to the same line and read it silently to herself.

"What? Tell me!" she begged.

"*Dignity* has three syllables," I explained. "Remember when you first learned about syllables? You were taught to put your hand under your chin and say the word?"

"Oh, yeah!" Jennie cried, smiling. "And the amount of times your hand moved down was the amount of syllables there were in a word!"

"Exactly. So what's the difference between a word like *wealth* and *dignity*?" I pressed.

"*Wealth* has one syllable, and *dignity* has three, duh! Who cares?"

"Shakespeare did. He cared *a lot*." I launched into a mini-lecture on iambic pentameter and watched Jennie's eyes widen as I told her to test any of the fourteen lines of the prologue.

"They all have ten syllables," I announced confidently.

"No freaking way!" She was counting on her left hand while

placing her right palm under her chin. With each line she tested, her smile became broader.

"Wow . . . ," she breathed. "He's, like, a *genius*."

"It is pretty cool," I agreed.

"It's so crazy how we just spent so long on just one line," Jennie remarked, but she wasn't complaining. Her eyes were shining, and she was looking at the prologue with the same intensity I had seen her give her *US Weekly* when I had first walked in the room.

"That's what I love the most about Shakespeare," I confided. "You can really lose yourself in just one or two lines and somehow every time you revisit you can find a new meaning or angle. He tells a story, but he sometimes gives it to us in riddles."

"Like a puzzle . . . ," Jennie said softly.

"Exactly!" I suddenly sat up straight. "That's why some students don't enjoy Shakespeare. They complain it's too much work to figure out each line's meaning. But they don't understand that's okay. It's fun to linger on lines and read them slowly. It's probably why Mr. Richards only gave you such a small amount to read."

As Jennie moved on to the next line, which was far more straightforward, I found myself unable to move past the last sentence I had just uttered.

It was so simple. And so very, very brilliant.

This "detested" and "terrible" teacher Mr. Richards gave small chunks of manageable reading to his students each night. They had no choice but to read *and* understand the material in depth because what most teachers gave as homework, Mr. Richards waited until the next day to present as schoolwork. In class. No tutors. No Internet. No sharing of homework or side discussions. The work he received from his students was simply that. The real work of his students.

Oh my God.

"What does *piteous overthrows* mean?" Jennie asked, interrupting my epiphany.

"What do you think it means?" I challenged. "If I just tell you, then there's a chance you may not remember. It'll mean so much more if you first look up the words in the dictionary and then give it a shot."

"Can I at least use dictionary.com?" Jennie asked, rolling her eyes.

"Dictionary.com is fine. I'm not a Nazi!"

By the end of the session, I was confident Jennie could have given a lecture on the prologue to a high school class.

"You're going to blow Mr. Richards away tomorrow," I promised. And I meant it. After bullshitting for so long, it was an utter relief to be able to leave a tutoring session feeling as if I had actually taught something. And because there was no physical writing assignment to turn in, there was no confusion as to my contribution. When it came time to show how well she knew the prologue tomorrow, Jennie would be on her own.

This Mr. Richards had made sure of that.

27

had to get to the Braxtons in under fifteen minutes, and there were no cabs on Madison. The remainder of the afternoon stretched endlessly. Four more clients. I would be tutoring till at least midnight because Whitney had a paper on *The Great Gatsby* due the next day and I knew she didn't even have a thesis for it yet. It was outrageous that she expected me to show up at her house at 10:00 P.M. and complete an entire paper with her. More outrageous was the fact that I would do it. I could just see her now, sitting hopelessly on her bed with the computer screen turned on to a blank Word document. Like half of my clients, Whitney preferred to *dictate* from the confines of her canopy bed: "Okay, for the next paragraph, say how, like, Gatsby thought Daisy was hot but that her husband Tom was really snotty and all. I sensed that from the movie." As I watched her flip the pages of *Vogue*, I imagined myself responding, "Okay, for the next paper, you little brat, how about you, like, *read* the book and actually sit at your desk to write it yourself? I sense that would be good for you."

But if Jake Herring's endless succession of tutors had taught me one thing, it was this: Manhattan tutors were replaceable. If I wasn't willing to write the paper, some other underpaid and frustrated teacher was.

Damn! There really were no cabs.

Walking over to Park, I found myself wishing that all my tutoring experiences were like the one I had just had with Jennie. True, she might have an unfair advantage in class tomorrow compared to any of her peers who didn't have a tutor. Working with a teacher would definitely give her an edge; but still, Jennie had worked, and I had actually taught. When I left her room, I had a feeling that Jennie might grow to appreciate Shakespeare, that she might actually enjoy figuring out what other lines meant. I couldn't help but compare my session with her with how I had handled the same prologue in my class earlier in the year. Unlike Mr. Richards, I had asked my students to write a fourteen-line translation for homework. The next day I had a stack of flawless translations on my desk, but no sense of who actually got it or who did the work. For all I knew, that one assignment could have financed the lease for some lucky tutor's BMW! All so I could read what they wrote the next day.

Finally spotting an off-duty cab down the block, I began running wildly and flaying my hands.

"Please," I begged, "I'll give you a five-dollar tip. Just fifteen blocks, *please!*"

"Off duty," the driver growled, beginning to roll up his window.

"*Ten!*" I begged.

It worked. Gratefully sinking into the back seat, I eyed his registration sticker and couldn't help but think that Omar Ahmed and I weren't very different. We were both suckers for bribes.

"It's *so* hot," Madeline grumbled as she slumped into class the next day.

The air conditioning wasn't working and it was unreasonably warm for May. May! I couldn't believe that there were only two months left of the school year.

"Ms. Abrahams is taking her class to the Guggenheim so they can buy Popsicles from the vendors. Can we go too?" Amy asked hopefully.

"Guys, we still haven't finished *Lord of the Flies*," I argued, a little nervous that with all the library visits, the school year would end and we still wouldn't have finished the book we had started in . . . oh God, in January! Strangely, none of the parents seemed to mind. If anything, I had been repeatedly complimented for my understanding pace and reasonable workload.

"Just give us a reading hall in class tomorrow and we'll finish it. There are only, like, four chapters left to go," Benjamin suggested.

I found myself weakening, but then I thought about Mr. Richards. He would do just the opposite. His students would read at night and would actually work tomorrow. Was it too late in the year to try something new? A lightbulb went off in my head.

"Okay, guys, we can go with Ms. Abrahams's class," I said brightly. They all started cheering and rushing for the door.

"BUT . . . ," I rushed to the front of the room and blocked the entrance, "first you will all sit down and take out your homework planners. I have an assignment. If I'm going to compromise, you're going to compromise."

I heard a few exaggerated sighs and moans—they were, after all, seventh-graders—but the promise of Popsicles caused them all to quiet down.

"I don't have a homework planner," Max whined.

"It's *May*." I rolled my eyes. "When were you thinking of getting one?"

"Like, never," he mumbled. I ignored him.

"I want you all to read the chapter entitled 'A Gift for the Darkness' tonight," I ordered. After five minutes of shuffling and requests to borrow pens and pencils, I watched most of them dutifully writing in their planners.

"And what's the assignment?" Charlotte asked.

"That's it," I replied flatly.

"Just read?" Jacob asked, his eyes shining. "Awesome!"

"Yes, I just want you to read. You are going to do the writing assignment in class tomorrow. And it's going to count as a quiz grade."

Silence. Deadly, pin drop silence.

Unsurprisingly, Benjamin broke it, but I was amazed to hear how polite his tone of voice was.

"Um, Ms. Taggert? We don't mind doing the assignment at home. Just tell us what it is?"

"Quizzes give me panic attacks," Madeline added.

"This is *a lot* of work," David agreed.

"No, it's not," I answered simply. "The chapter won't take you more than twenty minutes to read. So I don't want any of your parents calling me tonight and complaining that I'm giving you too much work. If I get a single call, I'm announcing whose parent it was in class tomorrow," I warned, looking around the room. I focused in on Madeline. "And the only way you will get a panic attack is if you don't read very, very carefully. Because the quiz will be easy. Ridiculously easy, actually. You should all get an A+ if you read. Of course, if you don't, it will be quite impossible."

Silence once again.

"Now let's get some Popsicles!" I said sweetly, walking out of the room.

Half of Langdon seemed to be at the Guggenheim. Harold Warner's and Randi's classes had gotten there a little earlier and I could see Sarah Waters's class walking ahead with a trail of high-school students who looked as delighted as my seventh-graders. Across the street I saw some other Langdon kids, but I couldn't make out their teacher as a bus was blocking my view.

"Is your school having a field trip to the museum?" an elderly woman asked me curiously as we approached. "How wonderful!"

"Sort of," I replied evasively, then walked over to join Randi. What was I supposed to say? No, we only come here for the ice cream?

Randi was, as always, a vision. She was wearing a buttercup yellow sundress tied daintily at the shoulders. Large white Oliver Peoples sunglasses covered half her face, and she carried the new Anya Hindmarch Perry bag. Lately I had managed to keep up with her in designer wardrobes, but I hadn't made it out of Whitney's apartment last night till 2:00 A.M. I had earned almost $2,000 writing that *Gatsby* paper, but once again I found myself paying for it in the morning. I knew Randi was eyeing my dark undereye circles and slightly crumpled shirtdress.

"Sweetie, what happened to you?" She looked genuinely concerned.

"Horace Mann is hard," I responded, deadpan. She knew all about how I was writing Whitney's paper. We both chuckled, loving the fact that no further explanation was necessary. "And it may be crumpled, but the dress *is* Marni," I added.

"Then you're excused!" She grinned, taking a lick of her Popsicle. Harold Warner walked over, holding a large salted pretzel in one hand and a Snickers ice-cream bar in the other.

"Look at them," he sighed happily, eating with his mouth open. "They're so happy. I love the community we have at Langdon. We work hard and we play hard." At that moment, the three of us were greeted with the most curious sight. As the other group of Langdon students I had seen across the street approached the museum, we all stared at the man they were following. Or was he a *model*? His dark hair was slicked back with gel, and he was wearing a pair of gold-rimmed Cavalli aviators. An expensive-looking white linen shirt was tucked into low-riding jeans. As he turned to make sure all his students had crossed the street, I saw the gold-studded snake on the back pocket. More Roberto Cavalli. His shoes were a light crème ostrich leather, and he was strutting like John Travolta in the opening scene of *Saturday Night Fever*.

"Mr. Mehta!" The kids started screaming, and suddenly he was surrounded by a pack of students. I noticed Benjamin giving him a high five. Randi and I stared, open-mouthed.

"Good gracious," Harold muttered, his eyes still wide. "Who is that man? Is he a *Langdon* teacher?"

"*That*," Sarah Waters informed as she walked over to us, "is the new math teacher. Ashok Mehta. Remember? He's from India? Wow, does he look fabulous or what?" She stood there beaming for no reason. It *had* to be the Prozac.

I caught Randi's eye. We both knew the reason behind

Ashok's alarming transformation. Randi pulled me away from Harold and Sarah and nodded in Ashok's direction.

"Fuck, fuck, fuck," she fumed. "I bet he's easily raking in over $400 an hour."

"Why would Ashok make more money than either of us?" Randi could be so dramatic sometimes.

"Because he's *Asian*," she seethed, taking off her glasses and now openly staring at him. "All the Asians make that much. Parents immediately assume they're smarter. Haven't you ever heard of the Indian S.A.T. tutor who makes $750 an hour? He can teach math and physics too. Some people have all the luck."

At that moment, Ashok Mehta strutted over with a posse of students who were following him like he was the pied piper.

"Hel*lo*, ladies," he drawled. "Looks like great minds think alike!" He gave us both a knowing wink.

"Excuse me, I have to check on my students," Randi muttered rudely and rejoined Harold and Sarah. Alone with Ashok, I found myself suddenly at a loss for words.

"What a year," he remarked gamely. "What a great year. Who would have thought that this teaching job would change my life?"

I smiled weakly and nodded. His days of smuggling the Langdon lunches were clearly history.

"We should go out sometime," he continued suavely, taking off his glasses and winking at me again. "Have you ever been to Bungalow 8? It is most great."

28

What a day. I don't know whether it was the burning May sun or Ashok Mehta's big reveal, but I had a splitting headache. I slipped out of Langdon after my two o'clock class and headed home for a nap. There was no way I could tutor for the rest of the evening without one. As I walked into the apartment, my cell phone began buzzing. Bridgette. I would call her back. Slipping my heels off, I climbed under my covers and closed my eyes. The phone was vibrating. This time she was texting me.

Pick up ur phone. Imp. V. urgent!!!!!

I knew I was going to have to call her if I was to get any sleep.

"Your answering machine is full," she accused, picking up on the first ring.

"Whatever, probably tutoring or parents," I mumbled sleepily. "This is the emergency you wanted to tell me about?"

"Well, I got a *little* weirded out," she admitted. "Plus I haven't seen you since you moved in. But that's not why. The *emergency* is . . . actually, guess! Guess what!"

"Bridge, I'm exhausted. Just tell me," I sighed. I was too tired to even walk across the room to my answering machine. Why the hell was it full anyway?

"Why the fuck are you tired? It's two in the afternoon. You're at home while the rest of the human race is still at work? Okay, whatever, it doesn't matter. Get your beauty sleep now because I want to fix you up tonight! There's this *amazing* guy at work—oh, Anna, he's really amazing. Well, I've been sort of seeing him, and well, we want you to meet his best friend. He's a lawyer and he went to Harvard. Don't worry . . . it's not technically a blind date because I met him last week and Anna, he's freaking gorgeous. Are you free for dinner tonight?"

Admittedly, my love life was nonexistent. Between teaching and tutoring, I was rarely going out. I had to admit, this guy sounded pretty fantastic.

"Sure," I said, brightening. Even my headache was fading. "When?"

"We have dinner reservations at Mr. Chow's at 9:00," Bridgette gushed. "Anna, you are going to *die* when you meet Brian!"

Wait a minute. I couldn't have dinner. I was tutoring till eleven tonight!

"Bridge, hold on," I ordered, now sitting up. "Can we do Saturday night?"

"Saturday is fucking bridge and tunnel night. Nobody in Manhattan goes out on Saturday. Why can't you do tonight? What are you possibly doing that is more important than going on the most perfect date in the world?"

I tried to think quickly. Could I cancel my tutoring? Maybe my 5:30 with Jake, but Katie had a project due tomorrow, and Keith's term paper for his history class was due as well. Plus I had overspent a bit last weekend and indulged in the same Maurice Villency couch I had admired at Bridgette's last summer. I needed that afternoon's cash.

"I'm tutoring," I said lamely.

"What?" Bridgette cried. "Easy. Cancel. You're so weird sometimes, Anna. It's a side job. What's the big deal?"

"My rent's due in a couple weeks," I admitted, feeling my headache come on again. "I really can't cancel. Let's please do Saturday? Or even Friday night? Remember, I'm *from* New Jersey so technically I'm ex–bridge and tunnel."

I could hear her breathing, but she didn't answer.

"Bridgette?"

"Forget it, Anna. Another time."

"Yes, another time for sure, I *really* want to meet him," I begged, lying down again. "And Bridge, I really appreciate it. Honest I do." It was then that Bridgette asked a terrible question. It would repeat itself over and over in my mind until I eventually had the courage to confront it.

"Anna . . . why'd you fight your parents so hard last summer? I mean, if ultimately it *was* all about the money?" Then she hung up the phone.

I really hated her at that moment.

Now unable to nap, I trudged across the room to my answering machine. The first message on my answering machine was from Dottie Parker:

"Ms. Taggert! This is Dottie Parker. Jennie just texted me from school. She received an A on her assignment for Mr. Richards's class! She has *never* received an A in his class! Thank you from the bottom of my heart! What a godsend you are!"

I couldn't wipe the smile off my face. For a few seconds, even Bridgette's nasty question ceased to bother me. The next twenty messages, however, were like a succession of daggers, all aimed at my head.

"Anna? This is Lynn Briggman. Max called me from school today quite upset. Apparently you have assigned a quiz tomorrow? Don't you think one day's notice is a little . . . daunting? Please call me back as soon as you get this."

BEEP.

"Anna? This is Lara Kensington. How are you, my love? I hope everything is just wonderful! Benjamin is a bit perplexed as to what you mean by a reading quiz. Is there any part of the chapter he should concentrate his attention? I thought you were one of the few teachers at Langdon who didn't believe in causing the children unnecessary stress?"

BEEP.

"Ms. Taggert, this is Madeline's mother calling. As you know, my daughter is prone to anxiety and often suffers panic attacks. She called me from school today about your quiz. I must warn you that due to her anxiety she feels like she cannot produce for you in class the same quality of work she is able to do in the comfort and solace of her bedroom at home."

The messages went on. I was ten minutes late for my tutoring, but found myself rooted to the spot. I hadn't gotten these many messages since . . . since I had actually been teaching. For the last several months I had followed Randi's guidance and simply given basic assignments that were to be completed at home. Coupled with the trips to the library and a few movies thrown in during class, the Langdon mothers had been silent. Now the sharks were surfacing again. My quiz was like fresh blood in the waters. I wouldn't be home till midnight again that evening, so there was no way I could call all these women back. And I didn't want to. I was giving that quiz tomorrow. Popping two Advil, I quickly slipped on a pair of jeans and a tank top and walked out the door.

By the time I got to Keith Morgan's house, I was cranky and miserable. It was 9:15 P.M. I could have been at Mr. Chow's meeting my future husband. Instead, I was sitting with a pimply-faced junior who didn't know the first thing about why World War II broke out. I wanted to kill him.

"Keith," I said as patiently as I could, "what exactly does your history teacher want this paper to be on?"

"I'm not sure." He shrugged, one eye on his cell phone. He was still wearing his soccer jersey, which meant he hadn't even bothered to shower when he came home. That explained the sickening odor in the room.

"Well, think hard," I pressed. "Or can you call someone?"

I watched him disdainfully as he put the phone to his ear. Not only had he left this paper for the night before it was due, he didn't even know what it was on.

"Hey, bro, it's K-Morg, what up, man?" He got up from the desk and started pacing around his room. His voice was completely different. Gone was the nervous teenager. "So, listen, man, I'm doing this freakin' history paper. What's the topic again?"

9:25. I could have been ordering appetizers and falling in love.

"Yeah, she's so hot . . . ," he drawled.

"Keith!" I barked.

"Sorry, dude. Yeah, that's my tutor. Yeah, so, I gotta go and all . . . you sure that's what it's on? Okay . . . thanks, man."

He hung up and faced me. "So we have to write a five-page paper on one reason we think World War II broke out."

"What's your reason?" I asked meanly. Usually I would give my students some slack, maybe offer a list of reasons and allow them to pick one. I wasn't in the mood.

"Well, like . . . give me some reasons and I'll pick one,"

Keith said, not meeting my eyes. Had this kid even been to his history class? I had serious doubts. I looked at the clock again. 9:43 P.M.

That's when it happened. I officially snapped.

"I don't know any," I lied.

Keith stared at me, open-mouthed.

"I can help you write this paper," I continued crazily, "but I'm not going to write it for you."

I didn't know what had come over me. Maybe it was the missed date. Bridgette's comment. Dottie Parker's voice message. The ones that had followed it. I felt recklessly self-destructive. Keith was looking extremely uncomfortable.

"Look, Anna, I don't know, okay? That's why you're here. You think I would have a tutor if I knew stuff like this?" His right eye started twitching.

"Keith," I glared at him, "do you even know what a tutor is supposed to do?"

"Dude! What's gotten into you! You're usually so cool!" he yelled, pushing his chair back. "Yeah, I've had tutors for years. They help me with my homework. Can we have this convo, like, next week? This thing is due tomorrow!"

"That's your problem," I replied calmly. It was strange. Just saying that had lifted a huge burden off my shoulders.

"Anna, look, you're being so weird. Can we just please work as we normally do? This is my term paper. I'm a junior. If I don't hand this in this could seriously hurt my chances at applying to Brown in the fall."

"Brown. What a joke," I laughed. I was sick of whoring my brain out so I could keep some fancy apartment that I never had time to be in anyway. And after seeing how ridiculous Ashok Mehta looked with all his designer labels flashing in every direction, I was quite certain I never wanted another article of overpriced clothing again.

"Anna, are you leaving?" Keith was now standing, blocking the door. His eyes were wide with alarm and I could see that he was starting to perspire.

"Yeah, I'm leaving. I'm done. I quit."

Not just Keith. With all of them. Even Jennie Parker. Because even though I had actually taught her, she wasn't my actual student. She was someone I got paid an obscene amount of money to help prepare a lesson that I was certain this Mr. Richards would still have preferred she do herself.

"If you walk out tonight, my parents are going to fire you," Keith threatened. "They're not home right now, but wait till I call them."

"You can't fire someone who quits," I pointed out, still maddeningly calm. I picked up my Chanel bag. Had there really been a time when I thought that spending time tutoring kids like Keith was worth a bag with a huge C on it? Which, I was now certain, could only stand for *chump*?

"ANNA! What the fuck! Please! Don't do this!" Apparently this was Keith's new tactic. Outright begging. I softened a little. Just because I was suddenly seeing the light didn't mean I had to take it all out on poor Keith. After all, I was guilty of writing several assignments for him. It wasn't completely his fault that tonight was the night I was finally rediscovering both my morality and my dignity.

"Listen, Keith. This is not about you. I'm just exhausted. I don't feel well. Look up the policy of appeasement, okay? It was because of that policy that so many world leaders turned a blind eye while Hitler grew increasingly powerful. You can do it. It's only five pages. You'll be expected to do a lot more at Brown, I can promise you that."

I left Keith speechless and rushed down the hall to the front door. Gone was the eerie calmness I had felt moments before. Suddenly, I couldn't breathe. I had to get out of this building. A part of me couldn't believe what I had just done. Even if I wanted to keep my other clients, once Keith's mother reported to Francine what I had done, I would never get another referral again. Did that matter? For a fleeting second I thought about going to Mr. Chow's, but instead I hailed a cab and went home. I had a new life to plan. Or, rather, an old self to rediscover. I didn't even bother to reply to the e-mail that was waiting for me:

Date: Monday, May 14, 2006 10:15 PM
From: "Clarissa Morgan" <cmorgan@newyorkersfor
dolphins.net>
Ms. Taggert,
Your quitting does not preempt the fact that Keith's father
and I fire you. After all this money we have thrown at you,
your decision to leave our son at such a critical juncture in
his junior year strikes us as entirely selfish. Because of
your decision, you may be destroying his chances to attain
many of his hopes and dreams.
I cannot think of anything worse than a human being who
would leave an innocent child to write his paper the night
before it's due by himself. BY HIMSELF!
Be assured we will be reporting your actions to Ms.
Gilmore. Moreover, his father and I will take every measure
to spread the word and make sure you never tutor in
Manhattan again.
                                    Clarissa and Spencer Morgan

29

My class was seated and eerily silent when I walked in the next morning. The kids looked nervous, and Jacob Stein looked like he was about to pass out.

"We're not really having a quiz, are we?" Benjamin asked. "My mom said you never called her back."

"You're right, Benjamin, I didn't call her back. I didn't call any of your parents back," I replied calmly. "I had you read a chapter last night. ONE chapter. I'm going to ask you one question in class today. If any of your parents find that unreasonable, you can tell them I don't care. Now. I would like you all to take out a piece of paper and a blue or black pen. Or a pencil. Not a gel pen. Not a glitter pen. Not a marker."

"You're acting different," Max commented. "Are you feeling okay?"

"I feel great," I retorted. "I'm not starting until everyone has done what I just asked. So whoever is not ready is wasting everyone else's time."

There was a frantic scampering as the seventh-graders rushed to "borrow" pens, pencils, and papers. It never ceased to shock me how the request to take out a piece of paper and a pencil could produce outright panic in a seventh-grade classroom.

"I need to go to my locker. I didn't bring anything," Charlotte whined.

I ignored her. How could anyone come to class with absolutely nothing on them? *Students who have been accustomed to going to the library or the Guggenheim for ice cream,* a voice in my head answered.

"Okay," I began, "here's the quiz. It's fairly simple. I want you all to use the rest of class to write one paragraph that covers what, *in your opinion*, are the three most important events in last night's chapter. That's it."

Once again, I had apparently asked them to do something completely unreasonable.

"Does spelling count?"

"Should we double-space?"

"Is it just opinion?"

"Can we look at our books?"

I held up both my hands to stop the barrage of questions. "Hey!" I ordered sternly. "I'm not repeating myself. You decide how you want to go about doing what I asked. And no, you may not refer back to the book. No more questions. That's final."

I retreated to my desk. From the corner of my eye I saw some of my students starting to write. Benjamin was eyeing Madeline's paper hungrily.

"Eyes on your own paper," I announced, looking straight at him. He opened his mouth to protest but I raised a finger in warning. Reluctantly, he picked up his pen and started writing.

It had taken me twenty minutes to get my seventh-graders to write, but finally they were all quiet and at work. I used the opportunity to open my laptop and write an e-mail to all the parents of the children I tutored. I had thought long and hard the night before about what I wanted to say, but in the end I decided to keep it short and simple. I figured if anyone wanted an explanation or was truly upset, they could call or e-mail me back. It took me under two minutes to write, and under ten to send to each of my families.

At that moment, Randi burst into the room.

"Hi, guys! Do you want to join my class? We're g—"

Fifteen heads looked up, startled out of silence.

"Shh!" I hushed in annoyance, then gestured to the table where the kids were writing. "They're taking a quiz." She gave me a curious look and shrugged her shoulders.

"She's being so mean," Benjamin muttered for her benefit, but returned to his paper immediately after I glared at him.

Giving me one last lingering look, Randi left the room. A minute later I saw her class fly past my door screaming about going to Central Park. I got up and shut the door, ignoring the tortured expressions on my students' faces.

Toward the end of class, they wordlessly came to my desk to turn in their paragraphs. The looks I received went from accusing to outright betrayal. Only Michael Worthington smiled as he handed in his paper.

I had two hours until my next class, and instead of Starbucks with Randi, I found myself blissfully free. Free! I could do whatever I wanted! Eagerly, I sat at my desk and began to read over the paragraphs I had just received. I had never been more interested to see what my students had produced because for once I was certain that what was in front of me was their own work. Jacob's was on top because he had been the last to finish. I could have sworn he looked like he was about to burst into tears as he had left the room.

> *Lord of the Flies is a very intersting book*
> *about boys on an island. All the adults die and*
> *the boys have to suvive. They make houses*
> *and Jack is really mean. Last night I read this*
> *chapter called present for darkness. It was so*
> *intersting that I couldnt put it down. It was*
> *also scary because who gives a present to*
> *the darkness? All in all the three things that*
> *happened were that the boys were scared,*
> *the night made it worse, and the present was*
> *mysterius.*

All year I had had a sense that tutored-in-six-subjects Jacob was not reading and writing at a seventh-grade level, but I had never actually seen anything he did on his own. Without the help of any of his other tutors, this was what Benjamin was capable of producing. I felt sick. Here was a child who would be protected, helped, and then sent to a prestigious Ivy League school where he would continue to be protected and helped, much like the college students I tutored over winter break. Then he would graduate and probably be placed in some important position in his parents' company where he would spend long days golfing while his team did all his work. And because he never knew better, he would most likely perpetuate the cycle with his own children and provide them with a team of tutors. Disgusted, I moved on to Madeline's paper. She was another student I suspected was not writing her own papers. Well, now I would know for sure . . .

"A Gift For the Darkness" was a deeply symbolic chapter. After cutting off a pig's head and placing it on a stick, Jack offers it as a sacrifice to an unnamed beast on the island. This gesture is noteworthy because it allies Jack and all who follow beneath him with an evil force on the island. In addition, Ralph and Piggy's continued resistance to Jack signifies their attempt to cling to a semblance of sanity. Finally, the imaginary conversation Simon has with the pig's head foreshadows future devastation. The pig warns Simon not to interfere with Jack and threatens to end Simon's life if he does. Therefore, the creation of the pig's head, Ralph and Piggy's resistance, and the warning Simon receives at the end stand apart as the three most significant events of the chapter.

Wow! So Madeline had been handing in her own work all year. Did her parents know how bright she was? What had I told them at the conferences? I couldn't even remember. By now all the conferences had blurred together in my mind. Flipping through the papers, I pulled out Michael's and read it quickly. His was just as well written, and even raised the point that Simon's imagined conversation with the pig's head was probably a result of his epilepsy. I wished I had paid him more attention!

As I read the rest of the paragraphs, I discovered that there was an honest range in the class. Michael and Madeline were clearly the best writers, and Benjamin's paper actually proved decent when I compared it to Jacob's and Max's appalling paragraphs. But in between these extremes were average papers that indicated a real need for lessons on how to write topic sentences and proper usage of commas. Maybe even a lesson on transition words . . .

"Anna?" Randi was standing at the door, hands on her hips. "Are you okay? I just passed a few kids in the hall and they said you were acting crazy today. You're just sitting there staring into space! What's going on?"

"Randi, come here and look at this," I said urgently, ignoring her question. I shuffled through for Madeline's and Michael's paragraphs. "Read these," I ordered, thrusting them at her.

Randi scanned both paragraphs briefly and then grinned. "Some people's tutors are sure working overtime!"

"That's just the thing!" I was more excited than I had been in a long time. "They just wrote them! Here! In class! These two kids can actually write like that! Did you know that?"

She immediately stiffened. "You had them write *in class*?"

"Uh huh. And *look* at this." Bravely, I gave her Jacob's paragraph. I watched her face closely as she read his paragraph. Aha! She looked as disgusted as I had felt! But when she finally looked up, she directed her disgust . . . at me.

"What's your point, Anna?" she asked coldly.

"I'm not attacking you," I said quickly, speaking fast. "It's just that this is the first time I had the kids write in class. It's amazing what the range is. I feel like there's so much I want to cover! For the first time I know for sure that this is their work!"

"Anna, it's almost the end of May." Randy was icy. "What are you really going to do about it now? And we discussed this already. You went down this path in October. Families like the Kensingtons aren't going to thank you if you tell them that their son writes at a fourth-grade level. They're just going to blame you. I thought we agreed that it's better to just play the game. Do you really want to go back to answering five hundred phone calls a night?"

"But what about Madeline's and Michael's parents? They should know how gifted their kids are," I pointed out.

"Okay, call them. God. Tell them. But just leave the others alone. You're being really stupid, Anna. The kids were right. What has gotten into you?" Shaking her head, I watched Randi reach into her new oversized Jimmy Choo bag to retrieve her vibrating cell phone.

"Hello? Yes, of course. Tonight? I'm not free till ten-thirty . . . what's it on? I'd have to charge extra . . ."

As I watched her expertly arrange an additional tutoring session for that evening, I felt like I was looking at the person I had become. I knew all about those middle-of-the-day cell phone calls. The last-minute appointment bookings. The mothers who wouldn't let you say no. Just last week I had told Jake Herring that under no circumstances could I see him for an additional time that week as I was booked solid. Mimsy's call had come an hour later with the promise of an additional $1,000 for my "troubles." I found myself incapable of saying no.

But I was saying no now.

To all of it.

Bridgette was right. If it was money I was seeking, I should have become a banker. Or a lawyer. I spent most of my days at Langdon abiding by a list of unwritten rules that I neither cared for nor respected. My evenings were a crazed blur of rushing from Park Avenue penthouse to penthouse, where I allowed myself to be manipulated into doing homework for hours at a stretch. After initial interviews, I rarely saw the parents, and often the only proof of their existence were the envelopes with my name on it that were left on foyer tables. I didn't even know what my job was anymore. Could I even call myself a teacher? And what the hell was a tutor, anyway?

The snap of Randi's cell phone broke my thoughts. "Look," she said reasonably, "you're probably just tired. Had a late night. Don't make any rash decisions." *Rash*? She didn't know the half of it. I was almost afraid to tell her what I had done.

"I am tired," I admitted. "And maybe what I did this morning is rash, but I'm not sorry I did it."

"Oh, one quiz never hurt them. We'll take them to the library tomorrow and all will be well. Although," she laughed, "you may have to deal with some nasty phone calls tonight!"

"I'm not talking about the quiz, Randi."

"Then what?" she asked, her eyes narrowing. "Anna, what did you do?"

"I quit my tutoring jobs. All of them."

There. I had said it. Her mouth dropped open.

"No, you didn't."

"Yes. I did."

"How are you going to afford rent? And . . . and . . . other stuff?"

"Honestly, Randi, all I do in that apartment is sleep. It may as well be my old place on 84th Street. I have no time to see my friends. Or my family, for that matter. Sometimes I feel like I'm rushing around like a madwoman for . . . nothing. I feel like I contribute . . . nothing."

"Let me get this straight," Randi said slowly, now absolutely expressionless. "So you're no longer tutoring. You're moving out of the building. I guess you're no longer doing the Hamptons thing either."

I hadn't thought about the Hamptons tutoring, but yes, I guess that was out too.

"Yeah. I'm finishing the year, then I'm quitting. I hate this world. I hate myself," I replied honestly.

We both sat there quietly, not moving.

"Do you think my life is also meaningless? That I contribute nothing?" Randi asked finally.

I couldn't answer her.

After a terrible silence, she turned and walked out of the room. I sat and listened to the sound of her Gucci stilettos clicking down the long hallway until I couldn't hear them anymore.

30

S o this was rock bottom.

I was Hester Prynne with a big, fat T branded on my chest. One by one, the families I had tutored had all managed to get back to me and inform me of what a terrible person I was. Amanda Carleton labeled my decision a "profound betrayal" and the Braxtons had threatened "to come after me with the force of all their money." Mimsy had simply whispered, "Fuck you." I didn't even know if I should finish the school year. The furious look Francine had given me as I passed her in the hall Friday afternoon made me never want to go back.

I hadn't had a weekend free in months. I didn't even remember what I liked to do besides shopping. Trying to be optimistic, I ventured boldly outside and made a left instead of my usual right toward Madison Avenue. The thought of purchasing another handbag or shoe made me physically sick. Instead, I found myself heading to the Barnes & Noble on 86th where I spent the afternoon drinking coffee and browsing through the new releases. It dawned on me that I hadn't read a book for pleasure—or for less than a thousand dollars—all year. Reading had always been my favorite pastime. How had I let it go so easily? Later, I wandered down Second Avenue past the restaurants and bars. All of them were packed with people sitting outside, eating and laughing. One group of three girls caught my attention. They were sitting outside Blockheads Burritos drinking margaritas. They looked to be about my age. All of them were dressed casually in jeans and T-shirts . . . not a label in sight. I must have been eyeing the empty chair a little too longingly because one of them suddenly looked in my direction and asked, "Can we help you?"

Embarrassed, I continued walking down the block. Could it only have been one year ago that I wanted to be a teacher more than anything else? Now here I was, contemplating walking into Dr. Blumenfeld's office on Monday and quitting. On Friday I had called the management company—I was surprised at how gracious they were when I said I had to break my lease. Then the overly chatty saleswoman told me that a certain "Mr. Mehta" had already inquired about taking over the remainder of my one-year contract. He could move in as soon as July 1st.

"I'm only telling you because he has the same school you work at listed as his place of employment," she said brightly. "Looks like you Langdon teachers love our building. Wow, they must be paying you *good* over there."

I hung up.

Did Randi tell Ashok about the apartment? It was too depressing a question to answer. Adding to my dark mood was the fact that I hadn't received a single e-mail from any of the families I had tutored. No expressions of remorse. Or even anger. While I was relieved to be no longer tutoring, it was going to be a little strange not seeing the students I had spent so many hours with after school. A part of me was hurt that they never bothered to write or call, and I even missed a few of them. But then again, I had been a service. Once again, easily replaced. Any relationship I had imagined to have forged with any of these children was just that: imagined. Francine had probably given all my clients to Ashok.

As I crossed Park Avenue and headed toward my building, I suddenly heard a familiar laugh.

Randi Abrahams.

I couldn't deal with her right now, either. We had avoided each other on Thursday and Friday, and the question I had left unanswered had created an ever-widening gap in our relationship. I quickly crouched behind a Range Rover and peered through the windows. It wasn't my finest hour.

Randi wasn't alone. Arm in arm with Ashok, who was holding as many shopping bags as she was, she giggled and stumbled into our building.

Looked like Randi had replaced me, too.

Feeling emptier than ever, I waited another few minutes until I was sure they had gone up in the elevator before I headed toward my building.

"Good evening, Ms. Taggert."

Even Tony's greeting, which usually thrilled me, did nothing to cheer me up. As I approached my door, I noticed a small Post-It someone had stuck.

Sweet Anna!
I move in July 1st, but would
you mind if I left a few
boxes in the apartment
next week? It would be
most helpful.
                    —Ashok

"Asshole," I muttered, ripping off the Post-It and slamming my door shut. Alone in my apartment again, I decided to call Bridgette even though I didn't really feel like talking to her. She wasn't home. I desperately needed someone to talk to or else I was going to go mad. My parents. No . . . I was not ready to deal with them just yet. Prozac-Sarah? Tweebles-Dorothy?

Tentatively, I found myself reaching for the Langdon directory and scrolling with my index finger for the Os.

He picked up on the first ring.

"Hello?"

"Damian," I started awkwardly. "Hey . . . it's Anna."

"I need at least three days advance notice for a date," he said and laughed hysterically at his own joke. To my horror, I began to sob.

"Hey . . . Anna? I'm kidding. Hey, are you okay?"

"N-n-no," I managed, "I'm qu-qu-quitting L-l-langdon."

"Meet me at the Starbucks on 88th and Lex. Ten minutes."

The phone went dead.

Damian was sitting toward the back with two cups of iced coffee in front of him. He stood up when he saw me and gestured to the empty chair across from him.

"Talk," he ordered, without a trace of sarcasm.

I felt the tears rush to my eyes.

"Hey," he said softly, "just sit and take a few sips, okay? Whatever it is, we can figure it out. We're teachers, after all." He smiled gently and waited as I melted into the chair.

"Thank you so much," I said, now more than a little embarrassed. "I just didn't know who to talk to."

He opened his mouth and then promptly shut it.

"You were going to say something about Randi, weren't you?" I laughed bitterly. He grinned sheepishly and shrugged.

"You got me, Anna. But believe it or not, even I know when it's a bad time to make a joke."

"I'm done with it all, Damian," I sighed. "I quit tutoring last week. I'm moving out of my fancy apartment. I'm leaving Langdon."

"Wow . . ." he breathed. "That's pretty heavy. I have to admit, though, two of those decisions sound good."

"What do you mean?"

"The apartment and tutoring stuff are bullshit. The leaving teaching part I'm not sure about," he replied seriously.

"Don't you tutor?" I asked. "I mean, you're clearly not into all the materialistic stuff, but you know the whole scene so well. You know, the *game*. The *shortcut*?"

Damian sighed and looked out onto the dark street, which was lit by one lonely streetlight.

"I say a lot of shit, sometimes," he said finally.

"What's that supposed to mean?"

"I don't know," he muttered, "I guess I've seen so much at Langdon that I shoot my mouth off. It's true, I don't have a lot of faith in the system or how it's run. But I still believe in teaching."

I didn't know what to say. We both stared at a woman picking up her dog's poop on the sidewalk.

"That's how I feel," I suddenly said. "Like one big old pooper-scooper."

We both laughed a little, and then Damian became serious

again. "I actually don't tutor, Anna. I had a couple clients years ago, but I dropped them after only a few sessions. They literally zapped my desire to be a teacher."

"That's exactly how I feel," I agreed. "But how can you continue to teach at that place? Year after year? It seems like nobody's happier than when we're just slacking off and letting the kids run wild. You know, with trips to the library . . . ice creams at the Guggenheim. The minute you give them actual work and tough assignments, you come home to endless parent phone calls."

Damian was quiet. "Not all the families are like that," he finally said. "And not all the kids are tutored."

"You know when I finally realized that?" I asked, leaning forward. "Just last week when I had them do an assignment in class. A couple of kids blew me away, but mostly their work depressed me. It just made me realize what I was avoiding all year. Most of the kids at Langdon are just like the kids I tutor after school. Manipulating other teachers just like me to do their work."

Damian didn't reply. But I could tell he was listening, and I still needed to vent.

"I would be completely happy just assessing them in class! That way I could be sure that what they did was their own work! But you should have seen the way the kids turned on me! Not to mention the mothers. It's like I upset the private school balance. How do you handle this?"

"By doing just what you said. I assess them in class," he answered simply.

"You do? How?" I pressed, crossing my arms. I remembered that he had won Best Teacher several times at Langdon. There

was no way he was winning something like that without cater-
ing to the parents.

"Look," he said seriously, "I'm not going to lie. I'm not perfect. I've had to turn a blind eye occasionally when I'm up
against a parent who clearly doesn't want to hear the truth.
Sometimes I'll get bitter around report writing and want to go
back to tutoring."

I could feel a very important "but" coming.

"*But*," he continued, "it's not like they startle you with a
shitty salary. You know to expect that from the get go, so if you
find that it gets to you, then you've lost sight of why you wanted
to become a teacher in the first place. I, for one, remember my
reason, and it keeps me coming back every year. Despite the
fact that I'm surrounded by buffoons who should never have
become teachers in the first place."

"You mean like Randi?"

"Like Randi. And no offense, for a while that included you. I
had a feeling the minute you came in that you wouldn't last
long, or that you would sell out."

"Looks like you were right about me," I said bitterly. "I didn't
last. So why are you here?"

"Besides the chance of a hot date at Starbucks?" Damian became serious again, a little to my disappointment. "Because
apart from me, I've never really seen a teacher go the tutoring
route and quit," he replied honestly. "It usually sucks them up
and they never come back."

After Randi's disapproval, Damian's obvious regard for my
decision to leave tutoring was encouraging.

"Here's my theory," Damian said, gesturing for me to lean

forward. "Most adults work nine-to-five jobs, right? I mean, let's exclude the overly intense investment banker or lawyer. Am I right?"

"Right."

"Then they're free at 5:00. To get drinks at happy-hour bars all over the country. Watch TV. Relax, unwind. Sleep."

"Okay." I listened intently. Where was he going with this?

"Then what gives us the right," he said with a burst of energy, "to expect *kids* to work harder than adults? Think about it. Most of our students don't go home to rest and unwind! They have after-school clubs. Sports practices. Religious school. Piano lessons. Whatever. So they get home around 6:30 or 7:00. Then they have dinner. *Then* they have to go back to work, in essence, and do their homework."

"Oh please." I rolled my eyes. "Tough life. They don't pay bills. They don't pay taxes. They have their summers off . . ."

"Yeah, they don't have adult stress, but you're delusional if you think they don't have their own stresses. It may not seem serious to us, but to them it's real," he argued, before breaking into his familiar grin. "Even if you're Charlotte, you still have to decide who gets blown on the party bus."

"Damian!"

"Different stresses," he repeated.

I remembered my conversation with Amy Greenberg in the bathroom. Okay, maybe he had a point . . .

"I'm listening."

"Soooo," Damian continued, "I figure that some of these kids are just fucking exhausted at the end of the day. The bright and motivated ones push through and do their work. Others slack off and sometimes they fail out. Then you have the majority of Langdon students, who have parents who are both rich *and* willing enough to provide their children with tutors who, any way you look at it, promote a system of cheating."

"So?" I knew all this already.

"That's my point. Homework is bullshit."

"So . . . you just teach," I said, moving my straw around in the empty coffee cup.

"Yeah. Don't get me wrong. It takes me *hours* to plan my lessons. I bring in newspapers, maps, and textbooks. Hold debates. Argue with them. Tell them stories. Draw timelines. Whatever it takes. In my classroom, I *teach*."

"How do you assess?" I challenged. I was starting to like what Damian said, but it sounded too utopian. "Don't you have to grade them?"

"Oh, there are tests," he admitted. "I tell them on the first day that at the end of every unit, there's a short-answer test. Four a year. And they're *not* easy. But *no* written homework. I *refuse* to grade work that I have no way of knowing isn't entirely their own."

I was beginning to warm up.

"It's still *Langdon*, though," Damian drawled, his old sarcasm returning. "They're gonna occasionally make you treat some kid differently. Or hand out an A when they deserve a C."

"That doesn't bother you?"

"Every time."

"So why continue?" I asked both for him and myself.

"It's like that hokey starfish story, you know?"

"What starfish story?"

"This man is walking down a beach," Damian began, "and he

notices that all these starfish have washed up ashore. It's burning hot, and they're drying up in the heat. Thousands of them, as far as he can see." Damian stretched his arms out to emphasize his point. "Then he sees this little boy who's throwing them back into the water. Slowly, one at a time. So the man shakes his head and walks up to the boy and says, 'Give it up, little boy. What's the difference? There's too many. You'll never throw them all back in.'"

I remembered the story. My mother had told it to me once, when I was very young. It was hokey, but coming from Damian's mouth it suddenly took on a different tone.

"But the boy says—"

"'It made a difference to the one I just threw in,'" I finished, beating him to the punch line.

"Exactly," Damian smiled. "If you try and win 'em all, you'll lose your mind. But that doesn't mean you can't make a real difference to a handful of students. Maybe more than a handful."

"Even at Langdon?"

"Even at Langdon," he confirmed.

Monday morning I made a stop at Krispy Kreme and bought doughnuts for my students. It was a scorching June morning and as I approached Langdon, I couldn't help but have a flashback to my first day. There they were again. The nannies with the dogs, the shiny Lincoln Town Cars, and the . . . mothers. Today they were all dressed in soft yoga pants and sheer pastel T-shirts. Without exception. The Hamptons season was right around the corner and the unspoken goal was, of course, to see who could hit a chic Nicole Richie—esque weight first. Lara Kensington pointed a skeletal finger at my doughnuts.

"I'm not sure Krispy Kreme is peanut friendly." Her voice was cold, and it drew attention from the other mothers. They descended like an angry flock.

"Charlotte is trying to lose five pounds before camp."

"Max does not eat sugar so early in the morning."

"Sugar interferes with Jacob's medication."

"Really, are doughnuts an *appropriate* message for a teacher to give her students?"

I froze. My resolve was melting as quickly as the glaze on the doughnuts, and for a terrible moment I contemplated just dropping the boxes and running. These were the women who had highlighted and Sarabeth-ed and La Goulue-ed me. Who had lavished me at Christmas with Chanel clutches and Barneys gift certificates. Who were true to only one principle: I-love-you-as-long-as-you-do-what-I-say.

Had there really been a time when I thought they were my . . . friends?

"Only a new teacher," a smooth voice behind me said, "only a new teacher remembers how much a kid likes some sugar every now and then. Aw, Ms. Taggert, did you buy those with your own money for our unruly middle-school charges?"

It was Damian. He was wearing the same jeans he had on at Starbucks and his hair looked a little rumpled. An unlikely ally, but my ally nevertheless. The mothers looked at him suspiciously.

"Damian Oren, high school history," he grinned affably, eyeing Lynn Briggman's perky breasts with undisguised appreciation. "Lara, I believe we already know each other. I had the pleasure of . . . seeing Eric through . . . How is he doing?" he asked meaningfully.

"Eric is doing, well, quite well," Lara mumbled, a flash of fear crossing her blue eyes.

"That's so good to hear," Damian nodded with grave concern. "Considering . . . ?"

Lara was positively ashen. The other mothers eyed her and my doughnuts were forgotten in the unexpected and glorious possibility of a Kensington flaw exposed.

"Anna, if I walk you in can I steal a doughnut? I need to fill out my bathing suit if I'm going to hit the ol' beach in a few weeks. Good morning, ladies," Damian said charmingly, then opened the door for me as if he were Rhett Butler incarnate. This time, the hushed whispers weren't about me.

"Wasn't Eric Kensington like a . . . *drug addict*?"

The possibility of a resurfaced scandal hung tantalizingly in the air.

"Damian, you're brilliant, thank you. But you can't keep saving me. I have to learn to do it myself." We walked toward the elevators together.

"You're just a puppy," he dismissed affectionately. "Let an old dog teach you a couple of new tricks. If they ask you a question, or accuse you of anything, never respond."

"What do I do?"

"Ask them another question. Preferably one laced with a little . . . sugar. We don't have those files for nothing, you know. Don't you agree?"

"Doughnut?"

"You learn fast."

"Who? Me?"

The elevator doors opened and I went in smoothly, leaving Damian chuckling with approval in the lobby.

Dr. Blumenfeld was waiting in the hallway outside of her office. Like the mothers, she eyed my doughnut boxes suspiciously as if they contained anthrax-laced confections. *Stay strong, Anna. You don't need Damian to fight your battles.*

"Ms. Taggert."

"Dr. Blumenfeld?" *Ask questions. Ask questions.*

"It's June and I'm still hearing complaints. Many parents are unhappy. Their children are anxious and quite frankly, paralyzed with fear. They feel as if your classroom has developed a *hostile* atmosphere. That you are taking a . . . how do I say this . . . *adversarial* role. I mean—*unannounced* quizzes? Really, Miss Taggert. This is not public school."

"Oh, are pop quizzes not allowed at Langdon?" I asked innocently.

Damian was a genius.

"No, it's not that at all." Dr. Blumenfeld was momentarily flustered. "It's just that it seems as if you're still clearly inexperienced with handling the demands of our parents."

"Which parents?"

"Excuse me?"

"Which parents are upset with me?" I repeated calmly, lowering the boxes on top of a nearby photocopying machine.

Dr. Blumenfeld played with her pearls and stalled.

"It's not about naming names, Ms. Taggert. It's about the *environment* you are creating. Too much homework. Too many anxiety-ridden expectations."

"So I should . . . ease the homework load?"

"Yes, Ms. Taggert. I think that would be a start."

"And . . . maybe limit my lessons so the expectations are more child friendly?"

"Why . . . yes." Dr. Blumenfeld looked relieved. Pleased, even. "You know, Anna, you are so bright and have the makings of a wonderful teacher. It seemed like you were really getting the hang of it earlier in the year. I heard so many praises, but then the uneven response from the parents began to worry me. I want very much to extend your contract and have you continue with us in September. I'm sure you understand that we need our parents to be constantly and consistently happy."

"Dr. Blumenfeld, I completely understand. I can assure you that I won't be making the same mistake again, and can only hope you can have patience with such a novice teacher. I *have* lost sight of the needs and expectations of the parents from time to time. After all, we have to please the customers, right?" I could imagine Damian rolling with laughter.

"Yes, Anna, that's absolutely right."

And there it was.

As if Langdon was no different from any other high-priced boutique on Madison Avenue. As if Blumenfeld was the benevolent store manager.

"Dr. Blumenfeld, I couldn't agree more. Can you give me a chance to prove it to you?" This was almost fun.

"Anna, my dear, we're a progressive school. And as much as I adore to see our students flourish, it makes my heart burst when a teacher finally sees the light!"

"I wonder why I didn't see it before?" I asked with exaggerated wonder. I picked up my doughnuts and, leaving Dr. Blumenfeld behind, headed confidently down the hall without waiting for a response to a question even I couldn't answer.

Grinning like a madwoman, I wanted one brief minute to myself before entering my classroom. I ducked into the bathroom and discovered, thankfully, that I was alone. And there in the mirror was the Lifetime heroine who had gone missing for so many months: it was true-story Anna Taggert, the Manhattan teacher who battled the odds. She had accrued some scars along the way, and okay maybe spent a little too much money at Bendel's, but there she was, golden highlights and all. True-story Anna Taggert knew all too well about the late nights, the endless assignments, and the empty demands of misguided parents that paid for each gigantic handbag and designer dress that hung in her closet. Let Randi have it all. There would be plenty left over for Ashok.

By now Bridgette had probably been in her cubicle crunching numbers since 6:00 A.M. so she could afford her own showroom apartment and sushi dinners and peach Bellinis. But she had been right about one thing: I had been so busy trying to keep up with their lifestyles that somewhere along the way I had forgotten about mine. What a hypocrite. It had been a very, very long while since I had taken a deep breath and felt . . . like myself. I could look my parents in the eye again. But most important, I could look back in the mirror and like who I saw.

I walked out of the bathroom and headed straight to my classroom. The halls were empty and clear and there was nobody to stop me.

As expected, when the seventh-graders walked in they immediately spotted the doughnuts on my desk and came rushing over.

"You're nice again!" Benjamin cried happily.

"Yeah, we were so scared!" Madeline cried. "You like totally freaked us out last week."

"You're the *coolest*!" Charlotte gushed happily.

I rolled my eyes and smiled, but this time it was at myself. I had been intimidated by them at the beginning of the year, but now I was really seeing them for who they were . . . *children*.

"Okay, okay," I said loudly. "All of you have a seat. I know I caught you off guard last week, and for that I'm sorry. We haven't done much in-class writing this year, and I wish it hadn't been so stressful. Maybe the doughnuts will make us all feel a little better."

I waited while they shouted with excitement again.

"And even though now it's June and things are winding down, I do want to talk to you about the next two weeks. They're going to be a little different, and I want to explain *how* so that you are not caught off guard again."

"Oh, no!" Max groaned. "So you *are* going to become quiz lady again."

"Not quite, Max," I said gently. "But I'm going to treat you all like *grown-ups*. No surprises. I'm going to share every aspect of this change with you so you all know what to expect."

They were staring at me intently. I knew a large part of this amazing attention had to do with the prospect of the impending doughnuts, but I noticed that many of them had sat up a little straighter when I mentioned the word grown-ups.

"Let's start with the fun part," I said slowly, anticipating the reaction to my first announcement. "No more *written* homework for the rest of the year in my class. Only reading!"

They went wild. Benjamin stood up and did a little dance while the rest of the boys hooted and the girls cooed "We love you, Ms. Taggert!" I just smiled calmly and let them go nuts for a few minutes because what was coming next, I was certain, was *not* going to garner the same response. I was making a bold change at the end of the year, and I had to tread carefully.

"But—" I raised my palms and gestured for them to calm down, "we're also not making any trips to the library or the park or the Guggenheim for ice cream. I think it's a fair trade, don't you?" I asked evenly.

A few heads started to nod warily.

"We have one chapter left in *Lord of the Flies*. I am going to give you the rest of class today to read 'Cry of the Hunters.' Some of you will finish the book. Some of you will only get through the first five or six pages. That's *okay*," I said earnestly. "Read at your own pace. It's not a race. If you don't finish, I'm also giving some class time tomorrow. When you finish reading, you will correct the paragraphs you did in class last week."

"What are you going to do while we read? Just relax like

Mr. Warner?" Charlotte asked accusingly. "No fair! Teachers have all the fun."

"Absolutely not," I stated firmly. "I will be calling all of you up one by one so we can have a mini-writing conference and look at your paragraphs together. I want to give you personal feedback in addition to the comments I wrote."

"Did you grade them?" Alexa gasped dramatically, covering her mouth with her hands. "Ohmigod I'm so nervous."

"Not yet," I said slowly. "You will all have a chance to rewrite your paragraphs after our writing conference. *Then* I will put grades on your *revised* copies."

Benjamin and Jacob looked delighted, and I knew what they were thinking.

"All your revisions will be made *only* in class," I said clearly, watching their grins fade. "They will not go home. They are not subject to outside help. I want to see what you are capable of doing on your own."

"You're doing this because you hate us!" Benjamin cried defensively. "No fair! You're like, a teacher Nazi!"

"I'm doing this because I care about you," I corrected him gently. "I want you to be able to have the confidence to write on your own."

"I *never* write on my own!" Jacob howled. "I *suck* at writing!"

There it was. Again.

Finally cornered, Jacob had just inadvertently voiced the single fear that was, year after year, motivating and strengthening the tutoring industry. Students had become so accustomed to their tutor's assistance that they were now conditioned to mistrust their own abilities.

"Jacob, I guarantee you'll see a small improvement in two

weeks," I promised. "You might even surprise yourself and see a drastic difference. But at least you'll know for sure that it's *you* who's responsible for the improvement. That's why from now on, all the learning and the work you do in my class happens here." I smiled confidently and took my seat at the head of the conference table.

"In school."

ACKNOWLEDGMENTS

Thank you first to my agent and dear friend Jeanne Forte Dube. You are truly one of a kind. At Hyperion, I am forever indebted to Ellen Archer for her immediate and overwhelming support and enthusiasm, and Brenda Copeland for her priceless humor and thoughtful editing. Also, my endless appreciation to my super publicists Christine Ragasa and Lauren Hodapp. Thank you also to Will Balliett, Kathleen Carr, Jessica Wiener, Navorn Johnson, and the entire team who worked on *Schooled*—an author could not dream for more. Love always to my father, Vinny Ahooja, and his beloved Benjamin Rory, the most handsome golden retriever in Hilton Head, South Carolina; my little brother Karan "The Chairman" Ahooja; and most of all to my mother, Anjali Khanna, without whom this book would never have been possible. The memory of the four of us at Soldiers Field will always be the best thing I have ever known.

© Mary Lee

Until 2006, **Anisha Lakhani** taught English at the Dalton School on Manhattan's Upper East Side. Soon after she started teaching, she was named chair of the Middle School English Department. Lakhani received both her B.A. and M.A. degrees from Columbia University. She lives in Manhattan with her beloved Shih Tzu, Harold Moscowitz.